Here Comes Trouble

Here Comes Trouble

DONNA KAUFFMAN

BRAVA

KENSINGTON PUBLISHING CORP.
www.kensingtonbooks.com

Chapter 1

Where was all the damn snow?

She'd even begged Santa, but none of the white stuff had magically appeared under her tree. Or any other tree in Pennydash, Vermont, for that matter.

"Enough with this gorgeous weather crap." Kirby Farrell drummed her fingers on the sides of her ceramic mug as she gazed out at yet another perfect, springlike morning. That would have been ever-so-lovely, really. If it were, you know, actually spring. Not the first freaking week of January. In the middle of high season. For skiing. Which was damn hard to do on bare grass and rock-strewn slopes, as it turned out.

What the hell had she ever done to piss off Mother Nature anyway? Or Santa.

She thought she'd done everything right. No, she *had* done everything right. She'd found the right house in the right location for the right price. She'd been smart with her hard-earned money, working for eight months straight, starting the last few weeks of the previous winter season. She'd done as much of the renovation on her weathered, neglected yet charming, and character-filled little Victorian as she could by herself. She'd worked with local contractors on the rest, which had earned her a good reputation in her newly adopted hometown.

Kirby had haunted area antique shops and flea markets, refurbishing some old furnishings and discovering secondhand treasures for use in her guest bedrooms and public rooms. She'd also found the best resources for everything from food and wine, to handwoven blankets and rugs, right down to organic soaps and shampoos. She wanted to offer a unique experience, enhanced by the use of local and regionally made products. One her guests could only get by staying at the Pennydash Inn.

She'd made sure her little inn would meet the specific needs of the hoards of skiers who would be descending on the new nearby Winterhaven resort, but who might prefer her more intimate, less pricey digs. Racks for guest's snow gear had been built in the detached garage, which was now accessible right from the house through a short, enclosed walkway. She had overhauled an aging Chevy Suburban for transporting skiers to the nearby resorts when needed, and was also available to rescue a stranded skier when the snow proved too much for their often unsuitable rental car.

Everything was in place. And had been for going on nine weeks now, since the beginning of November. She'd known it would take some time to reap the rewards of her hard labor, but she'd been fairly optimistic about her first season. Given the otherwise rural and, as yet, undeveloped locale, she'd envisioned her place bursting at the seams right now, with guests who preferred intimate and specialized care at a more economical price than the resort hotel could offer.

However, all the research, preparation, hard work, and reasonable, optimistic attitudes in the world were not going to have even the remotest impact on Kirby's one, unavoidable vulnerability: the weather. Or record-breaking lack thereof in this particular case.

Kirby continued drumming her fingers as she glared out the bay window of the breakfast nook. A freshly shaken snow globe. That was the view she should be having right now. Everything blanketed in a fluffy layer of white, with fat flakes swirling in the air, smoke curling from the chimney tops, the smell of homemade hot chocolate brewing in the kitchen . . . the picture postcard of a perfect winter wonderland playground.

Oh, it looked like a postcard all right. "But the only snow that goes with this picture is Snow White." In fact, all she needed was a few dancing butterflies and adorable chirpy bluebirds flitting about to complete the scenario. Walt Disney would be orgasmic.

Kirby Farrell, on the other hand, not so much.

She'd stopped listening to the news completely. If she heard one more report about this being the warmest winter in the history of recorded weather, she was going to throw something.

And to think how smug she'd been. This area had been about as goof-proof a location as she could have hoped to find. Well, east of the Rockies, anyway. Pennydash was tucked up against the highest peaks of the Green Mountains in such a way as to create a perfect winter effect. Even when other parts of New England experienced less than optimal snowfall conditions, Pennydash and the surrounding area were generally blessed with the most of whatever snowfall came their way.

Historically, it had been mostly a mining and farming community, until advances in technology made it possible to bring in the kind of supplies needed to build a world-class-level resort. One she'd known about through her connections back in Colorado before they'd even been publicly announced. It had been the exact break she'd needed at exactly the right time. And, historically for Kirby Farrell, the good breaks were very few and far between.

Now Pennydash, Vermont, would become an exciting new vacation spot for skiers, and at the moment, Kirby's inn was the only other game in town. She was well aware there were other start-ups under way, but she'd been the only one to open up on time for the new resort's inaugural season. A prime, once-in-a-business-launching chance to build a loyal customer base before the competition started.

Right.

She sipped her hot chocolate, defiantly made despite the seventy-degree temps, her own personal little nose-thumbing at Mother Nature, and studiously avoided going into the office she'd created behind her bedroom in what had once been the mudroom by the back of the house. Now the attached garage served that function and kept her from having to scrape clean her lovingly restored hardwood floors from all the muck her vast numbers of boarders would surely be tracking in, what with all the mud, snow, road sand, and salt out there. Or so she had planned, anyway.

Besides, she didn't need to look at the books to know how broke she was. And even after spending close to a year renovating the three-story, gingerbread-laced, lone house up on the hill, there was still a long list of things she needed to do. Those were slated for the off season, later this spring and summer, bankrolled by the profits made from her first successful ski season as an independent innkeeper.

Mm-hmm.

Now her main objective was to keep the bank from rolling over on her business, which also happened to be the roof over her head. Either the snow had better start falling, or she'd better come up with another way to keep a full house and quick. She didn't think she could handle having her dreams crushed twice.

Although, at least this time she'd see the end coming.

"Yeah," she muttered, turning her back to the window. "Like train lights in a very short tunnel."

She sat her half-empty mug down on the counter and walked into the front parlor where she'd been working on repairing a wedding ring quilt she'd found at a flea market the weekend before. It was going to make a gorgeous bedspread for the third-floor queen suite. But she wasn't feeling up for the intricate needlework required. And quite frankly, sitting around indulging in another pity party for one was simply too pathetic, even for the mood she was in. Instead she grabbed a notepad and pen and went outside. Might as well utilize the sunny skies and bare ground to plot out the design for her spring flower and vegetable garden.

Take that, Mother Nature.

She was crouching in front of the weathered mulch at the

base of a small willow, frowning at a tidy circle of crocuses that had the absolute nerve to even think about poking their little purple heads out of the dirt, when the loud, rumbling sound of a motorcycle vibrated through the warm, morning air.

She looked up in time to see a big, black, dust-covered Harley slow and swing into the narrow drive that led up the hill to her inn. The guy straddling the noisy monster was wearing a thick black leather jacket, jeans with what looked like black leather chaps over them, heavy gloves, heavier looking boots, and a black helmet that looked as dusty as the bike.

"Stealth biker," Kirby murmured as she straightened to a stand. She could only assume he was either lost, or . . . well, she didn't know any other reason why he'd be idling in her drive-way. When he didn't turn around at the leveled-out gravel lot area at the top and head back down the hill, she walked over to see what was up. Maybe he was looking for work. Which, good luck with that. The area wasn't an economic boomtown in the best of times, and while the excitement over the coming ski hoards had been palpable in terms of expanding the local work-force, that excitement had waned rapidly in the face of the re-lentless, unseasonably warm weather.

"So, I hate to disappoint you," she murmured under her breath, "but I'm definitely not hiring."

As she drew closer, he turned off the bike, settled the weight on the kickstand, and then threw his leg over the back and straightened. He looked . . . well, the word "powerful" came to mind. Maybe it was all the black leather, but he was a big man, easily over six feet, with or without the heavy road boots, broad shouldered, and just very . . . imposing. He slid off his gloves and laid them across the seat; then he turned as he unbuckled his helmet. Affording her a lovely view of a mighty fine back-side. She decided right then and there she was a big fan of what-ever those chap things were he was wearing. *Damn.*

Then he turned back, helmet off, and she forgot all about his amazing ass. She was too busy noticing the way his thick, dark curls, unshaven, hard-looking jaw, and lethal black sunglasses jacked up the intensity of his overall outlaw appearance. Her steps faltered, partly because he looked dangerous, and partly because, well . . . any woman with a pulse would probably have stumbled at least a step or two. Half of her wished there was a county sheriff close by, just in case . . . and the other half wished she could afford to pay this guy to tackle the list of odd jobs that were slowly piling up. Starting, of course, with the tasks that would require him to work with his shirt off. As often as possible. Warm weather might as well come in handy for something, after all.

She noted the bike had a Nevada license plate. Interesting. A bit longer than a day trip from Vermont. But given the amount of dust and dirt that had accumulated on the sleek machine, and on him she noted, it wouldn't have surprised her if that's how long he'd been on the road. So . . . not a local looking for work.

"Can I help you?"

He slung his helmet on the back bar of the bike. "You have any rooms available?"

His voice was deep, a little rough. He sounded more than a little road-weary. Or maybe he always had that kind of laconic drawl. Whatever the case, it only enhanced the whole road warrior vibe he had going on. He did things to her body just standing there that she hadn't felt in . . . clearly far longer than she wanted to think about. "You want a room?"

In retrospect, she realized how comical her honest surprise must have seemed. His smile was slow, but brief, more a quirk of the lips. Which were also kind of chiseled and perfect. She really needed to stop staring. Anytime now.

"You do rent them out, right?" For all his pulse-pounding, over-the-top sex appeal, he was actually fairly soft-spoken. If gravel could be soft. In fact, now that she was close up, she thought her early suspicions might be right. He didn't just sound road-weary, he looked downright exhausted. She couldn't see his eyes, but the lines bracketing his mouth, the flexing and tensing of his jaw, and just the way he stood there, shoulders hunched a little, all but shouted extreme fatigue.

He nodded at the carved wood sign, painted periwinkle blue and leaf green, and planted in front of the house. Under the name, PENNYDASH INN, it read: PROPRIETOR: KIRBY FARRELL. "Is that you?"

"I am. I mean, yes, that's me. I'm sorry, you just caught me by surprise."

His lips curved again, a bit wryly. "You not in the habit of folks wanting to stay here?"

She forced herself to snap out of the hormone fog that was clearly only affecting her—no shock there, as she had at least a dozen years on the guy—and smiled as she swept her arm to encompass the view of the very green looking Green Mountains. "Not exactly the vacation destination for the discerning skiing enthusiast this winter."

"Ah. My lucky day, then." That last part was said with a particularly dry note as he pulled out his wallet. "I don't ski."

Kirby smiled at that and quickly shifted gears the rest of the way into innkeeper mode. "Why don't we go inside, get you registered?"

"My bike okay here?"

Her smile widened as she continued to find her footing. He wasn't exactly the sort of guest she'd visualized hosting as she'd been slaving away all last summer and fall. In fact every single one of her instincts, both as a woman and as a business owner, were screaming that this guy was not what he appeared to be— or maybe too much of exactly what he appeared to be. But, given the current state of her bank account, she was in no position to get all picky-choosy about what kind of boarders she'd prefer to have under her roof.

"It would appear you have the run of the lot," she said, then immediately could have kicked herself. *Right, Kirby, just announce to the down-on-his-luck-looking, lone-wolf biker dude that there are no other guests in the inn.* Not that he would have to be Sherlock Holmes to figure that one out, but still.

He opened one of the side compartments on the back of the bike and lifted out a black gear bag, which he slung over his shoulder. Even that unconscious motion was sexy as hell. *Seriously, get a damn grip*. She was coming off like the stupid cliché of single, sex-starved, middle-aged innkeeper, when she was anything but that. Okay, so she was exactly that. But she definitely wouldn't have used the term "starved." Sex wasn't everything. At least, for the past two years and right up until five minutes ago she'd had herself firmly convinced of that.

She started up the cobblestone walkway, leading to the wide wooden steps, smiling as she always did when seeing the front of her newly restored place. It was probably hokey to some, and she seriously doubted this particular guest would even notice, much less appreciate it, but she loved the lacey gingerbread pattern that scalloped along the edge of the wraparound porch overhang. It made the place look lively and inviting to her. Very ski chalet. She'd painted the house in a flat, Wedgwood blue to offset the cream and pale green–painted adornment, so it wasn't too over-the-top cutesy, but it looked like a happy house. And that had been her goal. Both for herself and her guests.

She heard his heavy boots on the steps behind her, and a little tingle shot straight down her spine. Okay, so maybe she was a teeny tiny bit hungry. But she was also a well-educated, savvy businesswoman and any second now she was going to start acting like it.

She'd already decided to fax a copy of his driver's license over to Thad at the sheriff's office and get him to check the guy out. Smart business even if her hormones were acting stupid . . . and she was admittedly curious to know more if she could. Her new guest didn't exactly strike her as the chatty sort.

She stepped behind the small counter she'd had designed and built under the stairs where they made their turn up to the second-floor landing. "I'll need to see your driver's license or some other form of photo ID." She smiled as she turned the antique guest book around, hoping her chatter made him less aware of the fact that there weren't many names filled in before the line where his signature would go. In fact, other than Aunt Frieda, who'd come up from Florida over the summer to help her with the window treatments and the finishing touches of her interior design plan, and a small group who'd stayed for a wedding in the area around the holidays . . . well, the page wasn't exactly full of scrawled names.

"Interesting book," he said, surprising her with voluntary conversation. If you could count two words as conversation. He lifted the worn and faded leather cover to look at the front.

"I found it at an antiques market. It was the guest register for a hotel that was here back in the late eighteen hundreds when the town first started up. And, don't worry, I use more technologically advanced record keeping, but I kind of liked the idea of the more personal touch, too." She'd actually envisioned folks leaving little notes about their stay, perhaps coming back again and again over the years and looking back over previous entries. At the moment Kirby was just thankful that there was a stack of previously signed pages in the book. No one had to know that the signatures on those pages had been signed with a fountain pen. Well over a hundred years ago.

So, of course, he flipped back a few pages.

She kept the smile on her face and busied herself making a copy of the driver's license he'd slid across the countertop. Great, not only was he the only current guest, but now he'd realize she wasn't typically booked up. Ever. Made for a great setup for any number of horror movie scenarios.

Kirby turned back, smile still set in place, and handed his license back to him, belatedly realizing she'd been so distracted she hadn't even looked at it. She'd check out the photocopy just as soon as she was alone.

She began explaining the rates, but he stopped her with, "I just need a single. Top floor if you have it. Doesn't have to be fancy."

She nodded and snagged a key from the hook under the counter. "One key will be okay?"

He nodded and palmed the key off the polished wood countertop. His hands were broad, tanned, and surprisingly well maintained. In fact, the brief flash she'd had of his long fingers, she'd have sworn he had a manicure. That . . . so didn't seem to go with the rest of the persona. "How many nights?" She glanced up to find him looking at her, but she didn't think he was actually seeing her. Hard to say. He was still wearing his sunglasses.

"Not sure. Is that a problem?"

So many things about this guy weren't adding up. She could lie and tell him she was booked solid starting the coming weekend, but given the fact that he'd seen just how busy she'd been over the past month . . . or three, she didn't think she could pull that off with the sincerity required. "No, that's fine. How will you be paying? I take all major credit cards—"

"Cash," he said.

She tried—and was certain she failed spectacularly—not to gape when he pulled out a wad of bills being held together with a wide paper band. The kind of band that looked like a bank band. What the hell did that mean?

He peeled off several bills and laid them on the counter. "That should take care of the next few days." He wasn't trying to flaunt it, nor was he coming off with any braggadocio or arrogance. In fact, he tucked the wad away as swiftly as he'd pulled it out.

"I—um, yeah, I mean yes," she said, taking the bills—the one-hundred-dollar bills—off the counter. He hadn't even asked her rates. "That will be fine. Wine, cheese, crackers will be available in the front parlor at five and I can direct you to several local restaurants for lunch, dinner, depending on—"

"That won't be necessary," he said, sliding the strap of his gear back over his shoulder. "And don't go to any trouble for me with the wine. I doubt I'll be back down tonight."

"Okay," she said. Despite the mane of curly, wind-tossed hair, the beard stubble, and beat-up leather jacket, he seemed a rather decent sort. Quiet, mannerly. Then there was the wad of bills and salon-maintained hands. And the fact that she still hadn't seen his eyes yet. Eyes said a lot about a person. She tried to pull her thoughts together. After sliding the bills into the cash drawer under the counter, she stepped out from behind the desk. "Let me show you to your room."

He glanced at the key. "Number seven?" Then his lips curled briefly and he muttered something like "Lucky seven," under his breath.

"Yes, top floor, back corner, nice view down the valley and the front range from your window."

He curled the key into his palm and shifted his gear bag up farther on his shoulder. "I'm sure it will be fine. Thanks." He gave her a nod, then started up the stairs.

She watched as he turned at the first landing and kept climbing, his heavy tread on the steps at odds with his otherwise quiet demeanor. She briefly thought that perhaps she should follow him up for security reasons, but it wasn't like he wouldn't have ample time to explore the place, and she couldn't be everywhere at once. There were cameras installed discreetly in the top corner molding at the ends of each hallway, but they weren't hooked up to anything yet. The guests didn't have to know that, however.

As soon as she heard the creaking floorboards up overhead, she slid the paper from the copier and turned it over. "Brett Hennessey," she read, then skimmed the rest of the information. He was from Las Vegas. And, noting he'd just turned thirty right before the holidays, he was ten years younger than she was. She smiled at herself and all her fluttery little hormones. So he was a little older than she'd thought, but the only other surprise was that he hadn't ma'am'd her. If he'd noticed her reaction to him at all, he'd probably thought she was having a hot flash.

She penned a quick note on a small sticky pad, peeled it off and stuck it on the paper copy of his license, and then slid it in the fax machine and sent it off to Thad. Not that she was truly concerned, not really. Still, Las Vegas, long way from home, big wad of cash, dusty motorcycle–riding, road-weary, hunky rider in black chaps with a sweet ass and perfectly maintained cuticles . . . Yeah, that was not your typical inn guest. She might not ever find out what he was all about, but there was definitely a story.

That was actually, in part, her attraction to wanting to be an innkeeper. As a child, growing up in a small resort town in the middle of the Rockies, she'd always looked up at airplanes flying overhead and wondered where the passengers inside were going, what adventure or journey they were embarking on . . . or returning from. Of course, in her youthful fantasies, the stories were always fantastical. Nothing so mundane as a burned-out businessman heading back from a boring meeting on the coast. But, even in her far more mature, far less naïve forty-year-old mind, she still found people endlessly fascinating and wondered what their story was, what path they were on. As someone who provided a way station along that path, she'd get to find out.

Like the group who'd stayed through the holidays. Three couples, each in their late twenties, all of whom had begun dating each other while in college together, had reserved rooms to attend the wedding of the fourth couple in their college quartet. Two of the couples were simply enjoying the reunion and time spent catching up, but the third woman had confided in Kirby that she was hoping that watching two of their oldest and dearest friends tie the knot would prompt her significant other to finally pop the question. Kirby had kept her opinion on the likelihood of that happening to herself, but she'd enjoyed the confided secret nonetheless.

Not that she was nosy—okay, she totally was, but she didn't pry. Not exactly. Mostly because she didn't have to. She'd grown up inside a ski resort, and had literally done every job conceivable along the way, from cleaning rooms and working registration, to busing tables and even running the ski lifts. One thing she'd learned was that if she was friendly and outgoing, and tried to make her guests feel at home—a feeling that she hoped her bed-and-breakfast-style inn would encourage—people talked, chatted, and generally shared far more with her, a complete stranger, than they sometimes did with those in their own party.

She looked at Mr. Hennessey's license and wondered what his story might involve. Why was he such a long way from home . . . and where was he going from here? Why did he have such a big wad of cash? Had he gambled big in Vegas and won? Except he lived there according to his license. Had he stolen the money? And why had he biked cross-country instead of hopping a plane? Was he on the run? Or merely taking a long road trip, seeing the country? Plus, why did a guy wearing dusty biker leathers have the hands of a Wall Street investment banker?

She laid the paper down and entered all the information into the computer . . . and wondered if he'd be here long enough for her to find out.

Chapter 2

B rett Hennessey just needed a place to stop.
And think.

He was tired. Tired of running, tired of not knowing what the best course of action was, tired of worrying about the people he cared about. His life had never been normal, but he thought he'd finally gotten a handle on balancing the expectations that had been placed on him. Somehow, over the past six months, it had all spun out of control. He wasn't even sure when it had begun unraveling, really. So many little threads, he supposed. Threads he'd let go and ignored because they annoyed him and he hadn't wanted to deal with the bullshit they presented. None of them particularly important, in and of themselves, but collectively, they'd all seemed to unravel completely at once.

Easy to say now that he should have spent a little more time on the annoying bullshit part as it had come along, but he'd never been good at that part. He'd told them all that. The sponsors, tournament directors, media agents, casino owners, television producers. Repeatedly. They'd told him to hire people to handle the details. Delegate. But he wasn't comfortable with having people counting on him for their personal livelihood. Hell, he hadn't been all that crazy about earning his own livelihood that way. Not to mention the fact that the idea of people hanging around him all the time, looking over his shoulder, waiting to see if he would win big again, and thereby get to keep their jobs, would have driven him bonkers. There were already too many people, too much noise, too much . . . everything in his life.

It was true, he had a knack for cards. He'd grown up in Vegas casinos, literally, so of course he knew how to play poker. And yeah, when the Texas Hold'em craze had swept the nation, he'd swiftly become an attention getter, whether he'd wanted to be or not. He'd been a little—okay, a lot—younger than most back then, but he could hardly help that. It had been fun, in the beginning, sort of like a hobby. He'd been a kid, a minor, so there wasn't much he could really do with his innate skills other than show them off.

It hadn't been until later on that he'd started to think of it as a way to earn money. Even then he hadn't pictured it as a career. At best, it was a way to pay for college a little faster than just banging nails and hauling lumber on the renovation jobs he worked on for his best friend's dad. He definitely hadn't counted on winning often enough to make it pay long term.

He'd been around the game his whole life, so he knew better than most that when it came to cards, the odds would always balance things out. Often. And usually not in your favor. The trick was respecting that, not getting greedy, and being willing to walk away with a little and never banking on winning a lot. That was one fundamental rule he'd never broken.

Or wouldn't have, had it been necessary to heed it. Because when Brett Hennessey played, he tended to win. A lot. In fact, he won so often even he had begun to wonder what the hell was going on. Skill only accounted for so much, and nobody was that lucky. His life up to that point hadn't exactly been blessed. Which, granted, had partly been what had endeared him to the poker crowd in the first place. Young kid, tough childhood, a bit of a rebel. At least that's the way the sponsors played it. He didn't see himself as a rebel so much as a survivor.

The day he'd hit twenty-one he'd been hot bait for every cable show producer and online gambling site on the planet. It had been a lot after a long time of not much. He'd had a hard time—an impossible time as it turned out—saying no to being given a chance. Any chance. But no matter how much he tried to keep things sane, he didn't seem to have much say on where the white hot glare of the celebrity spotlight shined. And, for quite some time now, it had been shining on him.

He'd played his way through college, then grad school, and then figured that would be it. He'd call it even and walk away, having provided whatever the hell draw it was that he'd become in exchange for the chance to earn enough to better himself, better his life, give himself a chance to get up and finally out, once and for all. Win-win for both sides.

But it hadn't exactly turned out like that. College was long in the past, his degrees were gathering dust, while what had originally been a way to pay off school loans had, nine years later, somehow become a way of life. A life he'd long since grown weary of, but had continued to participate in because it never seemed the right time to walk away. He was always left feeling like he was leaving someone in the lurch. Someone who had helped him out when he'd needed it. But he'd finally burned out, wised up . . . and walked away.

Which was when things had gotten really interesting.

That good luck charm that had been his constant companion for the past decade had abandoned him, and rather swiftly at that. He hadn't really thought much about it at the time, not initially anyway, beyond being pissed off at the string of little incidences that had been more a nuisance than anything. He'd replaced the missing supplies on his current job site. Over the years, he'd never stopped banging nails, although his contributions to the renovation company his buddy, Dan, now owned, having taken it over from his father several years ago, hadn't always been consistent during the craziest of times. But Dan had convinced him to take over one of his easier contracts while trying to sort out what he wanted to do with the rest of his life, and Brett had been happy for the distraction.

The missing materials had been irritating, but he'd resolved that, only to have his work truck broken into. It was a pain in the ass to fix the jammed door lock, and he'd wondered what the hell anyone thought they were going to steal out of the old rust bucket, but it had never occurred to him to tie those minor annoyances to the barrage of requests that continued to pour in for him to come back to the tables and play.

The bad luck streak had continued, though, with the stakes escalating each time. Dan's brand-new work truck had been stolen and found in a drainage ditch, half bashed in, tires gone, one door missing, and another job site had flooded due to a water pipe break that hadn't been anywhere near where Brett's crew had been working at the time. Brett had begun to wonder what in the hell was going on, but the cops hadn't turned up any evidence on who might have been responsible for the stolen truck much less tied it to the job site problem he'd been sure was vandalism, so he'd done a little digging on his own, but got no answers. Then another one of his job sites half burned down, his landlady started having a string of trouble at the boarding house she owned and he lived in . . . and the demands for his return to the tables had taken on a decidedly . . . concerned tone.

And he'd finally put two and two together.

So he did the only thing he could do. He got out of Vegas, putting as much distance between the folks he cared about and himself as possible. He'd let it be known that he was leaving town, leaving Dan's employ, his leased rooms at Vanetta's place . . . all of it, behind him. If somebody wanted him that badly, they were going to have to come after him, and no one else.

And here he was, four, almost five weeks later, in Vermont, of all places, exhausted, confused, and no longer sure he'd done the right thing in leaving. Nothing else had happened since he'd left, which initially he'd taken as proof that he'd been the target all along. Only, as the weeks continued to pass, no one was tracking him down as far as he could tell, and no one was trying to contact him, either, much less pressure him to return. Apparently his blunt declaration of permanent retirement and the added step of leaving his hometown completely had been taken seriously.

He'd talked to Dan throughout his cross-country sabbatical, who'd been monitoring everyone Brett was worried about, and . . . nothing. Not a single incident. He'd begun to think Dan was right, that it was just a string of incredibly bad luck. That, maybe, after all his amazing good fortune, the odds had simply finally caught up with him. But there was still that niggle, that suspicion, that wouldn't entirely go away.

If he was right, and returned, as Dan was encouraging him to do . . . he was afraid it would stir things up again. And, to be honest, he didn't know if he wanted to return or what, exactly, he'd be returning to. Dan's renovation business was something Brett had done while figuring out his next step, but working for or with Dan wasn't the actual step he wanted to take. Not in the big picture, anyway. He wanted to finally put all his education to use, do something that energized him, that he could be passionate about. He just didn't know exactly how to go about doing that, or what form, exactly, that passion would take.

But it was time he figured his shit out. So he'd stopped running, stopped trying to second guess, just . . . stopped. He'd checked into Kirby's bed-and-breakfast because it was as good a place as any to stop his flight . . . and because the unique architecture of the old place called to him.

His thoughts turned to his hostess. Kirby Farrell. It was true that he'd been a little self-involved of late—okay, more than a little—but not so much so that he wasn't aware of the way she'd been watching him. And that, more surprisingly, he'd wanted to watch her right back. She hadn't recognized him, which he'd have never presumed she should, at least not outside Vegas. But on his trek around the country, he'd been amazed at the number of people whose paths he'd crossed who apparently had nothing better to do than watch a bunch of strangers bet ridiculously large sums of money on a card game on late-night cable.

He'd been relieved that Kirby wasn't one of them. Which was only part of why he'd been drawn to her. On the surface, she was a contradiction. Her frame was long, lean, and willowy; her hair a soft brown, her eyes an even softer gray. He'd seen his share of dancers and she had that long, lean dancer's body. Only she was all ballet and *Swan Lake* . . . not two pasties and a monstrous sequin-covered head piece.

She was all grace and refinement and he would have guessed her to be the quiet and reserved type. Very proper. Classy. Elegant.

But there had been nothing reserved about the way those soft gray eyes had cataloged every inch of him. She came across as educated, smart, her expression one of polite kindness when she smiled . . . and yet as he trudged up the stairs to his room just now, he'd have bet against the house that she was staring openly at his ass.

So, instead of thinking about the bed that awaited him, and the sweet oblivion of sleep, he found himself wondering how a real honest-to-God smile would transform that oh-so-serious face of hers, and what her laughter would sound like. And if she was as direct in all areas of her life as she'd been standing in her own driveway, giving him quite the once-over.

He dropped his bag by the door, yanked his clothes off, and let them drop where they fell. Then he debated for all of two seconds on the merits of taking a shower first, before giving in to the siren call of the huge sleigh bed with its soft-looking spread and mounds of pillows. At the moment, it looked like heaven on earth. And something told him, after meeting Ms. Inn Proprietor, who seemed attentive to detail, at least where his person had been concerned, she hadn't been any less so in her accommodations.

And he was right.

A long groan of abject appreciation rolled out of him without a conscious effort as soon as his weight sank into the heavenly perfection that was his new bed. He might not climb back out of it ever again.

He tugged a pillow under his head, tucked another one under his arm, his eyes already drooping before he could even contemplate getting under the covers instead of laying stark naked on top of them . . . but that was the last thought he had.

Until she screamed.

He shoved up on his elbows and blinked the cobwebs away. He had no idea how long he'd been out, and for a moment thought maybe he'd just been dreaming. Then there came a loud clatter from somewhere outside the back of the house, which had him instinctively moving off the bed and ducking to look out the window in his room before he really put thought to deed.

There, almost directly down below, was Kirby Farrell, Proprietor, hanging from a rather high limb of a huge oak tree. If it hadn't been for the season and total lack of foliage, he wouldn't have seen her at all. Her feet and legs were wiggling as she tried to get a better grip on the branch, but it was clearly much bigger around than her slender hands.

He shoved the window open and stuck his head out. "Hang on, I'll be right down."

She angled her head to look up, then her eyes rounded and she struggled even more furiously as the movement seemed to loosen her already precarious grip.

Brett turned and headed for his bedroom door; then he belatedly realized he wasn't wearing anything. He hopped into his jeans and snagged his shirt off the floor before running down the winding staircase, pulling the black tee over his head as he went. He had no idea where there might be a back door to the place, so just headed out the front and ran to the back. There he found a long ladder laying on the ground and the innkeeper still hanging on for dear life, far too high above him to drop safely to the ground, or for him to attempt to catch her. He didn't see where he could climb the tree and get her down without risking shaking her off, so he grabbed the ladder and lifted it off the ground and tried to position it as close to her as he could.

"I'll hold it steady," he called up. "Just let me get it against the branch, then swing your leg over so you get your footing. Then you can let go with one hand and grab the side."

To her credit, she wasn't squealing or obviously freaking out. She didn't yell back down to him, either, so he just worked to get the thing as stable as possible. "Okay, just swing your left leg over."

He could see the grit and determination on her face and found himself still marveling a little over the dichotomy that was Ms. Farrell. She of the cool elegance and cultured features who would look perfectly at home in tutu and toe shoes . . . was presently swinging from a tree in baggy khakis, a hoodie, and a pair of well-worn hiking boots. He assumed she'd been wearing the very same thing earlier, but he honestly hadn't noticed. All he remembered really were her soft gray eyes and prim-looking mouth, and the incongruous directness of her personality.

He heard her grunt, then lost about ten years off his life when one hand slipped off the limb just as her other leg caught the side of the ladder. "Grab the ladder! I've got you."

He planted his bare feet in the scruff of winter grass and braced the ladder as best he could. Fortunately, while the width of the limb had made it hard for her to grab on to, it made for steady support for the ladder.

A few seconds later, she was safely on the top rungs and he let out a deep sigh of relief. "I'll hold it while you come down," he called up to her.

As yet, other than grunting to get on the ladder, she hadn't said a single word. And, at the moment, she didn't appear to be in any hurry to climb down, either. Maybe she was just taking a moment to collect herself now that she was safe. But seconds ticked by and she still wasn't moving.

"Are you okay?"

"Fine," she said, the word muffled by the sleeve of her hoodie as she was ducking her head between her arms, which were clutching the rungs above.

Her back was to him—well, mostly it was her butt above him—but he couldn't see her face. "You thinking you might want to come down sometime soon?"

There was a pause, then, "I'm thinking that I need to get this damn kitten to get its claws out of me first."

What? "What kitten?"

"The world's stupidest one, who thought that climbing a big tree would be a great adventure, until it got stuck and then figured that climbing all the way out to the end of the limb would be a better bet than just climbing down the damn tree."

"Ah," he said, suddenly fighting a smile. "That kitten."

"Exactly. It's inside the front of my sweatshirt. Trying to climb me. I just need to—" She shifted a little, and the ladder wobbled, which made Brett jump back into action and brace it again, but that didn't keep his smile from growing when a rather superlative string of swear words erupted from his heretofore-thought-of-as-elegant innkeeper.

"Maybe your best bet is just to get you both down on the terra firma and then get untangled before either of you does more damage."

"Oh, I'm going to do some damage all right," he heard her mutter over his head, as she slowly began to descend, one careful rung at a time. And which he didn't believe for a second. People who dragged massive ladders out from God-knows-where in order to climb into a centuries-old oak tree to save a terrified kitten were doubtfully the abusive types.

As soon as she was on the ground, he let go of the ladder and took her arms, turning her to face him. "Here, let me get him."

"Her," she grunted, "which, I am well aware makes two stupid females stuck in a tree. Just let me pry this one claw out of my—ouch! Dammit, cat!"

Brett carefully unzipped the hoodie to find the most innocent looking, teeniest of tiny baby kittens . . . presently doing actual bloody damage to the front of its rescuer's torso.

"Damn," he muttered as he tried to pry the claws out of both fabric and skin, which brought a few more swear words, but given the situation, her restraint, otherwise, was impressive.

As Kirby was clearly past the point, Brett softened his own voice and did his best to calm the still-terrified kitty and de-prong the thing from the front of Kirby's body. But every time he got one claw out, the kitty would redouble its efforts else-where, as if it were past comprehending that letting go no longer meant a plunge to its death.

Finally Brett ripped his own T-shirt over his head and wrapped it around the kitten's body, so that when it swiped its feet, it got tangled up in his T-shirt instead. It took a few more very painful maneuvers, but a minute later, he had the little hel-lion wrapped up.

He crooned nonsense to the fluffball, then winced and swore himself as she got a few of his fingers through the shirt. "Blood-thirsty little thing, aren't you?" He started to squat down to let her go.

"No! She'll just go right back up the tree."

Brett stood but tried to keep the now-squalling, squirming ball of kitten and T-shirt away from his body. "What did you have in mind then? Kitten soup?"

"Don't tempt me."

She turned toward the back door, which he saw now led to a screened-in porch outside and what looked like the kitchen be-yond the door leading inside the house.

"Let's take her inside," she said, "see if we can get her calmed down, then I'll call Pete to come get her."

"Would Pete be the owner? Maybe he should have been the one climbing the tree," Brett said as he followed her up onto the porch, still holding the kitten bundle aloft.

"He's with animal control. Actually, he is animal control.

Only usually he deals with wild animals who get themselves in trouble. I think this one qualifies. These scratches sting like—"

Brett paused at the bottom of the porch steps.

"What?" she asked, turning back when she realized he wasn't behind her.

"You almost killed yourself getting her down and you're giving her to the pound?" He thought it was funny how he'd thought her gray eyes so soft before. Storm clouds were soft compared to the color of her eyes at the moment.

"You want to keep her? You're welcome to. But there's a surcharge for pets."

He grinned at that. "Okay. I'll pay for room and board. And any damages," he added as the storm clouds darkened.

She looked like he'd suddenly sprouted two heads. "You're really going to keep her?"

"Not permanently, but I'm thinking we might be able to do a better job finding her a home than the dog catcher. Maybe find out where she strayed from in the first place. Maybe somebody's missing her already."

Storm clouds parted. Momentarily, anyway. "Fine," she said at length. "You're responsible, then. I'm going in to clean up."

She tromped on into the house, apparently no longer concerned about him or the kitten. So why he was standing on the back stoop, grinning like an idiot—an idiot who'd never owned so much as a pet fish and had just apparently adopted a feral cat in the making—he had no idea. Maybe he was more road weary than he thought. Had to be it.

"Come on, Claw," he said to the still-squalling bundle. "Let's see if you stay this ornery in the face of some food and water. Maybe we'll feed both of us. Then figure out what our next step is."

He let the screen door slap shut behind him, still careful to keep the wriggling ball of cotton well away from his body. And thought maybe it was fitting, in a way. They were both outcasts, after all. Stuck in a limbo not entirely of their own choosing.

He stepped into the kitchen and discovered Kirby at the sink,

her hoodie gone and her long-sleeve shirt hiked up as she carefully dabbed at the bloody welts on her abdomen.

He winced at the damage done to such tender, pale skin . . .
but at the same time found himself thinking that if they had to
be stuck, perhaps both he and the cat could have done far
worse.

Chapter 3

The instant Kirby caught sight of Brett from the corner of her eye, entering the kitchen, she clumsily shut off the water with one hand and tugged her shirt back down with the other, wincing slightly as the cotton fabric rubbed over her raw, scratched flesh.

"Flesh" being the key word flashing through her head. And the fact that Brett Hennessey was sporting quite a lot of it at the moment. Not, perhaps, as much as the eyeful she'd gotten when she'd looked up at his bedroom window. Holy crap. She'd be picturing all that masculine perfection in her dreams—waking and sleeping—for weeks. Who was she kidding? Months. Possibly longer. It wasn't likely anything else would come along to top it anytime soon. It was a miracle she hadn't dropped like a stone from the tree the instant she laid eyes on him. So . . . so much of him.

She averted her gaze and gathered up the clutter of first aid supplies she'd pulled out of the little kit she kept under the sink for kitchen emergencies. It was silly to feel so self-conscious. After all, he was exposing a lot more than she'd been, and she seriously doubted he'd be as moved by the sight of her pale, scratched-up stomach as she'd been by his oh-so-perfectly-golden skin. So, so much skin . . .

"I—uh, I have some milk. In the fridge. For the cat. They drink milk, right?"

"I haven't any idea." He was just standing there, half naked. In her kitchen. The very same kitchen she'd fallen in love with for its roomy interior, high ceilings, and huge bay windows. Sunny, bright, and spacious. Suddenly it felt tiny, airless, and crowded. Very crowded. In fact, the only way to make a graceful exit was past his very big, very mostly naked body. At least she couldn't seem to look anywhere but at the naked part. And given she'd seen the parts that were currently covered by his jeans, it was just as dangerous to look there. So, she simply wouldn't look at him at all.

She shoved the first aid kit under the sink and swung around to the cupboards over the opposite counter. "I have bowls in here." She put one on the counter and then dragged the antique bread keeper over and rolled up the top. "Bread in here." She scooted over to the pantry. "I think I have tuna."

Kirby knew she was babbling. Realized she was acting like an idiot teenager who was stumbling over her words in the face of the school stud. Unfortunately, acknowledging the ridiculousness of it didn't seem to make it stop.

After assembling her cluster of kitten-feeding amenities, she floundered for a moment. "Are you sure I can't get you anything?"

When he didn't reply right away, she was finally forced to turn and look at him. Still packed a punch. Jeans, broad, beautifully muscled shoulders, a six-pack that wouldn't quit . . . and green eyes. Seriously? Didn't seem fair, really. All that and killer eyes, too? Which were twinkling a little at the moment, despite the wriggling ball of black T-shirt dangling from his fist. So, he thought this was funny. That she was funny. Or, at least, pathetically amusing.

Also fair. Because she was certainly behaving pathetically at the moment.

"I'm fine," he said. "I think I'll just grab a few things and take them upstairs. I'm not thinking it would be a good idea to let my, uh, roommate here, out, until we're behind closed doors."

Heaven help her, that was the last image she really needed at that moment. Behind closed doors with Brett Hennessey. Oh, yes indeedy, that visual would be guaranteed a starring role in those dreams she'd be having, no doubt. "Here, let me," she said, more to have something to do than because she'd really thought it through.

That came later, after she was trudging up the stairs behind him and the very annoyed kitten bundle, admiring yet another fine view and deciding that she really, truly, had to reconsider trying to develop some kind of social life here in Pennydash, and not just with the Friday-night ladies auxiliary bingo league.

Of course, any fantasy she might have harbored about possibly developing a nice, safe, temporary dalliance with one of the resort ski instructors, or emergency patrol guys, was, at the very least, going to have to wait a year, as most of them had either been let go or quit and headed west or overseas to find steady work where there was actually snow on the ground. Any other time, she'd have been okay with that. Or would have talked herself into being okay with it. After all, what were her alternatives, really? At the moment, however, staring at Brett's insanely perfect ass, she was thinking a year sounded like an impossible eternity. But cheered herself by acknowledging that possible alternatives could, potentially, turn up at any time. Just as he had.

Not that he qualified as such. He, her much younger, incredibly hot guest. But he had at least opened her up to the idea that something could happen. With someone else. At some point. Possibly.

She should thank him for that.

At the moment she was sort of caught up staring at the back of his 501's and wondering how that bit looked uncovered, as she'd pretty much seen everything else. Probably just as good. Or better, she thought with a long, mental sigh.

Naturally, this was when he topped the stairs at his third-floor landing and turned back, so that she was now staring directly at a part of his body she had, actually, seen unclothed, and immediately pictured again. She gulped, and might have wobbled back and fallen down all three flights of stairs, thereby ruining all of his best efforts at saving her from herself after all.

But he snagged her elbow as her tray full of goodies wobbled, and eased her up onto the landing next to him. He opened his door with his free hand, bumped it open wider with his hip, and motioned her inside with a tip of his head. "Trying to keep this one from being anywhere close," he said, still juggling the kitty bundle, which said kitty was trying to climb out of, as one claws-extended paw made it out of one of the gaps at the top where he was holding the T-shirt bundle mostly closed. "You can just set it on the bed. Or the dresser. Wherever."

She arranged the items on his dresser top, trying not to look at the mussed-up duvet that covered the sea of bed. The sea of bed that made his airy, sunshiny room feel suddenly just as small as her airy and sunshiny kitchen had a few moments ago. Yeah, she definitely needed a life. "Okay, I'll leave you two to get acquainted." The kitten chose that moment to give a particularly plaintive howl. "Good luck with that," she added, with a dubious glance at the kitten.

"We'll be fine," he said, but the quick glance he gave the still-squirmy bundle wasn't quite as convincing.

Which, somehow, was what restored her confidence. Big man leveled by a little kitten. Yeah, it might be small of her, but it helped her scrape at least a little of her self-esteem up off the floor.

"If you need anything else—"

"You'll be the first to know."

"Okay." She tried to find her calm, easygoing, polite innkeeper smile, but somehow they seemed a bit past that now. "I'll be downstairs."

He gave her a little salute and perched on the side of the bed. The big, fluffy, perfect-for-wild-sex sleigh bed.

"Right," she added, apropos of nothing, then turned and all but fled the room. Before he could read on her face what was going through her head. She'd been humiliated enough for one day.

Once outside on the landing, the bedroom door safely shut between them, she'd had every intention of retreating to the main floor, heading to her rooms and doing a better job of attending her wounds. Somehow, instead she found herself hovering outside the closed door. His closed door. And listening. She told herself she was simply being a good hostess and making sure her guest didn't get attacked by the ten ounces of terror wrapped up in that T-shirt. She told herself that. It was the making herself believe part that was a bit trickier.

There was a sudden spate of yowling, followed by the deep, soft rumblings of his voice that had her craning her neck, trying to hear what he was saying. Not that it mattered; he was obviously trying to calm the terrified kitten. She just . . . wanted to hear the words. She shifted closer, but it was all a softly spoken murmur. All the same, it did interesting things to her insides, listening to him. She had no idea how it was working on the kitten, although the yowling seemed to have stopped, but it would certainly have made her feel all warm and snuggly and content. Along with a few other things she doubted her four-legged guest would understand.

There was a rustling sound, followed by some other noises that she figured were Brett making something to eat for the little hellion. Just picturing him in there, being all domestic and caretaking for the tiny little furball, only served to further strengthen the warm fuzzies she was feeling. That softly crooning man, along with the one who had raced to her rescue, was such a far cry from the dusty, leather-clad, intimidating road warrior who'd shown up at her door a few hours ago. Or the man she'd ascribed him to be, given his appearance. Clearly those were at odds with the man himself. She recalled thinking upon checking him in that he'd actually been rather quiet and soft-spoken. A few hours of hard sleep, if his tousled bed head when he'd raced out to save her had been any indication, and a little shot of adrenaline had certainly livened him up.

Seeing him buck naked while she was hanging twenty feet up in a tree had certainly livened her up.

The sound of the phone ringing at the front desk on the main floor down below snapped her out of her reverie. Her heart skipped a beat, as it always did. It might be someone calling to book a room. Even though she knew it was far more likely a sales call, she clung to her optimism. Just as she turned to head down the stairs, the ringing stopped . . . and the door opened behind her.

She spun back around, wishing for the life of her she had something more official looking in her hands than the empty tray she'd left his room with. A clipboard, laundry cart, portable phone . . . something. Anything that would make it look like she hadn't just been standing outside his door all this time . . . listening. "Um, hi. Can I help you?"

He frowned for a moment, but was clearly distracted and thankfully didn't seem all that interested in following up on why she'd still be standing there. "I—wait." He stepped into the small, third-floor landing area and pulled the door behind him. "Just in case," he added, shuffling forward to completely shut his door, which crowded her back a little against one of the other closed bedroom doors.

The top floor basically emptied into a small landing area that fanned out toward the three doors leading to the uppermost floor's bedrooms. And though it wasn't big, it allowed coming-and-going traffic reasonably well. Providing all the guests weren't coming or going simultaneously. But she'd had to tear out and rework the floor plan so that each room could have a more generous closet and its own private bathroom, so it had seemed well worth the traffic risk. Until that moment, anyway. At the moment it seemed much, much more narrow a space than she'd realized.

"I was wondering, you don't happen to have anything like cedar chips, sawdust? Newspapers, even?"

Now it was her turn to frown. "I've got plenty of newspapers, but what do you need sawdust . . ." She trailed off as he nodded back toward his bedroom door and she realized he was referring to the kitten.

"I was worried a little on whether she was old enough to eat a bunch of regular food, so I mushed up the bread and tuna with some milk and the damn thing scarfed it up like it hadn't been fed in days. Then I got to thinking that, you know, what goes in . . ."

"Right, right," Kirby said, already on the same page.

"I could hit a drug store, or something, but thought I'd ask first."

"I'm sure we can figure something out. Temporarily," she added with a gauging look at his face. "Right?"

"Right. Of course. I figured I'd let her settle down some from her scare, then start making some calls tomorrow." He propped his hands on his hips. His very lean, narrow hips. At least he'd pulled on another T-shirt. Bright blue this time. Made his green eyes look almost electric.

She kinda preferred the black one. The black flashed her back to the leather and the motorcycle and all those visuals she really didn't need to recall. Especially when combined with the naked ones. Most especially. She realized he was waiting for her to respond and cleared her throat. "Good plan," she said, sounding like she'd been out in the desert too long with no water. At some point she was not going to be an idiot around this man. If, perhaps, he stayed long enough.

A few weeks might do it. Or kill her.

"Glad you agree." He folded his arms over his chest and smiled.

Okay, so kill her it was.

"Could you give me some names, places to start?"

"Sure. Let me go down and see what I can find for a litter box."

"Thanks. I appreciate it."

"No, no bother." She motioned to the stairs, making him aware he was going to have to move if he didn't want her plastered up against him as she made her way past him.

"Oh, sorry," he said, backing up against his door. "Hey,

Ms. Farrell?" he said after she'd made it safely to the top step without making any actual physical contact.

Great, she thought. She was fantasizing about him scooping her up in those strong arms, holding her against that ridiculously gorgeous chest, and carrying her in to the very delicious bed that she knew lay just beyond that door. And he was Miz Farrelling her. Lovely. She supposed it could have been worse. At least he hadn't ma'am'd her. "Yes? And please, you saved my life. It's Kirby."

"Kirby," he added with another brief smile.

He was both sex on a stick and cutely adorable all at the same time. There should be a law. She tried not to swoon.

"If you tell me where the stuff is, I'll get it." His smile flashed to a grin for a brief moment. "I figure you've done about enough for the little beast for one day." He nodded in the general direction of her body. Very general, very vague nodding . . . but that didn't stop some very specific points of her body from responding. Two, in particular.

Her long-sleeve tee was a bit on the thin side, so she folded her arms in front of her, just in case. It was only midafternoon, and yet it felt like an enormously long day.

"Some of those scratches looked pretty nasty. You okay?"

"Fine," she said, a bit mortified that not only had he seen her naked stomach in all of its not-twenty-five-anymore glory . . . he'd also gotten an additional eyeful of ugly, bloody scratches for the trouble. Yeah, that was the visual she wanted him to have. Definite fantasy material right there. If you were Stephen King. "They don't feel as bad as they look," she lied.

"If you say so." He paused for a moment, and she'd have sworn he looked a little uncertain about what to say next, but he wasn't ducking back into his room, either. Clearly wishful thinking on her part. Or he was trying to find the words to tell her something she didn't want to hear.

"Is there anything else I can get you?"

"Uh, no. No, that's all. I'd—follow you down, but maybe I

should go check on the beast. Make sure she hasn't shredded something irreplaceable."

"I'll be back up in a few minutes with a cardboard box and whatever I can dig up."

"Okay." But he lingered a moment longer, so she paused, but then he finally turned back to his door. "Thanks again."

"Sure," she said, then headed back down the stairs once his door was shut behind him again. So, had that just been her? Or had things suddenly gotten awkward there at the end? Awkward in that way where you weren't ready to end a conversation, but weren't sure how to prolong it without seeming dorky.

Except the dork in that situation had clearly been her. And yet, he'd been the one to prolong the moment past its natural comfort zone. *You're really stretching if you think he was somehow flirting, or wanting to keep your company.*

Besides, who knew why he was there, or how long he'd been on the road. Maybe he was just starved for any human interaction. He certainly had been nothing if not polite, not coming onto her in any discernible way. And he'd saved her life, or at the very least saved her an extended hospital stay. So . . . maybe it was just that. Not knowing what to say to someone you'd kept from breaking her own fool neck.

Didn't keep her from thinking about what it would mean if he really was coming onto her. Except a guy who looked like him, and was confident enough to spring into action and play white knight like he had . . . probably had very few awkward moments with members of the opposite sex. As polite and gentlemanly as he'd been since his arrival, she didn't doubt that if he wanted to spend more time with her, he wouldn't have been at all awkward about making her aware of it.

She went about gathering whatever she could find to make a decent litter box for the wee beast, making a mental note to give Pete a call later. She'd given her guest a hard time about finding a home for the critter, but she'd been bloody and a little annoyed at that moment. She actually thought it was pretty sweet that he'd cared one way or the other what happened to the kitten. Which, so did she, or she wouldn't have climbed, literally, out on a limb to save its sorry little fuzzy butt.

But she also knew Pete was a softy who'd have kept it at the animal control compound until he found a home for it; so turning the kitten over to him wasn't the heartless action it had come off as, either. She layered a stack of newspapers on top of the stuff she'd already put in the empty cardboard box and headed back up the stairs.

She knocked on his door with her elbow. "Room service."

He opened the door an instant later and essentially tugged her into the room by her elbow, then shut the door immediately behind her. Startled by the action, and thinking she normally didn't go for brutish kind of guys, but that he could manhandle her all he wanted . . . she stutter-stepped to a stop when he immediately let her go as soon as the door was shut behind her. Still staggering a little, she watched as he turned and dropped to his hands and knees to look under the wide opening beneath the sleigh bed.

Yeah, not exactly the next part she'd pictured in her fantasy scenario, right there. Although it did give her a great excuse to stare at his mighty fine backside once again. Which she did. Openly. It was like she'd reverted to some primordial version of herself that was merely a slave to her inner, baser instincts.

"Come on," he was crooning. "You really don't want to make a bed out of . . ." He trailed off on a sigh and then levered himself back up to stand. "Sorry for yanking you in there like that, but she's been tearing around the room like some kind of Tasmanian devil and I didn't want her ripping out the door."

"We could still call Pete, you know," Kirby said.

The quelling look he gave her was rather comical when you thought about it.

"She just needs some time to calm down. I just sort of wish she hadn't picked my sweater to do that in," he said, glancing back toward the area under the bed. "But . . . there are other sweaters."

He wore sweaters. He struck her as a faded, beat-up-sweatshirt kind of guy. Well, the guy who'd rolled in wearing dusty leather certainly had. This guy was . . . she really wasn't sure yet. But it was certainly a more interesting puzzle to worry over than, oh, say, how she was going to pay the bills this month. At least his being here was also making that part a bit less daunting. So, it was only natural, really, that she spent so much time thinking about him.

"You know, Pete isn't a bad guy," she said, fessing up. "He's not like the proverbial dog catcher. He'll find her a home."

Brett turned back toward her. "Which you knew, earlier."

"Possibly."

"Why did you let me haul her up here?"

"Post-traumatic stress from my tree ordeal?"

His lips twitched.

"Plus, you seemed pretty bent on playing white knight—which, if I didn't take the time to thank you profusely for that, by the way, I'm very sorry. I really can't thank you enough for being so quick on your feet." His bare feet, she recalled. Bare lots of things, in fact. She forced her mind away from that. Standing next to him, right beside a perfectly great bed, was enough of a test of her conversational skills at the moment.

"Anybody would have done the same thing," he responded easily, not even looking at the bed. Or her. In that way. Totally not distracted. "I'm just glad the ladder crashing woke me up."

She winced a little. "Not such a great stay in the inn so far. Again, my apologies. Why don't you let me get the kitten out of your hair, so to speak, so you can get the rest you checked in here for." She bustled into motion, setting the stack of litter box stuff on his bed to free her hands up for kitten wrangling. "I'm really sorry. I don't know what's gotten into me. I really am a better hostess than this, I promise."

"It wasn't like you purposely tried to fall out of a tree."

She had knelt on the floor on the far side of the bed to look beneath it, but his comment had her stretching back up to look at him across the other side of the bed. "True, but I'm sorry all the same."

"Nothing to be sorry about. And, to be honest, I think we should just leave the cat where it is at the moment. She's been through enough today without being taken somewhere else. We'll be fine."

Kirby ducked back down and peeked under the bed. The tiny ball of fluff was curled up in the middle of what appeared to be a very nice, very expensive cashmere sweater. She frowned. Cashmere? This guy? Then she remembered the manicured hands, the roll of money, and, well . . . he was an enigma wrapped up in a mystery, he was. The kitten was sacked out, and he was probably right about disturbing the poor thing again. She pushed up to a stand just as he was scooping up the box of stuff she'd put on the bed.

He rooted through it. "What is all this stuff?"

"Uh, just things I thought would make a good litter box."

He spread out the papers, a small, shallow plastic tray, a box of baking soda, several old towels, and an old blanket.

"And some bedding," she said, lifting one shoulder. "Which, honestly, I'd have picked the cashmere, too. Sorry. I'll pay to have it cleaned, or . . . whatever else might need done to it. Replace it. Once she gets up, just put that stuff under there instead."

"Don't worry about it. Thanks," he said, carrying the box into the bathroom.

She realized she was just standing there, watching him again, and snapped back to attention. "No, thank you. I—the least I can do is fix you dinner. For, you know, saving me. Earlier."

He paused in the bathroom doorway, his hands empty now. He looked remarkably . . . domesticated. All well worn blue T-shirt and faded jeans. Bare feet, tousled hair. He also looked worn out.

"I'll—let me get out of here so you can rest. Just say the word later and I'll bring a tray up for you. Pot roast. It's not much, but—"

"That would be great, actually," he said, surprising her. "What time?"

"Uh, anytime you'd like. Just ring down and I'll—"

"I mean, what time are you eating? Unless you'd rather eat alone."

"No," she blurted, even more surprised. "That would be fine. Usually a bit later for me, around six thirty."

"Sounds good. If I don't come down, if you wouldn't mind, just ring the room and wake me up."

"Are you sure you wouldn't rather sleep?"

He shoved his hands in his front pockets, the picture of laid back and relaxed. Or would have been if it wasn't for the tired lines creasing the corners of his mouth and eyes. "I'd have thought so, yes. But the distraction is proving to be kind of nice, too."

She stood there a moment longer than necessary, trying to figure out if he meant what most men would mean when they said something like that . . . or, if it was more like he was just being honest. Maybe he really was just hungry for some human contact.

Do *not* look at the bed, she schooled herself. There were all kinds of human contact. "I'd enjoy having some company, too."

"Good." He smiled. "Don't let me sleep through."

"I won't," she said, scooting around the bed and heading toward the door, before any of her thoughts dared play out on her face. Only once she was in the hall, door shut safely behind her, did she allow herself a sigh of relief. Now she had a few hours to figure out how to stop thinking about her only guest—her only paying guest—as a possible bed mate.

And how to make pot roast.

Chapter 4

Brett finally gave up on sleep and rolled off the bed, intent on heading for the shower. One peek under the bed showed that the kitty from hell was having no problem snoozing. "Good thing you look like you do," he muttered, looking over the snagged and balled-up cashmere sweater the little fuzz ball was now calling home. "Couldn't take my T-shirt or old sweats." He'd packed light when he'd left Vegas, putting everything else into storage until he decided what he was going to do with the rest of his life. Which meant that, short one sweater, he basically had nothing decent to wear down to dinner.

He dragged his bag across the bed and rooted around until he found the one T-shirt with long sleeves, and dug that out. He shook it out, shook his head, and took it into the bathroom with him. It was doubtful any amount of steam was going to make it look much better, but at least he'd make an effort to look halfway decent.

The hot, steamy shower felt like heaven on earth as it pounded his back and neck. He should have done this earlier. It was almost better than sleep. Almost. He'd realized after Kirby had left that he'd probably only grabbed a few hours after arriving, and he'd fully expected to be out the instant his head hit the pillow again. But that hadn't been the case. This time it hadn't been because he was worried about Dan, or Vanetta, or anyone else back home, or even wondering what in the hell he thought he was doing this far from the desert. In New England, for God's sake. During the winter. Although it didn't appear to be much of one out here.

No, that blame lay right on the lovely, slender shoulders of Kirby Farrell, innkeeper, and rescuer of trapped kittens. Granted, after the adrenaline rush of finding her hanging more than twenty feet off the ground by her fingertips, it shouldn't be surprising that sleep eluded him, but that wasn't entirely the cause. Maybe he'd simply spent too long around women who were generally over-processed, over-enhanced, and overly made up, so that meeting a regular, everyday ordinary woman seemed to stand out more.

It was a safe theory, anyway.

And yet, after only a few hours under her roof, he'd already become a foster dad to a wild kitten and had spent far more time thinking about said kitten's savior than he had his own host of problems.

Maybe it was simply easier to think about someone else's situation. Which would explain why he was wondering about things like whether or not Kirby was making a go of things with her new enterprise here, what with the complete lack of winter weather they were having. And what her story was before opening the inn. Was this place a lifelong dream? For all he knew, she was some New England trust fund baby just playing at running her own place. Except that didn't jibe with what he'd seen of her so far.

He'd been so lost in his thoughts while enjoying the rejuvenation of the hot shower, that he clearly hadn't heard his foster child's entrance into the bathroom. Which was why he almost had a heart attack when he turned around to find the little demon hanging from the outside of the clear shower curtain by its tiny, sharp nails, eyes wide in panic.

After his heart resumed a steady pace, he bent down to look at her, eye-to-wild-eye. "You keep climbing things you shouldn't and one day there will be no one to rescue you."

He was sure the responding hiss was meant to be ferocious

and intimidating, but given the pink-nosed, tiny, whiskered face it came out of, not so much. She hissed again when he just grinned, and started grappling with the curtain when he outright laughed, mangling it in the process.

He swore under his breath. "So, I'm already down one sweater, a shower curtain, and God knows what else you've dragged under the bed. I should just let you hang there all tangled up. At least I know where you are."

However, given that the tiny thing had already had one pretty big fright that day, he sighed, shut off the hot, life-giving spray, and very carefully reached out for a towel. After a quick rub-down, he wrapped the towel around his hips, eased out from the other end of the shower, and grabbed a hand towel. "We'll probably be adding this to my tab, as well." He doubted Kirby's guests would appreciate a bath towel that had doubled as a kitty straightjacket.

"Come on," he said, doing pretty much the same thing he'd done when the kitten had been attached to the front of Kirby. "I know you're not happy about it," he told the now squalling cat. "I'm not all that amped up, either." He looked at the shredded curtain once he'd de-pronged the demon from the front of it and shuddered to think of just how much damage it had done to the front of Kirby.

"Question is . . . what do I do with you now?"

Just then a light tap came on the door. "Mr. Hennessey?"

"Brett," he called back.

"I . . . Brett. Right. I called. But there was no answer, so—"

"Oh, shower. Sorry." He walked over to the door, juggled the kitty bundle, and cracked the door open.

Her gaze fixed on his chest and then scooted down to the squirming towel bundle, right back up to his chest, briefly to his face, then away all together. "I'm—sorry. I just, you said . . . and dinner is—anyway—" She frowned. "You didn't take the cat, you know, into—" She nodded toward the room behind him. "Did something happen?"

"What? Oh. I was in the shower. Shredder here decided to climb the curtain because apparently she's not happy unless she's trying to find new ways to terrify people."

He glanced from the kitten to Kirby's face in time to see her almost laugh and then compose herself. "I'm sorry, really. I shouldn't have let you keep her in the first place. I mean, not that you can't, but you obviously didn't come here to rescue a kitten. I should—we should—just leave you alone." She reached out to take the squirmy bundle from him.

"Does that mean I don't get dinner?"

"What?" She looked up, got caught somewhere about chest height, then finally looked at his face. "I mean, no, no, not at all. I just—I hope you didn't have your heart set on pot roast. There were a few . . . kitchen issues. Minor, really, but—"

"I'm not picky," he reassured her. What he was, he realized, was starving. And not just for dinner. If she kept looking at him like that . . . well, it was making him want to feed an entirely different kind of appetite. In fact . . . He shut that mental path down. His life, such as it was, didn't have room for further complications. And she'd be one. Hell, she already was. "I shouldn't have gotten you to cook anyway. You've had quite a day, and given what The Claw here did to your—*my*—shower curtain—I'll pay for a new one—I can only imagine that you must need more medical attention than I realized."

"Don't worry about that, I'm fine. Here," she said, reaching out for the wriggling towel bundle. "Why don't I go ahead and take her off your hands. I can put her out on the back porch for a bit, let you get, uh, dressed."

Really, she had to stop looking at him like that. Like he was a . . . a pot roast or something. With gravy. And potatoes. Damn he was really hungry. Voraciously so. Did she have any idea how long he'd been on the road? With only himself and the sound of the wind for company? Actually, it had been far longer than that, but he really didn't need to acknowledge that right about now.

Then she was reaching for him, and he was right at that point where he was going to say the hell with it and drag her into the room and the hell with dinner, too . . . only she wasn't reaching for him. She was reaching for the damn kitten. He sort of shoved it into her hands, then shifted so a little more of the door was between them . . . and a little less of a view of the front of his towel. Which was in a rather revealing situation at the moment.

"Thanks," he said. "I appreciate it. I'll go down—*be down*— in just a few minutes." He really needed to shut this door. Before he made her nervous. Or worse. I mean, sure, she was looking at him like he was her last supper, but that didn't mean she was open to being ogled in return by a paying guest. Especially when he was the only paying guest in residence. Even if that did mean they had the house to themselves. And privacy. Lots and lots of privacy. "Five minutes," he blurted, and all but slammed the door in her face.

Crap, if Dan could see him at the moment, he'd be laughing his damn ass off. As would most of Vegas. Not only did Brett happen to play high stakes poker pretty well, but the supporters and promoters seemed to think he was also a draw because of his looks. And no, he wasn't blind, he knew he'd been relatively blessed, genetically speaking, for which he was grateful. No one would choose to be ugly. A least he wouldn't think so.

But while the looks had come naturally, that whole bad boy, cocky attitude vibe that was supposed to go with it had not. Not that he was shy. Exactly.

He was confident in his abilities, what they were, and what they weren't. But confidence was one thing. Arrogance another. And just because women threw themselves at him didn't mean he was comfortable catching them. Mostly due to the fact that he was well aware that women weren't throwing themselves at him because of who he was. But because of what he was. Some kind of quasi-poker rock star. They were batting eyelashes, thrusting cleavage, and passing phone numbers and room keys because of his fame, his fortune, his ability to score freebies from hotels and sponsors, and somewhere on that list, probably his looks weren't hurting him, either.

Nowhere on the list, however, did it appear that getting to know the guy behind the deck of cards and the stacks of chips was of any remote interest.

And there lay the irony.

He was a guy surrounded by women. In the city that gave sin a whole new meaning. Complete with diagrams, video clips, soundtracks, and anything else a person might desire when indulging in a very wide range of wants or needs. Even the most casual observer would likely assume that Brett had a different woman in his bed every night. Possibly more than one. Or three. It wasn't a scenario that he was entirely comfortable with, but the promoters ate it up and pushed for more, so he tolerated the whole thing . . . for appearances. Because it helped the promoters get a bigger buy-in, which meant a bigger potential payday for him and everyone else playing the game. But that was just while he was playing.

Appearances aside, he generally went to bed alone. The dealers got more action than he did. Hell, so did the busboys, the bellhops, and every other damn person in the city. But then, the available action simply wasn't his thing.

Dan said he'd just needed to expand his horizons beyond the casino floor and try to meet women elsewhere. But there wasn't any elsewhere for him in Vegas. Except on Dan's job site . . . and there weren't many women swinging hammers and hauling lumber.

So, he supposed it made perfect sense that the more often he laid eyes on Ms. Farrell, the more often his thoughts strayed from figuring out what he was going to do with the rest of his life . . . to fantasizing about what he'd really like to be doing for the next few hours. Or days. Possibly even a week or two. Or three.

It had been a pretty long dry spell, after all.

"It's just dinner," he reminded himself as he trotted down the stairs a few minutes later, hair toweled dry, and the still slightly rumpled long-sleeve tee paired with his jeans. And the increasingly delectable innkeeper was not on the dessert menu. Even if she did look at him like he was dipped in chocolate. And she'd been craving a Godiva fix for weeks.

Funny, he thought, how all those women wanting him for nothing more than his looks or body in Vegas had been a major turnoff. But let Kirby run her soft gray eyes over his towel-clad body a few times and he was fully on board with whatever her little heart desired, no further questions asked.

Yep, that was downright hilarious.

He forced his wayward thoughts elsewhere so he didn't enter the dining room sporting uncomfortably fitting jeans. Which would have worked out just fine, he was sure, except the instant he entered the dining room, he found her bending over the table, all long legs and sweet heart-shaped ass staring him right in the face. She was wearing form-fitting, soft ivory khakis, an even softer looking, thin blue sweater, and had her hair pulled up off her neck—a perfectly beautiful, slender span of creamy skin that he was a lot more anxious to taste than whatever it was she was presently setting on the table . . .

Yeah, the plans for his immediate future were now solely focused on taking his seat as quickly as possible, and spreading that neatly folded linen napkin sitting on his dinner plate over his lap instead.

He cleared his throat so as not to startle her, which startled her anyway. She clattered the last dish to the table and turned quickly around, her hand on the table for support. "Sorry, I didn't hear you come in."

"I should have knocked, I guess."

"No, no. Don't be silly."

He took in the high color blooming in her cheeks and wondered if it was from the heat in the kitchen . . . or the heat he'd swear was cranking pretty damn good right here in the dining room.

Oh, Brett, my man, you are in very big trouble.

"Kitten okay?" he managed to ask.

"She's fine," Kirby said, her gaze running the length of him, then abruptly locking on his. "I, um, blocked off an area on the back porch and made a little bed, put some food and water out there. She's all set." The end of her sentence was punctuated by a crashing sound, followed by a rather petrified sounding yowl. "Okay, maybe not so fine." Kirby headed toward the kitchen and Brett followed.

They found demon kitty attached by its claws on the screen door that separated kitchen from porch.

"I should have mentioned," he said sardonically, "she likes to climb things."

"Very funny. I thought I had her penned by stacking some old empty moving boxes." She gingerly pushed the door open, kitty still clinging to the opposite side, and glanced out. "Well, they were stacked. For such a tiny thing, her climbing skills are already legendary."

Brett slipped out behind Kirby and tried to calm the still-yowling cat by stroking its head and scratching behind the ears. Instead of hissing and getting more frantic, she quieted, and eventually he could feel the tiny body relax, bit by bit. "That's right," he said, keeping his voice low, smooth, "it's going to be okay." After a few minutes, he was able to coax the kitten off the screen and into his hands, claws in for a change. "See? We're here to help you." He turned to find Kirby staring at him, a bemused expression on her face. "What?"

"Nothing."

"Something," he countered. "Why the look?"

She tried a "who me?" expression, then shook her head and said, "I'm just trying to reconcile the soft-spoken kitty whisperer with the leather clad biker dude who rolled into my driveway earlier today. I'm betting your biker buddies would have a few things to say about your new sidekick there."

"Possibly. If I had any biker buddies."

She lifted her eyebrows. "No?"

He just shook his head.

He noticed her gaze shift to his hands for a moment. Then she seemed to look at the rest of him all at once before turning back to the mess on the porch. He wanted to ask what she'd been thinking just then, but she spoke first.

"I guess we have to build a better kitty trap if we want to eat while it's still warm."

He could have told her that as long as they were in the same room together, he doubted anything would ever get cold, but it seemed a bit premature for that. He was still working out her apparent conflicted impression of him ... and, admittedly, he was feeling a bit the same about her. A shoot-from-the-hip, straight talker in a ballerina body. But then, maybe he did know a little about not living up to the packaging. She couldn't help her looks any more than he could his.

He moved in front of her and carefully handed her the kitten. She instinctively balked, and he couldn't exactly blame her given the fact that her wounds had probably not even scabbed over yet. But to her credit, she carefully took the little heart-breaker and did her best to croon something to it while he went about fortifying the kitty corral. He glanced back at her a time or two, then smiled privately to himself. She didn't hesitate to climb a towering oak to rescue a stranded baby animal, but he wouldn't exactly call her naturally maternal. And yet, she was an innkeeper, a caretaker by profession, presumably by choice. Interesting.

"I'll be right back." Before she could ask, he headed through the house and up the stacked flights of steps, taking them two at a time. He was back a minute later.

"You don't have to donate the sweater to the cause," she started to say.

He shook it out to show the destruction. "I already have. And don't worry about it." He knelt again and finished setting up shop, smiling.

"What?" she said, noticing the smile apparently, when he finally stood and brushed off his knees.

"Nothing."

"Something," she echoed back at him. "You seemed . . . amused by my kitty-whispering skills. Or lack thereof."

"No, no, you did fine." He took the now yawning little ball of fluff and nestled her into his sweater, where she instantly curled up and went to sleep. He straightened and stood next to Kirby. "They look so innocent when they're sleeping, don't they?"

He glanced over just in time to catch her rolling her eyes, which, perversely, made him grin all the more widely.

"We'd better eat while the little devil—I mean darling—naps," she said.

He laughed as he held the door open for her, then paused to check out the damage to the screen before stepping in behind her.

She looked back and sighed. "I'll have to tackle that tomorrow."

"If you have some extra screen laying around, I'll be happy to replace it for you."

She smiled now, but it was a wry one. He wouldn't have thought it would suit her aquiline features, but it did somehow. Or maybe he was finally adjusting his expectations. He wasn't sure which. But he knew he wanted to figure it out. Figure her out.

"I'm not in the habit of asking paying guests to do repair work on their guest quarters. And this was hardly your fault. I put her out there and constructed the failed playpen."

"I wasn't asking to be billed for the damage or offering because I felt guilty. I can do the job and thought it might help. I was just being . . . friendly." He smiled in the face of her dubious expression. "Are you always in the habit of not giving your guests the benefit of the doubt?"

"No, of course not." She immediately smoothed her expression and he almost felt bad for making her feel self-conscious. "I'm sorry. And thank you for the kind offer. But I can—"

"Handle it. Why is it," he said, as he gestured for her to proceed him into the dining room, "that I think you say that a lot?"

"I don't know that I say it, but it is true. I'm a pretty capable person, despite the damsel in distress act earlier."

"I don't doubt that. And accidents can happen to anyone. That you climbed up there at all either spoke of great confidence or—"

"—gasping idiocy."

He smiled as he took the seat across from her and spread the linen napkin on his plate across his lap. "I hardly think that would ever describe you."

"You'd be wrong, but I appreciate the gentlemanly response. Especially given you have actual proof to the contrary."

"Like I keep saying, accidents happen."

She took the lid off the serving dish. "Chicken and mushroom over rice. Salad, too. The dressing is there," she said, motioning to the small tureen. "It's Italian. I hope that's okay. Biscuits in the basket there."

"More than okay. Smells incredible."

"Sorry about the pot roast."

"I can't tell you the last time I had home-cooked anything. I'm more than grateful."

Her smile was a bit self-deprecating as she served herself salad. "Well, I did use the stove, but it's hardly cooking. Pour a can of mushroom soup over a few breasts of chicken. Make instant rice. Crack open a tube of biscuits. Not exactly going to give Rachel Ray a run anytime soon."

He smiled as he filled his plate. "Don't knock yourself. My specialty is ordering room service or takeout. Left on my own, I'd be surviving on peanut butter and jelly sandwiches and Captain Crunch. This is five-star for me."

Kirby lifted a quizzical brow and looked like she wanted to ask some questions, but continued to munch her salad instead. He'd have answered anything she asked him, but he had to admit he kind of liked that she had absolutely no idea who he was, and therefore was willing to take him strictly at face value. Her curiosity would get the better of her eventually, and then things would go in whatever direction they did. Probably not all that differently here in Vermont than back in Vegas. Money and fame tended to affect people the same no matter where they hailed from, he'd discovered.

It didn't occur to him until he was on his second serving of chicken that he'd naturally assumed he'd be sticking around long enough for her to find out anything at all.

"So," he said as he cracked open another biscuit. His third. "Is this the first place you've owned?"

"That obvious?" she said on a laugh. She was working on another biscuit herself.

He liked a woman who wasn't afraid to eat in front of a man. Not that this was a date, or that she was remotely concerned about his opinion of her eating habits . . . but he'd spent most of his life surrounded by women for whom eating was an elaborate science of carb totals and protein gram calculations that would give even the most anal retentive scientist a migraine, all while making sure nothing that contained actual fat ever crossed their lips. He swallowed a smile as he watched her slather on the butter, thinking how hated she would be in his hometown if she regularly ate chicken and biscuits and still looked like she did.

"No, it's not obvious," he said. "You have a really nice place here. All of it, inside and out. I just . . . when I was signing in. I noticed . . ." he trailed off, not wanting to insult her or make her feel bad. Quite rude given he was enjoying a meal prepared by her. "I'm sorry, none of my business."

"That's okay; it's a fair question. This is my first and only establishment. A culmination of a lot of hard work, a long ago dream . . . and quite possibly a large portion of that gasping idiocy I mentioned earlier."

"I'd call it flying in the face of fear."

"Terror, yes. Lots of that."

"I'm pretty sure that's a requirement. You're only afraid because it matters if you fail. And so that's a good thing."

She paused for a second, as if considering that. "I'll take your word for it," she said, and polished off the rest of her biscuit. "I wouldn't mind if the fear took a break. At least on alternate weeks."

He gave a short laugh. Then he reached over to dab a bit of errant butter from the corner of her mouth before he thought better of such a personal action. Her gray eyes widened a bit, but she didn't jerk from his touch. "Sorry, I just . . ." He smiled . . . and licked his finger.

She cleared her throat then and shifted back in her seat. "No problem." He saw the color steal into the smooth cream of her cheeks and figured he should feel badly about that. But . . . not so much, as it turned out.

"Would you care for another helping? More salad? I don't know who I thought I was feeding. Enough here for an army. Biscuit?"

He liked the nervous chatter. A lot. "I'm hungry enough to eat at least a platoon's worth."

"Please then," she said, all but shoving the serving dish at him. "Help yourself."

He did . . . but he was thinking how what he really wanted to help himself to wasn't on the table, but sitting at it. Although having her on the table wasn't exactly a bad idea, either.

Now he was stifling a smile at his own expense. Big talk for a guy who hadn't put moves on a woman in . . . well, it was too embarrassing to actually factor out. But, safe to say, a long while. Hard to put moves on women who were already draping themselves all over you. Then, with the string of bad stuff happening over the month or so after he'd left the casino world, that hadn't exactly been uppermost in his mind.

Unlike now. When it seemed to be all he could think about. Thank God he knew his poker face was unshakable. Because if she could read even a fraction of the thoughts running through his mind at that moment, a whole lot more than her cheeks would be turning pink. And he doubted he'd be a guest at her dinner table again anytime soon.

He'd read the stuff that had come tucked in the well-worn

leather folder on the dresser in his room. Or some of it, anyway. Pennydash Inn provided a gratis breakfast and evening après ski wine, cheese, and hot toddy hour . . . and box lunch service to order if placed the night before. Nowhere on there was any mention of dinner. Just a list of places in town, and at the resort, along with carryout menus for the local deli and pizza shop.

Dinner with Kirby definitely didn't come with the room.

Which meant he owed her. This was a debt he wouldn't mind settling. He wondered if she'd let him reciprocate by taking her out to dinner. She looked up just then, caught him staring, so he said the first thing that popped into his head. "What made you decide to open up your own place? Where did the long-ago dream begin?"

She was splitting open her third biscuit and paused, then tore it the rest of the way open and put it on her plate uneaten.

"That's okay, you don't have to answer," he said, realizing he might have stumbled into a sensitive area. "Just making conversation."

She flashed a quick smile, but it was polite, nothing more, then reached for the butter, keeping her hands busy. "No, that's okay. I basically grew up in a ski resort out west, in Colorado. Eventually got a degree in resort management, but thought I'd rather do something on a more intimate level."

It was clearly the polite, rehearsed answer, but for obvious reasons he didn't press. "Why Vermont and not Colorado?"

"Couldn't afford the property out there. And it's all pretty much developed at this point. I heard about the resort coming in here from some connections I had out west and thought it was the perfect opportunity to make the dream finally come true. So, I did my research, found this place, and the rest is history. Or would be, if it would just start to snow." She smiled, shrugged a little, then bit into her biscuit. Subject closed.

There was more to it. He could easily read from her face, to her body posture. But it wasn't his place to dig any deeper. And that right there should have been the moment where he pulled back, regrouped, and shifted his focus back to where it should belong.

It was nice of her to cook him a meal, but he was here to catch his breath, do some thinking, and make some very important decisions. Kirby was nothing more than a distraction, an excuse to put off doing the hard thinking that needed to be done.

He caught her looking at him from the corner of his eye as he polished off another chicken breast. And he had to admit that, as distractions went, she was a pretty damn good one. He wanted to know the story of Kirby. Clearly there was one. Everyone had one. The more he knew about the guys sitting around the table with him, the better he was able to read them. Of course, he wasn't trying to take Kirby's money. Or play her, for that matter.

Play *with* her; now, that might be a different story.

In fact, after all the emotional angst and worry of the past few months, maybe that's exactly what he needed. To just drop out, check out, take a break. Hadn't Dan been telling him that very thing? Well, when he wasn't telling him to get his ass back to Vegas, anyway. Take a vacation. Something he'd never done. Hell, he lived in vacation land, right? Of course Dan had mentioned beaches, blue water, and available, scantily clad foreign women . . . but Brett didn't see where that was all that entirely different from home. Plenty of women looking for a good time there, too.

Brett wasn't sure what he was looking for, but the idea of chasing after someone who was baiting the trap to be caught right from the get go, didn't really appeal.

He purposely caught Kirby's gaze as she reached for biscuit number four. He smiled. She flushed a little. His smile grew. No, what was appealing was a quirky, single, middle-aged innkeeper in the wilds of Vermont, who had no idea who he was or what to do with him. But she was thinking about it.

And so was he.

Chapter 5

Kirby was up early the next morning. Not because there was all that much that needed to be done. Which was unfortunate enough. But because she was tired of tossing and turning in her bed. Thinking about her only guest.

Dinner the night before had been a kind of excruciating gauntlet of arousal and denial, with her alternately thinking that there was no way she was imagining the sexual tension between them . . . and kicking herself for buying into the fantasy she was clearly so desperate to believe.

She'd refused Brett's offer to help with the dishes after they'd finished eating, knowing there was no way she was going to make it through being that deep in his personal space without making a complete fool of herself.

So, he'd collected his sleepy kitten in a ball of cashmere, like it was something he did every night, and headed up to bed. And she'd spent the next hour scraping dishes and kicking herself for not being more of a risk taker. Because . . . what if she'd been right about the sizzling undercurrent?

She stared at her computer screen, which was open to her banking file . . . then sent a baleful glance at the stack of unpaid bills and smirked at herself. Oh, she was a risk taker, all right. She'd sunk everything she owned, along with everything the bank would give her, into her new business, her new life . . . and look where that was taking her. Maybe it was just as well she hadn't jumped from frying pan to fire again.

She worked on believing that, which lasted for about . . . five seconds. Which was when she asked herself how she'd feel if Brett Hennessey checked out today. Would she be disappointed that she hadn't taken at least a shot at finding out exactly what might be going on between them? Embarrassing or not? Because the "or not" option was pretty damn likely to end with a very worthwhile memory.

Pride dictated that she at least make a go at pretending that a one-night stand with anyone, even a white knight in black leather like Brett, would have been an unfulfilling waste of her time, that she valued herself more than that, required more than that. But who was she kidding? Hadn't she come to Vermont, quite clear about what she wanted? Her own life, played by her own rules. And that didn't include a long-term relationship where someone else would have any say in how she ran her life. Which was what overly tanned ski instructors and randy touring Italian and French ski racers were for.

And, okay, so she hadn't exactly had the chance to take advantage of that last part. Not many European racing professionals dropping by to stare at ski runs covered in grass rather than snow. She could bide her time. After all, she'd been a little busy.

And so, here was her chance to make good on her promise to herself. Dropped, literally, right in her lap. She didn't even have to figure out the part about how she was actually going to get the hot Swede in the tight racing suit to lust after her forty-year-old ass.

But, as it turned out, the reality of jumping into a hot, sweaty, deeply satisfying, purely sexual, short-term relationship wasn't quite as casual, carefree, and easily entered into as her imagination had made it seem it would be.

That same imagination took a short detour from her banking crisis, as a series of images played through her mind. Vivid, highly detailed, quite erotic images. Nothing wrong with a little fantasizing. No risk there. Kirby had become quite fabulous at fantasizing about what she'd do if she could actually make herself do it. In fact, she was downright easy in her fantasies. And it sure beat the hell out of staring at a bank balance that wasn't going to change no matter how long she scowled at it. Deciding which part of her rapidly mounting debt to toss Brett's hundred-dollar bills at stood even less of a chance at distracting her. She could only spread them around so far, after all.

A far more entertaining use of her time would be imagining what it would be like to spread something else entirely. She lifted her coffee mug to her lips, deciding to extend her daydream for just a few more delicious moments, when there was a loud thwap, followed by a quick yowl and some serious swearing originating from somewhere in the back of the house.

She set the mug down as she shoved her chair back. "Now what?" She didn't even give the bright sunshine a passing scowl as she scooted through the foyer.

Another string of swear words colored the warm morning air blue as she moved through the sitting room to the dining room. "Hello?" she called out.

"In here."

"Brett?" She stopped on the threshold to the kitchen. "What are you doing?"

Her guest looked up from where he was crouched on the other side of the now screenless door leading to the porch. He was stretching mesh across the frame, or trying to. "I came down to see if I could grab a bottle of water, then saw the extra mesh rolled up on the porch—"

"I got it out this morning; I was going to work on that after I—" She broke off. He didn't want to hear about her chore list. "You really didn't have to do that."

"I know," he said, his expression tight. "Just trying to help out. You fed me dinner after all."

She stepped into the kitchen. "I was listening for you to come down so I could offer you breakfast. I'm sorry I didn't hear you on the stairs." She resolutely forced herself not to blush as she was reminded where her head had likely been during that time. "There's fresh coffee on, and I'll be happy to make you some eggs, toast, I—" She stepped closer. "Are you okay?"

He shifted in his still-crouched position so she could see his back. And the kitten that was lodged there. "Fine. Until Vlad the Impaler here decided to launch herself from the plant stand to . . . well . . ." He very gingerly turned a bit more. "Would you mind—I'm afraid if I try to stand up, she'll just dig in deeper."

Kirby sprang into action. "I'm so sorry, I didn't know you were—I thought you banged your thumb with a hammer or something."

He lifted the staple gun. "No hammer. But I'm thinking of using this on something other than the screen here."

"Right, right. I got it. I'll get her. Just . . ." She ran her gaze around the back porch to find something to put around the kitten so it wouldn't transfer claws from Brett to her. Her stomach was stinging in sympathy just looking at how fiercely the kitten was digging in. She knew just how fierce a digger the kitten was.

"No apologies needed. I was the one who turned my back on the little vampire. I should know better. She was sleeping mere seconds earlier, I swear."

Kirby slipped between the crouched pair and through to the back porch, where she grabbed the now completely gnarled and mangled cashmere sweater from the kitty fort and carefully worked the little mangler free from Brett's T-shirt. And his skin. "Got her."

Brett straightened, which kind of trapped her between the screenless door and . . . well, him. "Thanks."

"Why don't you let me get something to clean those scratches up? I know from experience they're going to sting." She inched out from the space between his chest and the door behind her, and went over to the kitty fort. "Did she escape from this?"

He shook his head. "No, I figured as long as I was right at the door, I'd give her some room to play a little." He lifted his hand. "I know, you don't have to say it."

Kirby deposited the kitten back in its safe room, putting her down, sweater and all, before turning back to him. "I wasn't going to say a word."

He gave her an amused "sure you weren't" look, which made her bat her eyelashes all innocently. He shook his head, she smiled . . . and suddenly there was all that tension again. Just like that. The silence stretched and then expanded some more. And she was pretty damn sure she wasn't imagining anything. Then he took a step toward her, and she was instantly rooted to the spot. Here it was. Her chance. No regrets this time. He was totally focused, intent . . . on her. The most tantalizing sort of awareness hummed over her skin and she prayed she didn't do anything stupid to ruin the moment.

It had been longer than she cared to think about since she'd last been kissed. Not that it would have mattered. Despite all of her personal mission statements where men were concerned . . . she'd never seduced, much less been seduced, by anyone like Brett. Casually or not.

He moved closer, and she tried to look . . . what, casual? Ready? Turned on? Needy? She was afraid she was all of those, except that first one. Could he tell? Did it matter? She fervently hoped not. There wasn't much she seemed to be able to do about it. As he closed the final bit of distance between them, she thought her heart might thump its way right out of her chest.

Her lips parted on a soft sigh as her gaze dipped to his mouth and lingered there. That perfectly sculpted mouth, which was attached to a perfectly sculpted body. And it was going to be touching hers, tasting hers, in just a matter of seconds. She had to curl her fingers in to keep from grabbing him. Had to lock her knees to keep her thighs from shaking. Wanted, desperately, to press her hand over her stomach, to make sure she wasn't going to be sick from the anticipation of it all. Because nothing says seduce me like puking on a guy's feet. That would be sexy, huh?

She really wished she could be a whole lot more *The Graduate* about this. But she was clearly no Mrs. Robinson, the experienced older woman, ready to school the younger man in the fine arts of seduction. But then, there was nothing remotely Dustin Hoffman–ish about Brett, either.

He leaned his head down, she tipped up her chin, and at some point her eyes drifted shut. But the next thing she felt wasn't his warm, oh so perfect mouth on hers . . . no, her lips were brushed with something that felt like—

She blinked her eyes open as he finished pulling his T-shirt over his head, then swiveled his back to her. "How bad is it?"

She blinked a few more times, then squeezed her eyes shut in abject mortification. *Please*, she silently prayed, if there is a God, let him be the kind of benevolent deity that uses his wise powers to keep her gorgeous guest completely oblivious to the, clearly, very wrong conclusion she had drawn regarding his sudden interest in her. That, or allow the earth to open up and swallow her whole. Or both. Before she did something else stupid.

It damn well wouldn't hurt if he'd stop disrobing every other second, too.

"You'll live," she choked out, feeling every bit as ridiculously foolish as she'd suspected she would last night.

No regrets. Right.

"I—I have some antiseptic spray in the kitchen that might be a good idea. We should clean up the deeper gouges." She winced as she leaned in to examine the scratches and punctures a bit more closely. "I think there's a little T-shirt fiber stuck in a few."

I also think I don't need to be spending any more time inspecting any part of your perfectly perfect naked skin, she thought as her gaze began to wander beyond the immediately affected areas. Which, in turn, had immediate effects on her. She abruptly straightened and did her best, which was to say made any effort at all, at sounding calmly efficient and otherwise entirely unaffected by him and his godlike body. Which, seriously, she was both breathing and female, so that was already overreaching where both goals were concerned. Still, she was proud that she actually spoke in complete, nondithering sentences. Something to build on, anyway. "Head inside and we'll take care of it."

He glanced over his shoulder. "Thanks. Then I'll get the screen done."

"No, that's okay," she said, perhaps a bit more forcefully than necessary, "you don't have to—"

"I know, but I can, so it's the least I can do." He headed toward the kitchen door, and Kirby followed behind. "You always have such a hard time accepting a little help?"

"No," she said, knowing that was only partly true. "It's just, you're a guest. You're here to relax, and . . . do whatever it is you want to do. You're not paying to stay here so you can help with chores. Much less rescue your hostess or be attacked by the local psycho kitten." She scooted around him as soon as they were both in the kitchen and went immediately to the cupboard below the sink where the first aid kit was stashed.

"I'm pretty sure feeding me dinner wasn't part of my room and board, either. I was simply returning the favor."

"I fed you because you saved my life. I owed you, not the other way around. We're even. Well, if you can consider chicken and mushroom casserole an even trade for a life." Knowing she was babbling, but seemingly unable to stop, she braced herself and stood up only to clutch the kit to her chest when she realized he was standing right beside her. She winced a little when the kit rubbed at her scratched stomach.

He took the kit from her and then did that quick, half-smile thing she was coming to realize he did when he was amused but trying to be polite.

If only he knew just how impolite she'd been with her thoughts of him.

"What?" she said as he placed the kit on the counter. She reached out to help him unclasp the safety latch on the front of the kit.

"I was just thinking that, in the end, all we were both trying to do was help the poor, defenseless little kitty cat, and look at the both of us." His tone took on a wry note. "I'm thinking maybe she'd have been better off left to her own defenses."

Her own lips twitched. "You might have a point." She went to draw her hand away, but his fingers brushed over hers as he went to lift the lid off the kit, then more deliberately when she didn't move them away. She looked at his fingertips as they lightly stroked over the backs of her fingers, as if she was having some sort of out-of-body experience. Except her body was experiencing all kinds of things at the moment and she felt every electrifying one of them. She didn't lift her gaze to his, not fully prepared for what she might find in those green eyes of his. Was she making this up, too?

"Kirby."

She took another millisecond to decide, so he lifted his fingers from hers, to her chin. One little glimpse of his eyes, that intensity, that focus, so close up, so . . . intimate. And she knew right then, if he asked her to clean his wounds, or . . . or something else that had absolutely nothing to do with kissing her senseless, well, she would not be held responsible for her actions.

"Am I the only one who can't stop thinking about this?"

"A-about—this?" she said, sounding more than a little breathless. She was okay with that. Sentence ability was gone, but at least she was still capable of forming words.

"This," he said, and began lowering his mouth to hers.

She let her eyes drift shut. Her body tensed. Everything tensed. Everything that wasn't quivering in anticipation, anyway. And all she could think was . . . *finally*. Well, that, and thank God she really wasn't a pathetic, sex-starved, hallucinating moron. Okay, one out of those three, anyway.

"Kirby!" a deep voice barked from the back of the house. A sharp rapping on the door to the backyard followed.

Brett jerked his head up just before his lips brushed hers and swiveled around to see who was calling her name.

Even through the thick clouds of pheromones, Kirby recognized the voice. She was tempted—so tempted—to just yank Brett right back around and demand he finish what he damn well started.

"Kirby? You in there?" More rapping.

Kirby swore under her breath and Brett's eyes twinkled in open amusement at her unladylike outburst, muttered though it was. She supposed she should be thankful he had a good sense of humor. Where she was concerned, apparently he was going to need it.

"Shouldn't you go see whoever that is?"

"I shouldn't, no. But it'll only postpone things." She cleared her throat, pushed her hair from her face, and tried not to look like a woman who'd just been prepared to be thoroughly kissed. Or ravished. Taken right there up against her own kitchen counter. Goddammit. "What is it, Clemson?" She stepped around Brett, who stopped her with a hand to her arm. Such a big, nice, warm hand it was, too. A shame it wasn't cupping her face right about now. Or more sensitive areas, for that matter.

"Need any . . . assistance?" he asked.

Oh, he had no idea the depths of assistance she'd like to have from him. "I'm fine. It's just the farmer who owns the land on the other side of the mountain, up the hill behind me. Stay here. No point in both of us being exposed to his crotchety attitude."

As if to underscore her statement, there was another sharp rap on the door, followed by, "Kirby! We need to speak! It's a matter of great importance."

"It always is, Clemson," she muttered softly. She caught the way Brett's mouth was quirking again, though not so subtly this time, and impulsively stuck her tongue out at him.

"Careful where you aim that thing," he warned, that green twinkle suddenly all glittery hot. He ran his fingertips up her arm to her shoulder.

She swallowed against a suddenly parched throat. It was the only thing parched about her at the moment. Clemson suddenly seemed like the easier task. At least she knew what she was dealing with where the old coot was concerned.

She scooted away from Brett, and his glittering green eyes, and big warm hands, and stepped onto the back porch, swearing she heard Brett chuckling behind her. "What can I do for you, Clemson?"

"You can start by telling me why you thought it was okay to poach one of my prime mouser's offspring. And don't bother trying to tell me a story, I can already see the thing right there on your porch. Same coloring as my Matilda. You got a mouse problem in this inn of yours, get your own damn cat. Don't come stealin' mine." The way he said the word "inn" made it clear what he thought of someone—namely her—running an establishment such as this, on property he'd made it perfectly clear was only suitable for crops and cows.

She'd long since given up trying to have any rational conversation with the man. Like explaining that she hadn't exactly come along and built the inn there, that the house had been on the mountain almost as long as he had, and that at least it was renovated, occupied, and being put to good use.

Kirby stepped out on the porch and glanced over at the kitten. Who was looking remarkably adorable and innocent, all curled up sleeping. Though how it could sleep through all of Clemson's banging and barking, she had no idea. Apparently it took a lot out of a kitten to play demon monster during its waking hours. She looked to Clemson, who was wearing a dark green John Deere T-shirt under a pair of denim overalls that had seen better years. Decades, possibly. And a heavy green and black plaid jacket. What was left of his white hair curled around the perimeter of the shiny dome of his head. He was tall and rangy, holding an old grease-stained tractor cap crushed in one fist and pointing at her with the other.

"Now, you see here," he began, only this time Kirby cut him off.

"Clemson, calm down. I didn't poach anything. Your little rat catcher there was up my tree and about to fall off. I climbed up and almost killed myself getting her down. I was just holding on to her until I figured out where she came from. How'd you even know she was here?"

A bit of a sheepish look crossed his face, but it quickly returned to a scowl. "Caught a couple of 'em a few days back heading over the peak. Figured when I couldn't find that one she'd headed down this way. Was headed down to find her and there she is, right on your back porch. What's a man supposed to think? And what the hell kind of contraption you got her in? She's no pampered house cat. She's straight from two of my best mousers."

"This does not come as news," Kirby said dryly, feeling her stomach twinge all over again.

"Well, hand her over and I'll be out of your hair."

Kirby pushed the porch door open and waved him inside. "Be my guest."

He clutched his hat more tightly and grumbled some as he came up on the porch, his progress hampered a bit by a bad hip.

"Matilda needs to do a better job monitoring her offspring," Kirby said as he passed by. "Or maybe you need to make a little kitten corral until they're old enough to know where they live."

He grumbled some more, but she couldn't make out exactly what he was saying, which was probably just as well. He reached down and went to grab the kitten by her scruff, causing Kirby to involuntarily suck in her breath. That earned her a glare.

"You got something else to tell me about handling barn cats?"

She thought about the scratches all over her body and Brett's, and shook her head. "No, but since you have to make it all the way back up the hill, feel free to just bundle her up in that sweater. We don't need it back."

She fully expected him to reject that offer, just on principle, but he surprised her by scooping up the sweater with the kitten nestled inside. The kitten yawned, stretched, seemed momentarily disoriented by what was going on, but didn't seem to struggle any further when he tucked the sweater, feline and all, against his bony chest. Kirby only hoped that plaid jacket and the denim beneath it were as heavy as they looked. Somehow she couldn't imagine the little terrorist remaining calm during their entire trek.

"I'll be on my way. You see any of this batch again, I'd appreciate a call next time."

"Oh, you'll hear from me, don't you worry." *And you're welcome,* Kirby wanted to add, but was happy enough to see this situation concluded that she managed to bite her tongue.

"Who's we?" Clemson asked as he made his way back down the steps.

"What?" Kirby asked, confused.

"Owner of this fine piece of sweater, I imagine." He jammed his cap back on his bald head and squinted back at her as the sun hit him in the face. "Heard you had a new boarder."

Kirby opened her mouth, then closed it again. He'd come down here to give her a hard time for saving his precious nextgeneration mouser and now he wanted to gossip?

"Seen that fancy bike. Tell him to stay clear of my property. Damn kids on dirt bikes last summer ruined more than an acre leaving tire ruts."

"I don't think you need to concern yourself about that in this case."

"Well, just see that he doesn't."

Kirby sighed a little, but didn't bother to explain that a Harley was hardly a dirt bike and she doubted her fully grown guest was going to suddenly decide to go off road with it up the back of her hill. "I'll make sure to mention it."

"Neighbors supposed to take care of one another," he said as he ambled across the expanse of groomed grass behind the inn. "Why I prefer not to have any. Can't count on anyone these days but yourself." Beyond the cut grass, the land turned into a grassy, rocky field, which then stretched up into trails that led to the top of the hill and beyond.

"Which is why I saved your damn cat, you miserable old coot," she said, but too softly to carry very far. "Careful on the trail," she called out.

"Been walking these hills all of my seventy-two years. Don't need some green little missie telling me how to handle myself. Just because I've been on God's good earth a mite longer than you doesn't mean I'm anything less than fully capable."

She stood on the back porch, the morning breeze carrying his grumbling and muttering back to her until he was well beyond her property line.

"Quite the character," came Brett's deep voice just beside her ear. "You weren't kidding about the crotchety part."

She startled at the sound of his voice, and he steadied her. With his hands on her hips. Which he left there.

"He's just mad because I snatched up this property before he could finally convince the town council to let him tear down the old house and add the whole parcel to the land he already owned. He'd have been king of the mountain then. Had I known what having him as a neighbor was like, I might have kept looking and let him have it." Again with the babbling. But, honestly, his hands were still on her, and she didn't know quite what to do next. Seemed easier to just keep talking.

She felt the heat of him, just behind her. All that bare skin . . . he was like a one-man furnace with that heat. Or maybe she was the one with the elevated temperature. She certainly felt feverish . . .

"You gave my cat away," he said, his breath warm on her neck. Her feverish neck.

"It, uh—it wasn't yours, as it turns out."

"So I heard. Good thing he's up on all the rules of being neighborly. Are the rest of the residents of Pennydash as . . . colorful?"

"Never boring, anyway." *Sort of like every second I've spent with you.* "I've met Matilda, the mom cat, by the way. It explains a lot."

"Psycho senior?"

"Something like that. Let's just say, I'm not thinking your little pet there was going to be domesticated anytime soon."

"Well, I think our girl has found a good home. She has a fine career ahead of her. One she can sink her teeth into."

Kirby groaned, but she was smiling.

"A real corporate climber."

Now she laughed.

"If there was a draft for mousers, she'd be a first-round pick."

Kirby ducked her chin and shook her head, but snickered anyway. "If you start in with the 'my kitten can beat up your kitten—' "

"Hey, I'm just trying to show a little paternal pride here." He bracketed her hips with his hands, careful not to drag her shirt across the raw skin of her stomach, and pulled her body back against his. "After all, I sent her into the world with the very shirt off my back."

Which was so very, very true, Kirby thought, feeling the heat of his very bare nakedness emanating right through her thin cotton shirt. "Probably just as well you sent her off when you did," she managed through a belly knotted up with lust. "She's already gone through two shirts in two days."

He pressed his lips just below her ear, and only a superhuman effort could have kept her from tipping her head back to rest on his shoulders. His very broad, very naked shoulders. Turns out she had a ways to go to achieve Wonder Woman status.

"Yeah," he said, the low rumble of his voice vibrating straight down her spine. "It'd be a real shame if I lost all of my clothes." He splayed his palms gently across her stomach, pressing the well-washed cotton to her ravaged skin like the softest of bandages. "Whatever would I do?"

"Indeed," she choked out, which was something of a wonder in and of itself, given the veritable avalanche of images that accompanied that little comment. Her poor imagination couldn't decide which clip in the erotic slide show to focus on first.

"Kirby," he said, rubbing his lips along the side of her neck.

She covered his hands with hers, trying, and failing, to find her equilibrium. Things like this didn't happen to her. She really . . . really . . . wanted them to, but as to actually happening? This was a first. "Yes?" she breathed.

"How many beds are there in this house?"

"Uh . . ." She tried to focus, but it was damn near impossible now that he'd started nibbling. "Ni—nine. Total. Including mine."

He caught her ear lobe between his teeth and pressed ever-so-lightly. "Would it be too forward of me to tell you that I want to have you on every single one of them?"

Had he not been holding her all but braced up against him, she was pretty sure she'd have slid right to the ground in a puddle of gooey, hormone-soaked lust. She tried to speak, but he was kissing the side of her neck, and all she could manage was a head shake.

How crazy was this? She'd only been fantasizing about this since he'd ridden up on his bike, but fantasies never came true. Not like this. He hadn't even properly kissed her yet, and he was talking about having her, taking her . . . dear Lord she wanted him to take her, have her. Anywhere he damn well pleased.

For all she knew, he was some kind of serial killer—a very good-looking, well-dressed, manicured, bank-rolled, hot biker serial killer—who rode around the country seducing poor, orgasm-starved innkeepers into having mind-blowing sex with him, so he could—so he could . . . well, she didn't know what exactly, but letting him do this probably was unwise on numerous fronts, the worst of which would be that one. Probably.

Except his hands were all over the front of her now, and she

really rather liked them there. Not enough to die a grisly death . . .
but then what, really, were the chances of that? Because, was
she really so pathetic that the only reason a guy could want to
make love to her on every bed of the inn was because he was a
raging sociopath? Had she such a low self-esteem?

He chuckled against the very heated skin of her neck. She
was one giant piece of heated skin at the moment.

"Don't worry. I'm not going to do anything against your will."
He slowly turned her around, then crowded her back against
the wall next to the screenless door. He grinned. "Unless you
like that kind of thing."

Her eyes widened. Holy hell, maybe he was a socio— He cut
off her wild thoughts with a kiss. A kiss so perfect, where his
mouth fit hers so effortlessly and beautifully, that by the time he
parted her lips and took the kiss deeper, she was pretty sure
even catching the glint of a silver blade being lifted over her
head wouldn't have stopped her. Not that her eyes were open at
this point or anything.

He lifted his head just a fraction, and she sighed a little at the
sudden defection of his lips from hers. "Do I really scare you
that much?"

"What? Why—" She broke off, certain she couldn't pull off
the necessary insouciance to make him believe she did this sort
of thing all the time, and, that, of course she wasn't afraid of
him. What he didn't realize, was that she wasn't so much afraid
of what he might do to her . . . she was more afraid of how
she'd feel about it when he finally stopped doing it.

"I don't—" She started, then stopped, then swallowed and
lifted her gaze to his. "I don't do this. Normally. I mean, I've
done this. Of course. Just not . . . not with a guest. It's not very
professional."

"I think we've established that, at least between us, the professional aspect of innkeeper-guest possibly doesn't apply. What
with that whole lifesaving-rescue-dinner part."

"I know it's been a bit unorthodox so far, but, I just meant
that, it's not how I'd normally, how I'd prefer to—"

"Would it help if I told you that this guest doesn't mind being an exception? And, don't worry, he's not looking for any special favors from his hostess."

"Define 'special favors.' "

His grin was slow, and oh so lethal to whatever was left of her sanity. "I'm not trying to duck paying room and board by giving up my bed for yours," he clarified.

"You already paid for your room and board."

"For a few days, yes."

"Are you planning on—"

"Extending my stay? Possibly."

There was a part of her mind that was still standing a bit separate from what was actually happening, trying to process everything, make sense of it, help her make rational and wise decisions. But the larger part of her brain, and pretty much all of her body, were totally in the moment. And they wanted what they wanted, and damn the bigger picture.

"And what would you be basing this decision on?"

"A number of things."

"Such as?"

"Such as I have some decisions to make, some pretty big ones. And I want the time and space to think things through, make sure the conclusions I draw are sound and suit me. And those I care about. This seems like a pretty good place to do that."

It so wasn't the answer she'd been expecting. She'd fully expected him to say whatever he had to say to get his immediate needs met. She was honest enough to admit that it would have worked with her. "You confuse me," she said, quite bluntly, and perhaps not entirely wisely given where her immediate needs were concerned. But if he was being surprisingly frank and open, no reason not to follow suit. "You have since you got here yesterday."

"How is that?"

"Oh, there's a list."

He cocked one eyebrow. "Really? I'm that much of an

enigma? I think I'm pretty straightforward. God knows I have been with you. No hidden agendas."

"Right. I don't know you, at all really, but that much I'm getting."

"What do you want to know?"

Everything, was the first thing that came to her mind.

Absolutely everything.

Chapter 6

So, clearly he was much further out of practice than he thought where the opposite sex was concerned. He'd been fairly certain at dinner last night, and pretty much a hundred percent certain this morning, that he wasn't the only one having wayward thoughts of a sexual nature. So much so, that, what the hell, he'd decided to act on them, see what happened.

Brett hadn't exactly thought things through much beyond that, but then, he'd sort of thought the direction would more or less establish itself. And he'd work from there.

He should have known that, where Kirby was involved, nothing was going to be simple. Had he admitted as much to himself, perhaps he'd have rightly talked himself out of making any moves whatsoever.

He really did have some important things to consider. And she was definitely clouding that process. It would be convenient to tell himself that this was all about cloud clearing, and using seduction as a means of regaining focus. Except he'd never had any problem focusing before. He was very, very good at that. Hence his current bank balance.

And he'd had his hands on her now . . . and his mouth. Well, on her neck anyway. Which had proven to be far more lethal than one would suspect. All warm and sweet and soft . . . with that rabbit punch of a pulse quivering against his lips. Told him a lot. A lot more than she was telling him, anyway.

At the moment, she was stalling. And he was letting her. Because he meant what he said about not forcing her. But ... he wasn't exactly letting her go, either. Was he?

"You come tooling up on this huge Harley, all dressed in leather. But you wear cashmere and keep your hands in better shape than most women I know. And every guy I know. So yes, you're a bit of a paradox."

"Well, the leather keeps the bugs from stinging and the dust from choking. Not to mention providing a far more decent barrier to road rash than the jeans and T-shirt I was wearing underneath them. As for the hands ..." He paused, and used those hands to slide up her waist, then cup her elbows, and urge her arms up around his neck. "Occupational hazard."

She frowned a little. But didn't move her hands from his shoulders when he circled his back around her waist. As foreplay went, it was admittedly not what he'd been picturing ... but he wasn't any less turned on because of it.

"So, what, you're a hand model? Or all model? I mean, you certainly could be. Would explain the tan, the body, the lack of modesty."

When he spluttered a laugh at that last part, she instantly blushed.

"I said all of that. Out loud. Right out loud."

"You did. And I'm flattered. I think. Although I'm far more modest than the amount of clothing I've worn the past twenty-four hours would imply. I claim special circumstances. I also claim to not mind it as much as I'd thought I would, had someone told me I'd be spending most of my time half dressed around a woman I'd just met and found intriguing."

She snorted.

"Did you really just ... snort at that? I was sincere."

"You certainly always sound sincere. I'll give you that. In fact, that's another part of the enigma."

"Meaning ... what, exactly?"

"Meaning for a dusty, leathered-up biker dude, you're actually rather soft spoken and polite."

"When you'd have expected what, exactly?"

"I don't know. I guess a fill-in-the-blank cliché. I don't actually know any bikers."

"Which clichés would those be?"

"Tall, dark, and Clint Eastwood–like silent. Or brash, cocky, maybe a little crude."

He smiled a little. He did that a lot around her. "Sorry to disappoint."

"Oh, but you didn't. I think . . . I don't know. Like you said, intriguing." She paused. "Wait, what did you mean about me intriguing you? What about me could possibly be intriguing?" She lifted a hand. "Wait, that sounded like digging for compliments. I was actually just curious."

"You're not what I expected, either."

"You have certain expectations of your innkeepers?"

He felt her hands tense a little, where they still rested on his shoulders. She wasn't holding on, much less coming on—more like holding in place. In fact, she seemed so caught up in what they were saying, he wasn't sure if she realized she'd been toying with the ends of his hair. Normally he'd say that was a direct type of flirtation. She seemed more . . . distracted. Until that last comment. "Why did you tense up just then?"

She looked him square in the eye. "You're not a serial killer, right? Because that would be my karma. I don't even know what I did to earn a snow-less winter, much less a complete jackass of an ex, but I'm pretty sure I didn't do anything in this life to warrant it ending with me being hacked up into little pieces. So just tell me you're not in the habit of going from little town to little town, seducing poor, unsuspecting innkeepers, then stashing them in the basement freezer."

"Have you ever considered becoming a writer? Because that's quite an imagination—"

"So, that would be a no? You're evading, actually."

"Well, if I was a killer, I'd just smile and tell you whatever you wanted to hear anyway, so you're not going to automatically believe everything I say."

"True. I faxed your license to the sheriff's office."

He couldn't help it. That made him pause. And he was pretty sure his smile had faded along with it.

"Uh oh," she said, and started to slide her hands from his shoulders.

He quickly covered them, but gently. "No, nothing like that. I just—you can ask your local sheriff everything he discovered about me. That's not it."

"You say that like there's a long list of things to be discovered. Anything you want to confess up front?"

"I've never killed anything. Or anyone," he added.

"Okay. Felonies? Pending charges? Assault? Robbery?"

"Wow. Either I made a really wrong impression on the bike, or you really have lousy taste in men. What, exactly, did this jackass of an ex do to you, anyway?"

"Did I say that out loud, too?" She sighed and shook her head when he nodded. "See, I don't have taste in men."

His brows lifted. "Really? Because I could have sworn—"

"No! I mean, I didn't mean it that way. I have interest in men, but . . . never mind. Let's just say that I haven't had to worry about my taste levels or lack thereof. Lately."

"Ah."

"Ah, what?" She ducked her head and sighed. "Clearly, this is a good thing. Accuse you of being a crude, serial-killing, bank-robbing biker with a manicure, and, just in case you're the type that is attracted to psycho basket cases, make sure you add lonely and pathetic to the list." Kirby did remove her hands this time, and then she stepped back before he could keep her close. "Why don't I stop while I'm already so far behind there's no recovery? Because, given another few minutes, I wouldn't be the least surprised to discover I could actually make it worse."

He laughed. Which clearly surprised her. It even surprised him a little. Because psycho basket cases most definitely were not high on his list of women he wanted to go to bed with. No amount of good sex was worth that. Which went a long way toward explaining his prolonged celibacy of late. Not a lot of sane and normal in the casino life.

Maybe not in Pennydash, Vermont, either, as it turned out.

"Not that I'm not relieved you have a sense of humor, but why the laugh?"

"When I said you weren't what I expected, either, it wasn't as an inn owner. I was going based on appearance. Like you were with me. You're tall and graceful, with such quiet features and serious eyes. Seeing you, without ever meeting you, I'd have pegged you as somewhat culturally elevated, perhaps even a bit snooty, definitely over-educated, traditional, conservative . . ."

The corner of her mouth kicked up in a dry smile. "Ruined that perception pretty good, huh?"

"Mostly. Maybe. But that's what drew me." He reached for her again. "Draws me."

She moved back a half step. "I'm really not a psycho basket case. Over the past two years, I've been more sane than I've probably ever been, well certainly given the ten or so odd years that came before it. Speaking of which, I'm a lot older than you."

"Okay."

She cocked her head. "Okay?"

He shrugged. "I'm not sure I get the significance. Unless it bothers you. People are people."

"Age is just a number?"

"No, not at all. The number of years a person has put in should impact them in some way. Hopefully with increased wisdom, but not always. With life experience, to be sure. Sometimes where they are on their path doesn't match with where I am on mine, but otherwise, people are just people. I don't limit my exposure to them, or my attraction to them, based on how old they are. Or aren't."

She continued to look at him.

"Bad answer? It's the truth."

"No, not at all. Possibly the best answer."

"What then? Are you hung up on my being younger?"

She shook her head. "Not as it pertains to me, anyway. I can say I wish I'd had your more advanced worldview when I was your age. Would have saved me a ton of grief and loads of unfulfilled expectations."

"The jackass ex again?"

She shook her head. "No, I was talking about me. Jackasses are jackasses. It's not so much their fault when they do nothing to pretend otherwise. Then it's on the one who keeps thinking they'll change. It was that age-equals-wisdom thing that hung me up. Well, that and a pretty good case of insecurity and inexperience. Also on me."

"Clearly you figured it out at some point. How long ago did your epiphany come about?"

"Oh, about two seconds after I walked in on a private meeting he was having with his assistant—you know, one of those clothing optional meetings?—whereby he was telling her that of course there was nothing to worry about. I was too busy running around doing everything he told me to do to keep his fabulous resort running like a well-oiled machine while desperately trying to win his respect and continued support to ever imagine that he would be unfaithful to me.

"Or maybe it was a second or two after that, when he laughingly responded to her question regarding his ever marrying me by stating that why would he ruin the best thing that had ever happened to him? He had someone he could count on to be loyal, hardworking, and give him the very best both at work and at home, all for a less than commanding salary. He'd have to be an idiot to marry me." She tapped her chin. "Yep, it was pretty much right about then. Of course, the kicker is he was completely right."

Brett grinned. "So . . . maybe the real question is whether or not you've committed any felonies that I should know about."

She blinked and looked rather mortified by her outburst for a second, and then grinned right back at him. "Fortunately I managed not to ruin the next fifteen to twenty years of my life, no. I'd already given him ten." She lifted a hand. "And please, I am not asking for or expecting pity. You can't be surprised when folks treat you like a doormat when you never stop them from walking all over you. Some of us just have a much steeper learning curve than others. Walking in on that *meeting* was the best wake-up call of my life." She smiled even more broadly then and he loved how it animated those eyes of hers. "See? Totally not a psycho basket case."

Brett laughed, and so did she. "See, that's what intrigues me."

"I'm afraid to ask, but clarify?"

"You're a straight shooter. You don't mind speaking your mind, and you seem to be pretty self-aware, although you're almost too willing to cast yourself in an unflattering light."

"Hey, if the light shines dimly . . ." Kirby shrugged.

"We're all human. But you picked up the pieces and turned around and took your own dreams and did something about them. You're constructive, not destructive. You learned from past mistakes, and then you moved on. You're not a wallower."

"Wow. All that from a few babbled stories and a total lack of finesse where half-naked men come into play?"

He tightened his hands on her hips and pulled her a fraction closer. "I'm pretty good at reading people. Did I get any of that wrong?" He ducked his chin to keep her eyes on his. "Be honest. It's okay to toot your own horn, too, you know."

"I'd like to think your assessment is right. We'll see how things play out after this winter is over and whether or not I have to yet again find a new dream to build on."

"Fair enough."

"What about you? These decisions you have to make."

"See, this is where I envy you. You knew what your dream was all along. I know I want to finally have mine come true, and that I'm ready to do whatever it takes to make it happen . . . but I'm not sure what shape the dream is going to take." He laughed again. "So, I guess you're the psycho basket case with a jackass ex and I'm the aimless drifter with no idea who he wants to be when he grows up. Perfect match, right?"

"We're all human," she said, tossing his words back at him.

"So then," he said, feeling rather ridiculously content, which didn't bear examining given how newly acquainted they were . . . but rather than turn him off by her sudden revelation of a painful past, it had only served to further underscore his attraction. She was real. That was the bottom of it, he realized. She was honest, direct, and not particularly worried about his opinion. She told it like it was, even if that didn't paint her in the best of lights. He doubted, given the look on her face immediately after the fact, that she shared that story often, if ever. He liked it—a lot—that she'd shared it with him. Made him feel like, perhaps, she'd take him for who he was, too . . . even when his less-than-normal background finally came out. Which, given the faxed license, he figured was more likely to happen now.

"So . . . ?" she urged.

He snapped back to the moment and nestled her more fully in his arms. "So, I guess . . . we've established age isn't an issue. And that I'm not a serial killer or a crude biker. You're not dancing ballet at the Met or hosting snooty cocktail parties in the Hamptons. You don't take shit from cheating jackasses. And neither of us should probably ever own a kitten. Any other obstacles?"

She laughed. "To?"

"Me finishing what I started before your neighbor interrupted?"

"Other than wondering why in the hell you'd still want to? No, absolutely not."

"Human is good, Kirby. I'm not interested in plastic perfection, or any attempt at pretending to be it, much less achieving it."

"Well, there's a huge relief." She grinned and he really did love what it did to her eyes. That was going to take a long time to get old.

"What else?" he asked when he sensed there was something she wasn't saying. When she didn't immediately respond, he knew he was right. "Come on, no point in holding back now."

"Right," she said dryly. "However good or bad that is." She lifted her hand from his shoulder before he could say it. "Human is good, I know. But there are limits. I was just thinking that one of the deals I made with myself when I came here was that I was going to make it on my own first before contemplating whether or not I wanted to get into another long-term relationship. It seemed like the healthy thing to do. But in the meantime, I wasn't planning on being a monk, either."

"Okay."

"So, I have been a monk, but only because time and opportunity for the no-strings, weekend flings I'd imagined myself having weren't exactly presenting themselves."

She truly had no idea just how charming and adorable her complete and utter candor really was to him. "And now?"

"Well, now it seems like, possibly, maybe, that little problem might resolve itself. For which I'm very happy, by the way. Because you . . . well, come on. I couldn't have dreamed you. Only . . . you know, now I'm worrying that it might turn out to be a little harder for me to reconcile myself with that after-the-fling part than I thought it would."

"Well, I don't know what to tell you about that part. I'm not sure what I'm going to do about it, either. You see, I didn't even have a game plan in place to start with. Short- or long-term. So you're one up on me once again. But I do see one potential problem with your plan."

"Which is?"

He brushed her hair from her face and tipped her chin up. "Am I only allowed to stay for the weekend?"

Her pupils punched wide with desire, and her color rose again to those pretty porcelain features of hers. He wanted to see what other parts of her body he could make blush.

"I—I don't know. I mean, no. You can stay as long as you

want. I just meant, you're . . . temporary. That's all. This . . . whatever we do, can only be temporary."

He crowded her back against the wall by the kitchen cupboards. "We have no idea what this is, or could be. We haven't even started yet."

If it was possible, her pupils expanded further, until they almost swallowed those soft gray irises whole. He felt her fingers flex on his shoulders and saw her throat work.

"Are you opposed to starting something that has no definite path?" he asked. "Or an end date already all planned out?"

"No."

He cocked his head, surprised by the swift certainty of her response.

"Commitment issues?" he asked. "Understandable, after all, given everything."

"No. Just the continued desire to be more self-aware, make better choices for myself. And I don't know if I'm there yet."

"Fair enough. But how will you know when you are, if you don't try?"

"True, I suppose. You?" she countered.

"Commitment issues, no. I'm very loyal to those who matter to me."

"And are there many? Who matter, I mean?"

"I don't know that it's a long list, but there are some very definite names on it. Yes. You?"

"No issues with loyalty. Although what and whom I choose to be loyal to . . . that has changed."

That intrigued him, too. He wanted to know the rest of her story. He wanted to know what led a woman, he was guessing in her late thirties, to launch an enterprise in a small mountain town she had no prior connection to, far away from her original home, all by herself. One that would require a huge personal commitment, given she would literally live and breathe her work. And seemed content with that choice. And it wasn't just about location, or wanting to run a place her way. Or even starting over after a devastating breakup. There was more to it; he felt it clear down to his bones. And he was suddenly dying to know the rest.

One thing he did know was that Kirby Farrell did not lack the commitment gene. Her inn was testament to that. He was more curious to know who would make the loyalty cut in her life these days. And what it would take to get that close to her.

"Understandable, also," he said, "though I think we all make those adjustments as life progresses, for a variety of reasons."

"Is that what happened with you? These choices you need to make, the things you need to ponder . . . commitments changing?"

"As it happens, yes."

"And figuring it out meant a cross-country trek?"

"The journey was part of it. It wasn't just a flight. Well, it might have started out as one, but it became part of the process."

"So, is this just another layover, or a turnaround point?"

"I wanted it to be the latter. Felt it, when I stopped."

"And now?"

"I don't know. More to figure out, I guess. What about you? Is this a beginning point, or an end point?"

"This. You mean the inn? An end point. At least that was the plan. We'll see how that pans out. It's funny, I guess . . . I came across country, too. But I knew where I was heading. And why."

"I thought I knew. Why I was leaving, anyway, if not exactly where I was heading," he said. "Now I'm wondering if I've just been fleeing . . . or maybe hiding, the whole time."

She looked curious, but, to her credit and his relief, she didn't push. There was time, yet. Or would be, if it was still important to either of them. Later.

After.

The silence expanded, but it wasn't an uneasy one.

"What are you thinking?" she asked.

"That this might have been easier without all the talking first."

She smiled a little, but there was a hint of disappointment in it. "Men hate foreplay."

"Some men, maybe. Not me. But that's not what I meant. I didn't mean it was tedious."

"Then what?"

"Personal. Makes it more personal."

"Exactly what I was getting at. Maybe we both wanted something more nameless/faceless."

"I don't know what I wanted. I didn't even know I was going to want at all."

She smiled briefly. "You mean you haven't left a string of broken hearts across the country?"

He shook his head. "Haven't disturbed—or severed—a single body part, I swear."

"What about back in Vegas? Is there someone there who is waiting to hear about your commitment decisions?"

"If you mean a wife or significant other, no. It's not about that." He watched her face. "Would it matter if it did?

"Yes."

"Good."

"I was raised to play well with others and share my toys, but some things aren't meant to be shared. I didn't like it when it happened to me and I sure as hell wouldn't be a part of doing that to someone else."

"So, then I suppose I don't have to worry that someone other than Clemson is going to come banging on your door, asking nosy questions?"

"Oh, there might be all kinds of nosy questions." She watched him this time. "If that's a problem, I understand."

"I'm not the one who lives here, who'll keep on living here. It doesn't bother you?"

She lifted a shoulder. "It's not the kind of thing I would let bother me, no. I'm a grown woman and can do what I want with my private life. If they have issues with my business or how I run it, that's one thing, but about me personally?" Again, she lifted a shoulder.

His smile widened a little. He noticed she'd said "would let bother," indicating she hadn't actually had any experience with small towns and even smaller minds. "How much do you know about small towns?"

"Enough," she said. "Ski resort towns are very small towns."

"Although a bit more cosmopolitan than, say, a small town in Iowa, given the international tourist aspect, don't you think?"

"Possibly, but the resort itself is like a village within a small town, and there are no secrets, and gossip is second only to the skiing and golfing as a favorite form of entertainment. I lived under an enormous amount of scrutiny when I was working for Patrick. I was twelve years his junior, and despite being more than qualified for the job, both by my upbringing and by my college education, absolutely everyone naturally assumed I'd slept my way into the job as resort manager at such a young age. The irony was that Patrick was considered quite the prodigy himself for being an internationally renowned resort owner at such a young age . . . but no one thought he'd gotten there by anything other than hard work."

"Or the hard work of others, from the sound of it."

She shrugged off the intended compliment. "Bottom line is, if you're asking if I'd be bothered by what the locals here might think of how I conduct my personal life, then the answer is no. Both because it truly isn't their business and therefore their opinion is none of my concern, but also because I don't plan on conducting myself in any manner that could be considered questionable, no matter how conservative and small the mind. I'm a grown, single woman and can see or sleep with whomever I wish. It's not like I plan to jump your bones in the middle of the town square."

"Does Pennydash have a town square?"

"Are we in New England?" she teased. "Yes, it does. Actually, it's quite charming and one of the draws for both the resort planners and me. It had fallen on some pretty hard times since the town's inception a hundred years ago, but the resort is bringing a rejuvenation to the shops and empty properties. A few good winters and I think it will turn into something as special as the western resort towns, but with its own distinct East Coast feel. Which I think it is a good thing, despite my western background."

"Actually, I think it sounds pretty nice. I have a thing for town square architecture and development."

She looked surprised. "You do?"

"It's partly why I turned up the drive to your place. I liked the look of the old structure. We don't have this kind of architecture out west and I thought it was both charming and interesting."

"Hunh."

He chuckled. "Still an enigma?"

"More all the time, it seems."

He smiled, but didn't ask if that was a good or a bad thing.

"What about you? You sounded like you had small town experience. Did you live somewhere else before Vegas?"

His laugh was dry, short. "Oh, don't be fooled. Vegas is the smallest of small towns. Especially if you've lived there your whole life."

"Have you?"

"Until recently, yes."

"Oh. I thought you were still a resident. Where did you move away to?"

He nodded in the general direction of the front of the house. "That bike in your driveway."

"Ah," she said again. "The running away that became a journey."

Her hands were still on his bare shoulders, and his body was painfully aware of just how close she was, and how badly he wished there was a whole lot more contact points between them than his hands on her hips and hers on his shoulders. And he let himself get caught up in that for a moment, so she caught him off guard. It was the only reason he could think why he answered her so openly.

"You paused, a moment ago. When I said I'd sent your license to the sheriff's office. I do that as a precaution. One of the good things about small towns is we all look out for one another, but I'm a lone woman running a business and times aren't exactly flush, so while I am appreciative of the business, I'm also careful. No insult intended."

"None taken."

"So . . . why the pause? We've established you haven't hacked anybody up recently, and there aren't any angry exes chasing you—" She paused, and looked at him.

"What?"

"You just did it again."

"Did what?"

"Paused."

"I wasn't talking."

"Your body, something. You stilled, then. You sure there's not someone in Vegas waiting for you to decide if you're coming back?"

"I didn't say there wasn't anybody waiting, just that it wasn't a woman. Or significant other. There are a few other folks waiting."

"The ones on that list?"

"Them. And a few others."

Now she paused. Then she said, "You're right."

"About?"

"Knowing too much. Maybe we should have skipped right past it. Just enjoyed the moment."

"Maybe."

She let out a short, self-deprecating laugh. "Although, in retrospect, I don't know why I thought I'd be any good at this."

"This?"

She played her fingertips along his shoulders. "This."

He swore his entire body vibrated. They might be having a seemingly calm, casual conversation. But there was nothing remotely casual about what her touch did to his body. "No complaints from me."

She laughed. "Except all the talking."

"You're not doing all the talking."

"True."

"So, back to the question. What, exactly, don't you think you're good at?"

"Spontaneous, casual sex."

The directness caught him off guard, though why, he had no idea. She certainly hadn't played coy up till now. Maybe it was hearing her acknowledge, out loud, that she knew where this was heading, expecting it to, in fact, that jacked his body—and his mind—to an instant fever pitch.

"You look disbelieving, but you don't know. I mean, we're standing here, you half naked, us touching each other, chemistry off the charts, at least from where I'm standing. And for the past fifteen minutes, all we've done is talk."

He didn't tell her that the disbelief wasn't about her supposed lack of seduction skills. She had him right where she wanted him. If where she wanted him was all the way naked and buried deep inside of her, anyway. "The most direct things come out of that oh-so-classically shaped mouth."

"I learned the hard way to just say what you mean and state what it is you want. I could have saved myself a lot of grief if I'd stood up for myself as fiercely as I stood up for my job."

"Direct has its virtues, most definitely. It's a large part of why I'm standing here, half naked, with my hands all over you."

Her lips quirked then and the most mischievous, tantalizing light kindled to life in those heretofore soft gray eyes. "Not exactly all over."

His grin was slow, and he thoroughly enjoyed watching what it did to her expression. "Just wait."

"I think I've been very patient."

"With me?"

"With life."

"So, what, you've been waiting for someone to come along and seduce you?"

"The lack of snow has thinned the herd a bit."

It shouldn't bother him, her talking about herds. Herds consisting of other men. Standing where he was standing, touching what he was touching. And it didn't. Not specifically. As long as there weren't any currently waiting in line for their turn, what did he care?

More than he should, was the answer. At least if the way his hands reflexively tightened on her hips meant anything. Which was ridiculous. Not to mention foolish.

"And then I come along."

Now her fingers tightened a little, pressing her blunt nails into his shoulders. "That you did."

"And, prior to that, you'd decided that spontaneous sex would be the rule, not the exception, even if it meant accepting the advances of one of your guests."

"Well, given the thin herd and all," she said wryly. "Sometimes, rules have to be adjusted."

"So . . . where's the glitch?"

"Well, we're not having sex, for one thing. And at this point, even if you do get me naked on any of the beds in this establishment, we can't exactly call it spontaneous."

"And this would be a deal breaker? I'm confused."

"No. But . . . clearly, I'm not good at it. Talking about it. Thinking about it. Wanting to have it. All those things I obviously excel at."

His lips curved. "Thinking about it," he repeated. "With me?"

"Endlessly."

His body leapt. He wanted to roar. "See? You blush one second, and then say the damndest things the next."

"Talking about it. Check."

"You know," he said, slowly backing her up against the cabinet. "You're not the only one stalling. With the talking."

"Stalling. Is that what we're doing? Or trying to talk ourselves out of it?"

He pressed his hips a little closer. "I'm not interested in stopping."

"So . . . why the stall? I know why I'm doing it."

"Why?"

"Because I'm all talk, scared a little more about the action. This kind of action. Okay, maybe more than a little."

"Why?"

"The after-the-action part. Like I said. You?"

"I wanted it to be spontaneous sex. Maybe lose myself in the physical, dodge the mental for a little bit. I don't know. We're both consenting adults, so what's the problem, right?"

"Exactly. So . . . ?"

"So . . . I don't do spontaneous, either. Apparently."

"Which leaves us where? Exactly?"

He grinned and reached up to touch her face. It was so smoothly defined, so elegantly shaped. He touched her bottom lip, felt her sigh more than heard it. "Overcoming our fears?"

"Bold plan."

"Wouldn't be the first one I've made."

"Success rate?"

"Enough to be wary, but relatively confident."

"Are you always wary?"

"Depends on the stakes."

"And these?"

"Higher than I thought they'd be."

Kirby's eyebrows lifted. "Now who's being direct?"

"Bold plans sometimes require bold moves."

"Somehow, despite the quiet demeanor, I'm not getting much of a shy or retiring vibe from you."

"I'm more of both than you might think. Certainly than most people think."

"And why is that?"

Brett didn't answer right away. Wasn't sure how to answer.

He had no problem telling her who he was, what he did, what he'd come from, why he was confused about whether to go back. In fact, he'd bet against the house that her responses would be open, honest, insightful, and without an ulterior agenda. Maybe he shouldn't be trying to get her into bed so much as fixing her a cup of coffee and inviting her to sit a spell. He wondered if sleeping with her would change that ulterior agenda thing.

On the one hand, it was a good bet to take. What he'd learned of Kirby Farrell so far didn't lead him to believe she was ever anything but open and honest. Maybe to a fault, but it was refreshing enough that he found it more flattering than flaw.

On the other hand, once she knew more, that would influence her. It always did. She was direct, but some things were hard not to judge or be influenced by.

"I'm going to ask you something," he said. "Something I really don't have a right to ask, but I'm asking anyway."

"Go on."

"At some point, I'll answer any questions you have. If you still want to ask them. But . . . for now, I'm more interested in what you think than what anybody else thinks."

"About?"

"Me."

"Okay. So . . . what about you?"

"Nothing nefarious, I assure you. Just . . . get to know me. Form your own opinions based on what you come to know."

"Isn't that what I've been doing?"

He nodded. "I'd just . . . like to keep it that way. A little longer."

"Okay," she responded easily. "Can I ask why?"

"Because it matters to me."

"Because you think it will help with those decisions you have to make? I'm just one person. And I don't even know you. How could my opinion, whatever it might be, carry any real weight?"

"Because it would be an honest, unbiased opinion."

"Ah." Kirby was nodding, but he could see that she didn't really understand. "So, what, exactly, is off limits?"

"I'll let you know."
"Okay."
"Okay?"
She smiled. "For now."
"How long is for now?"
Her smile grew. "I'll let you know."

Chapter 7

It was laughable, really, that Kirby had ever truly imagined herself seducing or being seduced by some randy ski instructor or ego-assured international racer. She had no problem being direct. That was one part of her New Life Plan that she'd stuck to pretty religiously since coming to Vermont. And the payoff had been pretty decent, if you measured that by her success in getting her inn ready and open for business in record time, and building good relationships with the locals—Clemson notwithstanding—while doing it. Sure, her social life was a bit lacking, but she'd planned on fixing that just as soon as she got up and running, found her rhythm, her routine.

She'd fit in. She'd make friends that went beyond business acquaintances. And there would be the occasional lover to fulfill her other needs. And she would be in control. Her life, on her terms. Yep . . . she'd had it all planned out all right.

And now the occasional lover part of the plan was literally standing right in front of her, primed and ready, if his body was telling her anything . . . and it wasn't just telling her. It was literally prodding her with the information.

And here she stood. Talking. Negotiating, for God's sake.

So what if he could have the same picture, same pose, on every calendar page of a hunk-of-the-month calendar, and still make it an instant best seller? He wasn't really intimidating, once you got to know him. In fact, he seemed just as hung up on the casual and easy part of the equation as she did.

And now he was all, "get to know the real me." Which begged the question, what—or who—was the fake Brett?

Was it the mysterious and surprising layers to him that were tripping her up? Or the fact that only one of them had gotten even partially naked so far? She was hardly a twenty-something any longer. Gravity was doing its thing. There were parts that she would no longer label pert or perky.

I want to have you on every bed in this place.

She shivered a little, replaying those words through her mind. That's what she needed to remember, to focus on. She wanted her uncomplicated needs met. And just looking at Brett . . . boy, she had needs.

He traced a finger along the side of her face. It made her shudder with pleasure, with anticipation.

"So," he said, letting the rest trail off, letting her set the pace.

Great. "One of us has to start the transition from talk to action."

"One of us should, yes," he agreed, that twinkle sparking in his eyes. "Any ideas?"

"Well, you're the one with the bold moves."

He smiled. It was sexy and sweet at the same time. She looked at him and still saw the unbelievably hot Brett Hennessey, but there was more there now. He was also the somewhat vulnerable Brett Hennessey. Possibly a guy who also had his professional game a lot more together than his personal one. At least that's how she'd taken his comments about how others saw him versus what he knew to be the real him. Although how a guy with his genetic gifts could be anything less than cocksure of himself mystified her.

"Climbing up that tree was a pretty bold move," he countered.

"One that almost got me killed."

"Good point."

"Perhaps I shouldn't be the one setting the bold move standard."

"Well, I could make the obvious guy statement here that if your bold moves in bed led to my imminent demise, then . . . what a way to go! But that would be cliché."

"True. And you're not a cliché."

"I try not to be."

"You've definitely busted a fair share of them so far."

His broadening smile sparked that twinkle to an even brighter level. "Then my work here is almost done."

"Almost?"

"Almost." He framed her face with his hands, tilted it up so he could look directly into her eyes . . . and she directly into his. There was amusement, desire, want . . . and a very definite sense of purpose.

And, just like that, she was right back on that edge of the unknown that had made her leap into the safety net of prolonged conversation in the first place. Only this time, whatever potential danger there might be in spending her immediate future with him seemed far more titillating than scary. "Maybe the extended verbal foreplay part helped after all," she murmured as she stared into his eyes.

"Kirby."

"Yes?"

"No more talking." He lowered his mouth.

"No more talking," she agreed.

He finally, blessedly, kissed her. It hadn't been a fluke, or her imagination. He kissed her perfectly. His mouth was a perfect fit for hers . . . and he knew what to do with it. If anything, it was even more perfect than their first try. Whether it was because of their little getting-to-know-you byplay, or because, well . . . he was perfect, she wasn't sure. Didn't much care. As long as he didn't stop doing what he was doing. Ever, actually, would be nice.

He pushed his fingers into her hair, slanting her mouth beneath his, kissing her so slowly, so thoroughly, and with such deliberation, her knees, quite literally, went weak.

He crowded her against the cupboards, sliding his hands down to her shoulders, then over her arms, to her torso, trailing his thumbs so they brushed along the outer swell of her breasts, pausing a little when she moaned, then shifting them so his thumbs could lightly brush over her nipples. She jerked a little against such direct stimulation, and he stilled his hands. So she moved, pushing against him, just slightly, but enough that he knew her reaction had been one of pleasure.

She supposed, or would later when she thought back over things, that it was his very directness, coupled with his sensitivity to her every little reaction to what he was doing, that ultimately made her comfortable enough to . . . well, to let someone she hardly knew have such intimate access to her body.

She hadn't really thought about that part when deciding that casual lovers were going to be it for her from now on. That by its very nature, casual would also imply someone she didn't know well. Because, if she knew him well, it could hardly be all that casual, now could it? Had she really thought that this casual person was going to sweep her up in his arms, where the two of them would become suddenly naked and assuage their needs, then over and done, sorry gotta run now? She hadn't calculated in that part where there would be all this touching, and acquainting of selves, and exploration of, well, everything. And, eventually, everywhere. It was how sex actually worked. It was necessarily and quite specifically intimate. Which was the exact of opposite of casual.

How had she managed to overlook that crucial part?

How did anybody actually manage to have casual sex? She wasn't feeling remotely casual now that he was playing with her nipples. And . . . and stuff.

Then he was moving his mouth off hers and along her jaw. And using more than just his thumbs on her nipples to make her thighs quiver. And it felt so damn good. He felt so damn good. She wanted this. Wanted him. This was perfect. Brett was perfect. Possibly the most perfect of her illusory phantom lover ideals.

And if Kirby was going to do this, she damn well wasn't going to be a passive participant. So, she slid her fingers into his hair, both disconcerted by the fact that they were trembling as strongly as they were, and proud of herself when she continued anyway. Because it wasn't like she'd never done this before. She'd done this plenty. Just . . . with only one person. Ever. Well, if you didn't count her initial loss of virginity, at the startlingly advanced age of twenty-four, with her college roommate's brother, Mike, at their graduation party. She certainly didn't want to count anything about that horribly awkward, fumbling night. Getting her master's degree had been easier than achieving orgasm. Or even faking one. Maybe if he'd taken his horn-rimmed glasses off . . . and his socks.

Still, it was like riding a bike, pretty much, right? Even if this bike was flashier, shinier, faster, and built for a far more experienced rider. He wasn't pushing, wasn't coaxing, either. He was simply taking, enjoying.

So, she would, too.

She took a breath that was supposed to be steadying, but instead was remarkable only because she could suck in a breath at all, and shifted his head down . . . and then down some more.

He caught on quickly, her shiny new bicycle did, and he worked open the buttons on the front of her camp shirt, kissing her along her collarbone as he did, then pushed up the thin, long tee she wore underneath till his warm palms bracketed her waist. She held her breath for the moment when he inadvertently hit her scratched skin, not wanting to ruin the building moment with a moan of pain versus pleasure, but that moment never came. He slid his hands—and her tee—slowly up her sides, as his mouth moved lower along the scalloped edge of the deep neckline.

She'd never felt so intensely female, or desirable, as when her fingers slid from his hair to his nape and became aware of the insistent throb of the pulse along the side of his neck under the pad of her thumb. His hands were so gentle, but that rapid beat against her sensitive fingertips told another story. It shouldn't have been so thrilling. Given what she'd felt pressed against her earlier, she knew she wasn't the only affected party here. Still . . .

Kirby arched her back as Brett slid her tee higher, finally pushing it over her barely there bra that she barely needed. Her lacking there didn't seem to slow him down in the least. For which she was profoundly grateful. Size didn't alter sensitivity or need . . . which he seemed quite in tune with.

She closed her eyes as his mouth enveloped one tightened nipple while his fingers played with the other. Honestly, it was like she'd dreamed him up. Maybe she was dreaming. Hell, maybe she'd really fallen out of that tree and was dead and this was all happening in her afterlife.

Well, if that were true, at least it was good news. She'd gone to heaven.

He unclasped the front of her bra and slowly peeled the now damp, flimsy fabric from her skin. She gasped as he closed his warm lips back over the taut bud. And then, when she wasn't sure how much longer her trembling legs would hold up, he moved lower, placing the softest of kisses in between the scratches on her stomach. There was something both tender and erotic about the way he moved down along her torso. His wide palms were bracketed low on her hips as he pinned her back to the wall and continued downward.

Kirby purposely kept her thoughts focused on the moment, in the moment. If she allowed herself to think about what she was doing, in her own kitchen, with a guest, no less . . .

Brett plucked open the button at the waistband of her khakis, and any concern she had about the choices she was making were drowned out by the strident demands of her body. It had been too long . . . and this was simply too good. So . . . so good. She released a long, shaky breath as he dropped heated kisses along the tender skin of her lower belly being slowly exposed as he pulled down her zipper. His lips were warm, firm, and in command . . . and he was taking so damn long to get to where she needed him to be, she had to curl her fingers inward against her palms to keep from sinking them back into those thick curls and urging him to get on with it already.

His own low groan of appreciation as he tugged her pants down to her hips, hooking his fingers around the thin band of her panties and taking those down, too, had her splaying her palms flat against the wall, digging her fingertips, seeking for purchase, anything to help keep her upright on shaking thighs and—*Oh!* "Yes," she gasped as he found her.

Her hands moved instinctively then, fingers sliding through his silky curls, not urging—no need, he was doing everything right—but simply for balance, to keep from sliding down the wall and into a—"Oh!" Her hips bucked against his hands, her whole body trembling now as he slid his tongue against her . . . then into her. She moved against him, with him, establishing a rhythm that drove her easily, swiftly, straight up to the edge. Right there, she thought. Right. There.

And, keeping the dream lover scenario alive and screamingly well, he moved right there . . . and her gasps quickly turned to loud moans as the climax roared through her. She bent over as he continued driving her well past the point she thought she was capable of going. Her hands slid from his hair to his shoulders, her blunt nails digging into the firm muscle there as he wrenched ridiculous amounts of pleasure from her body. "You . . . wow," was as coherent as she could be. When the rippling waves finally peaked and began to subside, he surprised her by pushing her pants and panties the rest of the way down her legs, urging her silently to step clear of them.

No fool she, she did anything he asked.

As he stood, he pushed off his own jeans, and even in her post-climactic, pleasure-drenched state, she paused to marvel—okay, possibly it was more like goggle—over his unbelievable physique. Hanging from a tree, a twenty-foot drop from death, she really hadn't had time to appreciate him the first time she'd seen him naked.

She most certainly was appreciating him now. Wow. Santa

hadn't come through with the snow, but he was damn well making up for lost time right now. In fact, she owed Santa a present. Big-time. Big, being the key word there.

His hands came back to her hips, and her gaze finally lifted to his. She wasn't sure what she'd expected to see there. Probably not arrogance or cockiness; he hadn't struck her as the type. A knowing smile perhaps, a sexually charged twinkle in his eyes . . . something like that. A silent, perhaps even humble acknowledgment that if she'd experienced pleasure so far, she could definitely look forward to more of the same.

What she found was his focus entirely and directly pinned on her. As if his godlike body wasn't really a factor here, other than how it was about to be directly involved with hers. There was nothing nonchalant or offhand about it, either.

No, there was . . . a whole lot of other things going on there. Personal things, deeper thoughts, thoughts about her.

As if reading her mind, and perhaps he could—nothing would surprise her at this point—his hands tightened on her hips. "Upstairs? Or your room?"

She'd been thinking that right here up against the wall would work just fine. Possibly the counter. Or the floor. His eyes flared and she really started to wonder if he could read her mind. He might be focused quite intently on her, but there was no lack of sexual desire. Which was easily proved by his ready—very ready—body, but somehow, seeing it there, in the way he looked at her, pushed it beyond the merely physical. Made it personal. Which made her nervous.

And, perversely, that turned her on even more.

"I—uh—" was pretty much the extent of her verbal ability.

He moved in closer then, the extremely hard length of him pushing up against her belly, reminding her just how much taller and bigger he was than her. He pushed his hips in, pinning her to the wall, then slid his hands up the sides of her waist, brushing his thumbs over her still tightly budded nipples, making her twitch, gasp, then framed her face. Her gaze was riveted to his, her body his to do with whatever he pleased.

"I want you right here . . . right now. But while spontaneity is great . . . I didn't come down here prepared for this."

Oh. *Oh!* "I'm safe," she said. "And I can't—I won't get pregnant." She didn't illuminate. Let him think she was otherwise protected. The end result was the same.

"I am, too. Safe, I mean." He slid his hands into her hair. "Will you trust me, then?"

He was a biker, from Vegas. She had no reason to trust him. For all she knew he'd slept his way across the country. But that's not what her instincts told her. And certainly not what she wanted to believe. And . . . he'd asked. He could have just taken. But he'd asked.

And then that twinkle surfaced, glittering playfully, and she was so gone, and not just her body. "Race you to my bedside nightstand," he said, giving her the graceful out, and in such a way as to make it fun, easy. Not awkward.

And she knew then that it was never going to be awkward. Not with Brett.

"I'm fine . . . here," she said, answering the trust question her own way. It was that or shake him and beg. And she was trying to at least pretend not to appear desperate and beyond needy.

"Really," he said, that slow grin easing back across his handsome face. He tilted her head, lifting her mouth up to his. "Well, then . . ." He closed his mouth over hers, and all she could think was that it was always, always going to be just that good. Better, even.

Kirby wound her arms around his neck, and let herself go, let herself take, and open to him, and just sink into the pleasure that could be had just from kissing.

But Brett had other ideas. He gripped her hips and pulled her thighs up, urging her to cross her ankles behind his back. He hiked her up farther, until her face was even with his. He took advantage of the shift and took the kiss deeper. Then he slowly slid her down the wall . . . and onto him.

She sucked in a deep breath, and he slowed. "It's okay?"

"Very," she gasped.

He grinned against the side of her mouth, but said, "You sure?"

"Very."

He took his time, given that gravity alone was pushing her down on him, and lifted her hips away from the wall a little so she could have some control over the movement.

And then, oh, there was movement. Heavenly, wonderfully invasive, incredibly fulfilling movement. If she'd thought she might die from the bliss of having his tongue on her . . . in her, well, this . . . ? This was pretty much proof that she really had died and gone straight to heaven.

Their kiss was broken by the necessity of him arching his hips to keep her pinned so she could move. He still gripped her hips, she held on to his shoulders, her own head tipped back now pressing against the wall as her back arched away . . . pushing her more deeply onto him.

They found their rhythm, and she lost track of who was moaning, who was growling. His hands were wide, warm, and secure on her hips. He was deep, and strong, and steady in taking her. She'd never felt so wanton, so wanted, so purely sexual in her entire life.

She felt him gathering, and he pressed her back against the wall then, pinning her there with every part of his body. His mouth was on the curve of her neck and she felt devoured, invaded, claimed . . . and thrilled at the very intensity of it all.

When he came, he found her mouth, and took her there, too. She was gripping his shoulders so hard her fingers cramped; her legs shook from holding him so tightly. She took his pounding release and reveled in every pulse, every beat of her heart and of his.

They were both breathing hard, clutching each other, when he said, "Hold on."

She already was, so she wasn't sure what he meant. But as he slid from her body, he hiked her up higher again, and she instinctively tightened her legs around him. He turned, leaning his weight against the wall as he fought to regain his regular breathing. "Bed?" he said, nudging at her hair, her face tucked against the rapid pulse still beating in his neck. "Or shower."

She might have growled a little at that last suggestion. A growly groan. It was a primal response and she was feeling nothing if not absolutely primal in that moment.

"Shower it is then." He pushed away from the wall, holding on to her tightly. "Closest?"

"Mine," she said, and when his hands reflexively tightened at the word, she instantly had a flash, a blink, of what it would be like if he actually was. "Front hall, first door," she managed, thankful her face was averted from his. He saw too much with those soulful, wicked, sexy green eyes of his. She doubted the world would look the same to her after today; that was how altered she felt. Like the colors would be brighter, the sounds crisper, the smells sharper. All of her senses felt ignited to the point of hyperawareness and she wondered if they'd ever really return to the way they'd been before. At the moment, it didn't seem possible.

She was a changed woman.

She slid her arms more tightly around his neck, knowing this was all some kind of hormonally induced nirvana. And given her past experiences, it was normal, even, at least for her, to feel these ridiculously out-of-place, over-the-top things. So it was good he didn't know what was going through her mind. She'd just have to make sure he never knew.

She tried her best to maintain her balance, wrapped around him as she was, so he wasn't hefting dead weight as he made his way to the front hall, to the door leading to her bed and bathroom. He adjusted her weight to free a hand up to open the door.

"You can put me down, you know."

"Yep." But he didn't. He pushed open the door and kicked it shut behind them.

"Bathroom is the door on your left."

They made it as far as the bed.

"But—" she started, then stopped as he lowered himself down next to her.

"I'll do the laundry. I thought our legs could use a pit stop."

She laughed. "I don't care about the laundry part. And, now that I'm laying here . . . you're right. My legs are shaky."

"Mine, too," he said, smiling.

"I should have told you to bring me in here before; I'm sorry."

He rolled to his back and sighed with what sounded like deep appreciation. "Please, don't be sorry for one second of that. Lord knows I'm not."

She smiled. He slid his hand over until it found hers, and covered it. Something about that, about his wanting to still feel connected, sent her shooting willy-nilly into very dangerous territory. The fact that she knew it was the hormonal rush, the lack of male companionship, on all levels, and . . . well, a culmination of a lot of things she'd refused to let herself think about for the past few years . . . didn't make it any less terrifying. More, perhaps.

Kirby wondered again about him. About his story. What had led him to her inn, what it was he had to work out while he was here. She wanted to just be curious, but not really care. Only when his fingers traced little patterns on the back of her hand, she felt her heart squeeze a little. And she knew that if they kept this up, even for a little while longer, it was going to hurt like hell when he left. And he would leave.

She closed her eyes. Dammit. Had she really thought she was cut out for casual relationships? Had she really thought that what life had handed her had changed her so profoundly that she could control this, too?

The simple answer was yes. Yes, she had. She'd been numb. So numb. For so long. Of course she thought she could call the shots, control the emotions. Hell, she hadn't really thought she'd have any of the latter. She'd been thrilled just to have gotten back to the place where she was wanting the fundamental pleasure that sex could bring. If not anything beyond that. Surely she could control that. Most especially with a complete stranger. Simple.

Right.

To her horror, she felt that tingling burn gather behind her eyes. No. She absolutely, positively was not going to ruin what had otherwise been a stellar, stand-alone, exultant moment in her life. One she'd call upon for months, no, let's be honest, years to come, when she needed a little pick-me-up. Or some good fantasy fodder.

Fantasy. That's what she needed to latch on to. This was, for all intents, a pure fantasy. And as they went, it was pretty much the apex. So she'd fix her mind on that, on enjoying that, on being lucky enough to get that. Because, really, when she thought about it, it definitely beat not ever having had it. Emotional threat or not.

There. She squeezed her eyes a bit more tightly and focused on how lucky she was . . . and the threat subsided.

"Kirby," he said in a drowsy, perfectly sexy, gravelly kind of way.

She rolled her head to the side, looked at Brett, just as he did the same. Their gazes collided. Then he smiled. And it wasn't knowing, or a come-on, or even post-coitally dazed. Nope. It was sincere and honest. And . . . well, sweet.

Yeah. She was totally screwed.

Chapter 8

Brett had promised Kirby a shower. And, in theory, it sounded like one of his better ideas. If only he could will himself to move off the bed. He could honestly say that he'd never met anyone like her. And he'd definitely never had sex like that.

How it had seemed perfectly natural to carry on a lengthy conversation while standing that deep in each other's personal space, all that sexual tension leaping off them both, without just ripping each other's clothes off and having at it . . . he had no idea. But he was pretty damn sure it wouldn't have been nearly as spectacular, or just plain damn fun, if they'd gone about it any other way.

She was singular, Kirby was. Nothing like the women who normally crossed his path. There was no fear in talking about what was going through her mind . . . and yet beneath all that, or actually right there on the surface along with it, there were some pretty hefty vulnerabilities as well. He wasn't sure whether or not she thought she'd done a good job of hiding the fact that her past still colored her present. But he'd pulled too many marathons at too many poker tables, staring at hundreds if not thousands of faces, to not be good—damn good—at reading people.

He'd been curious about her before. After the tree. And dinner. And psycho kitty stuff. But now, after having her, tasting her, taking her like that . . . He closed his eyes. *Yeah. Like that.* Damn, that had been fucking amazing. She'd been fucking amazing. And he wanted her again.

Which he'd do something about. Just as soon as his body recovered. It had been a while since he'd played like that, and he was still dog tired from the past couple of weeks. Months. Hell, longer, to be honest, if he factored in mental fatigue. But she'd stirred up more than his long-neglected libido. She'd stirred his mind up, too.

Since she didn't seem to be in any hurry, either, he laid there, lazily stroking the back of her hand, liking the contact with her warm skin as he listened to her breathing even out. And, despite the fatigue, the worry, the concern, that had been dogging him for what felt like ages now . . . at that moment, he felt almost peaceful. Certainly more relaxed than he'd been in a long time. He smiled. He could hear Dan now. *Well, of course you're feeling mellow. You finally got laid.*

He was still smiling as his eyes drifted shut. He sure as hell had.

He thought about what he'd tell Dan about Kirby. The two of them went back so far, there was very little if anything one didn't know about the other. So it was kind of foreign, this feeling he had, of wanting to keep this, keep Kirby, to himself. At least for now. Maybe it was part of the whole thing about her getting to know him outside of his professional persona. It felt pretty damn good, he had to say. And in ways that had nothing to do with sex. Though he knew that played a role, too.

He'd tell Dan about her eventually. After he'd taken off. Right now, he didn't want any outside influence at all. He just wanted this.

To that end, he covered Kirby's hand and tugged her gently until she rolled toward him. He tucked her easily, and almost too naturally, against his side. He'd never necessarily thought of himself as the post-coital cuddler type, if he even was a type, but there was a lot to be said for having the warm body of a naked woman tucked up against him. Didn't happen all that often. No point in sleeping alone if a guy didn't have to.

Yeah, right. He tucked her head beneath his chin and she mumbled something in her sleep. He pressed a kiss against her hair. She drew her leg up over his thigh. He let sleep claim him, well aware of the big smile on his face.

The ringing phone jerked them both awake some indeterminate amount of time later. She groaned when her head connected with his chin, and they both sucked in a quick wince of pain as their cat-scratched skin stretched when they moved apart and sat up too quickly.

His eyes went to the jagged, flame-red marks that streaked across her stomach. His back probably looked much the same. He didn't mind his so much, but he hated seeing all that creamy skin of hers, skin he'd tasted now, all raw and ravaged. He was happy the little heathen's attack skills would come in handy in her new life . . . and equally grateful the cat would never get a chance to mark up Kirby's champagne-sweet skin again.

Skin he was thinking of sipping, much like the finest Perrier-Jouet, and was dipping his head to put thought to deed, when the phone rang again. It occurred to him as the muzziness of sleep cleared with the continued ringing that she was running a business here, so he reluctantly aborted his mission. "You need to get that?"

All he got in response was a grunt, which made him smile. There wasn't much about her that didn't make him smile, he realized. She rolled to a sitting position, her lovely naked back to him, her hair all sexy in a mussed-up, bed-head kind of way. The kind of way that made him want to pull her back down and roll her underneath him. He felt his body come to life at the thought, and his smile widened. So, maybe he wasn't all that road weary after all. Or she was the elixir of life. Either way, things were looking up for him. Literally.

The phone continued to ring. "Yes," she said at length, fighting a yawn. "I should. But the machine will pick up. I'll screen it."

"Do you have more than one line? I mean, a private one for you?"

"My cell is my private line, and I have the line here forwarded to that one if I am out or away. But that line, the ringing one, that's for the inn."

He could have pointed out that, given the dearth of guests at the moment, possibly she didn't want to avoid taking the call. But if ignoring the phone meant he had her all to himself a little while longer? Well, he was all for that. Who was he to tell her how to run her business?

The phone cut off, mid-ring, and he thought the caller had hung up until he heard the echo of a voice—a man's voice—coming from the room beyond. There was a door between this room and that one, partially opened now. He vaguely remembered seeing the other space that looked like an office before he'd kicked the door shut and dropped them to the bed. He hadn't really been paying attention, as he'd had a naked woman wrapped around him at the time.

"—know who that is staying at your place?"

Brett's attention was immediately yanked from Kirby and all the wonderful things he wanted to do to and with her, and directed to the disembodied voice coming from the next room. He felt his spirit sink, like his entire body kind of just caved in a little. He could have spoken up, said anything, and drowned the voice out. But it would only have delayed the inevitable. He'd hoped, thought, that being the only guest here and not having left the inn since checking in, that he'd keep his anonymity a while longer. Like, until he decided to leave. He'd been in Vegas for so long, where everyone knew who he was. The thrill of being unknown hadn't worn off yet.

But he remained silent and watched as Kirby slowly turned enough so she could look at him.

"—Brett Hennessey. *The* Brett Hennessey. He's like the Tiger

Woods of poker. Guy's won millions." The man on the phone chuckled like he'd personally hit some kind of jackpot. "Hey, maybe you should get him to do some kind of commercial for you. Or at least autograph something to hang on your wall. Guests would love that kind of stuff. When you get guests, that is. Anyway, just letting you know you have nothing to worry about." There was a pause, then, sounding highly amused with himself, the caller added, "As long as you don't play five card stud with the guy." On a final, self-satisfied chuckle, the call finally, mercifully, ended.

Brett held Kirby's gaze and braced himself, even as he mentally began packing his bags and wondering where he'd head to next. Maybe Dan was right, and he should just head home.

But she merely lifted her eyebrows in question. He lifted a shoulder in response.

And, rather stunningly, she didn't ask a single question. Well, she did ask one.

"You still thinking about taking that shower?"

He stared at her a second longer. As if he wasn't entirely sure he was hearing things properly. Or maybe he'd just hallucinated that entire phone call. His worst fear. Well, not his worst, not given what was going on back home, or had . . . but in this particular intimate situation, certainly up there on that list. "Who was the guy?" he asked, wondering both who knew he was here . . . and, maybe, what he was to Kirby.

"Thad. Deputy Johnson," she clarified. "That's who I faxed the copy of your driver's license to."

Brett supposed he'd been kidding himself, thinking he'd remain some kind of phantom lover or something. Although, outside of Vegas, unless you were a gambler, an online player, or a late-night watcher of ESPN, it would be kind of unusual to know of him. He wondered which category Deputy Thad fell into.

"It does explain a few things," she said, apparently mistaking his silence for a desire on his part for her to say something, anything.

"Like?"

"The cashmere under the leather. The manicure. The bank-wrapped wad of cash."

His lips curved briefly. "Worried that I was a bank robber?"

"Not worried, no, although you don't see a bank roll like that every day. Or ever. At least in my line of work. I was curious, mostly. But I'm always curious. Everyone has a story. It's partly why I run an inn. You meet a lot of people, hear a lot of stories."

He cocked his head, watched her. "Why not be a journalist?"

She smiled then. "I have no aptitude for storytelling. And I'm not particularly compelled to share the stories. I just enjoy hearing them."

He nodded. "You said partly. What's the other part?"

"Long story. Boring story."

Now she was bluffing. It might be boring to him, but that had been an entirely different sort of vulnerability flashing across her face just then. The kind he'd bet went much further back than the stinging blow her former boss and lover had delivered to both her pride and her heart. That other part of the story, whatever it was, was a whole lot of things to her, but he doubted boring was one of them.

"And since we agreed not to delve into any more personal stuff where you're concerned, that mercifully saves you from having to listen to mine," she said, smiling as she scooted off the edge of the bed and headed toward what he presumed was her bathroom.

So. Conversation closed. For now, anyway.

He wondered what she'd say if he told her he didn't necessarily want to be saved? That he wanted to know every last thing about her?

The shower came on. Would it be different now? Awkward when he thought it wouldn't be? Would Thad's call and her obvious duck just now become the elephant in the room—or the shower—that they would stumble over not talking about? He supposed there was only one way to find out.

He slid off the bed and walked to the bathroom. She was already under the spray. He hadn't paid much attention to how she'd decorated her own space, being somewhat preoccupied, but he did now. Her bedroom was just as tastefully decorated as the one he occupied. Warm, polished antique bedstead, with a carved head and footboard. Hers was covered with an old quilt and lots of linen-covered pillows with handstitched patterns along the hem of the slipcovers. There were colorful, handwoven rugs on the hardwood floor, mismatched old lamps, the odd knickknack or crafted art piece placed here and hung there. Dried flowers mixed with potted plants. It wasn't overtly feminine, or masculine, for that matter, but he knew it was her. Her taste, her style. Classic, but a little offbeat, a good eye for design, mixed with a bit of whimsy.

He liked the attention she'd paid to detail, to making the whole place feel more like someone's home than a sterile, cookie-cutter, hotel environment. He'd stayed in his share, more than his share, including some of the most ridiculously over-the-top suites one could imagine. He'd rather have this.

It was one of the reasons he still rented rooms from Vanetta and had never gotten his own place. Vanetta would like Kirby's inn, he thought, though he couldn't picture the older woman living anywhere but at the edge of the desert. He already knew she would never even consider leaving Vegas. When all the trouble had started and he'd begun to piece together the possible origin of the threat, he'd tried to talk her into retiring, maybe moving to Palm Springs or something. He'd known she wouldn't go for it. He'd tried to get her to retire before, but she said she'd shrivel up if she didn't have work to keep her honest.

And she did work. Harder than anyone he knew. She had both a razor-edged tongue and the biggest heart of anyone he'd ever known. Not that she'd want anyone to know that. As close to a mother figure as he'd ever had, he'd done his best to repay her for everything she'd done for him. Not that she'd made that easy on him, either. He smiled, recalling the tongue lashing he'd taken when, after winning his first seven-figure pot, he'd used the winnings to pay off the bank loan on the boarding house and set up a retirement account for her. He'd made sure that Dan and his father kept the place in good shape so she wouldn't take out yet another loan for upkeep and repairs on the old place.

When all the trouble had started after he'd quit playing poker last year, he'd also taken out a rather large, high-risk insurance policy on the property. If she wouldn't relocate or retire, then he'd protect her the best he could anyway.

Thinking about Vanetta, about home, drew his mind right back to why he'd stopped here in the first place. He'd call Dan later today, talk things over, start working on an endgame to all this. But, at the moment, there was a naked woman in a shower waiting for him.

And that was an easy bet to take. He was going all in.

He stepped carefully through the opening in the circular curtain set inside the long claw-foot tub. His bathroom upstairs had been far more recently renovated; it was modern, with more current amenities, like an oversized tub and a big, drenching showerhead. He rather liked the style of this one. It suited the feel of the old place.

Kirby was standing forward, beneath the narrow spray, her back to him, head ducked so that the water pounded on her back. She didn't immediately react to his joining her, and so he took the moment to simply drink in the sight of her. All of her. She was slender almost to the point of skinny, but there was a hint of hips, albeit not much ass, a bit of graceful breadth to her shoulders. Her neck . . . that long, pale, slender column, made his mouth water. Plus, she had legs that went on forever.

All shiny wet and slippery looking, he ached to run his hands over her, bring her up to that fever pitch, the way he had in the kitchen. She'd responded to him so honestly, so openly, it had driven him half crazy. Her plea for him to take her where she stood had pushed him the rest of the way there. At the moment, though, she was simply standing, not even looking at him, seeming lost in thought. Was she wondering about him, after that call, or having second thoughts about the choices she'd made, getting intimate with a virtual stranger? He could hardly blame her, he supposed.

But, right now, he was more distracted by the fact that even doing nothing, she had his undivided attention. Okay, so she was nakedly doing nothing, and he had just been buried deep inside that slender frame, being held so tightly he'd thought he might just die from the pleasure of it. But still . . . he'd had sex before. Even good sex. Usually he found his mind drifting to the next game or event, or to a job-site issue with Dan, or . . . something other than the partner he'd just been intimate with.

And that's when it hit him, the difference. Not that he'd made love to her in that kitchen. That had been all about sex, about slaking needs and taking and pleasuring. But, right now, watching her, thinking about that vulnerable part, the part that had taken a good long time to get to where she could let her defenses down with him completely, the way she obviously wanted to. Yes, he was thinking about that part, all tangled up with the way she'd followed his request to leave the rest of him out of the equation and just take him as she got to know him . . . he had a lot of respect for that. Especially given her self-proclaimed curious bent.

But it was that first part, the vulnerable part, that had kept her talking for a lot longer than most women would have, given his ready state and the fact that he had all but pushed her up against the wall in his desire to have her. He'd wanted to take her, to have her, to slake needs, his . . . and hers. And they'd done all that, and more.

So, it was curious now, not that he wanted her again, but that the needs behind it were different. He wanted to . . . what? Romance her? That wasn't really it. And he didn't know her well enough to call it lovemaking. That felt like something that required at least reaching some deeper level of affection. And it wasn't that he felt sorry for her, for what the last person she'd trusted with her heart, her body, had done to her. He hated that, to be sure, but that wasn't why his heart felt all kind of wobbly and weak when he looked at her.

He merely knew he wanted to give her pleasure, and take care of her in a way that wasn't just about slaking needs and having mind-blowing sex. He wanted to give her . . . more. Get her off that wobbly, vulnerable edge, at least where this was concerned. Bring that other part he knew of her, the direct, confident part, to this. All of this.

He was reaching for her without really knowing what in the hell he was actually thinking, or even wanting. Maybe this wasn't about her at all, or that sad look he'd seen in her eyes, or the way she'd had to talk herself into having sex she obviously wanted. Maybe this was about him. He wasn't sure he really cared. And he knew he was tired, damn tired, of thinking about every last thing. He just wanted to feel. To do what felt natural, what felt right, and to hell with everything else.

Because, for once, maybe for the first time ever, there was nothing else.

He took her shoulders, gently, in his hands, and she didn't jump, so she'd been aware he was standing behind her all this time. But she hadn't turned, hadn't looked at him. He turned her to him, into him, into his arms. It was a confined space, a small circle of curtain surrounding them, filled with steam and the spray of hot water. He tipped her mouth up to his and took it slowly, in a deep, searching kiss. It wasn't about demanding or claiming, or anything even carnal, really. It was just about connecting, joining, feeling. His eyes had drifted shut, so it took him a second, or maybe two with the water cascading down over them, for him to taste the saltiness on her wet lips.

He paused, opened his eyes, and blinked away the water to see that there were tears on her cheeks. Confounded, he didn't know what to say, or do for that matter. But then she was weaving her fingers into the hair at his neck, urging his mouth back down to hers. And he knew he should be concerned, should worry that whatever this was for him might be construed differently by her. But her mouth was on his, seeking, tasting, feeling. And it was exactly what he wanted.

So he kissed her back, pulled her more fully into his arms, and kissed her until the salty tang went away. She was slick and lithe and perfect in his arms. Her fingers dug into his scalp, and their kisses became deeper, longer, if not more urgent. His body recharged slowly, and grew achingly, fully to life. She moved against him, trapping the length of him between her belly and his. He thought, briefly, about the scratches, but when he tried to shift back, she dug her fingertips in deeper and urged him to stay where he was by sliding her tongue more deeply into his mouth.

This was what he wanted. Her, all of her, the parts that were direct, the parts that were a bit needy, all wrapped up into this. Into him. Eventually he shifted and reached for the soap that hung from a rack hooked to the overhead spray. He squeezed some in his hand and began stroking the lather into her skin. The tight quarters prevented him from moving too far down, much less crouching, but what he could reach he took his time with. She was making small whimpers, deeper moans, when he slid his hands between her legs. He pulled her back against his chest and soaped her breasts with one hand, while bringing her to a slow, shaking climax with the other.

She tipped her head back on his shoulder as her body continued to quake and shudder. He leaned down to kiss her throat, but she turned, captured his mouth . . . then squeezed soap into her own hands.

Never in his life had he felt anything like this. Her hands were warm, slippery, foamy, searching, sliding . . . stroking. She moved in against him, used her shorter, smaller stature to tease his nipples with her teeth, her tongue, while sliding her hands around his hips, sinking her fingers into the rounded cheeks, careful not to stroke his back, even while trapping the throbbing length of him between them.

He groaned, long and loudly, tipping his face up to the spray as she slipped her hands around the front, and moved enough so that she could stroke the length of him, again and again. He ached to feel her mouth on him, or better yet, bury himself inside of her again. But their confines made both an impossibility.

She stroked and kissed and nibbled her way across his chest. He sunk his fingers into her hair, framed her face, and then finally reached up and gripped the circular shower rod over his head as her hands worked their magic on him. He wanted her, to do this for her, but hadn't expected the tables to turn so swiftly, so erotically, so . . .

Her grip tightened, oh so perfectly, and he didn't even have a chance to prepare. Climax surged up, ripped through, and was upon him before he could even catch his breath. He grunted, growled, and shook as he came. Her hands never left him, her mouth shifted to soft kisses to the center of his chest. Just over his heart.

His knees were weak, but he pulled her to him, into his arms, and just held on. She slid her arms low around his waist and held on just as tightly, her face buried in the crook of his shoulder.

He could feel both of their hearts thundering, but neither spoke. The water gradually turned cool, and he somehow found the wherewithal to grope behind him and spin the antique lever knobs to off without freezing or scalding them.

She started to move, but his hold on her instinctively tightened. He wanted to say . . . something. Let her know what he was feeling, find out what the tears were all about, and about a million other things he'd never once been compelled to want to find out. Easy enough to say that it was the mind-blowing climaxes doing the talking, but it felt like a cop-out, even now.

"Kirby—"

The damn phone chose that moment to start ringing again.

He supposed he should be happy it hadn't lit up five minutes earlier.

But this time she did move, did reach through the damp curtain for the towels folded on the rack just beyond the side of the claw foot. "I really should—"

"Kirby," he said, a little more insistently this time, tipping her chin up to his.

She didn't avert her gaze, but what he found there didn't answer any of his questions. The tears were gone, but in their place was something he couldn't see through, couldn't read. "Please," was all she said.

He let her go.

She didn't flee, exactly, but it was close to it.

He stepped out, dried off, and wrapped the towel around his hips. He wasn't exactly sure what to do next. He could hear her in the next room, her office, talking quietly on the phone, too quietly to hear the actual conversation. He could only assume it was business. He thought about waiting, but maybe it was best to give her some room. So, after giving a quick scan of the foyer, making sure no one had suddenly shown up looking for a room while he was having the time of his life in a little claw-foot tub, he ducked through to the kitchen, scooped up his clothes, and hers, left hers draped across the back of the kitchen chair, and found the back way up the service stairs to the third floor. Handy to know, he thought, as he made the climb carefully in the tight little turnabout and high, stubby wooden steps. Good thing he wasn't claustrophobic.

He entered his room, saw the remnants of the kitty supplies, and thought it felt like about a million years had elapsed since containing demon kitty had been his immediate concern. "Amazing what can happen in a single day." And he knew. He'd won millions in less than twenty-four hours. Lost a bit, on occasion, too.

He couldn't be entirely certain until some time had passed for him to think on it properly, for it to sink in properly, sort of like winning another championship bracelet or a record-breaking pot. But he was pretty sure this was going to rank right up there.

He pulled back the bedspread, dropped the towel at his feet, sprawled face first onto the fresh, cool, white linen, and dropped immediately to sleep.

Chapter 9

Well, Kirby had gotten it half right, anyway.

The whole wild and crazy spontaneous casual sex thing—that part she'd figured out. The part about not falling apart and crying afterward because she was already getting emotionally involved? Yeah, that part she had to work on. She wondered if Brett even knew. He'd stood behind her, under the spray, for quite some time before reaching for her. She'd tried, desperately, to stop the tears, but in the end had worked on being really quiet about it. Had he known? Is that why he'd reached for her?

He'd been . . . different, that second time. Less intent and hungry, more . . . she wasn't sure how to describe it. Not as intent, no, but maybe all the more intense because of it. He'd been . . . gentler. Thorough. Like he'd had his appetite slaked the first time and now just wanted to savor the intimate contact. She wasn't sure which had been more effective in destroying whatever defenses she'd built up in the past few years. Any physical defenses she'd built were gone before he'd pulled her pants down in the kitchen, but she'd thought, after waking up next to him on her bed, that her emotional defenses were shot, too. Hence the tears in the shower as the totality of the step she'd taken, and what it meant, what it signified to her, personally, hit her fully.

But that second time . . . yeah, she'd still had emotional defenses left to shatter as it turned out. She was thankful for the phone ringing and the stupid vendor asking whether she was wanting to stock up on wine and champagne for high season. She wasn't sure what she'd have said to Brett. As it was, she'd asked the vendor if perhaps he was high, or if he'd bothered to notice that with no snow, there was no season, of any level.

Yes, perhaps it was best that she'd said her first post-earth-shattering-moment words to a salesman . . . and not to the man who had been responsible for all that world shaking.

At the moment, she was hiding. Unashamedly. She'd stayed in her office for a bit after ending the call, chicken that she was, and when she'd gone back to her room, Brett was gone. She'd dressed, paced, laundered towels and bedspread, paced some more, then finally climbed the stairs to his room. His door was closed, and there was no sound coming from behind it. His bike was still parked out front, so she assumed he was in there. Probably sleeping.

She'd crept down the back way to the kitchen, only to find her clothes and panties folded in a pile on one of the kitchen chairs. Mortified and kind of amazed at herself still, she'd added them to the laundry, set out a bottle of wine, along with some cheese and crackers, in the front parlor, in case he came down. It was part of his room and board, after all.

Then she'd grabbed the legal pad and pen she'd started her garden design on and headed outside again. Kind of full circle, a bookend to how and where it had all started. She sat, cross-legged, between the trees and the open hillside on the side of the house, supposedly dreaming up her garden pattern and subsequent planting schedule. But the pad remained empty of sketches and lists. Instead, she found her gaze drawn to Brett's bike. Again. And her mind replaying what Thad had said on his answering machine message.

What happened next? she wondered. Was that it? A casual, if mind-blowing, fling? Did he hop on his bike now and head out to parts unknown, never to be seen again? Much less go to bed with. Or . . . did he stay? And, if he did . . . then what? How did she act? How should she feel? More importantly, how *would* she feel? She drummed her pencil eraser on the yellow lined paper. She didn't know what to do with what she'd done. She supposed she'd always assumed her casual lover assignation, when she'd finally had one, wouldn't be at the inn but somewhere else. That she'd come back, resume her life, then decide if and when she would see the guy again. Control. Calling the shots.

She laughed, but it was a hollow sound. "Yeah, I'm in control all right." He was under her roof and very admittedly already under her skin. She sucked at casual. One time—okay, technically two times—and she was already spending way too much time thinking about him. All of her time, actually.

Not that she had much to distract her, Kirby argued silently. After all, it was the most exciting thing that had happened since . . . well since she'd almost killed herself falling out of her own tree, but before that? In a very, very, far too many verys, long time. Naturally she was going to think about it, ponder it, analyze it. She felt the weight of her cell phone in her hoodie pocket and was tempted, for about two seconds, to call Aunt Frieda. Frieda wasn't her actual aunt. Kirby had no idea if she had actual blood relatives left anywhere. Frieda, who had worked at the resort and taken Kirby in when she was sixteen and had left her most recent foster family when they'd told her they were packing up and moving to Texas.

Frieda had been one in a long line of resort folks who had kind of adopted her after her biological mother, a teenager working at the resort, had left her in the manager's office with a note pinned to her onesie and taken off for parts unknown. She'd bounced in and out of foster homes and state-funded homes, but had always stuck around the resort because that was really home to her. Frieda had let her stick around until she finished her college degrees, and had become as close as anyone had ever come to being Kirby's family. Longest she'd ever stayed in one place, that was for sure.

But while Frieda was solidly supportive of Kirby's goals, and proud of the career she'd launched after graduation, and the business she was trying to start now, she hadn't been a huge fan of Kirby's relationship with Patrick. Given the way it had ended, clearly Frieda had been the better judge of character. So Kirby couldn't quite imagine how she'd start a phone conversation that needed to be steered in the direction of how she'd had wildly satisfying animal sex in her own kitchen with a virtual stranger. Who happened, apparently, to be kind of famous. If you liked poker. And was also maybe filthy rich.

Of course, Patrick hadn't exactly been hurting, but this was a different scale and sort of wealth. At least so she imagined given what Thad had said. Patrick was born into money, but he always seemed to have all of his ready assets tied up in this investment scheme or that new development deal. She had no doubt he'd always be successful as he was a born wheeler and dealer. Why she hadn't realized that skill would naturally extend from the boardroom to the bedroom, she had no idea.

Complete naïveté where men were concerned was only a partial excuse for her inability to see what had always been right in front of her face. She supposed it had more to do with her wanting what she'd never had. Stability, a family, someone she could truly count on. A foundation. And in her mind, the older, more mature, well-established Patrick was easily all those things. And he'd chosen her.

She sighed and thought again about the man who was sleeping right now on the top floor of her inn. Brett hadn't chosen her, he'd just taken advantage of an opportunity. As had she. She had no idea if he was stable or wise, or what he did with his earnings, much less what had put him in such a quandary that he'd taken off on his motorcycle and headed out for parts unknown. Certainly if she was looking for stable and steady, a new foundation, so to speak . . . he certainly didn't seem like a very wise candidate. But then, on paper, Patrick had been perfect.

And Patrick had never once made her feel so . . . understood. Not in the way Brett had within their first five minutes talking to one another. Possibly merely a side effect of launching a relationship with one of them rescuing the other from a near-death experience, but that instant intimacy couldn't be completely discounted, either. She'd had a more frank, open, and intimate conversation within a day of knowing him than she'd had with . . . well, pretty much anybody, save Aunt Frieda. In years. Even where Patrick was concerned. Not that she hadn't been open with him, but she realized now, after seeing the intent way that Brett focused and truly listened, that Patrick hadn't been paying the least bit of attention to her. Not really. Other than as he had to do to get her to do whatever he wanted.

"Damn, I was a pathetic idiot, wasn't I?" It was a rhetorical question. She just wished she could be more certain of the decisions she was making right now. It was a bit disconcerting, more than a bit really, to realize that even after everything she'd been through, both with Patrick and with launching the inn, there were still going to be things she had no clue how to deal with.

Which, of course, would all resolve itself when Brett got on his bike and rode right out of her life. But what she did between now and then could matter afterward. And moving forward. Why make more stupid mistakes if they could be avoided?

She glanced at the house and wished she could convince herself that continuing to mess around with Brett Hennessey wasn't going to be a mistake.

The fact that she'd cried—cried, for God's sake—in the shower was proof enough she couldn't handle this . . . whatever the hell it was. It certainly didn't feel casual, but what the hell else could it really be? Sure, it was understandable to get emotional. She was forty years old, and Brett Hennessey was only the second man she'd ever let—who'd ever really touched—ever gone—the first to truly . . . She closed her eyes.

Yeah. It was understandable.

She opened her eyes again and forced her attention back to the legal pad. Did she want vegetables? Or just flowers? Was she willing to do the work to have fresh tomatoes on her table? She decided she was. But mostly she wanted flowers. Aunt Frieda had taught her the joy to be found in planting with her own hands, growing things in the dirt . . . and enjoying the vivid colors, the spicy scents, the organized chaos of beauty that was a well-planned garden.

So first . . . the flowers. She was sketching out an outline of the house, the property lines, and had just started to fill in a few dotted line areas for proposed beds, when her phone buzzed in her pocket.

She pulled it out, shaded her eyes, and read: Front Desk. Which meant the call was from a guest. And she only had one of those.

She froze. The phone vibrated in her hand again. What did she do? Pretend to be Kirby Farrell, hostess? Or Kirby Farrell, recent recipient of a multiple orgasm in her own shower, thanks to said guest on the other end of the line?

Yeah, she was never going to try having a fling with a guest, ever again. Ever.

It vibrated again, which did other vibratory things to her senses that she really didn't need to be reminded of at the moment. She pressed TALK before her nerve gave out. "Front Desk," she said, then made a face at herself. She was such a loser. A dork loser who suddenly felt a lot more like a woman who'd only had two lovers in her whole life, than a woman who'd single-handedly bought, built, opened, and was running her own business. Sort of.

"Ah, yes. This would be Room Seven."

God, just his voice was enough to make her melt into a puddle of goo. Good thing she was already sitting down. "Yes, what can I do for you?" She squeezed her eyes shut and swore under her breath. Double dork!

To his everlasting credit, and her merciful thanks, there was no sexy chuckle, or knowing retort. Although maybe that she could have found a way to respond to outright.

"Well," he said, then it sounded like he groaned a little.

Stretching, maybe? Which meant, what, he was just waking up? From sleeping? In that big sleigh bed . . . naked, maybe?

"Since you treated me to dinner last night, I was thinking I could return the favor."

"I thought we'd already gone over that. I owed you. Certainly more than a dinner." Okay, so she really, really needed to just shut up. Right now. Because Lord knew she'd given him a lot more than dinner, all right. She sure hoped he wasn't misconstruing—surely he wouldn't think that she'd ever—

"Then can I just ask you to join me? I eat alone a lot, and I kind of liked having some company last night." He said it sincerely, not a shred of innuendo in his tone.

It was like the whole interlude in the kitchen, in her shower, hadn't happened. Like they'd jumped from dinner last night to right now. And, to her surprise, she was very okay with that time-space continuum. "I—yes," she answered, no analysis this time, going with her gut. "I'd enjoy that." It was, after all, the honest truth. Perhaps not the wisest course, but . . . it was just dinner. And who knew? Maybe it would get them back on some kind of host–guest footing that she'd have a clue what to do with. "What time? Did you need some info on the local places?"

"I just need directions to the closest market. Grocery store."

"Grocery—you're cooking? Here?" She might have sounded a bit squeaky on that last part.

"I prefer smaller crowds." There was a pause, then, "Is that okay? I promise I won't burn the place down. And I clean up."

"You really don't have to go to the trouble. There are several places that have good takeout if you just want to—"

"I'd really like to cook. You wanna help?"

"I, uh—" *Yes, Kirby. Yes, you do. Just say yes, for God's sake.* It didn't have to be so complicated, did it? It was just dinner. "Sure," she said. "Okay. That sounds like fun." And it did. See, simple. Right. "What time?"

"What is it now?" She heard him make a little groaning noise as he, what, rolled over? In bed? Naked?

Her body reacted like it had been zapped with a live wire. And the wire's name was Brett. She closed her eyes and shook her head. Nothing was ever simple.

"It's almost four thirty. How about we head out at five?"

"We—wait, what?"

"To the store? I thought you were going to help?"

"I thought you meant cook." Now was when she might want to explain about her lack of actual cooking skills. There was a reason her inn didn't serve dinner. But he was talking, so she didn't push it. She'd tackle the jobs she could.

"I did. But shopping is part of the deal. Or can be. You can show me around. Cut down on errand time. Are you game?"

You have no idea, she thought, wanting to swat at her treacherous body, which was so game he could have stripped her naked right there on the lawn. Yeah, she was definitely going to have to figure out what her code of conduct was going to be . . . and how in the hell she was going to pull it off.

Maybe in public wasn't such a bad place for them both to be, to kick off the evening. Give them both a chance to find their footing, figure out what the new status quo was going to be. "Sure," she said. "That sounds fine."

"Meet you out front at five, then." And he clicked off.

She stared at the phone for a second, then sighed as she tucked it back in her pocket. She had thirty minutes to do a complete overhaul on her emotional balance and well-being. "Good luck with that." She got up off the ground and brushed off her pants. Then she realized she looked like a reject from an Earth Day rally. Beat up khakis, worn-out canvas flats, an old T-shirt with a faded frog making a peace sign on the front. Topped off by her lovely garden hat, which was more like an old fishing hat, but it was comfortable on her head and provided shade for her fair skin. Since moving to Vermont, she hadn't really had to concern herself with the aesthetic value of the clothing she wore any longer.

It had been a wonderful and welcome surprise side benefit of escaping the trendy, label-conscious world of resort management. Even if the labels she wore then were attached to casual sportswear, there had been nothing casual about the not-so-unspoken pressure from Patrick to always look her trendiest resort and skiwear best. She'd always found a little private humor in the fact that she was a disaster on the slopes, and she hadn't actually skied again past the age of eight or so when she'd almost broken her neck. Again. Thankfully you didn't actually have to ski to understand how to best serve the needs of those who did.

She stopped for a moment and asked herself if Patrick ever even knew that about her . . . and realized he'd never once asked. How was that even possible? she wondered now. They'd lived right on the damn slopes. She'd always had the latest gear, courtesy of their vendors, but had never once actually used it. Of course she'd always been swamped. She supposed Patrick had just assumed . . . like he'd assumed so many other things.

Wow. She shook her head and smiled a bit ruefully, amazed that she could still discover things that made her feel ridiculously stupid all over again. How had she ever been so blind?

And how had it taken a renegade professional poker player of all people to make her see that? She couldn't imagine living under the same roof as Brett for ten days, much less ten years, and not have him know every last detail about her. And vice versa.

Crap. She was wasting precious time. She had—she glanced at her watch—twenty-five minutes to overhaul and find a balance with her internal psyche as well as her entire outward appearance. "Yeah. I'm not holding out much hope for that," she muttered under her breath. She collected her clipboard, notes, and pens, and then headed back to the house.

Twenty-four minutes later, she walked down the front steps wearing freshly pressed, much nicer khakis, a pink-and-cream-plaid long-sleeve blouse, and had tied her hair back with a piece of gingham ribbon. She might have even made an attempt at mascara. Possibly there was a light smear of lipgloss as well. She felt like a complete idiot. It was the grocery store. Not exactly a date. And he'd surely seen her looking far worse. In far less. In fact, she'd always looked far worse.

She imagined him watching her approach, being highly amused at the trouble she'd gone to, possibly assigning all kinds of meaning to it that she certainly hadn't intended. Was it wrong to not want to look like a garden troll when going shopping at the local food mart?

Then she rounded the path out to the parking area . . . only to see him standing next to his bike. He was wearing black jeans and what looked like a freshly pressed long-sleeve, dark green shirt, buttoned up over a short-sleeve white T-shirt. He was freshly shaven and smiling. At her. She found herself smiling, too. But more nervous than if he'd shown up in ratty jeans and a faded sweatshirt. Because now they were both being amusing. And she didn't know quite what to do about that.

Then he held out a helmet.

She slowed her steps. "I—assumed we'd take my truck. Where would we put the groceries?"

Now his smile was amused, but she found she didn't mind so much.

"We're just feeding the two of us, right? We can fit whatever we get in the saddlebags."

She glanced at the bike, remembering now the gear bag he'd stowed in one of the side compartments. "Right."

He lifted the helmet in her direction. "Ever ridden on one before?"

She looked from the black helmet to him, then to the bike. The big, black, beast of a bike. "Uh, no, no I haven't. Never had the opportunity."

His smile spread. "Well, we can fix that."

She took the shiny black helmet out of his hands and then turned it to see what was on the back. "Playing cards?" She didn't really know much about card games, much less poker, but she knew enough that the two cards emblazoned across the back of the helmet didn't seem to make any sense. "A queen of diamonds and a three of hearts." She looked at him. "Do they mean something, or are they just symbolic?"

"Those are the cards I won my first bracelet with."

She frowned. "What kind of bracelet?" She looked at the cards. "And what kind of game wins with a hand like that?"

His smile spread to a grin, maybe a hint of cocky there for the first time. Only it was kind of adorable on him. "Exactly."

"I meant with only two cards, but you meant . . . oh, you bluffed, didn't you?"

"Biggest one of my life."

"And . . . it paid off. With a bracelet?"

"Super Bowls have big gaudy rings, boxing and bull riding have big gaudy belts. We have big gaudy bracelets."

"Do you ever wear it? Wait, you said the first one. How many do you have?" She lifted her hand before he could reply. "Never mind. None of my business. No probing questions."

"You can probe all you like. I'll answer anything you want to know. But I'd rather you just get to know me. I'm more than what I do. Or used to do."

"You don't play at all anymore?" She smiled and shook her head. "Sorry, I can't seem to help myself. But isn't that how people get to know each other, asking questions?"

He took the helmet from her hands and stepped closer until she had to look up to keep hold of his gaze. "I can think of at least a dozen questions I'm dying to ask you, just off the top of my head, but none of them have to do with your job as an inn owner."

"Well, that might be because my job isn't as interesting as yours."

"Why people do what they do is always an interesting story. Some happier than others, but a story all the same, and you're right, it provides insight. But there's all kinds of insight. And why people do what they do for a living is just the tip of it."

"But people find out what you do and pass or make judgments without getting to know anything else. Is that what you're saying?"

"Let's just say it distracts them. And then we never seem to get back to the whole getting to know the rest of you part. There's more there than just a poker player."

"I would never have thought otherwise. Doesn't anyone take the time to figure that out, to find out the rest?"

"Bright shiny objects tend to blind a lot of folks."

She smiled. "They can't get past the bling, huh? Well," she gestured to herself, "as you have probably figured out, I'm not much of a bling type. And, for what it's worth, I've never gambled or been to Vegas." She studied his face for a moment longer, and he let her. "I also know there is a lot to you. And I'm curious about all of it. But trying to tiptoe around parts makes it hard to see the whole. Like a jigsaw puzzle with a bunch of pieces missing so you can't see the entire picture."

"Kirby—"

"Just let me ask you this. If I promise to ask about other things, take the time to probe your brain about how you feel about things like environmental awareness, or do you prefer crunchy or smooth peanut butter, who you voted for in the last presidential election, are you more excited about the Super Bowl or March Madness, and if you've ever been to Paris, or Sydney . . . which are both high on my personal list, would it be okay if I also asked questions about what it's like to win big gaudy bracelets by playing cards?" She made the sign of an X over her chest, then held up her hand, little finger crooked. "Pinky swear?"

He stared at her a moment longer, his smile growing, until he finally shook his head and laughed. "You think I'm making a mountain out of a molehill, and maybe I am. I haven't been away from the mountain long enough to put the molehill in perspective."

"Pinky swear," she repeated.

He ducked his chin, still chuckling. But he surprised her by shifting the helmet under one arm and extending his own little finger. "Okay. Deal. But it goes both ways."

"Deal," she said, hooking fingers with him.

He tugged her closer with their linked fingers and then unhooked them and tipped her chin up. "You're an original, Kirby Farrell."

"I'm just me." She smiled, even as her body shot right past tingling awareness to full throttle take-me mode. "Maybe you should get out more."

"That part I figured out. That's how I got here."

"Some folks just get a hobby, you know. Broaden their social circle."

"I think, in my case, I needed to shrink it. Drastically."

She thought about the world he'd lived in and really couldn't wrap her mind about what it would be like, to live, work, and play in that environment all the time. "You never really got away from it? Didn't you have somewhere you could retreat to, pull back, hang out?"

"I thought I did. It wasn't enough."

"I guess it's hard to escape the bubble there."

"Something like that." He leaned down and kissed her.

It was short, and more tender than hungry, but it was also more poignant than sweet.

"Thank you," he said when he lifted his head.

She had to blink her eyes open, clear the fog a little. He really was kind of entrancing. And maybe she needed to get out more often, too. "For?" she asked.

"This. You. Hanging out, pulling back, escaping the bubble, and retreating. It's better now. With you."

She felt her skin flush, both with pleasure and a little embarrassment. "I'm not, I mean, I haven't—thank you," she said, wisely breaking off and opting to shut up and accept the compliment. She could obsess and stress over all the possible implications and potential meanings behind it later.

He slid the helmet onto her head. "Come on. Dinner awaits." He put his own helmet on, and she saw that there was no adornment on his. He slung his leg over and settled his weight. "Put your foot here for leverage," he said, motioning, "then kick your leg over—right."

She settled in behind him, but wasn't sure what to do next.

He settled that question by reaching back for her arms and nudging them forward. "Hold on. Lean when I lean, move with me when I move. Don't work against me."

Oh, she thought as her thighs snugged around his and put her hands on his waist, I want to work against you, all right. Visions of everything they'd done in the course of the past day and a half clicked through her mind like a rapid-fire slide-show display. She squirmed a little in her seat.

He pulled her hands from his waist to his stomach, which snugged her front up against his back.

"Your back, the scratches," she said, raising her voice so he could hear her with their helmets on.

"Feels better with you against it," he responded, tugging again until she was literally wrapped around him.

So much for taking a step back and reassessing her place in this situation.

"Hold on tight," he shouted.

And she instinctively tightened her entire body around him—legs, arms, torso pressing tight—so that when he lifted his weight and came down on the throttle, and the bike roared to life, it was only by some miracle she didn't come right then and there.

Holy crap.

She could only hope that when he started moving the damn bike she didn't fall apart entirely. Would he even know she was back here, climaxing all over the place?

They coasted down the long drive, and she sighed in relief. Then he pumped them out onto the main road, and she squeezed her legs, tightened her hold . . . and prayed she was able to concentrate well enough to hold on and not become Pennydash roadkill. Of course, she'd be the only roadkill who'd died with a smile on her face, but still.

Once they were up to speed—a very fast speed, if you asked her—the vibrating smoothed out a little, even if the effects continued to linger. She eventually managed to let go with one hand long enough to give him hand signals on which way to go, but silently freaked out every time a car or truck passed by. They arrived at Harrison's Food Mart about ten minutes later, but that was plenty of time for her entire life to flash before her very eyes. Several times. In the end, she'd been thankful for the physical distraction he'd provided. It was the only thing that had kept her from losing her cool entirely.

He parked and got off the bike first, then helped her off, cautioning her to be careful not to brush her leg against the exhaust pipe. Once safely on two slightly shaky feet, they took their helmets off. He was grinning. She . . . forced a smile.

"So, what did you think of your first ride?"

She was tempted to tell him that the only ride she wanted him to give her was the kind they'd had earlier, back at the inn, but he seemed so excited to share his apparent love of motorcycles with her that she didn't want to disappont him. "It was . . . an adrenaline rush," she said, quite truthfully. She just didn't add the part about needing to go throw up now.

"You probably know the back mountain roads pretty well. Maybe we can plan a little day trip. Winding mountain roads, have a little fun on the tight turns."

She tried not to turn green, but it was really beyond her control. "Um, sounds like a plan." One she would find a way to politely decline when she wasn't being put on the spot.

He took the helmet from her and strapped it to the backrest. Then caught her hand before she could start across the parking lot. He tugged her back beside him and bent his head. "You're too nice, you know."

She glanced up at him, eyebrows raised in question.

"Your face, just now?"

"That green, huh?"

He nodded. "You can say no thank you. You don't have to do something because I like it." He pulled her another half step closer still, until her hip bumped his and leaned even closer. "I'm sure there are plenty of other things we'd both like to do," he said, then glanced at her and laughed. "Much better face."

She laughed, too, but part of her cringed. "Good to know I'm that transparent."

"Hey," he said, bumping her with his hip, then taking her hand as they set off across the lot. "Don't feel too badly. You're playing with a professional."

She couldn't help it, she just shook her head and laughed again. He really was incorrigible. Incorrigible and sweet and ridiculously sexy.

It wasn't until they were stepping up on the curb to head into the store that she grew aware of the looks. It took her a second to process, then she realized what she was doing. Holding hands. With Brett Hennessey. Not that probably anyone in Pennydash, Vermont, knew who Brett Hennessey was in terms of his poker fame, but what they did at least see was her, clearly attached to a much younger, hot motorcycle guy.

That part didn't bother her, but before she could consider any other possible ramifications to their public display, Helen Harklebinder was calling her name.

"Kirby!"

She casually slipped her hand from Brett's as he opened the door for them and the trailing Mrs. Harklebinder. Kirby stepped into the store and turned back as the older woman caught up. "Hello, Helen, how are you?"

Helen had already forgotten all about Kirby. She was too busy beaming up at Brett. "Well, aren't you the nice young man. Too many of your generation don't know their manners these days."

Brett nodded. "My pleasure." He stepped forward and un-stuck a cart from the queue and rolled it to her, handle first.

Helen's smile deepened and Kirby swore there was a bit of a pink flush to her feathery cheeks. "Why, you're just a big Boy Scout, aren't you." She turned to Kirby. "Aren't you going to in-troduce me to your new friend?"

Kirby had been caught up in the byplay, watching the spell Brett so effortlessly wove and was thinking he probably did that, rather pied piper like, everywhere he went. So it took her a split second to switch gears. "Oh, he's not my—I mean, he's—"

Brett stepped forward and extended his hand. "Brett Hennessey."

"Mrs. Harklebinder," she said, eyes twinkling now. "But, please, you can call me Helen."

"Helen, it's a pleasure to meet you." He rolled another cart out, which Kirby grabbed like the lifeline it was. "Have a nice evening," he said to Helen, and then expertly guided Kirby and her cart toward the fresh vegetable department.

Kirby threw a little wave over her shoulder. "Nice to see you," she said, then so softly only Brett could hear, added, "Thank you."

"Actually, I should apologize."

She glanced up, honestly confused. "For?"

"Not thinking. Small town. And your town. I know what you said about it not bothering you, but I don't want to put you in a deliberately uncomfortable or awkward situation."

"No, no, don't—"

"Stop being nice," he said, but was smiling as he said it.

Which made it easier for her to say, "Well, to be honest, I hadn't even thought about it, beyond the general not caring about other folks' opinions on my personal choices."

"But you haven't actually encountered them yet. Right?"

"True. So, yes, I guess I'd like a little processing time." She took a steadying breath and added, "and more time to get to know you."

She risked a glance up, and found him smiling but looking at her quite intently.

"What," she asked, wishing she could read him as well as he apparently read her.

"Good," was all he said. Then he nodded, and his expression was . . . happily content. "That's good." He covered her hand on the handle of the shopping cart and steered her toward the lettuce. "You get stuff to make a salad. I'm heading out to find us some pasta. Meet me in the bread aisle."

"Ten-four," she said.

"Horrible hand. I'd fold with that one," he called back to her as he headed off.

She frowned. "It's a radio sign-off," she called after him. "Not a poker—never mind." He'd already ducked down the soft drink and chip aisle. She turned and resolutely rolled her way through the fresh vegetable bins, choosing a fresh head of romaine, a few decent-looking tomatoes, some thoughtfully preshredded carrots, an onion, and a bag of croutons. She had no idea what kind of dressing he liked, so she picked out a ranch and a spicy Italian. Not so bad. A salad even she couldn't screw up. Probably.

She pushed the cart along the aisles, heading toward the small bakery and bread area on the far side of the store. She heard Brett before she saw him. He was talking to somebody. She pushed the cart a bit faster, then slowed before she rounded the end of the last aisle and peeked around the corner first. Crap. Thad had Brett cornered between the dairy and the bread rolls. Thad, who knew exactly who Brett was. And had no idea he'd prefer no one else did.

Thad was pumping Brett's hand, and to his credit, Brett was smiling easily enough, but it wasn't the same kind of twinkling, truly sincere smile he'd favored her with. This was more . . . well, it was hard to say, exactly, because he looked quite sincere as he listened to Thad ramble on about something. She pushed the cart around the corner and headed their way, her mission plan to extricate him—them—as soon as possible. Maybe this hadn't been such a good idea after all.

"You in town for an exhibition of some sort?" she heard Thad ask.

She winced inwardly as she noticed a few other shoppers shamelessly listening in on the conversation. If she didn't do something quickly, he'd have folks asking him to autograph their grocery lists or something. Everybody loved a celebrity, even if they had no idea who he was.

"No, nothing like that," Brett was saying. "I don't think Vermont even has a gaming commission," he joked with an easy smile. "I'm just taking a break, doing a little sightseeing."

"Hey, Thad," Kirby said as she closed ranks.

"You get my message earlier?"

She forced herself not to so much as glance in Brett's direction or she was certain a neon sign would pop up over her head, announcing exactly what it was the two of them had been doing right before he'd left said message. "Sure did, thanks."

He nudged her with his elbow. "Coulda told me you had a celebrity booked at your place."

"It wasn't an advance booking. And Mr. Hennessey here was looking for a bit of relaxation and a chance to get away from Vegas for a bit. If you know what I mean." And she hoped to hell Thad did. Unless he'd already blabbed it across town. Which, come to think of it, he probably had. She should have thought of that and headed off this little excursion at the pass.

"It was a pleasure to meet you, Deputy Johnson," Brett put in, setting the box of pasta and cans of tomato sauce he'd been juggling into Kirby's cart.

"No, the pleasure's all mine. Thanks for the tips," he said, clearly loving the idea of feeling he was suddenly a poker insider.

"Catch you some other time," Kirby said, rolling the cart forward a bit and hoping Thad would catch on and move himself and his little handheld basketful of items on along.

"Sure, sure." He glanced at the cart. "You making your guests do their own grocery shopping now, Kirby?"

Thad was about five or six years older than Kirby, divorced three times, no kids, and had made more than one attempt to get her to go out with him since she'd moved to Pennydash. She'd always politely but firmly declined. Thad was nice enough, in an overly-loud-but-friendly kind of way, but he had "lonely divorced guy looking for number four" all but made into a badge and pinned to his chest right next to the real thing. That was not a combination she was interested in tangling herself up with.

Thad had always taken her kindly worded rejections well, and he'd seemed to back off once the season had begun, or had geared up to begin, anyway. Word was he was seeing the new twenty-four-hour video store night manager. Kirby wished them both well.

"I needed a few things," Brett interjected in response to Thad's jibe. "Kirby was headed this way, so I tagged along. She's a very accommodating innkeeper."

Kirby almost choked on her own spit; then she quickly pasted a smile on her face when Thad looked at her with concern. "That's me," she said brightly. Probably too brightly. "Well, you're probably wanting to get home before the game."

"What game?" Thad asked, confused again but mercifully no longer ogling their comingled cart items.

"Uh, hockey." There was always a hockey game on this time of year. "Tip-off is soon."

"Face-off," Brett said under his breath.

"Right," Kirby said, smiling as she maneuvered her cart between Thad and the huge display of muffins and cinnamon bread. Once clear she gave the universal sports fist pump. "Go, uh—"

"Bruins," Brett offered, and she could see his lips twitching now and that twinkling light was back in his eye.

"Exactly," she said, unable not to smile back. Until she caught Thad looking between the two of them and snapped right back out of it. "Go New England!" she said, giving another little fist pump and then swiftly angling the cart when Thad shifted his feet a bit, looking at her like she'd lost her mind. At that point she didn't care if she ran his toes over or cleared off half the display stand. She shoved the cart the rest of the way past the display case and kept on going. Brett was just going to have to save himself.

Which he apparently did, as he was beside her before she reached the bakery counter. "Sorry about that," she said.

"About what? He seemed like a nice enough guy. And it's Boston. You know, in case you ever get stuck again."

"Boston?" Then her expression cleared. "Oh. Boston Bruins. Well, Boston is in New England. I was close."

Brett just chuckled.

Kirby rolled her cart to a stop beside the baskets of French bread. "And you're right, Thad is basically harmless. Thanks for being so nice to him. You probably just got him at least a half dozen free beers down at Swingert's Pub on that one story alone. Of course, it will probably sound a little different by the time he's telling his buddies. By that time he'll have been the one giving you poker tips. Fair warning."

"Warning taken." He was still smiling.

"I just—I thought you'd rather not have it blabbed all over about . . . you know. And Thad is worse than an old woman when it comes to gossip. Mostly because he makes it his business to know every last thing about everyone within a fifty-mile radius of the town limits, and given we're not exactly riddled with crime, and with the resort hotel more than half empty, he doesn't have much else to do except run his mouth. So I'll apologize up front if you're suddenly inundated with questions from nosy townsfolk."

He slid the long loaf of bread from her hands and merely smiled at her as he put it in the cart. "There's only one nosy townsperson I'm interested in talking to at the moment. What do you say we blow this pop stand? Do we have everything we need?"

"I have wine back at the inn, so . . . yes, I think we're good." She looked in the cart. "Wait, where is the spaghetti sauce?"

He pointed to the cans of tomatoes and tomato sauce. "Right there. You have a decent spice rack?"

"Um . . . well. Like what, exactly?"

"Oregano, salt, maybe a little garlic to make garlic toast with the bread. Butter?"

"Maybe we should hit the spice aisle. Just in case." She silently groaned, thinking that getting there entailed crossing to the opposite end of the store again. All she needed was for them to cross paths with Thad again, or Helen, or anyone else Thad had cornered in order to share his latest piece of news.

Brett's long-legged stride kept up pretty easily with her sprinting pace. "Hungry?" he asked as she took the spice and condiment aisle almost on two wheels.

"Just not big on dawdling."

He plucked the appropriate spices off the shelf so easily it was clear he'd made his way around them in the past. "Or cooking," he said, half teasing, half asking.

"I do okay." As long as it came out of a box, can, or prepackaged tray. And was only responsible for feeding herself. There was a reason the only actual full meal she offered was a box lunch. Sandwiches and chips she could do. Bagels, muffins, little boxes of cereal in the morning, some hot coffee and juice? Check. She'd been doing setups for that stuff since she was six years old and had proved to Mabel, the resort dining room manager, that she could reach the countertops without knocking anything over. But cooking where actual ingredients and a hot burner or three were involved? Yeah, the fire department could only do so much. Why risk it? Not to mention that poisoning her guests by actually preparing full meals from scratch generally wasn't seen as a good business-building tool.

"Just okay?" he asked, that teasing glint surfacing again. And she realized then what she'd missed before, when he was talking to Thad.

His smile had been easy enough, his body language friendly and open, but his easy smile hadn't reached his eyes. She wondered if it was sort of like a role he played. It went past just being polite to charming enough that most folks probably didn't notice they were bothering him. Both Helen and Thad had surely felt like he'd personally connected with them.

"All right, barely okay," she said, figuring what difference would the honesty make at this point. "I'll be in charge of chopping up the fresh things that don't require a stove."

"Ah," he said. "Got it. But you're safe with knives?"

"I can chop anything from an onion to firewood. But you're only supposed to burn the latter one. I know my limits."

"Ah. So was that the reason for the last-minute change in menu at dinner?"

"In my defense, the pot roast barely fit in my Crock-pot after adding the potatoes and other stuff. I'm usually good with the Crock-pot. Okay, I usually only use it for mulled cider, but it just didn't look all that hard."

Brett was grinning again. "Well, I appreciate the effort. And the chicken and biscuits were wonderful."

She gave him a little curtsy. "Thank you." They moved to the front of the store and she scanned the check-out stands but didn't see Thad or Helen, or anyone else likely to interrupt their progress in getting out of the store without being further accosted.

Brett leaned in as she stopped her cart by the conveyor belt. "So, how is it that a person who dreamed of being an innkeeper doesn't know how to cook?"

She started setting items on the conveyor belt. "It's not for lack of trying. I learned early on to go with your strengths. I figured if I ever became wildly busy and folks were clamoring for home-cooked food after a day on the slopes, I'd hire someone. Frankly, running a full house doesn't really leave any time for that anyway." She glanced up at him as he leaned past her, his chest brushing her shoulder, to help her unload the cart. "So, how is it that a professional poker player also knows how to make his own spaghetti sauce from scratch?"

"Man can only live on room service for so long."

She pretended to pause and think about that, then said, "Right. I could see where that would get old. Ordering from an extensive menu and having one of the world's best executive chefs in a world-renowned Vegas resort hotel whip something up, then having it delivered to your door, and, oh, right, no cleanup, either." She patted him on the arm. "I don't know how you managed."

He smiled. "It's a trying existence."

He resumed putting things on the conveyor belt, but Kirby was left thinking about his life. He was a professional poker player, which essentially translated to professional gambler. It was funny, but she'd always kind of pictured gamblers as either a seedy, desperate bunch, spending their days and nights in smoke-filled rooms, never knowing if the sun was shining or the stars were out, drinking too much, losing too much. Or the opposite, with flashy bordering on tasteless fashion choices, overly groomed hair, too much jewelry, expensive dental work, and at least two surgically enhanced companions hanging on their arm at all time.

Both were the extreme clichés and she should be embarrassed by thinking like that, because, clearly, Brett Hennessey with his fine cashmere sweaters and well-maintained cuticles was hardly seedy or trashy-flashy. Actually, he was more college professor-ial than anything else. She hid a private grin. Yeah, if there was such a thing as a really hot, Harley-riding professor.

Still, it made her wonder what it was really like, to be a high roller, to live like that. Although technically she supposed high rollers were men who had made their fortunes in other realms and simply enjoyed the luxury of risking gambling huge chunks of it away whenever the whim struck them. Men who made huge fortunes usually were risk takers, so she could see the draw.

But that wasn't Brett, either. He did it for his livelihood. What must that be like? According to Thad, Brett was very successful, so it was doubtful he was scrabbling to keep a roof over his head these days, especially if that wad of bills was anything to go by. But he had to have started somewhere. And where was that, she wondered? What led a person to that career path?

"Kirby?"

She blinked and looked up to find their purchases bagged,

paid for, and back in the cart. "Oh. Sorry, my mind was drifting there."

Brett and the check-out guy both smiled indulgently, but only Brett's expression was tinged with a little something else. He knew where her train of thought had gone. She sighed inwardly. So much for keeping their respective jobs off the conversational table. If she was going to spend continued time with him, then there were things she was curious about, wanted to know. She'd just have to find a way to make him understand that whatever money he did or didn't have, wasn't of any interest to her.

He was. All of what he was. Or wasn't.

Chapter 10

Brett stirred the simmering sauce, but his mind wasn't on whether or not he needed more basil or oregano. His mind was on the woman presently on the phone in her office. He hadn't been thinking, when he'd invited Kirby to go to the store with him, about her small town, the folks in it, and what they might have to say to her stepping out with her only guest. Not that hitting the grocery store together was like a candlelit dinner for two, but why would she be shopping for the ingredients for one with a paying guest if that wasn't her intention?

No, all he'd been thinking about was spending more time with her before she latched on to whatever grip she was clearly looking for and stopped spending time with him. He was her source of income at the moment, and he hadn't discounted that she might be willing to play tagalong for that reason alone. But what had happened right over there next to the fridge, and in her shower, made him think otherwise.

Plus, she was too straightforward for that kind of subterfuge. She was such a refreshing change from the life he'd led, one that demanded straight faces and a lot of bluffing. He didn't think Kirby was capable of pulling a bluff. Everything she was thinking was out there to see. Good and bad. And, in the store, he could tell that she'd felt a bit put on the spot, having to figure out how to play off their joint venture. He wished he'd planned things a bit better . . . but his thoughts had been on getting her on the back of his bike—and wrapped around him. He didn't want to put her in a bad spot . . . but he didn't want her finding excuses for walking away just yet, either.

But where the bike had been a great idea . . . the store, and the folks in it, not as much. On the bike ride back she'd kept things more chaste. And before he could set her up next to him with a cutting board and a good chopping knife, the phone had started going off and she'd had to go take what was presumably a business call. She'd disappeared into her office shortly after answering the phone. Which was where she'd been ever since.

Hiding? Or taking a particularly difficult call?

He turned the pan down to simmer and thought maybe he'd go find out, when his own cell phone hummed on the clip on his belt.

There was only one person who'd be calling him. He checked the read-out anyway and smiled before answering it. "Hey, what's going on?"

"That's what I was calling to find out," Dan said. "You on radio silence? Something up?"

"Not in the way you mean," he said, thinking he'd been more up in the past twenty-four hours than he'd been in the past twenty-four years. "I was going to call you later this evening. How is everything out there?"

"Fine, good. You all done with the Brett Hennessey USA tour? Coming home anytime soon?"

"I—I'm not sure. That's what I stopped here to figure out."

"And here is exactly where?"

"Pennydash, Vermont."

Dan chuckled. "Right. Because you suddenly had a craving for snow and wanted to learn to ski, desert boy?"

"I hope not," he said with a chuckle. "There's no snow here. It's a warm winter in New England."

"Ah." Dan paused, then said, "So, what's her name, then?"

That caught Brett off guard and he took a moment too long

to respond. Not that he knew what he'd have said. And not that he wouldn't tell Dan about her, just . . . he hadn't figured out what he was thinking about her just yet.

Dan hooted. "Wow. And the best bluffer in the world can't even pull off a simple denial. She must be something."

Brett fought a brief internal battle, then said, "She definitely is that."

There was another moment of silence, then Dan said, "You're not kidding, are you?"

"I haven't kidded about anything now in quite some time. If you didn't really want to know, you shouldn't have—"

"Whoa. No, I want to know. Everything, actually." There was a short whistle, followed by another laugh, only this one sounded kind of stunned.

"Is it so impossible to believe?" Brett asked, both amused and a little surprised.

"That a woman would go for you? No. Assuming she's breathing, that doesn't surprise me in the least. That you noticed? Yeah, that surprises me."

Now Brett smiled. "It was hard not to notice."

"That hot, huh?"

"Something like that."

"How did you meet her?"

"She . . . kind of fell right into my lap."

"They have those kinda places in Pennydash, do they?"

"Very funny."

When he didn't add anything else, Dan sighed. "I want details and you're not going to give them to me, are you? My closest buddy finally trips over his own heart . . . or some body part anyway, and I get nada."

"When I figure things out, you'll be the first to know. So, listen, how are things otherwise? Your dad good? Vanetta okay? Did you get the buy-in numbers for me on the Omaha series?"

"I'll let you change the subject, but be forewarned, we'll be circling back."

Brett smiled briefly. He and Dan had always shared everything with each other. Dan was both best friend and brother. His father was the closest thing Brett had ever had to the real deal, with Vanetta there to keep him walking the straight and narrow. "Fine," he said, "just give me the latest."

Dan sighed. "No news is good news, right? Dad's good, his golf game still sucks, and Vanetta is riding herd on a bunch of college students who have shacked up in her place looking to make their college tuition at the casinos this summer."

Brett laughed. "Well, they picked the right place to stay then. If they win anything, she'll be the one to see that it actually goes for classes and books." Vanetta was pretty much single-handedly responsible for keeping him focused on the prize. Which was not a shiny diamond-studded bracelet. No, he owed a good chunk of his degrees to her riding herd on him to keep his studying up to par and learn to say no every once in a while to the promoters and marketers. Born and raised in Vegas, she'd seen it all in her seventy some years. Her boarders were all her babies, regardless of age, background, length of stay, or reason for coming to the gambling capital. If those students staying there now thought they'd come to Sin City for something other than college tuition, they didn't stand a chance with Vanetta holding court. Might be the best education of their lives. "And the Omaha buy-in?" There was another silence and Brett snorted. "That good, huh? Dammit."

"It was down over thirty percent from last year when you competed."

"Who are they marketing? Who's the new poster boy?"

"You mean whose soul are they sucking from?"

Brett didn't rise to the bait. By not bailing out sooner, he'd essentially allowed them to do the sucking, while he quietly or not so quietly really, went about making a shit ton of money. So, he could hardly complain about that now, could he? "What about that Irish kid, Iain Summerfield?"

"You mean the kid with only two measly championships wrapped around his wrist? He's like, what, twelve?"

"He's twenty-five."

"And you had, what, like nine of them by then? Now you could cover both arms with them, Brett. It's going to take a very long time, if ever, before they stumble across anyone who is the dream machine you were. And are." He paused. "No . . . urges?"

"Other than to mess up your prettier-than-average face right about now? No."

"Good."

"You that worried about me?"

"It was a surprise when you walked away like you did, you know that."

"You'd been telling me to for years."

"And you'd been ignoring me. And I sure as hell didn't expect you to walk all the way to freaking Vermont. So sue me if I'm making sure you're okay now that you've had some time away. What are your plans?"

"Who's asking?"

"Me. Dad. Vanetta. Folks who care. There are a few that exist who want you back for reasons other than making dime off your pretty face and freakish ability to get good cards. Don't forget that."

"Trust me, I haven't. It's why I stopped. I needed to think."

"If you're waiting for them to latch on to somebody else who can do what you do, then you might as well set up camp in Vermont. I doubt they'll come hounding you there." He paused, then said, "But if you're thinking you might want to come back to the place that is also your home, you know they'll hound you for a while. Given what you've done for them, they'd be stupid not to try. But it'll settle down; at some point, it has to."

"Or they'll burn your house down."

"Goddammit, Brett, we told you, me, Dad, even Vanetta. We're not buying that bullshit. Shit happens, sometimes bad shit. Believe in bad karma after so many years of good, whatever. But even the most desperate manager, promoter, or casino owner wouldn't reach to that extreme."

"Your naïveté is both touching and amusing, but also dangerous. Wait," he said, before Dan could launch into a refrain of the argument they'd had far too many times, never with a new result. "I know that world; you don't. You think I'm living in a fifties' movie and I know it's still very real. It's all beside the point. It's more about what I want, what I'm willing to risk, and how much shit I'm willing to put up with if what I want is to still live in Vegas."

There was a much longer silence this time, then, "You think you really might not want that?"

"I don't honestly know," Brett said, never more utterly truthful.

"You have some other place in mind where you think you should be?"

"Again—"

"Like Vermont, where the mountains apparently aren't snowy and a guy can get laid regularly?"

"Because you're pissed off and worried about me, I'm not going to beat your face in when I see you, but . . . tread carefully there, my friend."

"So . . . it is like that."

"It's like . . . I don't know. But I know enough to realize that it's like something I've never encountered before."

"Okay," Dan said, this time sounding more sincere . . . and considering.

"And don't even think about putting Vanetta on my ass. She knows I worry and you know I worry and I don't need her worrying about me."

Dan snorted. "Right. Like saying that will make it so. You know she worries about you day and night. Until you come home—"

"I might not, Dan," he said. It was the first time he'd let himself say it, even think it, really. And it wasn't as scary and weird as he thought it would be. In fact, it was kind of . . . exhilarating. In a way that nothing in his life had been up to that point, maybe other than the day they'd handed him those diplomas . . . or in the early days of winning at cards. But there was another really high-stakes game he might want in on . . . the kind where you risked something other than your bank balance.

"You don't mean that," Dan said, sounding far more subdued, maybe even a little hurt. "This is your town, your people, your family."

"Sometimes people grow up and move away from their families."

"Brett—"

"Dan . . . it's not about you. Or your dad, or Vanetta."

"I know that. We all do know that. We just . . . we can't imagine you anywhere else."

"I think that's been my problem all along. It's why I got stuck for so many years, doing what I never expected to be doing, not for that long. I really couldn't imagine myself anywhere else."

"And what, working for my dad, or with me—"

"Was good for my soul, and saved it. Regularly, Dan. You know that. Your dad was the closest thing I ever had to a real male role model. You're my brother. And, in her own way, I guess Vanetta is like my crazy old grandmother. You are my family, always will be. At least I would hope so. But maybe in order to figure out what I'm supposed to do, or what I really want to do, the thing that will truly satisfy me, fulfill me . . . I need to not be there. Where routines and patterns and ruts—no offense, you know better—aren't there to pull me back into that sense of complacency. Because it doesn't feel complacent any longer. It feels suffocating. Not the people, the work. And I need . . . I need more than people."

"I wish it was different," Dan said quietly. "I don't like it, and I wish there was more for you here, but . . ." They both took a break, and a breath. Dan spoke first. "So . . . it's Vermont, huh?"

"For now. I need to stop running. I need time. To allow myself to just be, to think, to figure out what works. Or what might work. But, right now, what works isn't being in Vegas. That much I do know."

"Okay," Dan said. He didn't sound happy about it, but he sounded, well, resigned to it. Which was a start.

"I still need you to keep an eye out, just . . . don't let your guard down. Okay?"

"Sure. But I swear to you, nothing's happening. I really think it was all just a freak bad streak."

"All the same—"

"Right, got it. I will. Has anyone been in touch? Anyone hounding after you?"

"No."

"Good. Then maybe, at least, while you're sitting there contemplating your navel, you can let that part go. We're all fine here. We miss you, but mostly we just want you to figure out what comes next. Consider what is, not what might be. Okay? Promise me that much."

"Dan—"

He sighed deeply. "Right. I'll keep an eye, okay? I have to get back to work. Enjoy your . . . stay."

"I already am." Then he hung up before Dan could piss him off again, or worse stick his nose in, and his unwanted opinions, about Kirby.

Speaking of which, she walked, just then, into the kitchen. He had just clipped his phone back on his belt and was stirring the sauce again, but he stopped when he saw her face. "What's wrong?" She was pale, well, paler than normal, and she looked . . . hollow. "Is everything okay?" Which was a stupid question, given everything clearly was not okay, but what else was he supposed to say? He didn't know enough about her yet, or anything really, to know what to ask about.

It was right then, however, that he realized that he wanted to know. Wanted to be more involved.

He put the sauce spoon down and walked around the center cooking island to the kitchen table where she'd stopped. She was looking at him, but it was obvious her thoughts were somewhere else completely. "Kirby?"

It was like the little bubble they'd created had burst. First with Dan's reality check and now with this, and suddenly he didn't know what the boundaries were or what she'd accept from him. But what the hell, he thought, he'd saved her from falling out of a tree. He'd made love to her. He figured that gave him some options. At least ones he wouldn't have to apologize for making assumptions about later.

So he did what he instinctively wanted to do, which was take her hand and tug her gently forward. She stutter-stepped into him, still looking poleaxed, and he put his arms around her and nudged her face up so she looked at him, but it was more like through him. "What's wrong?"

Her expression shuttered then and she ducked her chin.

So he lifted a hand to her face, cupped her cheek, and tipped her face up again. "Maybe I can help. Or at least listen. Tell me what happened."

"It's . . . not your problem." And then her eyes got glassy and he tensed, because that's what guys did when women cried, or looked like they were going to. Except this wasn't about him, or even them, like it might have been in the shower . . . so he stuck with it.

"It doesn't have to be my problem to listen, does it?"

"I—you want a nice dinner. Not to hear about—about—" And then her bottom lip was quivering and he could see where this wasn't so much about not wanting to tell him as about pride and integrity. And being made to cry in front of him about it, when she clearly wished she was being strong, was just making it worse.

So he did the only thing he could do. He kissed her.

And it took a moment, several actually, before she kissed him back. He shifted her arms up to his shoulders and pulled her more deeply into his arms. He let her guide the kiss at first, then slowly took over, taking it deeper, coaxing her to be more aggressive, until he was pretty damn sure they weren't thinking about anything except the kiss and what it was doing to them, what it was making them want, making them feel.

When he finally lifted his head, his breathing wasn't all that steady, and there was color in her cheeks now. He stroked her cheek with his thumb, pushed the hair from her forehead, and searched her eyes. "I get that living here, running this place alone, makes you a very self-reliant person. And someone like that probably has a hard time even sharing a problem they might be having. It's hard to lean once, because there is a fear that the urge to lean would become stronger, and that would make you weaker, if you gave into it like that."

Now her gaze sharpened on his, and he thought he'd hit right on it. But then she said, "You say that with utter confidence and more understanding than simply being a compassionate person would imply. So . . . I take it that you know whereof you speak."

Ah. He was in such a hurry to help take that stark hollowness away, so used to his ability to see into others, to intuit more than the average person, that he hadn't taken into consideration that he might leave himself vulnerable. He never showed his hand. That was more than a little unnerving. But trust had to be gained somehow. He supposed it wasn't too big a risk to take. So he took the bet. "You could say that. Maybe more than a little."

"You're right, but you know that. I don't lean. Not anymore anyway."

"It's not always a sign of weakness, you know."

Now her eyes crinkled at the corners and her lips quirked. "Where did you read that? I have a hard time believing you actually practice what you just preached."

"You might be surprised about that. I certainly didn't get to where I did all by myself."

"Me, either."

"So, you have a support network? Is there someone you want to go call, to talk with, someone you can trust with whatever it is? Dinner can wait."

"I heard you talking when I was coming through the foyer. You sounded . . . animated. Your support system?"

He smiled more fully this time. "You'd make a good promoter."

She lifted one brow. "But not a player, I take it?"

"You'd have to work on your poker face a little." He grinned. "Okay, a lot."

To her credit, she smiled, too. "So, why a good promoter?"

"You are good at keeping the focus where you want it, which is usually not on you but on what you want."

"And what do I want in this instance?"

"To keep whatever just happened on that phone call to yourself."

Her expression turned considering. "You're very . . . formidable. When it comes to reading people. It shouldn't be a surprise that people might be uncomfortable confiding in you."

"Why is that?"

"You already know too much as it is. See too much. It would be hard to know exactly how much you'd be handing over, even with the smallest of revelations."

"And what is it, exactly, that you think I'm going to do with whatever information I'm able to ferret out? I'm harmless."

She laughed outright at that. "You've been under my roof less than forty-eight hours and you've already gotten me naked. Hardly harmless."

He stroked her cheek again, touched her lips. "I haven't done harm, have I?"

She shuddered under his touch, and his body sprang more fully to life.

"Maybe just to my peace of mind."

He appreciated the honesty, but it didn't keep him from pushing. "So, what else then? You share details, whether tedious or important, and you're afraid I'll . . . what, exactly?"

"Play Good Samaritan again. You're very good at that."

"You say that like it's a bad thing."

"It can be, to a person who maybe doesn't want to be rescued every time a problem crops up. Falling out of trees notwithstanding."

"Rescue is something a person does for someone in a situation beyond their control. Like the tree. Otherwise, it's just called help. We all need that from time to time. It's not a bad thing. It doesn't signify failure. Sometimes it's even a good thing. You learn who you can count on, who is really there for you."

"And just how often are you the one on the receiving end?"

"Often enough to know it's there for me when I need it."

"So, what, are you like the Yoda of poker?"

"Hardly. Just trying to make you feel better about bending an ear or using a shoulder if you need to."

"You think it should be easier. Or is easy. Asking for help, I mean. Even if a willing ear is all that is needed."

"That's what friends, family, are for. I guess I don't understand what there is to gain from persevering alone if help is available."

"You gain the peace of mind and security from knowing you can be self-reliant when things get tough. That you can take care of business, no matter what. That's not a small thing. In fact, it can be everything."

"So, once you've figured that out . . . is that still the only way it goes?"

"If there are no shoulders to lean on and ears to bend, then sometimes that isn't a choice."

He let his hands fall to her shoulders and squeezed gently. "You have that choice at the moment," he said quietly. "Is that good enough?"

Her lips curved a bit, but her expression remained mostly shuttered. "You sure you're not an event promoter? You're pretty good at being focused yourself."

"It's a wonder we get anywhere in conversation, I suppose."

"Actually, I think I've had deeper, more thought-provoking conversations with you in the short time I've known you than I've had with anyone in a long time."

He tilted his head, searched her face. "But, at least from where you sit, that's not entirely a good thing, is it?"

"It can be a disconcerting thing. I haven't quite decided on whether or not it's good for me." She straightened and took a step back.

He toyed with the ends of her hair, then reluctantly let her go.

"And, for a guy who didn't want to talk about himself much, you sure don't seem to mind nosing in my business."

"I don't think I'd mind. Anymore. If it was you asking the questions.'" He was surprised by how easily that truth just popped up. But now that he'd said it, he knew that he meant it. "If you think it would help, or just distract you from whatever it is that's worrying you—" He spread his arms. "Ask away. Open book."

She smiled easily then, and it almost reached her eyes. "One night only?"

"We can figure that part out later."

Her smile faded. "See, that's the part that trips me up." She held up her hand when he started to speak. "I hate to renege on dinner; I really do. It smells amazing. But there are some things that require my immediate attention. I'm afraid I'll have to take a rain check."

For once, he didn't push. Knowing when to fold was just as important when it came to winning the bigger prize. "I'll put some aside for you. You can heat it up later, if you want."

She nodded. "Thanks, I appreciate that. And . . . thanks for the rest, too. It's not that I don't want the help, or even the ear. I appreciate the offer of both, I do. No insult intended."

He nodded and shoved his hands in his pockets. "None taken."

"Good. It's just . . . it's complicated."

"Most trying things are."

She ducked her chin, then looked back at him, and some of her defenses were clearly wavering. But he still didn't push. That wouldn't be fair. To either of them. If and when she wanted his help, or just a sounding board, she'd ask.

"You're almost too good to be true. Maybe that's part of it. Things that are too good to be true rarely are. Or rarely last."

"I'm just sincere. And honest. The offer stands, okay?"

She nodded, and the defenses crumbled a bit further when she folded her arms in front of her chest, tucking her hands tightly under them and against her sides, as if giving herself comfort and support. She stood there a moment longer, and he was just about to go against instinct and reach for her again, when she turned on her heel and walked away. "Don't worry with cleaning up," she called back. "I'll take care of it later."

"Just like you take care of everything else," he said under his breath as he heard her bedroom door close on the other side of the front foyer. "Including yourself."

He turned back to the stove, back to his sauce, which had cooked down further than he'd wanted it to. He stirred, added a bit more water, a bit more tomato sauce, tasted, then pinched a bit more oregano into the mix and kept on stirring. As did his thoughts.

He should just take a giant step back and leave Kirby to her business. After all, she had a point about things not lasting. She didn't want to allow herself to lean on someone who might not be there a week, or even a day later. Hard to fault that. Then there was the bigger issue at hand, which was that she'd only be concerned about that if she was worried she'd come to care about how long he stayed or when he might leave.

Which meant maybe she already did.

He tasted the sauce, but was too busy deciding his immediate course of action to pay any real attention to flavor. He knew, if he examined his own behavior right now, he'd be forced to admit that maybe, just maybe, this mental back and forth wasn't purely about his fascination with Kirby . . . but also a convenient substitution for his own problems. He'd told Dan that he needed to stop, to think, to figure out what came next. But there was no timetable on that. For once, there was no place he had to be. Not today. Not tomorrow. Not ever, if that was the way he wanted it.

Right that very second, he was exactly where he wanted to

be. With no plans whatsoever to go anywhere else. It was a nice change, to be certain of at least one thing. He'd figure out the rest.

He tasted the sauce again, and smiled. Yeah. But in the meantime, he still wanted to know the rest of Kirby Farrell's story. Find out what was the best way he could help. Which meant, for now, he wasn't going anywhere.

Chapter 11

Kirby sipped her coffee and shuddered at the volcanic strength of it. But she desperately needed something to kick-start her into the day. Day One of her personal thirty-day death march. Well, her inn's death march, anyway.

She stared at the computer monitor and the online bank statement she'd opened up; then she finally slid her glasses off and closed her eyes. She'd been juggling bills for almost three months now, pretty much since the day she'd opened. Initially, she'd still had a little something to juggle with. She'd known that without a sudden drop in temperatures and some snow, she was courting total failure. But she'd been trying to remain hopeful, positive. After all, how long could the damn heat wave last? It was unnatural. She'd honestly thought that things would turn around.

The call yesterday evening from Albert, a local tax accountant she'd hired early on to help her set up her books, had made it clear that her turnaround time was pretty much over. Her tax bill come April was going to be the felling blow, but the bank was already grumbling about her loan payments and Albert wasn't sure she'd even make it long enough to be worrying about the IRS.

At the moment, she was numb. Too numb to even cry. She'd poured so much of herself, of . . . well, everything she'd had left in her after the disastrous end with Patrick, and every bit of what she'd been able to summon up after her life had taken such a drastic new course. She'd been determined to look at the ending with Patrick as the beginning of herself.

This was her rise from the ashes; this was her celebration of what her life could be. This was the middle finger she'd given to Patrick, to fate, and anyone else who'd ever made her feel like she couldn't take care of business. Which, when it came down to it, she'd realized, was all on her. As Aunt Frieda had said often enough, "Just because folks don't understand, respect, or support what you think is true about yourself doesn't mean you have to listen to them." Kirby had only needed to listen to herself. But she'd let the other voices, so many of them, drown her own out.

It had taken seeing her chosen partner for who he really was—who he'd always been if she'd just been more willing to see the truth—and the following hard look at what she'd allowed herself to believe, to accept as okay, for her to finally, at the age of thirty-seven, examine her life, her choices, and what she was going to do about it—moving forward.

And she had moved forward. She was proud, almost fiercely so, of what she'd accomplished here. The one thing she knew now was that if the current combination of events conspired to end this new dream, this new path . . . well, she'd simply find another one.

She dropped her forehead to the edge of her desk. "I just really, really don't want to." It would be so easy to wallow, to blame fate, to sink into that place where it was all about being the victim and not being in control of her life. She wouldn't do that. Couldn't. But, right at that very moment, she simply didn't know where she was going to find the strength to rise again.

On a surge of anger, aimed at both the world in general and at herself in particular for not having an immediate plan of action, she shoved her chair back, took up her mug, and stalked into the kitchen. She hadn't eaten since the middle of the day before and that wasn't helping the hollow pit of dread in her stomach. Of course, the thought of food at that moment was abhorrent, but it was something she could do instead of staring and swearing. She popped the fridge door open and saw the neatly stacked containers of pasta and sauce. Her stomach gurgled. Pasta for breakfast. She reached for the container. Why the hell not?

She was heating up a bowl of noodles when Brett walked into the kitchen. "Hey," he said.

"Hey." She kept her gaze on the microwave door. As if that was going to speed things along. But she didn't know what to say to him, so it was a handy distraction. The bell dinged and she slid the bowl out.

"Pasta for breakfast?" he said, coming closer but stopping at the cook island.

"Sounded like a good idea at the time." She fished in the silverware drawer for a fork. "Thank you for saving some for me. And for cleaning up. You didn't have to do that."

"I didn't mind." He took another step closer. "Kirby—"

He broke off, and she paused in the act of forking up her first mouthful and glanced at him directly for the first time.

"I'm sorry," he said, surprising her.

She lowered her fork. "For what?"

"Whatever's going on with you. And for pushing last night. I just wanted to help out. I still do."

"If I don't fill this inn to capacity by the weekend and keep it that way until at least the middle of April, I'm going to lose the place," she said, putting it out there without meaning to but too tired to get back into the verbal cat and mouse game they had played last night. "I don't think there's anything you can do about that, but I appreciate the concern." She realized she sounded less than gracious and was certainly not on good hostess behavior, not by a long shot, but there didn't seem to be much she could do about it. Brett was a guest, but he wasn't exactly a guest. And he'd asked for the truth, so she refused to feel bad about giving him what he'd asked for.

"Actually," he said, just as calm as he'd been before her less-than-cheerful reply. "I could. Help, that is."

"How? You have a lot of poker buddies who need a place to hole up for a few months, get out of the desert for a while?"

He smiled at that. "You know, that's not a bad idea. If Vermont had a gaming commission, I could probably get a game going out here, make you all kinds of revenue."

"We have a lottery, but no gambling that I'm aware of."

He didn't respond right away, and it was clear his mind was spinning on something.

"What are you thinking?"

"I was thinking maybe something for charity. There are ways around the rules, or to make them work for you, anyway."

She straightened from where she'd been leaning against the counter by the sink. "That's—well, that's actually a very nice idea, but if anything like that even looked like it was going to happen here, I can bet you the resort would find a way to co-opt it. They'd be equipped for it."

"Yes, they would. And that would be exactly the way to go."

She took her bite and then gestured to him with her fork. "So, how would that help me?"

"Because putting on an event like that isn't just about bringing in a few players. It's a lot more complex, and there are a lot of tentacles. I'm sure your place and any other place around here with rooms to spare would have no problem booking."

"Is professional poker that big a draw?"

He didn't say anything to that, and the light dawned.

"You're that big a draw."

"Do you want me to look into it?"

It was both a non-answer and all the answer she needed. Maybe it was time to do a little research on Brett. She'd been curious, but out of respect for his request, she hadn't done any digging. Besides, in the past twenty-four hours, her thoughts had been on other issues. But with this offer, it appeared all bets were off when it came to leaving the past in the past.

"Could you honestly set something up that quickly?" She immediately waved a hand. "Forget I said that. I'm sorry. I have no business exploiting your fame, or livelihood."

"I'm pretty sure I offered. That's not exploiting."

"You came here to get away from that. You're a good guy, Brett, an incredibly nice guy, but I don't want you to do something that you otherwise wouldn't do." She waved off his response again. "It's amazingly generous of you to even offer. And I am appreciative, even if I don't sound like it. But even if I was willing to let you do that, I think it would be too late to save me—the inn, I mean. And then you'd have done all of that for nothing."

Now he closed the gap between them. He carefully took the bowl of pasta out of her hands and set it on the counter. Then he stepped right up into her personal space, pinning her back against the counter before he'd even touched her. Kirby could have scooted away. She could have done a lot of things. But she didn't. And what that said about how much she'd learned regarding what she should accept, and what she should stand up to, she didn't want to know.

But sticking her ground, at that moment, felt like the right thing to do. And if she was just lying to herself about that, well she could add that to the list of things to beat herself up over later.

"I want to help you, Kirby. One of the things about having achieved the successes I have is that I am in a position to do things like that. I kind of thought it must be something pretty drastic when you walked in here last night and, barring bad news about a family member, your business was the only thing I could think of that would put that look on your face. So, I gave it a lot of thought, but until just now, I didn't see a clear path on how to help. Other than just hand you a chunk of cash to bail you out, if that was the problem, which I'd do. Hell, I'll buy the damn place and you pay me back instead. I'm a lot friendlier than the banks. But I figured you'd be too proud to do something like that, despite the fact that I wouldn't think one iota less of you for doing so. It won't put a dent in my world, and it could make all the difference in yours."

"You're right. I couldn't accept that kind of offer." She

looked past his shoulder, then made herself look back at him. "So, you'd already spent time thinking about this before you came in here?"

"Yes. If it was something with your family or a friend, I'd just do whatever I could to ease the situation, but if it was your business, the inn, then I figured a more direct kind of help would be better. I just didn't know how to do that. But the charity event is perfect. It's a way to do good, all the way around, without much of a downside."

"Except putting you back in the world you just drove cross-country on a bike to get away from."

"That's my decision."

"It feels like all of this is your decision."

"That's where you're wrong. You can decide whether or not to take what I'm offering. I can't force that solution on you. All I can do is let you know it's available if you think it would help. But it's your choice, your business to keep or lose, your life. If you have other ideas, then that's great. I'll help you there, too, if there is any way that I can."

"Why?"

That stopped him. "What do you mean, why?"

"Why is it so important to you to help me? I realize we had sex, and I realize that you're going to move on to whatever it is you decide to do next. This is merely a stop on your journey."

"What in the hell does that have to do with me helping you? Do you think this is some kind of angle for some other . . . I don't even know. What other agenda could you possibly think I have? I know you have some issues you're dealing with, and I'm not talking about the inn now but with going forward with new relationships. You were totally up front with me about that. But I'm being totally up front with you. I have no other agenda other than I can help, I see you need some, and so why wouldn't I step up?"

She'd pissed him off. Which she was sorry for, but it also was kind of fascinating to see. He was typically so laid back, matter of fact, but so soft spoken in the way he stated his thoughts. So this . . . this was different. And she wasn't going to lie, it had her attention in more ways than one.

"I'm sorry," she said. "I was out of line, but I didn't mean any insult. You're right. I'm not as evolved as I thought I was. I still have some hang-ups—"

"I said issues. We all have them."

"Whatever the case, you're right. I've been too complacent in the past, too willing to let others dictate the course, even when I didn't agree with it. I don't want to do that anymore. So, it's important to me to find my own solutions. To figure things out on my own."

He surprised her by smiling. "Okay. So . . . you found me."

"Actually, you found me. Or the inn, anyway."

"Chicken and egg. The bottom line is I'm in your life and if you're someone who looks at fate or things having a bigger meaning, then maybe that's why I'm here. The point is, you are in control of this. I'm just saying I could be the solution to this problem." His smile grew and it made that twinkle come to life in his eyes. "Maybe you're just supposed to be smart enough to recognize a solution when there is one and use it to your advantage."

She couldn't help it, she smiled, too. "Either you really believe what you're saying, or you're an amazing bullshit artist."

"It's possible there is a little of both there."

"So, what's in it for you? You probably already know that your chances of getting lucky again are in your favor. And I doubt you're looking for a free ride on your room charges."

"Actually, I'm not certain of anything where you're concerned. A pushover you are not."

Now she smiled. "Well, then I'm making progress."

"As for what's in it for me? It'll make me happy to help you out, to see you push through this stumbling block and have the chance to make this place be what you know it can be. You can't help the weather." He finally reached up and touched her face.

It took remarkable control not to rub her cheek into his palm.

"Let me do something good here. It helps me, too. Okay?"

"You make it really, really hard, you know that?"

He reached for her hips, tugged her up against him. "Well, then, I'd say we're even."

She laughed even as she blushed, which was kind of funny given what they'd been doing in this very kitchen just yesterday.

"Eat your pasta," he told her, reaching past her to pick up the container.

"Now you're going to ride herd on my food intake?"

He tucked the container into her hands and then framed her face and kissed her. Hard. "No," he said when he lifted his head. "I just think stamina is probably going to be a good thing."

"You think so, do you?" she said, going for sanguine, missing by a mile. He was . . . hell, she couldn't even quantify any longer what he was.

"Let's just say I'm hoping." He pressed a finger to her mouth, then stroked her bottom lip. "And if you say anything else about my offer to help being some kind of insurance for extra favors, I will take that as a direct insult. Other than being one of the many reasons why I'm all wrapped up in you, this," he said, dropping another hard kiss on her mouth, "has nothing to do with that."

"Wasn't going to say a word," she said, looking a bit stunned.

"Good." He nudged the bowl at her. "Eat."

"Not all that hungry all of a sudden."

"Hmm. Well." His smile spread slowly. "Maybe we should focus on building your appetite, then. As it happens, I have quite an appetite. Where you're concerned, anyway."

Her entire body responded to his suggestion in ways that the best comfort food in the world couldn't have appealed to her. "Shouldn't we be working on . . . whatever it is we have to do to see if your idea will work?"

"I just have to make a few calls, find out what the time frame will have to be. It won't take that much to generate interest; then it's just a matter of figuring out the logistics."

He kissed Kirby's knitted brows. "Don't worry. I'll set it up so it works out for the best. For both of us."

"Okay," she said, still torn between massive relief and being a little worried that he was leaping before he was looking. "So, what happens next?"

"I'll make those calls; then we'll have to wait to get some feedback. I don't think it will take long." He brushed her hair from her cheek. "I know we can make this work."

She took a short, shaky breath. "Okay. Wow, but okay." She looked at him. "You're sure?"

"One hundred percent sure. The question isn't will it work, but how long it will take to put together."

"All right." She smiled a little, then, more confidently. "All right."

He laughed. "See? Not all that hard, right?"

She laughed, too. "Oh, I didn't say that. But I appreciate this, Brett. All of it. Your proposed solution and making it easier to say yes to accepting your help. This is the best solution I could hope for. Win-win." Then she held his gaze in steady regard and grew more serious. "As long as you promise me this isn't going to put you in a place you don't need to be. I don't know all the reasons you stopped playing, or why you left Vegas. But I can't move forward with fixing my problem if it adds to yours."

"I'm a big boy. I know what I'm doing."

"Okay."

"Okay." He bracketed her hips and tugged her closer again. "So, I was thinking, we could either stand around here in the kitchen and talk about not eating my very fine pasta, or . . ."

Her stomach chose that moment to growl. Loudly. They both laughed.

"I'm not sure, but I think I was just flattered and insulted all at the same time."

She shook her head. "But maybe I should at least make an effort. Is there anything I can do . . . with the rest of this? Any calls I can make locally to get the ball rolling?"

"Once I get things started out west, then yes, it's definitely going to have to be a team effort."

"Team efforts are good." She picked up the pasta and found that she was kind of ravenous all of a sudden.

"Agreed." He stepped back, gave her some space, and went to fix himself a cup of coffee.

Too late, she thought to warn him about the toxic level of caffeine she'd been shooting for earlier and had to apologize when he gagged. "Sorry."

"Wow," was all he said after he finished choking. "Sort of like a caffeine Slurpee."

"Pretty much. I didn't sleep. I needed a boost."

"Astronauts need a boost. This is . . . wow."

She sat down her bowl. "Let me make another pot."

"I can do that. Eat."

She saluted him with her fork. "Yes sir, captain sir."

"It's not so much about bossing you around as it is about me making a cup of coffee that won't keep me up until 2025."

"I'd call you on that, but you might have a point." She gestured to the cupboard over the coffeemaker. "The beans are in there, and the grinder."

His eyebrows lifted. "Freshly ground coffee?"

He looked like a kid on Christmas morning. She went back to forking up her now cold pasta. It was quite possibly the most delicious thing she'd ever eaten. "You know, and I'm not trying to butt in or anything, but given that you have apparently cashed in more than a few poker chips in your day, you could go out and get your own grinder and coffeemaker and have freshly ground and brewed coffee every single morning. Just saying."

"For that I'd have to stay in one place for more than a week at a time. And remember to buy beans."

"So you travel a lot? Are famous poker players like rock stars where you have a list of things you request that have to be in your dressing room?"

"We don't get dressing rooms."

"Right, you get actual rooms. Humongous suites in fancy hotels. Well, if the movies are to be believed."

She looked at him expectantly. He didn't refute her supposition, other than to say, "Little inns in Vermont are more my speed."

"So, in these big, fancy suites, can't you make a few demands?"

"I could try."

"But you don't."

"Never thought I needed anything that badly to be a pretentious ass about it."

"Back to that arrogant-cocky argument."

"Something like that."

She made a humming noise and continued to regard him while she ate and he went about making the perfect cup of coffee with his new bright, shiny object. Boys and their toys, she thought. In Brett's case, that included bikes and, apparently, bean grinders. She wondered to what other realms his interests extended.

"I can hear the wheels," he said as he flipped off the grinder.

"That was the coffee grinder."

He shot her a smile over his shoulder. "No, that was you, trying to figure out which of the million questions you have were okay to ask."

She waved her fork at him. "Now that could be mistaken for arrogance."

"Only if it wasn't true." He continued to look at her.

A little flush climbed her cheeks. "Okay, okay. Guilty as charged. But I wasn't going to say anything, or ask anything." At least not right that second.

"Well, now that I'm bringing my world to yours, I can hardly ask that you take me separately from all that. And you might as well know what you're really getting into."

"Such as?"

"In order to pull this off, it needs to be an event. A big event."

Kirby still hadn't wrapped her mind around all of the ramifications of Brett's offered solution as yet. Heck, she hadn't even
wrapped her mind around the basic concept that Brett would be
willing to do any of this for her in the first place. They hardly
knew one another. She didn't know him well enough to know
for certain if this was a truly selfless act, or perhaps a step he
wanted or needed to take for himself. Then again, if it got her
what she needed, and helped him in some way, wasn't that a
win-win proposition? What did she care what he got out of it, if
it solved her immediate problems?

"How big is big? I assume it will help the resort, since they're
hurting pretty big, too. And their continued success is vital for
my continued success, so that's all a good thing. And the town
wins, too, with increased revenue, however briefly, from more
visitors coming and spending their money here. What else do I
need to know?"

He ducked his chin for a moment, and Kirby wondered again
about his stake in this. He had, on the surface, anyway, left
poker playing behind. Did he want to go back? Was this a way
to ease himself back into the limelight and possibly garner the
goodwill and support of event coordinators who might have
been less than thrilled with his sudden defection from the game?

But then he was looking at her again, and there was nothing
in his expression to help her decide. Only what he had to say,
which was, "You know from Thad that I'm well known in that
world."

"All I know is what Thad said. If that's what you're wondering. I haven't Googled you or anything. But yes, I did get the impression that you were something of a rock star in Vegas."

"Poker tournaments are played all over, but even outside of
Nevada, there is always a Vegas element to it all. I call it seedy
glamour. Those are our roots, and while we might have dressed
it up quite a bit over the years, scratch just below the surface
and it really hasn't strayed too far from that."

"Are you saying that Pennydash is too conservative to handle
a little flash?"

Brett chuckled at that. "Sweetheart, where I come from there's no such thing as a 'little flash.' But no, I wasn't speaking to the conservative bent of the area, though that might make a few folks uneasy, so it shouldn't be discounted. I meant that it will be a spectacle by anyone's standards, and everyone on board would need to understand that."

She sat her empty container in the sink. "Define spectacle."

"In addition to some very flashy players and, in some cases, the ridiculous entourages that come with them, you'll have the promoters, who rarely say no to bling in any form, and that includes the complete media circus in all its many forms."

"So, you're saying we'll be overrun with paparazzi or something?"

"Possibly."

"For poker?" She lifted a hand. "That sounded like an insult, it wasn't. I just meant—"

"The sports media will be there for the regular pros. The paps come out for the Hollywood celebrities. You might be surprised by how many of them play at a pretty high level. Promoters love them because they raise the buy-in."

"Buy-in?"

"Players have to pay to enter the tournament. A ten-thousand buy-in is normal once you get to a certain level. And the more players buying in, the bigger the pots."

"Ten thousand? Dollars? Just to play?"

He nodded. "And for many celebrities, that's chump change, so it's like their version of going to Disney for the weekend. Only the rides are a little more exciting."

"So . . . you're planning on inviting celebrities? I mean, ones known outside your field?"

He nodded. "It's for charity. It will be a no-brainer, trust me. And I'll get some pretty serious poker names here, too."

"Because of charity?"

"Partly. There are some pretty big philanthropists in the upper echelons."

"Including you?"

"I make it a point to give back, yes."

"So, am I your current charity, then?" She wasn't exactly insulted by it. She could hardly afford to be, and she knew his heart was in the right place.

"I don't look at charity perhaps the same way you do. I like to give a helping hand or a leg up when I can. Folks did that for me, so it's just giving back. I simply have the good fortune of being able to give back a lot."

"That's pretty great. And even greater that you do. I'm not even sure where to start in saying thank you. You've saved my life. Twice."

"Just help me get this thing up and running. If it helps you get through this initial hump with the inn, helps the town and the resort get through this opening season, and supports a worthwhile cause at the same time, then it's all worth it. You have many more winters to weather. I'm just helping you through this first one."

"As leg ups go, it's a pretty big one. I don't know what to say."

"I think we're good on that score."

She felt her eyes begin to burn a little, and she'd be damned if she cried in front of him every time things got a little emotional. She felt like an idiot for the whole shower thing yesterday. Sure, it had been a monumental moment for her, but he must have thought she was at least a little pathetic. And now, today, he was trying to rescue her. Again.

She felt, strongly, that this . . . relationship, if she could call it that, wasn't anything like what she'd fallen into with Patrick. With what she'd allowed her life to become while being part of his. She tried, hard, to cling to what Brett had said, about finding opportunities and choosing to take advantage of them. He was here; he was willing to help. And whatever he got out of the deal would have nothing to do with her when it was all said and done. Totally, completely, different from Patrick. Not a rescue. More like a joining of forces. Because she was a force.

Even if, at the moment, she felt like a force on the verge of becoming a failure.

Brett finished brewing his coffee and she thought back over what he'd said. "The other players," she said, thinking out loud, "you said some of them would come to support a good cause, but most of them are going to come to get a chance to play against you, aren't they?"

He took a careful sip of his coffee, then turned back to face her. "Yes." Neither humble nor arrogant. He'd said it like a simply stated fact.

"How long has it been since you played?"

"Long enough to make folks hungry."

She didn't push, but she was unabashedly curious to know more about his world. "You've really thought that part of this through? I don't want you doing anything rash in the heat of the moment."

"I'm very well aware of what I'm doing."

She tilted her head. "That's kind of a non-answer."

"It's the truth."

So, she decided, this was how he was going to go with it now. He'd made his past fair game for her, but he was going to be all about the facts and just the facts, ma'am. She could hardly be picky. But it only served to make her more curious, not less. She decided it might be less awkward all around if she did her own digging on the subject of his career, get her own answers. And, if possible, do as he'd initially asked, and use what time they did have together to get to know him, outside of all that.

"What's on the agenda today for you?" he asked.

"Cleaning the rooms."

He lifted a questioning eyebrow.

"Yes, I'm aware the inn isn't exactly overflowing, but the rooms have to be dusted, swept, polished, fluffed. I can't have someone just stroll in unannounced and then make them wait in the foyer while I rush up to make sure there's no dust on the furniture. I need to keep it guest-ready at all times."

"I think about what the workload would be like if the place was full. Were you planning on hiring help? Like cleaning or cooking?"

"I was, during the busy season. But I planned on doing as much of it myself as I could, too. I like keeping busy—the busier the better. Less time to think." She hadn't meant to say that last part out loud, and when his gaze narrowed a bit on her, she rushed on. "It's actually kind of fun, all the rushing around and making things right for my guests. I enjoy the noise and the general chaos of it all. It feels . . . vital. And I like being in the middle of all that."

Brett's gaze stayed quite focused on Kirby, and she realized she was holding her breath, waiting for whatever question he lobbed her way. She could hardly duck it, given the open stance he'd now taken with her where anything having to do with him was fair game. He already knew about Patrick, but all he understood was the basic context, that she'd been betrayed by someone who was supposed to have her best interests at heart. And she was good with that.

He saw a lot, too much, at times, so she was braced. Which was why what he did say came as a complete surprise. "Other than the screen, do you have any other stuff that needs to get done?"

"You—have got to be kidding. I couldn't possibly ask anything else of you."

"You aren't asking. I'm offering. I am generally happiest when I have projects to work on."

"I'd say you have a pretty big one at the moment."

"Initially it's going to be a bunch of phone calls." He smiled. "I like to work with my hands."

She couldn't help it, she smiled, too. And flushed, maybe a little. "Yes, well, that's great, but I can't just—"

"Kirby." He sat down his empty coffee mug and walked over to where she stood, still by the sink.

She liked how much bigger he was; it gave her this private little thrill every time he got into her personal space. She wondered if he could read that on her face, too. "What?" she replied gamely.

"You *can* just. You like to stay busy because it keeps you from having to think. I like to stay busy because it helps me think. I can't sit and stare at the walls." He stepped even closer. Then he lifted the hair from her neck and ears with the backs of his hands as he slid his fingers around to her nape.

It was all she could do not to moan a little as he brushed his fingertips over such sensitive skin.

"So, you can either go clean rooms while I bang nails into something . . . or we can go mess up a few rooms first. And I can work off this pent-up energy in an entirely different way."

By banging me, she thought, and her entire body stood up and shouted yes. Emphatically so. She had every intention of smiling and saying no. She had an inn to save. Now was not the time to be frolicking naked with carefree abandon. So, it came as a surprise to them both, if the look in his eyes was anything to go by, when she put her hands up on his shoulders and slid them around to the back of his neck and said, "I've found that dusting and scrubbing is a highly overrated method of distraction."

"I find I couldn't agree more." He leaned in and kissed her, quite soundly, then made her squeal by lifting her up into his arms.

"Brett—"

He managed to nudge open the door to the narrow back stairway. "This feels rather indecent somehow, doesn't it?" He looked down into her face, and his eyes were fully sparkling, his smile wide, and he'd never looked more handsome to her.

"Wicked, yes," she said. "Having your way with the back-stairs help."

"Hold on." He slid her legs around, but when they both wouldn't fit on the skinny risers, he made her squeal again and grab at his belt loops as he slipped her over his shoulder.

"I can walk," she said breathlessly.

"Where's the wicked fun in that?"

They passed the door to the first floor. He wasn't even out of breath. She still hadn't found hers. "Where are we going?"

"I thought we'd start at the top. My room." He pushed through the narrow door at the top of the stairs, then bumped open his own door, which he hadn't closed all the way, and kicked it shut behind him. He laid her out on his bed and followed her down. "Then we can work our way down," he added. "What do you say?"

He was already pushing up her shirt and sliding down her body.

"I think . . . working our way down . . . could be a very good idea," she said on a breathless laugh.

He unzipped her pants and slipped them down her hips, taking her panties with them.

"Inspired, even," she managed to gasp as he kissed his way back up her inner thigh.

It was impossible to believe that a mere hour ago all hope had seemed lost . . . and now, not only was there a plan to save her inn, but the gorgeous, sexy man responsible for saving it was about to make love to her. Again.

He slid his tongue over her as his hands moved up under her shirt and over her rock-hard nipples. She arched her back and lost all track of any thought she might have ever had as he took her body on that sweet, sweet climb. So effortlessly, so perfectly.

Distractions, indeed.

Chapter 12

Definitely beat the hell out of banging nails. Maybe Dan had been onto something about that.

Brett moved up and kissed Kirby just beneath her belly button while her body was still twitching in the aftermath of her climax. He loved how responsive she was to him. Loved. He rolled to his back and tugged her over on top of him.

She slid down effortlessly over him, taking him deep and making them both groan as he hit all of her still-twitchy spots.

"Sit up," he urged.

She lifted her head from where she'd been most delightfully kissing the side of his neck. A little wrinkle furrowed her very lovely brow.

"What?" he asked.

"Gravity," she answered rather succinctly.

It took him a moment to figure that one out, then he laughed. "Right. I want to see you. I want to see you while we do this." He moved more deeply inside of her.

"You can see me right now."

"I have seen you. All of you, I might remind you. From most angles. But right now, I'd really love to see you—" He groaned in deep gratification as she pushed on his chest and sat up, taking him even deeper as she did so.

Her hair was wild, her face, usually so perfectly aquiline and so proper looking, was all flushed and damp, hair clung to her temples. Her nipples stood out boldly from her small but perfect breasts, and she truly looked, "Beautiful."

Her gaze was on his, and she smiled a little at that, then her eyes closed as he moved underneath her. She picked up his rhythm as perfectly as she'd suited him in every other way. His own eyes threatened to roll right back in his head, but he wanted to watch her. Watch her take him, come apart for him.

He tried to think about what he was doing here, about his insane idea to launch the charity event, and why he was doing all of that, even this, with a woman he hardly knew.

Then she opened her eyes and caught him staring at her so intently, while they were moving so intimately, so in sync, with one another. And she smiled, then she laughed, and leaned down to brace herself on his chest as she moved on him, her smile bolder, more confident, than he'd ever seen it. He gave himself completely over to her, to the moment, as she took him, directed the action, rode him . . . and damn, but a confident, bold, sassy Kirby was a thing to witness indeed.

She tightened on him and her movements turned from commanding to sultry as she tipped her head back, arched into the movement with him, and allowed herself to simply be taken over by the moment. It was all he could do to hold on, to hold back, long enough for her to climb that peak again.

She'd barely gone over the edge when he was yanked right to the brink of it himself. He tugged her down and rolled her beneath him, her moans and gasps as he kissed the hot skin on the side of her neck as he drove himself even more deeply inside of her only served to yank things up a notch, to the point he thought he might pass out from the sheer force of it when he finally came. He drove hard and deep and she met each and every thrust with equal fervor. Her legs were wrapped tightly around his hips, her nails digging into his back as she nudged him from her neck to her mouth. Their kiss, in that moment as release pounded through him, was intensely primal and so very perfect.

He'd never once considered himself a possessive man, but right then, inside that very instant, that kiss, that final thrust, with her . . . he'd never wanted so badly to lay claim to another soul, to another heart, as he did with her. In fact, it was the only time he'd ever felt that way about anyone. He wanted her. In every way a man could want a woman. He wanted to have her, hold her, thrust so deeply inside of her to where he might lose his mind and all of his control, knowing without a shred of doubt that she'd take it, take him, and keep him right where he wanted most to be. He wanted to laugh with her, tease her, be teased by her.

He wanted to love her.

Their bodies slowed, but his mind kept racing.

When he slid from her and rolled to his side, she followed, her body curving perfectly into his. He wrapped his arm around her, keeping them pressed closely, their slick skin gradually cooling as their heartbeats slowed.

There were no words for that kind of communication, that effortless, natural union of mind, body, and soul. It had nothing to do with the incredible sex, and everything to do with finding that person, that one person, you could commune with on any level, by any means, verbal, nonverbal, physical, all of it, or none of it. It was just there. And he had to believe it was just like that for her, too.

For that, for the continuation of that, for as long as was humanly possible, he discovered, he was willing to do almost anything.

He kept her close as her breathing steadied. He stroked her hair, watched her face, knew her thoughts were winding around, and wondered where she was inside her head. "Knock knock," he said, gently tapping on her temple. "What's going on in there?"

She pushed him to his back, shifting against him so she could prop her chin on her hand, which was laying on his chest. He thought perhaps all conversations between them should take place just like this.

She smiled at him, looking so content, so relaxed. But her thoughts were already on to other things. Not that he could blame her. She was facing rather critical circumstances. He was just happy she was more willing now to talk to him, with him, about it.

"You're really wonderful, you know. Stepping in like you are, to help me save my place."

He didn't stop stroking her hair as it soothed them both. He wished she wasn't so hard on herself, about accepting help, especially his help, but he didn't know much more about her past than how her last relationship ended. And that it had also been tangled up in her business career at the time. He was getting that it had to have been complicated and that there was probably even more, deeper below the surface. But those were all layers he wanted to know, too. She was imperfect. So was he. So he'd give her whatever time it took for her to work it out. But he'd also let her know that he wasn't her past. He was, at the very least, her present. And he wasn't going anywhere while they saw this through. "But?" he queried when she didn't continue right away.

"I know it's your call, your business . . . but, be honest with me, would you have returned to playing poker if not for this generous offer of yours?"

"I don't mind playing poker." Which, he realized, saying it, was the truth. "I don't plan on playing professionally any longer, but for charity, and helping out a town in need, I don't mind playing. I like the game itself." Also true. "It's endlessly fascinating to me, in fact."

"Why? What about it appeals to you?"

He knew she wasn't asking the obvious question, or expecting the obvious answer, which was usually some variety of "because I'm good at it" or "because it made me rich."

"It makes me think. I like the randomness of it, and the specificity. There are only so many of each kind in each deck, only so many hands you can draw, and yet add in the mental element and the emotional element, and it's not just about doing the math or playing the percentages. You're also playing the people sitting around the table, who don't have to be winners to rob you of the pot. I like the mathematical challenge; I like the mental challenge. But mostly I like the people challenge. And how the outcome is never obvious."

"Interesting." She smiled, like she'd figured something out about him she hadn't already known.

He smiled back. "Interesting how?"

"You never mentioned the risk. Or the high you could get from pushing all that money around, the thrill of winning."

"That's never been why I played."

She nudged him with her chin. "Easy to say for the guy with all the chips."

"You don't just get those handed to you, you know."

"True. So, you're not a risk junkie. Thrill seeker?"

"No. Risk is simply a factor of playing the game. One element, like all the rest, to be looked at, analyzed, and played accordingly. You can either seek to minimize the risk or exploit it. Everyone at the table is facing the same odds you are. You can play that angle, too."

"So, it's all angles, math, people, perception."

"Yes."

"And winning," she said, her grin daring him to disagree.

"It was a handy by-product of my fascination, yes."

"You sound so . . . clinical about it. Assuming you've had above-average success, I guess I'd have assumed you'd be more passionate."

"About the game itself, I have been. Maybe not so much of late. But keeping a clear head—clinical if you will—is key. At least for me. Lose your head; lose your wallet. And your heart. I never wanted to be in a position where a game had the power to break my heart."

"So . . . what happened to change that? Did you burn out or decide to get out before it did break your heart?"

"I love the game of poker, just not the rest of what comes with it. However, it's given me pretty much everything I have, outside of family and friends that is. And it's provided for them as well. So I have to respect it, respect that."

"But?"

"But, it's not what I pictured myself doing, or being. Not long term. It just sort of happened, and at a time when the income was needed and the help for others was needed. Then, it sort of took on a life of its own. And, I guess, to some degree, I felt kind of responsible for keeping it going, even when I was well past needing it for myself any longer."

"So, why not walk away? At some point, you're not obligated to help anyone else, right? It can't always be about putting everyone's needs above your own. What you want and need has value, too. The people you care about would respect that, want that even. And if they don't, well that's something to think about, isn't it? But even worse would be if *you* don't—" As soon as the words were out of her mouth, something struck her. Her expression shuttered almost immediately, as if long used to the protective measure, but not before a stark look of pain had flashed through her eyes.

"What's wrong?"

She blinked and looked at him. "Nothing," she said too quickly.

He brushed a soft thumb across her cheekbone. "Not nothing," he said quietly.

She held his gaze then. "I'm not used to anyone being so in tune with me. It's . . . flattering. But also a little disconcerting."

"I'd offer to look less deeply, but you compel me, Kirby. And I can't help what I see."

"What do you think you see?"

"Tell me what just ran through your mind, when you said at some point I shouldn't feel obligated any longer. It wasn't about my helping you out now." He didn't make it a question.

She shook her head. "Though maybe it should. I—it just, thinking about the position you were in made me think about my own past."

"Patrick?"

"More me, actually. Who I was with him, who I was before him. I just realized something about myself. Maybe you and I are both a little alike. At the time, I certainly wouldn't have said that I was doing everything because of some misplaced sense of obligation to Patrick. But . . ." She blew out a short breath. "Now, looking back, I have to wonder." She lifted her gaze to his again. "I was with him for over eleven years, Brett. The last eight, almost nine of those we lived together."

"A rather substantial chunk of your adult life."

"Almost all of it, certainly up to that point."

"The same with me, only my significant other was my job."

"I was very career oriented, too, and all that time I saw the two of us, Patrick and I, as a team, united toward the same career goals. Albeit his were far more expansive than mine, but when it came to the resort, we were a united front."

"And?"

"You know, you finally came to your own realization that your relationship with your career was not a fulfilling one, that this wasn't enough, or possibly all there could be for you."

"Is that what just struck you, that maybe you'd have never figured that out for yourself if you hadn't discovered that Patrick wasn't as united with you and your joint goals as you thought?"

"Partly, yes. I don't know that I would have," she said. "If I ever did, it certainly would have taken me much, much longer, before the dissatisfaction set in. If it ever did."

"You can't beat yourself up if your goals were clearly stated and you were doing everything in good faith, believing—rightly—that your partner was being truthful with you about sharing those goals. It's not about being blind or stupid, or even self-unaware, when someone you absolutely believe you can trust takes advantage of that."

"Thank you for saying that," she said, "but I'm not even really talking about Patrick's duplicity in this. Yes, it was both a devastating blow and a huge big beacon of illumination into what was really going on with my life. But it's really my part in all of it that still throws me, still keeps me wondering about myself."

"What do you mean?"

"I mean . . . here I was, with a man for over a decade, enjoying what I thought was a fully realized, healthy relationship. I absolutely assumed that we'd get married, have a family, but that we were both focused on achieving other goals, career-oriented ones, first. I had moved in, we were all but joined in holy matrimony in my mind . . . so I just sublimated the rest."

"The rest of what?"

"The rest of what I wanted from us as a partnership, but wasn't getting. I was constantly compromising my wants and needs for his, but he always made it seem like it was our idea, not just his idea. And I'm far, far from being an idiot or the kind of person who just blindly trusts and adores without any return of the same."

"But?"

"But that's exactly what I did. For a long time. A very long time. Why did I do that? It's so not who I am, and yet I was totally that girl, that woman. And just now, what I said about not being obligated forever, and that making yourself happy should be a valid goal, too. It's all about balance. You give; you get. I had no balance, yet I still felt obligated."

"Why? What did he do that made you feel that way? Give you the job?"

"The job, his heart. Or so I thought. He was like this bright shining beacon of everything I wanted, everything I was working toward, and there he was, willing to shower me with all of my dreams come true, both personally and professionally. It was really pretty heady stuff for me. I couldn't believe I was going to be that lucky."

"But you were giving him something as well."

"See, I guess that's where I never quite really grasped that equity. I always felt I had to live up to it, earn it."

"It being what, exactly?"

"Happiness. In my case, in my mind, that meant making Patrick happy, or making him love me. And that sounds so deeply pathetic. Like I didn't think I was worth anything just by being myself. But I did. At least where the business part of it was." She fell silent again, her thoughts clearly drifting inward.

"Just maybe not with the relationship part, huh?" he asked quietly.

She looked at him, and her eyes were stark again. "Yeah," she said, her voice softer, a bit rougher. "Just maybe not with the relationship part."

He stroked her hair a while longer, let her epiphany simmer a bit longer inside her head. Because he was pretty sure she already had most of this figured out long before this conversation. She'd felt duped, used, both in their private life and in their professional one. He couldn't imagine the pain of that, coming from the most trusted person in her world. It had to have been the deepest blow imaginable. But Brett assumed she already figured out why she'd hung in there so long on a promise that was never delivered upon, the one of marriage and family.

That flash of pain, of sudden, stark awareness, had been some other link, some other connection, she'd finally made within herself. It made him want to know more. She'd said it made her think about who she'd been with Patrick and who she'd been before him. So, this went deeper into the past, he thought, to her childhood maybe. Something to do with the link the love of her adult life had to the love given to her in her childhood.

A pain that stark, a sadness that profound, had to reach pretty deep. He knew that part from personal experience. Experience he was no more excited to delve into and share than she probably was. It was enough that she'd gained a bit of insight, perhaps put a few more puzzle pieces of herself together. He'd thought about things like that a lot on his trek. Who he'd been, who he'd become, who and what were important to him. And what would truly make him happy.

He didn't know how it would affect how she felt about him, but he was beginning to see the struggle she faced. Having loved a man for so long who, in reality, had never fully loved her back. Now getting herself involved with him, a man who, at best, didn't even know what he wanted for himself, much less in a relationship with someone else.

It bothered him, more than a little, to realize that he was not, perhaps, someone she should invest herself in emotionally. He might not have had anything close to a traditional upbringing, and adulthood, thus far, certainly hadn't changed that path. But he'd always known himself to be a good, honest, decent person, with a strong heart and solid dedication to those he loved. He had pride and integrity. He was a good man who felt worthy of giving and getting love.

So it was hard to accept that he might not be worthy of her. That, because of the kind of life he led, the uncertain future ahead, he could never be the right man for her.

More stunning still was the realization that, for the first time, outside family, he wanted to be the right man. There was a brief sensation of *finally*, and the relief of knowing for absolute certainty he did have that inside of him. He'd wondered. More than once. But there was no continued glory or joy in the discovery . . . because his *finally* was with Kirby.

Dammit.

She reached up and tapped his chin gently with the pad of her fingertip. "Now who's lost in thought?"

His lips curved briefly, but for once he didn't feel much like smiling.

She shifted a bit higher until his gaze met hers. "We're quite a pair, you know."

"Why do you say that?"

"I think we both have some stuff, in our past, that makes us a little misfit for traditional roles."

"I don't know why you'd say that about yourself. You're running a place trying to make it a home away from home for other people."

"Right," she said softly, "because I haven't figured out how to make one for myself. So this gives me one by proxy."

It made his heart tight. "Kirby—"

"Don't go feeling all sorry for me; that's not what I meant. I just meant, we've both reached a certain age, we've both had our successes in life, but we're both still trying to figure the rest out."

"Maybe that's what life is anyway. Trying to figure out what comes next. Life changes; goals change."

"True. But I know some of the things I want. Or wanted, anyway. And I couldn't get them."

"So you make new goals."

"I did."

"But?"

She smiled, but there was a definite wistfulness in her eyes. "Life goes on, and you try and move along with it, but you realize that maybe the old goals are still the ones you wanted all along." She slid up a bit farther until she could take his face in her hands. "Don't look all worried on me. I'm not going to try and mold you to fit my dreams, okay? I know you've got your own things to work out." She kissed him, and it was sweet and stirring and achingly poignant, all at the same time. "I'm not going to get in your way, okay?"

He pulled her the rest of the way up, then rolled so she was under him again. He kissed her, and there was nothing sweet or tender about it. She responded to him instantly. And his body, so recently sated, roared to life again. He didn't know what he was doing, just that he was suddenly angry and scared and uncertain and he didn't want to be any of those things. What he wanted was to be buried deep inside Kirby again, where everything felt intensely, perfectly right.

If she seemed surprised by his sudden ardor, by the ferocity in the way he took her, she didn't show it. Instead she rose right to the occasion and matched him thrust for thrust. She was moaning and he was all but growling when he came. It was wrong, venting his fear like this, but she was there to take it, to accept it, to make it all seem so very, very right.

She clung to him, her heart thundering against his, their breath deep and raspy gasps.

"Brett," she whispered, her lips hot against the slick side of his neck.

"Mmm" was all he could manage. Only when he felt her hands on his face did he finally find the strength to open his eyes again.

"That was . . . unbelievable. But . . . what was that?"

He could have bluffed. And he knew he should. At any other time in his life, with the stakes insanely high, he would have done exactly what he knew had to be done. And he'd have won.

So why, when it was the most important game of his entire life, he went with the truth, he had no idea. Because the minute the words were out, he knew he was going to lose. And that was going to cost him the only thing that might have ever really mattered.

"That was me," he said, still panting for air, but locking his gaze absolutely intently on hers, "telling you, that I want you to get in my way. Because, right or wrong for each other, I plan to get in yours."

Chapter 13

Kirby hung up the phone and looked at the clock on the wall behind the check-in counter. A little after nine p.m. Hunh. She sat down on the stool and slid the registration book a little closer. She was still reeling over the changes that had taken place in . . . what had it been? Not quite forty-eight hours. Most of those had been spent glued to the phone, taking room reservations for the next five weeks. It was crazy really.

Apparently, when Brett Hennessey decided he wanted to do something, it got done. People jumped. Plans were made. Things happened.

And phones started ringing.

She hadn't seen much of him during that time. Which was probably just as well. Even with the frantic burst of business, his heated declaration was still uppermost in her thoughts. And every damn time she replayed those last few minutes they'd spent together through her mind, it gave her the exact same heady little rush.

Which she hadn't yet decided was a good thing, or a really foolish thing.

While she'd been tied to the phone the last two days, taking reservations and frantically contacting vendors to make sure she could get in the supplies needed to support her suddenly full house, Brett had been over at the resort, hammering out all the actual event details with the folks there. Which was fine, really, as she'd been rather busy herself. So busy, in fact, that she was a little afraid of what she might have gotten herself into. "Careful what you wish for, Farrell," she murmured as she flipped through the remainder of the January log and the first half of the February log.

Almost one hundred percent capacity, starting two and a half weeks from tomorrow and lasting for three full weeks after that. In some cases, folks were even staying after the event. She'd been very specific in making sure they knew that, as of that moment, it wasn't exactly going to be a ski paradise if they were sticking around in hopes of getting time in on the slopes. More than a few had just laughed, making some comment about the Hennessey Fortune Factor and booked an extended stay anyway. So she'd smiled and taken their credit information. And hoped they didn't check out early when confronted with the green slopes of the Green Mountains.

The phone rang again. She glanced at the clock. "Seriously?" But she already had pen poised as she answered the phone. "Pennydash Inn, this is Kirby, how can I help you?"

She listened, registration book at the ready. A few seconds later, the pen clattered to the book, her hand still frozen in place. "I'm sorry," she managed to choke out, "did you just say you wanted to book a room for Jackson Deverill? *The* Jackson Deverill?" Jackson had been the hottest thing in Hollywood for at least the past decade. He was George Clooney, Hugh Jackman, and Brad Pitt all rolled into one amazing package of charm and good looks.

She quickly grabbed her pen again when Jackson's assistant made it clear that yes, she was calling for *the* Mr. Deverill. Kirby quickly regained her professional footing and finished taking the booking, which would be for two. She racked her brain trying to remember who it was he was dating these days, but with her self-imposed news blackout, she honestly couldn't remember. Not that it mattered. *Holy crap* was all she could keep thinking. During all those years spent working for her childhood resort-slash-home, then for Patrick, she'd crossed paths with both the very rich and the very famous. It just somehow seemed completely different when they wanted to stay in her very own quaint little Vermont inn. She hung up, let her mouth drop open again, then got up and danced a little jig around her stool.

Which was how Brett found her as he walked back in the front door. "Snow dance?"

She didn't even care that he'd caught her acting the fool. "No, that's the 'my inn is booked up thanks to you' dance."

Grinning, he walked over to the desk. "Congratulations; that's fantastic."

"I just got off the phone with Jackson Deverill's personal assistant. The Jackson Deverill."

"Oh, good, Dev called. He bought in last night and I mentioned he might like your place. He prefers to keep a more 'out of the way, under the radar' profile when he's playing."

"You know Jackson Deverill?"

Brett nodded. "We've played at more than a few tables together over the years, sure. He's one of the good guys. Hard to find a lot of those in his line of work, especially at his level of celebrity." He caught her still staring at him, gaping was probably more like it, and chuckled. "What? I'm sure working at that resort out west you came across your fair share."

"It was a little different. Okay, a lot different. I was just overseeing their stay. I wasn't exactly on a first-name basis with them."

"Well, you'll love Dev. Everybody does." He walked around behind the desk and scooped her easily into his arms.

She didn't even question the easy familiarity, mostly because it felt just as easily and comfortably familiar to her. She looped her arms around his neck and he hiked her up his body so she could plant a kiss on his lips. "Thank you."

"You might want to hold off until you have to manage this hoard for a few weeks," he said, laughing, but he didn't let her slide back down his body. Instead he pinned her back against the wall under the stairs. "Dev will probably be the easiest guy you have. Depending on who he brings with him, anyway."

"I thought you said he was a good guy; doesn't he have good taste in women?"

"He's like the perennial pushover, that guy. Sort of Charlie Brown and Lucy, always believing they have his best interest at heart. Usually it's just his bank account they have their eye on."

"Come on, he's got a lot more going for him than his money."

"I agree, one hundred percent. I'm just telling you like it is."

He lowered his head, but before he could kiss her, she said, "Is it like that for you? Is that why you were so adamant about me getting to know you for you?"

"Money always tends to complicate things," was all he said. Then his mouth was on hers and she really didn't care to continue the conversation as it turned out.

When he moved from her mouth to her jawline, he murmured, "I need to head up and shower. Wanna come help me wash my back?"

"I'm not sure that's part of the room services we offer here at Pennydash Inn," she said, tipping her head back against the wall to allow him greater access.

"You have no idea how happy I am to hear that." He nudged her higher up the wall and kissed down the side of her neck, to the tender spot between her neck and shoulder, nuzzling the collar of her shirt aside as he continued his exploration. "I'd like to think it's just a personal favor. Between the two of us." He kept dropping little kisses, then undid the top button of her shirt. With his teeth. "I'm really good at returning favors, by the way. In fact, I insist upon it."

"Do you?" she said, her eyes drifting shut as he pushed her higher and slid another button free, allowing his mouth access to the soft fabric cups of her filmy little bra. "I think that sounds fair." Then she groaned as he suckled one nipple through the pale pink silk.

"I missed you," he murmured against her skin as he moved to the other side.

The deep rumble of his voice, the softly spoken confession, made her heart clutch. Maybe she should have figured out that whole fun or foolish thing before she let him do this to her again. Because she most definitely was not feeling remotely casual about Brett Hennessey . . . and he was making it clear that the feeling was quite mutual.

"Me, too," she said, figuring it wasn't right to play chicken when the man was currently making her feel incredibly fabulous.

He ran the tip of his tongue over her and slid her down his body and kissed her, so passionately, so deeply, that when he scooped her up in his arms and carried her up every single step to his room, she simply put her arms around his shoulders and let him.

Instead of the shower, he laid her across his bed and followed her down, rolling them both to their sides, legs intertwined.

"I thought we were exchanging shower favors."

"I have to get back to the resort in a few hours for another meeting, so I thought perhaps I would get you good and sweaty first so we both could use a good back scrub."

"We're limited to each other's backs?"

"I see it more as a starting-off point."

"Ah," she said, then giggled when he tugged her under him and rolled his weight on top of her. She was happy. Deliriously so. In fact, she couldn't remember ever feeling so lighthearted before. She'd never had this kind of spontaneous connection with anyone, and it felt pretty damn fantastic. Surely, given that they were being so open and honest about where they were in their respective lives, enjoying this—him—wasn't foolish. She was well aware of the possible painful outcome, but the simple question of would she rather not have spent time with him at all was an easy one to answer. This time, she was putting her happiness first.

"So," he said, returning to his devastatingly seductive exploration of her collarbone. "Who all has registered for rooms?"

He continued to work his way down, opening buttons as he went, making it rather challenging to keep track of the conversation. She listed a few names, paused to gasp as he nipped the skin below her belly button, then somehow managed to dredge up a few more. It was on the last name that Brett paused and looked up.

"Did you say Uri Maksimov?"

She blinked, realized his wonderful tongue was not going to go back to doing what it was doing along the open line of her pants zipper, and lifted her head up to look at him. "I'm pretty sure I have the name right."

"That's his name. When is he arriving, do you remember the date?"

"I'd have to double check to make sure, but I think he's scheduled to arrive first."

"Which is when, exactly?"

"Little over two weeks from now."

Brett dipped his chin and Kirby was pretty sure she heard him swear under his breath. She pushed up on her elbows, then leaned her weight to one side so she could reach out and stroke the side of his face. She urged his gaze back to hers. "What's up? Do you want me to call him back and tell him I made a mistake and the room is already booked? I'm pretty sure I can fill the opening. At least enough that it won't matter."

"No, don't do that."

She waited a few seconds, but when he didn't chime in to explain his obvious distaste for the situation, she nudged. "Wanna tell me why we don't like Uri Maksimov?"

He did glance up at her then, but his attempt at a smile fell far short of reaching his eyes. "Have I told you how much I like it that you're on my team?"

"You do a very good job of showing it, yes," she said, wiggling her hips a little.

He dropped his chin for just a second; then he looked back at her. "I'm sorry, I ruined the mood."

She laughed. "I'm pretty sure if you just breathe on me, we'll go right back to being there. Or I will." Her expression sobered when he didn't immediately come back with a cute remark. She stroked the side of his face and ran her fingers through the hair at his temple. "It's really not an issue to reverse the booking. We overbooked all the time when I worked the reservation desk at the resort. I'm very good at managing the guests so they don't feel managed." She paused and then dryly added, "And you really don't want to make any jokes about my guest relations skills at this particular moment."

That got a small chuckle out of him. "I wouldn't dare."

"So, I take it that Mr. Maksimov isn't exactly a welcome guy. Is he a player?"

"He works for the owner of one of the newer casinos. Kind of the liaison between the owner and the promoters. Only been open a couple of years now."

"Did you give the rights to some part of the event to one of the casinos in Vegas?"

"Yes, but not his."

"Ah. So, why is he coming? And how will it work, combining the resort holding the event, with a casino . . . what role exactly does the casino play?"

"The resort here gets the event booking and all that goes with it, including a nice increase in guests. But since we're in Vermont, I need a team to be able to come in and actually produce the event who knows what they're doing."

"So, like a sponsor or something?"

"Not exactly, though we'll have them, too. This is more like the resort here is the producer and I'm hiring the director. They'll get billed as event promoter, working in conjunction with the charity organization and the resort here in terms of it being used, more or less, as a satellite location to their resort in Vegas."

"Right."

He did smile now. "Clear as mud?"

"Let's just say I trust that you know what you're doing."

"Thank you."

"Oh, no, thank you. I've been involved in helping, planning, and overseeing very large events, usually racing oriented, with all kinds of international vendors, where I worked before, so that element isn't new to me, but I understood the arena. I wouldn't have the first clue what to do with what you're handling. Even the charitable functions we had were all skiing and snowboard related in some manner."

"It's probably not much different, just different vendors and sponsors, different kind of sport, but more or less the same end result."

"I guess you're right. So what's the deal with Maksimov? Why would he come out if he's not part of the deal?"

"I'm sure he'll have some pretense, but now that I've raised my head, no doubt he's coming out to try and schmooze me into doing one of his upcoming events."

"Do different hotels hold different poker events?"

"No, it's usually one resort that gets the license to host the big events. But other hotels definitely have exhibition events, usually tied to a charity or bigger event of some sort, and bring us all in. It's good exposure and the pros usually kick in. It's good philanthropy, too, and the celebs usually come out as well. For the promoters, it's good to get as many headliners locked in as early as possible. Ostensibly it's for charity or some such, but if regular folks think they're going to be rubbing elbows with celebrities while playing the five-dollar slots, then they tend to book into whatever hotel is holding the next upcoming widely advertised event."

"Have you played for this guy before? Is there something wrong with how he does things?"

"Yes, I have, and on the surface, no."

"But below the surface?"

Brett lifted one shoulder. "There are a lot of rumors, possibly some shady dealings. There is Russian backing with the resort that's never been entirely on the up and up, at least that's the word. There's rumor of other questionable European backing, Pacific Rim, too."

"That's . . . rather broad in scope. Is that common?"

"Not quite to that degree, and it's not necessarily true, either. Other than the Russian part. No one has ever been able to prove anything, but the talk persists. It's been several years now, and talk doesn't usually stick like that unless there's something to it. And my gut tells me there is. So, when Maksimov comes knocking, I usually find somewhere else to be."

"Is it just you, or all the pros?"

"Most of the guys at the top tend to steer clear, or only get involved when the outside support is unimpeachable."

"I imagine that doesn't sit well with whoever owns the place. To be shunned. Are there other, I guess you could call it privately blacklisted resorts?"

"Some, especially the oldest ones, have never been able to shake some of their early connections to organized crime."

"Is that still a thing? Really?"

"Not in the way of the past, no. It's taken on a far more international flavor these days. Not to mention highly sophisticated. You have both syndicated, organized action, as well as independent problems."

"I guess I thought that would have been dealt with a long time ago. I know the town has really tried to build up a more family-friendly atmosphere."

"Because it plays well. But don't be fooled. When you have that much money concentrated in such a small, controlled area, it would be foolish to think they don't have a hand in."

"And you think Maksimov works for that kind of outfit?"

"Directly or indirectly? No proof, but I trust my instincts."

"A Russian Mafioso. Great. And, of course he's staying here. Are you sure I can't rework the books and block him out?"

"He's harmless enough, especially if he wants something from me."

"And when he doesn't get it?"

"He never gets it. It's par for the course. He just keeps getting sent out to try. Not my problem if he goes back empty-handed. And, chances are, to be honest, if he doesn't get a verbal commitment from me, he'll be able to schmooze it from any number of other players."

"I thought you said—"

"I said some of them, mostly the ones who can afford to say no. Most players can't. Maksimov will do fine on his recruiting mission. He just won't be recruiting me."

She continued to look dubious, and he bent down to kiss her nose.

"I'll let you know if I think anything has changed where he's concerned. But while I'm not happy he's going to be here, it's just an irritation. At least if he's staying here, you keep an eye, too, maybe help run a little interference and keep him off my back." He wiggled his eyebrows. "Use those guest services skills you're always bragging about."

She merely arched a brow, but said, "I'll do whatever I can."

He bussed her on the mouth. "See? Good teamwork."

"Speaking of teamwork . . ." She smiled against his mouth as he was already kissing her before she could finish the sentence.

There would be a lot going on over the next few weeks that would take a fast-lane learning curve to deal with . . . so she definitely could get used to having someone around who was so in tune with her.

She gasped and arched off the bed as he moved lower down her body. Especially when his thoughts were tuned in to doing this . . .

Chapter 14

Brett leaned into the turn as he eased his bike around the bend, then up another steep, winding curve. When he'd left the desert, he'd headed east, across the flat prairie of middle America, before encountering his first swell of hills and mountains. Nothing like they had out west, but he'd never taken off in the direction of the Rockies, so he'd found it a bit exhilarating, all the twists and turns, steep ascents and swift downhill drops. When he'd taken off from the resort a few hours ago, he'd intended to go home, back to the inn, but instead he'd found himself turning up a side road that led into the hills, where he'd been tooling around the winding back roads since.

Thinking.

About things like why he'd so easily and naturally thought of Kirby's inn as home. It hadn't been a casual thought, either. He'd never once thought of his hotel rooms as home, or even a home away from home. Though he'd stayed in the exact same rooms many, many times over the years, and they'd been familiar to him, they had always remained exactly what they were. A place to crash, eat, and sleep between sitting at tables for endless hours. And giving interviews, teaching seminars, doing local promotion for the various event hosts and sponsors. Whatever was required of him to help give back to the sport that had given him, well, pretty much everything.

If ever a place had felt like home it had been his rooms at

Vanetta's, but for the past few years, they'd come to feel like more of a hideout than home and hearth. He hadn't thought of it that way at the time, of course. It had been the only real home he'd ever known. But now . . . now . . .

He thought about the inn, about Kirby. And maybe it wasn't that place, either, specifically, though his feelings about the inn itself were definitely filled with real affection. Maybe it was Kirby. Thinking of her, wanting to return to her, wherever she was. That's what felt like the haven he'd always thought a home should be. A place where the world dropped away and he could relax, be completely and utterly himself. And, more importantly, would know, without a doubt, that that was exactly who he was supposed to be.

Being with Kirby wasn't hiding, not like Vanetta's had become. He'd been seeking serenity, he realized, which was something rare in his profession, given both the intensity of the game itself and the actual location of the events. Bright lights and endless noise was life inside a casino.

But it was a serenity that went deeper than creating a peaceful environment. It was serenity of the soul. Where he could discover a completely different kind of fulfillment. Where all sorts of needs that had nothing to do with money and repayment of debts, real or imagined, existed. It was about feeding into something entirely different. And he knew that all of those things existed for him, or could exist for him, wherever Kirby Farrell happened to be.

He took the next curve a bit more deeply, enjoying the thump of adrenaline that pumped into his veins as he leaned into the turn, unsure if the cause was the tight curve or the thoughts of Kirby, or both.

These past few weeks, since the two of them had decided on launching the charitable event, had been a new form of chaos for him, and not a little frustrating. He hadn't gotten to spend much time with her as the demands of putting together the event as quickly as humanly possible had kept him at the resort almost full time, and on the phone more often than not the rest of the time. Kirby, meanwhile, had been more than a little busy herself, preparing for her onslaught of guests, all slated to arrive in just a few short days now.

Though the temperatures in the evening were dipping lower and lower, the daytime temps had remained unseasonably warm, and yet that hadn't curbed the enthusiasm of the guests wanting to come out and be part of the event. He was thrilled for her, as that had been the goal all along, but, personally, selfishly, he was missing her, missing their alone time in the seclusion of her empty inn.

And yet, that same passage of time had been grounding, and illuminating, for the precise reason that it had frustrated him. He wanted to be with her. Needed to be. More. Often. All the damn time. And not just for the sex, or even the conversation, though he had swiftly come to wanting and needing both all the damn time, too. He wanted to play house with Kirby Farrell. Cooking dinner, doing odd chores around the inn, reading the paper over the breakfast table, hauling mounds of bed linens down the basement stairs to the industrial-size washer and dryer.

Sitting next to her on the porch in the evening, sipping a glass of wine, enjoying the crisp bite in the air as the sun finally ducked behind the surrounding peaks. Talking about what she was going to plant in her spring garden and the final improvements she wanted to make to the inn, watching her face as she listened to some of his ideas, seeing the light enter her eyes as she realized he was as invigorated by the architecture and character of the old place as she was. Like spirits, crossing paths by chance or divine design, now moving forward, with barely restrained anticipation, on a newly created path of their own.

Yes, he wanted to play house with Kirby Farrell. And not just for the next few weeks, either. A good-size part of him couldn't wait for the damn event to be over so he could go back to . . . what, exactly?

Hanging out with Kirby? Sleeping with Kirby? Living with Kirby? He didn't rightly know. He didn't know where her head was at, regarding him, her future, or any possibility of their future.

Hence the spontaneous road trip this morning.

He couldn't stop thinking about it all, about what was going to happen when the event was over. He had people waiting for him back in Vegas. Family, at least to him. But now he also had Kirby. And with all these thoughts and emotions swirling through him, he wasn't sure he could face her without blurting it all out. And when he did that, he wanted all those thoughts and emotions to be a bit more cohesive than they were at that moment. Because this time, when he went all in, the stakes were going to be the biggest of his life.

And then there was that other part, too. The rest-of-his-life part. And what the hell he wanted to do with that. And if there was any way that rest-of-his-life part could find a place here in the mountains of Vermont. A place that would give him the chance to see what could come of a future with Kirby. A place far, far away from flashing lights, endless noise, and playing cards. But also far, far away from the only other people on the planet he loved and cared for.

His gut knotted—or more precisely the knot already in his gut tightened—at the thought of actually playing again. Not the game itself. In some odd way, when he was playing, at least against a good table, the world shrunk down to that green baize surface, the cards in front of him, the stacks of chips being flipped, toyed with, shoved in, raked out. Everything else fell away.

He slowed his bike as it hit him, that it was that feeling, that solitude among chaos, that, in and of itself, was the bigger draw for him. Not of winning, or involving himself mentally in the challenge of the game itself. He wondered when that shift had actually happened. A long time back, that much he knew now. When money had ceased to be the reason for playing. When there was no real need to win, other than to keep all those folks who had given him a shot in the first place happy. He slowed down further as another realization sunk in. That place out of time was exactly what he felt when he was with Kirby.

Did that mean she was simply another escape hatch from the real world? Was that feeling he had when he was with her merely one of . . . what, relief?

Partly. He had to admit that was partly it. There were two places in the world where he absolutely knew who he was. Sitting at a poker table . . . and sitting across from Kirby Farrell. But there was more to it. Nothing in his life had ever stimulated him on so many simultaneous levels as playing in a high stakes game did. Until Kirby.

She reached all kinds of places that no game could. There were simply no other stakes that could climb that high . . . or penetrate that deep.

But what did that say? Was he merely trading one fixation for another? Was that healthy? Would it make him any happier in the long run?

He honestly didn't know.

He just knew he wanted the chance to find out.

Brett sped up and took the next turn at a scream. Then he slowed as a glint of sun off glass from somewhere deep in the trees on the slopes high above caught his eye. He slowed further, but after a quick flash of a building—a home, the prominent structure of which made it appear as if it were thrusting out beyond trees, soaring, almost—vanished as the road took another turn.

He couldn't have said why it mattered, or why he suddenly had to see more of it, but if it blessedly took him out of his own head for a few minutes, then he welcomed the distraction. On the next curve, he spied another road, a narrow, roughly paved track, snaking up the hill, in the direction of where the house had to be. He took the turn without asking himself why. Thinking wasn't getting him anywhere. So, for the next hour or so, he planned to just go, follow his gut, turn off his brain, and the hell with what came next.

*   *   *

It was early afternoon by the time he rolled back into Penny-dash. His brain wasn't going any slower than it had when he'd taken off that morning, but the thoughts running through it right now had taken on a decidedly new slant. One that might lead to a few answers. And probably a whole lot more questions, too. But he was excited about that part this time.

He discovered he'd had a call as he'd descended back into cell range, leaving him with a voice mail. It was from the resort, telling him there was a guest there, impatiently waiting for his return. Brett knew Maksimov was due into town shortly, and he had purposely put off thinking about the conversation he was sure to be having with the stubborn Russian. But Brett hadn't been in any mood to contemplate. Too many other, far more tantalizing thoughts crowding his brain. He'd known he would handle whatever the hell Maks wanted when he finally saw him face to face. No point in dwelling on it.

And now it appeared that the happy event was imminent. Lovely. Kirby had shifted Maksimov's reservation from the inn to the resort after all, telling Maks after the fact. She said the transition had been smooth and he had seemed fine with her apology for over-booking. A light fib at the time, but she'd filled that room since, so all was okay. At least until he had to talk to the man himself.

He sighed. As much as he wanted to race back to the inn, back to Kirby, share with her the million new thoughts racing around inside his head, get her feedback . . . he decided he'd get this out of the way first.

So he leaned into the turn heading up to the main resort hotel and conference center and gunned it up the steep, winding entrance into the ski resort. Winterhaven wasn't nearly as fancy or over the top in design as the resorts he'd grown up prowling around, but it definitely had an inviting air about it. It was styled to look like an extended series of Swiss chalets, all curved in a giant arc along the base of the slopes, allowing guests to ski right from their rooms to the slopes. The main resort building containing registration, shops, restaurants, and other guest services was tucked into the center of the chalets. It was designed to look like a larger, more complex version of the rest. This unique concept offered a rather intimate, more casual-slash-village feel to the place, while at the same time making guests feel they were staying somewhere special.

His thoughts drifted immediately to Kirby and he found himself trying to picture her running a resort the size of Winterhaven. Very likely the one she'd helped manage in Colorado had been decidedly bigger than this one. And though he was well aware she was competent enough to handle whatever she was thrown . . . he thought the small, quaint inn atmosphere suited her personality better. Like its owner, Pennydash Inn was an openly warm and welcoming establishment that made you feel instantly at home . . . yet housed in a quietly elegant, beautifully detailed structure.

He'd never really thought about all the elements that went into running a successful hotel, whether it be resort, chain, inn, or even boarding house for that matter. Not that he hadn't realized how hard Vanetta worked to keep her place going, but there were all kinds of elements that he'd never considered.

Over the past few weeks, he'd gotten a true glimpse of what Kirby's life would be like if the inn was operating as it was supposed to be. He selfishly and unapologetically wanted more time with her, before the true insanity descended upon her little adopted burg.

And that was going to add another layer of complexity to all the thoughts swirling inside his head, but at that moment, he had to switch mental gears and focus on dealing with Maksimov. Then Brett could work on getting the hell back out of the resort before someone else sidelined him with a myriad of new details that needed his immediate attention.

He missed her, dammit.

He was thinking about stopping by the Food Mart on the way back to the inn and showing up with a couple of steaks, maybe an assortment of local cheeses, a decent bottle of wine—

Kirby had introduced him to some very nice local labels there, too—and negotiate a stop-work measure where they both turned off their cell phones and locked themselves inside his top-floor bedroom for the rest of the day and night. Surely everything wouldn't fall apart if they went AWOL for a few hours.

He was quite happily playing out that delightful scenario as he tooled around the loop that led to the main lobby. So he missed the doors sliding open.

"Well, it's about time, buddy."

Brett almost laid the bike on its side as the familiar voice— one without any Russian accent whatsoever—reached through the carnal haze that had swiftly been clouding his brain and clicked his synapses back to reality.

He managed to steady the bike until he brought it under control and stopped it. Then quickly parked and climbed off as he saw, quite clearly, that he hadn't been hallucinating.

"Dan?" His face split into a wide grin. "What the hell?" Then he immediately sobered. "Wait, is everything okay? Your dad, Vanetta—"

Dan lifted his hand to stall Brett's concern. "Fine, fine. Though Dad is threatening to come back from Palm Springs to take over the company again." He chuckled; however, his expression was anything but lighthearted. "But then, you know he never did believe I could do the job he did with it."

Brett didn't chuckle along with him. "Is there something going on? I mean, with the company? Why the hell are you all the way out here, anyway?"

Dan lifted a shoulder. "If Muhammad won't come to the mountain . . ."

"So, something is wrong."

"No, no," he said, but it wasn't entirely convincing. And when Brett merely folded his arms, Dan relented. "Okay, so two of my higher end clients lost their financing. And, with that, things are a bit tight. But that's the deal these days, with the economy the way it is, what can you do? I'll make it through; I always do."

Brett knew better than to offer his financial assistance. Dan had made it clear years back, when Brett had really moved into a realm of income that most folks simply couldn't wrap their heads around, that he never wanted to be one of Brett's charity cases. Brett had argued that it wasn't charity, simply what family did for one another. Like what he'd done for Vanetta. Brett understood pride; he had his own. Which was why he'd handled Vanetta's situation discreetly, as he would any assistance he sent Dan's direction.

But that conversation had been definitively closed some time ago. Dan wouldn't take handouts, as he called them, no matter how much Brett tried to explain that it would make him feel good to do something to repay the kindnesses Dan and his father had extended him throughout his teenage years.

And knowing that it was a dead issue, he was loathe to bring it up again now. But he could do something, he could help. It was hard not to offer. "Dan—"

"That's not why I'm here, Brett," he warned. "I'm fine."

"Okay," Brett said, though he thought it was anything but. "So, why are you here?"

"To talk some sense into my closest friend's thick skull."

Brett understood Dan's frustration there, too. Dan wasn't big on change, which was partly why his business didn't thrive as much as it had under his father's hand. Brett had tried to get him to be a bit more of a risk taker, to think bigger, see farther, but Dan was traditional in his approach to building his business. The problem was, Vegas wasn't a traditional town. "You supported my decision to get out," he said.

"Out of casinos, out of playing cards for a living, out from under the pressure the promoters were putting on you. But not out of Dodge all together."

Brett sighed. Dan had been a part of his life for the entire duration of his poker-playing career, from the early rise, to the continued rise, to finally the retirement before he fell apart. But while his good friend had consistently told him that if he was miserable he should get out and find something else to do with his life, especially if his to do list included working for his good buddy, Dan had never really understood, not really, what it was about Brett's career that had made him so stressed out, much less feel unfulfilled.

Of course, Dan would have taken full advantage of the perks, namely the ones who came with perky assets, which had been another bit of a friction between them. More than once Dan had tried to goad him into "sharing the wealth" as he termed it. Brett would have handed them all over to his buddy, gladly, but he wasn't about to pimp for the guy and he wasn't interested in double dating.

Not that Dan was hurting for female companionship, at least when he could make time for it. He was a bit shorter than Brett and stockier, but in that muscular, beefhead linebacker kind of way that women who wanted a big strong man to protect them really went for. And Dan was more than willing to give shelter. The shelter of his bed, anyway. He wasn't exactly the go-to guy for long-term commitments. A holiday weekend would be considered a long relationship for him.

But while Dan might not have always been a stand-up guy where the opposite sex was concerned, he'd been absolutely loyal to Brett, even if they didn't always see eye to eye. Brett always hoped Dan would find "the one" and jump off the merry-go-round of women he kept circling around him all the time, just as Brett had hoped "the one" would enter his own orbit at some point. At least when Brett did go out, it was with the hope it would last. He wasn't sure Dan was interested in anything long term that didn't come with dollar signs attached.

"I had to leave," Brett said, retreading ground they'd been over many, many times. "You know that."

"No, *you* know that. Or you think you do. A few spots of bad luck, and you freak out and think the Mafia or something is after you."

"I didn't freak out. And it wasn't just a string of bad luck."

"How the hell would you know? You don't have bad luck."

Brett felt his own temper edge up and worked to quell it. "I think I've had my share in my day, enough to know when it's just fate and when someone has their hand in it. I did what I thought I had to do to protect the people I care about." He lifted his hand to stop Dan's rebuttal. "And even if those things hadn't happened, I might have taken off anyway. I had a lot of thinking to do."

"And you couldn't have done that while swinging a hammer?"

"I tried that," he reminded his friend. "And you have always known that my future was not down that path. Not full time. I respect what you do, Dan, what you and your father built, but that's your future. It's not mine."

"Says the guy with the fancy architectural and design degrees. Too good for us? You've got the money, the education—"

"Whoa, whoa. Where the hell is this coming from?" Brett was sincerely surprised, but also more than a little pissed off. "That was way out of line and you damn well know it."

Dan ducked his head, held his hands up, palms out. "You're right." He lifted his gaze. "I'm just frustrated. We make a great team. And I guess I thought, despite what you said, that when you left the tables for good . . ." He let it trail off.

And Brett felt his heart squeeze hard inside his chest.

He thought Dan had truly understood. Had he thought, all along, that Brett was really going to come work with him? Or was he just frustrated now that things weren't going well? Because what Brett knew, what Dan had to know as well, though they'd never spoken of it, was that on the occasions when Brett went to work with Dan, between tournaments, or when he just needed a break from the tables . . . Dan's ability to find folks who wanted to hire them tended to increase exponentially. Brett was well known throughout the world of poker, but nowhere was his fame as strong as it was in his own hometown. Word got out he was working with Dan, and well, folks liked to be associated with a winner. Some approached out of curiosity, but most just enjoyed whatever it was they got out of working with a recognizable "name."

Brett had never minded that. Though he'd never openly pro-
moted himself or their partnership that way, lending what
celebrity he had, to help Dan land the higher-end, more lucra-
tive clients was about the only way he could share his good fortune with his childhood friend.

But, as much as he wanted to do anything he could to help,
he drew the line at giving up the dream to build his own future.
Not when there were too many other ways he could help that
didn't require that kind of sacrifice. It hurt him to see his friend
disappointed, and in trouble, but he was feeling a bit betrayed
himself.

Maybe it was the time he'd taken, or the distance he'd finally
put between himself and the only life he'd ever known, but he
could see more clearly now that not only did Dan not seem to
have really gotten that Brett's path was not his best buddy's
path, but he almost seemed . . . well, a little pissed off that Brett
was going to go his own way.

And yes, that hurt. It also pissed him off a little, too.

"I'm sorry. You know I will do anything to help you out."
Brett pushed on when the mutinous expression crossed Dan's
face. "And don't go blowing up on me, you know I don't see it
the way you do."

"I work for what I get. I make the right choices for my business, to keep it strong and growing. And that means not being
an idiot and letting you walk away. That's why I got on a plane.
I'm not here for a handout, Brett. I will never take your money.
But I will take your honest work, because it's good for all of
us."

Brett blew out a long breath and swore silently, but he didn't
look away from his one and only true friend. Dan deserved at
least that much. "It's not good for me." He hated the pain that
flashed through his friend's eyes, but was bolstered by the anger
he saw there, too. "There are other ways for me to help that
allow us both to live the lives we want. If you won't let me help
you financially, there are other things I can do that are in line

with your work ethic. I'm not trying to insult your pride or your integrity. But I can help you, goddammit. So let me. I can finance projects; I can do marketing for you. I'm not coming back to work for you, but there are so many other ways I can drive business your way. All of which I want to do."

Dan didn't say anything, and the moment spun out until it felt pretty damn uncomfortable for both of them.

Dan was the one who finally broke the silence. "You know, I never thought you had a problem. With gambling, with cards. You were more like some kind of professor of the game or something. It was all math and numbers and angles. Probably why you did so well in school. And took to building houses as well as you did."

"I don't have a problem with gambling," he said, confused by where Dan was going with this. What else was the guy he loved like a brother angry about?

"Well, see, I kind of have to wonder about that. You won't come back and help out a friend. But you'll bring the card game to you. In fact, you're bringing it all the way across the goddamn country."

"I'm not going back to the game."

Dan snorted. "Could have fooled me."

"This is a one-time thing. For charity."

"Is that her name, then?"

Brett curled his fingers tightly inside his palms to keep from destroying anything else between them by planting his fist in Dan's face. "I'm helping out a friend." His gaze narrowed. "I'm like that."

Dan did have the grace to look slightly abashed, but he was already too far gone to rein himself completely in. "Well, looks to me like you've traded a lifelong friend for one who can scratch a certain itch. No worries. You're not the first one to get lead around by his—"

Brett stepped in closer, but didn't touch him. "You're going to want to think very hard about the words spouting out of your mouth right now. You, your dad, and Vanetta are the only family I've really had. It's because of you that I even know the meaning of the word family. Of what it means to love."

"Are you saying you think you're in love with this woman? Jesus, Brett, you just got out here. She must be one amazing f—"

"She is amazing," Brett said, using every bit of willpower he had to keep his voice level. "In every sense, she is exactly that. But you're missing my point. I love you all, you, and Vanetta, everyone back home. And I will always do whatever I can to be there for you. You know that. But, beyond that, I want something different than you do. Our goals are different. If our friendship, our life history, means anything to you, then you'd want me to achieve those goals the same way I want you to achieve yours."

"What the hell does that have to do with some chick you're shacking up with?"

Brett might have snarled. "She's one of mine, now, too. And I take care of what's mine. But then, you should already know that." Brett turned and stalked back toward his bike before he said or did anything else to further unravel a situation that had already gotten so far out of hand, he wasn't entirely sure how they were going to patch it up. He felt blindsided. A not a little sick.

"Brett, wait."

He paused, but he didn't turn around.

"Look." He heard Dan blow out a long, deep sigh. Then, "I'm sorry, okay? I—I guess I'm not used to anyone else mattering to you. No one else ever has."

Brett turned to face him.

"Even you have to admit that's a new side of you. You'll have to cut me some slack for not getting it right off. But I do now." His mouth curved just a little then, but he was shaking his head as it did. "I guess it's only strange that it hasn't happened sooner."

"To be honest, I don't know what this is. Or where it will go," Brett said, putting voice to at least some of the thoughts that had been rattling through his mind all day. "I just know that I want the chance to find out. About Kirby. About myself. About what's next. On all fronts." He faced his friend squarely. "It would mean a great deal to me if you understood that. I mean really understood it."

Dan held his gaze just as squarely. "I want to. That's about the best I can give you, because I've never been where you're standing. I just know where I'm standing. And what I see as the best possible future for us both. Your education, skill, your name, matched with my background, the history of my company, can take it to whole new heights. Your vision, the foundation I've built in the community. It can't miss. You're the one telling me to think bigger, see a better future. And when I do, that's what I see. So, no, I don't really understand. You say you want to build your own future, but you don't even know what the hell it is. And now, out of nowhere, you want to just jump into some new life thousands of miles away, with a woman you've just met. I mean, come on, Brett. It would be odd if I wasn't a bit mystified, and yes, pissed off, about that. It's going to take some time, I guess, to get used to. I can try."

"I can't ask for more than that." Then Brett was quiet for a moment, trying, as best he could, to hear what his friend was saying, to see it from Dan's point of view. After all, fair was fair.

The tension eased up, but only a little. Finally, Dan turned and gestured to the hotel. "You got rooms here?"

Brett nodded. Even though he was booked in with Kirby, the resort had comped him a suite here as well while they were working on the event. He'd slept alone in the huge king-size bed more times the past few weeks than he'd have preferred. "Nice suite, top floor." He pulled his wallet from his pocket and slid one of his card keys out. "Here, I'm not using it." At least he wasn't planning to that night. "Unless you already made other arrangements."

"You staying down in town, then? At—what's her name again, Kirby? At her place?"

He nodded, then tried a smile. "I'm kind of burned out on the whole luxury suite thing."

Dan chuckled, and things finally felt at least something resembling normal. "Never did understand how anyone could get tired of that, but if it's just sitting there unused . . ." He reached out and took the card.

Brett knew even taking that much was hard for him, so he joked, "Well, there are a few other benefits to staying down in town that the resort doesn't provide."

Dan's grin was knowing. "Now that's more like it." He slid the card in his back pocket. "You gonna tell me something about this mystery woman who's already got you whipped?"

Brett let that one go. "I'll do better than that. I'd like you to meet her." If nothing else, he thought, maybe Dan would at least understand why Brett was sticking in Vermont for a while. He didn't think his friend would behave as obnoxiously in person. At least he hoped not. It had been an interesting conversation so far. Regardless, he thought, Kirby could hold her own. It was yet another reason why he was anxious to get back to the inn.

He checked his watch. "Speaking of which, I need to get in touch with her, anyway." His forgotten dinner plans resurfaced, but though he regretted having to put them off—again—it was important to him that Kirby meet Dan as well. "How long are you planning to stay?"

"Well, since I'm out here, I thought I'd watch you play. Been a while since I've done that."

"Because you work too hard."

Dan grinned. "No such thing, brother."

"At the very least, you have to admit you need to get out and play more."

"I'm here, aren't I? Hell, if I had a clue how to play the damn game, I'd sit in on a few hands."

Brett didn't mention that the buy-in was ten thousand dollars. "I've told you many times, I'd be more than happy to teach you. I hear there's a vacant seat at the tables back in Vegas."

Dan shook his head. "It'll take bigger britches than mine to fill your seat."

"So, if you're out here, who's minding the store?"

"I'm handling things, don't you worry. That's what cell phones and laptops are for. Everything is under control." When Brett continued to look dubious, Dan added, "Wasn't it you who told me to delegate? See? I do listen to you."

Brett smiled, but privately he wondered just how bad things were for Dan. The one way he was just like his old man was in his work ethic. Neither of the Bradley men put much stock in leisure time. In fact, Brett was still stunned that when Dan senior had retired to Palm Springs, he hadn't been back in Vegas before the month was out. Either that or had started his own new company out there. But, as far as Brett knew, the elder Bradley was happily playing golf and being the much-sought-after companion to any number of retired widows and divorcées.

He also wondered if Dan senior had any idea of how bad things were.

Brett didn't give voice to any of that. If he wasn't willing to be a partner in his friend's business, then he had no right to tell him how to run it. Still, that wouldn't keep him from worrying.

"Well," he said, at length, "at least something of what I said is penetrating that thick head of yours. Why don't you head on up and relax a bit. I'm going to head back to the inn, talk with Kirby, find out what's on tap. I'll give you a ring so we can meet up later? I would like her to get the chance to meet you."

"Sounds like a plan." Dan shot a glance over his shoulder, in the direction of the lobby that was anything but calm and relaxed.

He caught Brett looking at him as he glanced back and replied to the unasked question. "Maksimov's here. I spotted him in the lobby. He was looking for you. Have you two talked?"

Brett shook his head. "Not yet. In fact, that was what I was on my way back here to do. I had a message someone was waiting to see me; I assumed it was him."

"Well, we both know why he's here."

Brett shrugged. "Won't net him anything. He wants to waste a plane ticket, nothing I can do about that."

"So . . . you're not thinking about—"

"No," Brett said flatly, not even letting Dan finish the thought. "I told you, this is a one and done."

"Charity, right. Speaking of which, when you get back at the tables, it's like I said when we were on the phone, you know they're all going to come begging." He laughed, but there was no warmth in it. "Hell, they'll probably all line up some kind of 'very special' charity for you to play for, if that's what it takes. You know it's going to start things up all over again."

"I was well aware of that, so I made certain everyone knew, from the first conference call, that this was a one-time thing. They can come after me all they want, but I won't be taking their calls or scheduling any meetings. Besides, I'm almost an entire country away from there now." He saw the pain flash through Dan's eyes and felt a twinge. But he remained resolute. "This is, for all intents, my turf. I've invited them here as my guests, handed opportunities to the few who I wanted to handle things."

"There will be return invites, you have to know that. They'll sweeten the deals whatever way it takes and you're handing them the charity angle. They'll make you feel guilty for not using your celebrity to fix everything from third world hunger to saving the humpback whale if it will get your name back head-lining their event marquee. Buy-ins are down since you left, and that's not changing anytime soon. Takes time to groom new su-perstars and no one is going to match your record for a very long time. As long as you're breathing, you're live bait."

"If they want to waste their breath, fine. Hopefully the dead silence they get in return will give them a clue. And not being around town won't hurt. Out of sight, out of mind."

Dan snorted. "Right. And if it helps you sleep at night, then sure, you'll be yesterday's news any day now."

"Trust me, when they realize that I'm not coming out of re-tirement, they will move along quickly to latch on to the new up-and-comers. Even if it's not something to make bank today or tomorrow, they have to move on. It's just good business. And they're nothing if not good businessmen."

Something flashed through Dan's eyes, and once again, Brett felt the nick of guilt pinch his heart.

After a beat, Dan said, "So, you coming in to break Maksimov's heart?"

Brett shook his head. "Later. You go on up. Don't let him sideline you trying to get to me."

Dan just shrugged it off. "Give me a little credit here."

"Okay, just trying to save you the grief."

"I can take care of myself."

But Brett didn't miss the second glance at the lobby. He thought about changing his plans, heading inside now to deal with Maksimov. But he was already going to lose dinner alone with Kirby, he wasn't about to give the rest of his time away to the annoying Russian. "Okay. I'll call you in a little bit. Dinner at the inn tonight."

"I hope she's a better cook than you."

Brett smiled. He wasn't about to throw Kirby under any bus. Besides, he thought he made a pretty damn good chicken marsala. "You won't leave hungry."

Dan smiled back, but Brett could still see the underlying tension. He knew he should resist the urge to call Vanetta. He didn't want her worrying. But she was his only other source. Woman knew every damn thing that went on in that town. Possibly because she'd lived there longer than anyone still alive. Brett didn't know for sure; he'd never questioned her sources or how she kept track of so much flotsam and jetsam while simultaneously and almost singlehandedly keeping the boarding house running. She probably new more about Dan's business than Dan did. And his, for that matter. So . . . he'd make the call.

There was more than one way to help out a friend.

Chapter 15

Kirby pushed her glasses up on top of her head and rubbed her eyes. She'd been going over the revised business plan her accountant had dropped off a few hours ago after his meeting with the bank. She was satisfied with the outcome, but her eyes were crossing at this point. She needed a break.

Naturally, her thoughts strayed directly to Brett. He'd been a guest of her inn now going on three weeks, but most of the last two he'd spent at the resort. Working to help her out, she knew, but that didn't mean she selfishly didn't miss his presence here. They'd had a few meals together and a couple of well-timed, very steamy, shower interludes, but most of the former had been spent talking about the charity event planning and the latter had been spent . . . well, not talking much at all.

She'd told herself time and again that it was for the best, their keeping things light, casual, and spontaneous. She was already far more invested in him emotionally than was healthy, knowing, as she did, that he'd move on after the event was over. She was forever grateful for the leg up he was offering her, the chance to keep her business afloat . . . so it was really wrong of her to want more. To want it all, frankly. She knew that.

But it didn't seem to stop her from wanting anyway. Dammit.

And who could really blame her? Other than the fact that he was thirty years old and had no clue what he was going to do with the rest of his life, he was perfect. And hell, she hadn't really embarked on realizing her own dreams until she was five years past that mark herself. And it wasn't like he hadn't already made quite a success out of himself. She just wished . . .

Well, she wished for things she couldn't have, is what she wished for. That he'd miraculously decide to go from the glitz and glamour of a high-rolling lifestyle in Vegas to wanting to live in a rural mountain village in Vermont. With her.

Yeah. That was going to happen.

As she reminded herself. Far too many times. Every day. Hourly at times.

She clicked the reservation screen up on her computer again and looked, once more, at the fully booked schedule she had coming up. In two days, they'd start coming in, and by the weekend, when the event started, she'd be fully packed. And finally, mercifully, she'd be too busy to think about pretty much anything other than keeping her guests happy.

And that would make her happy. Lonely, perhaps. But happy. Dammit.

Which was the other thing. She'd been perfectly content since coming east, to forge her own path, make her own choices, rule her own roost. Alone. It had been both a relief and a triumph. She knew she'd forge new relationships as time passed, both with the locals and in her private life as well. She hadn't come here determined to be a social shut-in or anything. Far from it. She just hadn't really seen herself falling into another long-term, serious relationship. Yet. Or maybe even ever.

She'd more or less left that part up to fate. So it seemed kind of unfair, she thought, being as she'd been so open-minded and honest and decent about the whole thing, for fate to go and hand her the perfect man on a platter . . . only, too bad, you can't keep him. You can only lust and need and taste and remember what it was like to want that in your life on a regular basis.

Damn damn dammit.

She sighed and clicked off the screen, then groaned as she turned to look at the clock only to feel how stiff her neck had gotten. She'd been hunched over this desk for what felt like days. She shoved her chair back and stood, rubbing her lower back and rotating her shoulders and neck a few times.

Time for a shower and then a hunt through the kitchen to see what she felt like dredging up for dinner. Her thoughts got sort of tangled up on that shower part as she walked out of the office, memories of the very wonderful one she'd shared with Brett— had it been yesterday? Seemed like forever ago now—swimming through her mind. He was attentive, and he made her laugh. And moan. A lot of moaning, really. She sighed and detoured the other direction, toward the kitchen. She was in no mood to stand in the shower and feel sorry for herself. She was just pathetic enough at the moment to indulge in a good, long, pity sob, and there was simply no excuse for it.

Her inn was going to be full, the air had a distinct touch of chill to it of late. At night, anyway. If her luck really was turning, then possibly by the time the event was over and all the attendant hoopla had ended along with it, there might be snow on the ground. Or, at least enough of a nip in the air during the daylight hours for the resort to finally put their bazillion-dollar snow-making system to work covering the newly designed slopes.

"Think positive," she murmured under her breath. "Optimistic thoughts only." Straightening her shoulders and resolutely not thinking about showers, muscled chests, or big, strong hands slipping and sliding all over her steam-slicked skin, she marched into the kitchen . . . and went straight to the wine rack. So she needed a little assistance with the resolutely not thinking part. "Sue me," she muttered.

After pouring a half a glass, she savored a few sips while looking out the rear kitchen window. Her gaze strayed to the big oak. Hard to believe it had only been a few weeks since she'd chased after that damn kitten. It seemed almost forever ago now. So much had happened since then. Her quiet little life here was anything but anymore.

Her lips curved in a slow smile. In fact, if her entire body could curl into a big smile, it would have. Sure, she was tired, but it was the good kind of tired that came from the hard work she'd been waiting for months to put in every day. After almost a year spent in the hard physical labor of getting the place into shape and ready to open, it had been difficult bordering on insanity-making to find herself sitting around . . . waiting for guests, for snow, for . . . something, anything, to happen. With no funds to continue crossing off anything else on her to-do restoration list, she'd been forced to putter. She was not a good putterer. She was a doer, not a sitter.

And then she'd climbed a tree, almost died; Brett had saved her and shown her a slice of heaven. Nothing had been the same since.

She sighed again, savored another slow sip . . . but the smile wouldn't go away. She was happy. As long as she lived in the moment, where there was no room at her inn, and Brett was still in residence, officially anyway, then life was good. Pretty damn good.

She sipped some more . . . and thought there was something to be said for living in the moment. Enjoying the good parts while they were happening. Not wasting them thinking about the less than good parts that were just out there on the horizon, headed her way. Yep, as long as she was standing here, sipping wine, and happy and content with her world, it didn't matter what the next day was going to bring.

"Looks like I didn't need to stop and get this on my way in."

She startled at the sound of his voice, almost sloshed the rest of her wine on her shirt. And didn't care in the least. Because she was happy. And living in the moment. And that moment had just grown exponentially even better. Way, way better.

She spun around, knowing she should be smart, play it cool, casual, like a woman who enjoyed his company when he was around, but didn't think about him incessantly when he wasn't.

Fat chance. If she'd been happy a moment ago, she was bliss-ful now. So she lived in that moment, too.

"There can never be enough wine," she said, crossing the kitchen toward him.

His leather jacket hung open to reveal a rumpled T-shirt and well-worn jeans. No leather, butt-framing chaps today. A pity. There was stubble on his cheeks and a decided case of helmet hair going on with his increasingly shaggy locks. She kind of liked him all stubbly and shaggy and rumpled. Made her want to get him into the shower. Or into bed. Or, well, the kitchen table was looking pretty damn good.

Feeling far too giddy and frisky, she set her wineglass down. Half a glass was apparently her limit.

"What else have you got there?" She tipped up on her toes and tried to peek inside the Food Mart paper bag, but he sat it on the counter and spun her into his arms instead.

"Stuff to make chicken Marsala. We're having company."

"Company? *We?*"

"Don't worry, I'm doing the cooking."

"Was that a less than subtle dig at my mad kitchen skills? Because I do have cans of cream of mushroom soup in the pantry, buster, and I'm not afraid to use them."

He laughed and tugged her up so her face was closer to his. "I miss you," he said, rubbed her nose with his, then claimed her mouth in a kiss so hot she was pretty sure her pink toenail polish got a little scorched.

It only took half a second to return the kiss with equal enthusiasm.

Words were beyond her when he finally lifted his head. She looked into his twinkling green eyes, and all she could think was, I'm going to miss you, too. Something fierce. She shoved that thought right out of her head. This was her moment—their moment—dammit, and she was going to live it to its fullest. This was no time to contemplate the less than rosy future they weren't going to be sharing. Besides, apparently there was a dinner to prepare. And company coming.

But before she could ask him what the plan was, he said, "Sorry I was AWOL all day."

"I just figured you got caught up in more planning meetings."

"I snuck out early," he said, "with every intention of coming back here and stealing you away for a few hours."

"What happened? Would it be something to do with the company we're having for dinner?"

"No, actually, that part came later. I . . . I was heading back here, but ended up taking a random turn off the main road and climbing into the hills for a little impromptu ride."

She could hardly be miffed that he hadn't asked her along. He was well aware of her comfort level regarding riding shotgun on his motorcycle. But still . . . "How was it?"

Surprisingly, his eyes lit up with some kind of . . . well, inner joy was the description that came to mind.

"That good, huh?" she said, unable to keep from smiling right back.

"Better."

"Well, the mountains are a pretty spectacular backdrop, though even better in the spring when things get green again."

"It was a gorgeous drive, but that's not what made it better."

She cocked her head. "So . . . 'splain it to me already."

He scooped her up against his chest, wrapping his arms around her to keep her feet dangling a foot off the ground. He spun them both around, making her squeal, and him laugh. Then he parked her backside on the counter and slid her hands around his neck as he moved between her thighs.

He braced his hands on the counter on either side of her hips. "We need to talk."

Surprised by the unusually ominous statement, her fingertips, which had been toying with the shaggy hair at the nape of his neck, stilled. "About?"

"So many things." He tipped his head back as if trying to corral all of his thoughts, and when he looked at her again, his expression was serious . . . but that banked excitement was still alive in his eyes. It couldn't be horrible if he was excited about it, could it? Unless he was excited about some opportunity to go back and play poker in Vegas again.

She tensed, despite trying to remain casual. She'd known,

after all, that this part was coming. She'd just thought she had a little more time, that was all. But if he was already thinking about the next thing on the horizon, she could hardly blame him for being excited about it. She might wish he shared that enthusiasm with someone else. Anyone else, quite frankly. But given all he'd done for her, she could hardly refuse to be there for him when he so obviously wanted to share his big news.

That also explained the long, spontaneous bike ride. He probably needed to figure out how he was going to break his news to her.

"And?"

He leaned in and kissed the side of her temple. Then he kept his face next to hers, pressing his cheek against the side of her head. "And my very oldest and closest friend, Dan, flew in and surprised me this afternoon. So I invited him over to dinner. I hope you don't mind."

"No, I don't mind." She thought she might scream from the tension building inside of her. Did he not have any clue how badly he was torturing her at that moment? "Is that what it was you wanted to tell me? Something about Dan?"

"I want you to meet him, but no, there's other stuff I want to talk about. I had thought a bottle of wine, some Marsala, some conversation. But then Dan was there, so now . . ."

"Dinner, and company."

"Right."

"Are you going back to the hotel with him afterward?"

He shook his head. "I was planning to stay here."

She didn't even try to ignore the hot little thrill that sent shivers down her spine. "Should I get another room ready for your friend?"

"I gave him my suite. He'll enjoy it." He lifted his hands to her face, pushed her hair back, and then framed her cheeks with his palms. "Not that I was trying to keep a paying guest from being under your roof . . . but I kind of selfishly wanted you all to myself for tonight."

"As it happens, I'm feeling a bit selfish myself." She smiled as he leaned in to kiss her again; then she swatted him across the chest as soon as he straightened.

"What was that for?"

"Taunting me with this big talk you want to have, then telling me I have to wait. Like my patience hasn't been tested enough over the past two weeks." As soon as that last part left her mouth she could have kicked herself. There was living in the moment, and there was being clingy and needy. And she was both, no doubt about it, but no need to broadcast it.

But then his eyes lit with that mischievous twinkle and she found she didn't mind so much when he tugged her hips forward so he could snug himself more tightly between her thighs. "How impatient are you feeling, say, right about now?"

What the hell, she thought. And she grinned right back at him. "How long does it take to make chicken Marsala again?"

"You know, Dan is a bachelor . . . I'm thinking cream of mushroom soup chicken could be just as popular a menu item this evening."

"Do you?"

He scooped her up off the counter and wrapped her legs around his waist as she wrapped her arms around his neck. "Indeed, I do."

He didn't ask his bedroom or hers . . . but took her up the backstairs to his bed. For which she was privately grateful. Not only because it took her farther away from the phone and her office, but she kind of liked being in his space, in his bed. So to speak.

He followed her down onto the bed, onto her, and she reveled in his weight on top of her. There was that thrill of all their body parts lining up so deliciously right, but even more, there was just a sense of . . . reassurance? Comfort? It was more complicated than that, but also as simple as that. She'd missed him, too. But rather than say it, she tugged his head down to hers and showed him.

He had his hands buried in her hair a moment later, returning her kiss with every bit the same intensity and enthusiasm. Oh, the wonders of being wanted like he wanted her. She didn't think she'd ever get to a point where his attention didn't move her like that. So focused . . . and so fun.

He was smiling as he lifted his head, and she couldn't help but smile back at him. "What?" she queried when he simply continued to stare into her eyes.

"I used to think I was one very lucky son of a bitch. And I was. For a very long time."

"I think that's great. That kind of success has to feel incredibly rewarding."

"It does. Or did. But you know what?"

She shook her head but found herself too busy tracing the laugh lines creasing the corners of his mouth with her fingertip to respond verbally. It was far too easy to get caught up in him. And she was so very, very caught.

He traced his own fingertips down the side of her face, and his expression took on a whole new light she'd never seen before. Her fingers paused as she got caught up in looking back.

"What?" she finally said, the word barely more than a whisper.

"My ridiculous good luck is holding," he said, caressing her bottom lip with one fingertip, then replacing it with his own lips. Only this time the kiss was slower, softer, deeper. Almost . . . reverent. He took his time, claiming her in a way . . . well, that felt like it was all about being claimed.

"Brett," she said as his lips left hers, slowly, so they continued to touch, even as their breaths comingled.

"I am the luckiest son of a bitch on the planet," he said, sounding almost a little stunned. Then he took her mouth again, only this time there was heat, and passion, and absolute intent.

And if she'd felt soulfully claimed a moment ago . . . she was feeling absolutely primally claimed now. She didn't know what it meant, or what he was thinking. Did he mean the great sex? It was pretty damn incredible. Or was there some deeper meaning. It felt a lot . . . deeper.

But that was as analytical as her poor, hormone-besieged brain could be. The rest of her was far too intent on doing some claiming of its own to be worrying about things like motivation and meaning.

The only thing she was motivated to do in that moment was to get them both out of their clothes and get him as deep inside of her as possible. He was like some kind of narcotic. Every time she got a little, she wanted more. And it took more to get her that fix she needed, craved. He was insatiable with her, which was heady, heady stuff . . . and she was equally voracious in return.

Clothes were peeled off, pillows shoved aside as he pushed her farther across the bed and moved between her legs. There was no talking, no laughter. This was hot, hard, so fierce she thought she might pass out from the intensity of it. And then he was burying himself hard inside of her and her guttural growl of satisfaction vibrated against the slick skin on the side of his neck, where she was nibbling, biting, licking.

He pinned her hands down beside her head and moved faster. She dug the heels of her feet into the backs of his thighs, urging him on, rising to meet him, reveling in the hoarse groans coming from somewhere deep inside his chest, matching him grunt for grunt with her own half wild growls.

Their bodies pistoned, her hips thrusting up, his pinning her back down, until the sweat and internal combustion made their bodies so slick it was hard for her to keep any grip on him at all. He solved that by gripping her thighs and pushing her up the bed.

"Hold on," he commanded, jerking his chin at her hands, now clutching at the sheets beside her head.

She reached blindly up until she found the headboard and grabbed on to the heavy rolled edge now above her head.

He held on to her thighs and lifted her higher, farther onto him, as he continued to take her. And she continued to take him in.

They were both half grunting, half shouting, as she felt him gather inside her, building . . . which took her screaming right over the edge. He was swearing, loud and long, as he climaxed right as the shock waves were still spasmodically jerking her body beneath his.

The force of it was so strong, so intense, they continued pumping even as they both shook with exhaustion, until finally he braced his weight over her on his elbows, sweat dripping from his brow onto the base of her throat, as he slid from her, emitting another deep groan of satisfaction as he did, making her quiver involuntarily . . . then sliding down her body so he could press a reverent kiss directly over her heart.

She managed to pry her grip from the headboard and buried her fingers into his thick hair as he sprawled across the bed, his cheek pressed against her stomach, one arm splayed across her hips. He slid his free hand up to cup the side of her face, cradling her in his wide palm, as he stroked along her cheekbone with his thumb.

She had never been so utterly and completely spent in her life. There was no actual thought, and a complete inability to form words. So she just laid there, sated in a way that went so far past the physical, she was grateful that her brain was too saturated to figure out the true deeper meaning of it all.

So she simply enjoyed the weight of him, half draped across her body, feeling his heartbeat against her thigh as her own finally began to slow to some semblance of a normal pulse pattern. As she toyed with his hair, he continued to softly stroke the side of her face. She felt incredibly well loved . . . and, again, it reached past the physical. She closed her eyes and floated, purposely letting go of all thought.

Because if she'd dwelled, for even a second longer, on how well loved she felt in that moment, on the richness and depth of emotion that he brought to her heart and soul, in a way she'd never even knew existed, much less ever experienced, then that burning sensation would build and well up behind her eyes again, and that deep, unending ache would bloom inside her heart. And it was too fine a moment to spoil with even a tinge of pain or sadness.

Because Kirby was one lucky son of a bitch, too. And, for right that moment, that was damn well going to be enough.

But, like all moments, fine or otherwise, this one had to come to an end. She felt Brett sigh even as she heard the sound of it, and his touch paused along the edge of her cheekbone.

"Kirby," he said, and the sound of her name, said in a voice so raw and raspy from the force of his lovemaking mere moments ago, threatened to bring those tears on anyway. Only now she couldn't tell if they'd be of joy, or anguish . . . or some pathetic mix of both. She just knew she'd give a lot to hear him say her name, just like that, again. And again.

"I—" She broke off, finding her voice raw, but her throat even tighter against those unshed tears. God, he was going to think her a basket case, unable to keep her act together whenever they had sex in a damn bed. She eased out from under him, knowing she was running away, but feeling retreat was, in this case, the better part of valor. Or at the very least, in retaining her some shred of her dignity. "I need to . . ." She didn't finish, but hoped he'd fill in the blank as she slipped from the bed and ducked into the adjoining bathroom.

She clicked the door shut softly behind her, praying he was spent enough that his awesome powers of perception didn't see past her surface excuse and cause him to follow her.

She went straight to the pedestal sink and ran cool water, sliding her hands under the steady stream and splashing the water lightly onto her face, then doing it again, hoping to quell the threat. When she finally felt like she was getting some semblance of a grip, she slowly lifted her face to the mirror. Her eyes were clear, not even a hint of pink. Good, she thought, and turned off the water as she grabbed a fluffy washcloth to pat her stubble-abraded cheeks dry.

Now, she thought as she straightened, if I could only cool off my heart with a good cold splash.

She took a steadying breath and turned away from the mirror, leaning back against the sink as she drew another breath, then another. She'd go back in there, crawl back into bed with a smile on her face, say something light, something funny, make him smile . . . and shift the tone back to one of teasing and playful banter. And away from . . . whatever the hell had just happened between them. Which was anything but light or playful.

She wondered what he was thinking out there. What had he been feeling while he was taking her like that? What had it meant?

She ducked her chin as a small, wry smile twisted her lips. He was probably just horny after not getting any regular time together with her, and right this very second, he was out there sound asleep with a stupid grin on his impossibly handsome face. And here she was thinking silly, pathetic romance and roses thoughts.

But then she sighed and tipped her head back, and her smile grew into a grin that couldn't be contained or twisted into something else. Maybe she didn't know for sure what had been going through his mind during the last half hour, but that didn't change what had felt like a life-altering moment for her. Even if, for him, it had just been stupendous sex, for her it had been once-in-a-lifetime special. She'd never been made to feel like that, not ever. And she refused to feel foolish for wanting to cherish the moment, savor the memory of it. Even if it was destined to never be repeated, she had that one time. And, oh my word, was it ever going to be memorable.

Pushing away from the sink she stood, rolled her shoulders, and turned and finger-raked her hopelessly snarled hair as she stared defiantly at her reflection. "Living in the moment. That's what I'm all about." She gave up on the hair, thinking maybe she could con Brett into going down and starting dinner while she ducked into her own room and did a better job of making herself look like she hadn't just been thoroughly ravished before his friend arrived. Her defiant expression dissolved into another helpless grin. "Except you were just thoroughly ravished. And you loved it."

She turned away from the mirror and opened the bathroom door, bracing herself for whatever was going to come at her next, only to find Brett sitting on the side of the bed, his back to her, with his cell phone propped against his ear.

"Right, no. That's fine, just . . . are you sure you're okay?"

Kirby leaned in the doorway, not wanting to intrude, but other than ducking back into the bathroom, having nowhere else to go at the moment. So she hung back and let him finish.

"Tomorrow then? Okay, I'll be over in the morning anyway for a meeting, we'll—okay. Right. Night." He clicked off his phone, stared at it for a moment, and shook his head and tossed it on the nightstand.

"Everything okay?"

He looked over his shoulder, his expression more bemused than anything. "Actually, I was just about to come in there and find that out for myself when my phone rang. That was Dan. He begged off dinner, claimed jet lag. He figured he'd enjoy room service and then crash. I invited him over for tomorrow, but whatever works with your schedule is fine with me. I was thinking maybe a late lunch after I get done with what I hope is the last coordination meeting in the morning. It's only supposed to last an hour or so, but they get to talking and you know how it is."

She just stood there, taking him in, in all of his ridiculously casual glory, and marveled all over again that this was—that he was—somehow part of her day-to-day world. She had no idea what stupid expression was on her face, but he gradually trailed off as he realized she was not participating in the conversation but just staring at him. Standing naked in the bathroom doorway, arms folded, just . . . looking her fill. What would her life be like if this really was an everyday part of her normal routine?

She watched him get up and walk toward her, equally unconcerned about his magnificent nakedness, a hint of that mischievous twinkle glinting in his eyes, an amused curve to his lips . . . and thought there was no such thing as a life that was this perfect. No one was that much of a lucky son of a bitch.

"I have no idea what that cat-and-canary smile is on your face for," he said, his voice still all deliciously gravelly, "but if it's because you're thinking anything like what I'm thinking, I say last one to the hot, pulsing shower spa is a rotten egg."

Then he made her squeal by darting forward and tugging her from her resting spot, snagging her around the waist and carting her into the bathroom and straight into the shower before setting her down again.

"What if I don't want to—"

"Duck or get sprayed." He flipped on the water levers and the three big shower heads all burst into life at the same time, just as she dove behind his back to keep from getting hit full force in the face. And to think the drenching shower spas had been her idea.

Although as the water turned hotter and the steam started to rise, she had to admit it had been a pretty damn good one.

"Mmm," was as articulate as she could get as the pulsing spray thrummed along her back and shoulders.

Brett turned and pulled her into his arms so they were both positioned in a way to get the maximum effect from the opposite end shower heads. "Agreed," he said, and tipped up her chin to kiss her. "Did I mention that I miss you?"

She smiled against his wet mouth as water beat down on her head and ran down her cheeks. She was certain she had nothing on a drowned rat at the moment, but since he didn't seem to care, neither did she. "I think you made that pretty clear a few moments ago," she said. "Almost tempting to go a few more days apart just to see what that reunion would be like, but I'm not sure I could survive the bliss."

He chuckled, and when she blinked the water from her lashes to look at him, she could only think how purely happy he looked. She knew what that felt like.

"Kirby," he said, turning her just slightly so he blocked the water from her head and face. "Bliss is exactly what I'm feeling right now."

"Good to know the shower spa was a wise investment, then."

He smiled but ran his fingertips over her lips, making her shudder and her body leap right back to life again, which should have been anatomically impossible at that moment. But clearly was not.

"I wasn't talking about the shower spa, wonderful as it is. I was talking about you. Us. This."

She blinked a few more times, though it wasn't water from the shower getting in her lashes this time. He really wasn't going to do this now, here. Was he? The "it's been incredible and you're amazing, I'm going to miss you" speech? Now? Here? She wasn't ready. Not yet. Not so soon after . . .

"Kirby," he said, his finger still pressed to the fullest part of her bottom lip.

Which was now quivering, despite her best efforts not to. God, seriously, and she was supposedly the mature one here?

His expression had grown serious. "What's wrong? Too much, too soon? I know it's a lot, but I can't . . . I mean, I know I should probably pull back, go slow, or more slowly, but . . . God, there's just so much there. So much more than I thought. And today . . . it all kind of came together and crystallized, and I couldn't wait to tell you about it. That's when I knew. I mean, I thought I knew before, missing you, wanting to be here more than anywhere else, all of it. But I couldn't figure out the rest of the bigger picture. Until today."

"What are you talking about?" she said, pulling his hand down but unable to make herself pull away when he simply wove his fingers through hers. "Is this that thing you wanted to talk about before?"

"It is. Only I was picturing telling you all about it over a quiet dinner, with wine and candles and no interruptions. Somehow we ended up here instead."

"Imagine that," she said dryly, and not unkindly. He was too excited about whatever the hell it was he had to tell her for her to be upset, even if she was going to come out the loser at the end of it all. He was simply too pure, too genuine, and what you saw with Brett Hennessey was definitely what you got. And it was just so much. And all so good.

How could she be upset? So what if it felt like one good tap and her heart would shatter into a million tiny pieces? She'd put it back together and move on. She was a champ at moving on. It was just . . . for all she thought she'd loved before, or wanted to love, nothing had come close to tapping into the part of her that Brett had so effortlessly reached with just a smile, a laugh, a twinkle in the eye. Could she have fallen that hard, that fast? She would have said no . . . but it was hard to break a heart that hadn't been given.

"I found a house," he said, looking like a kid on Christmas morning.

"You—what?" She hadn't a clue what he was going to say, except that wasn't even close to it. "Were you looking for one?"

"No. I took off today, on my bike, so I could get away from the resort, the folks, everything, and just try and sort out what I wanted."

"Hasn't that been the point of your whole journey?"

"Yes . . . but this is the first time I was finally in a place that I didn't want to leave."

Her heart started thumping, so loudly that between the shower and the thrumming in her ears, she couldn't hear him. "You . . . want to stay? Here?"

The ultimate grin that had been on his face a mere moment ago froze for a second, then faded. "I—maybe I presumed too much. I should have talked to you first, I know, it was just . . . you'd rather I not stay?"

Her eyes widened. "No! I mean"—she paused, trying to calm herself down before she blew this—"I knew you probably wouldn't, so I've been sort of trying to keep myself prepared for when you left. You've been here longer than I thought in the beginning, because of the event, and it's made it really difficult to not . . ." She trailed off, knowing if she tried to explain even a fraction of her growing feelings for him, he would run fast and far. And she wouldn't blame him. No one spouted stuff like that only a few weeks after meeting someone. Even if they had pretty much been living together since about eight hours after laying eyes on one another.

God, when she thought it through like that it all sounded more than a little crazy and unstable. Only it had always felt anything but. Being with him, from the very first moment, had been easy and good and normal. And perfect.

He tipped her chin up so their gazes met.

"It's been too good to be true," she told him. "And I'm not the same lucky son of a bitch you are. Stuff like that doesn't generally go the way I'd like it to."

There was so much in his expression she didn't know if she dared allow herself to believe in it. There was hope, and joy, and this kind of deep well of affection she'd never seen directed at her, not like this.

"Well, I am. And I know when to hold and when to fold." He tugged her closer. "Kirby, I know I rolled into town and into your life without so much as a plan for my own. Not the best of situations to get yourself tangled up with, given how hard you've worked to get where you are to put roots down here. I knew I wanted to put down roots, to start building something to last a lifetime . . . I just didn't know it would be here. And I didn't know it would be with you."

Okay, now her heart was simply going to burst. "What are you saying?"

"Were you planning on my leaving?"

"I thought it was a given."

"How would you feel if I didn't? If I stayed? I'm not saying I have to stay here, underfoot. I know we've kind of gone about this whole thing backward, and I'm not asking for some kind of commitment up front. Okay, maybe that's wrong, maybe I am.

Because I don't want to share you. Or wait. But I am willing to work from the start, and build on this the right way. Whatever the hell way that is."

"What are you saying, Brett?"

"I'm saying I want to stay here. I know what I want to do, and I've already found the first step in making it happen."

"The house?"

"Not just any house. Kirby, wait until you see it. I wanted so badly for you to be there when I discovered it. I want your advice and input. In fact, I'd like you to help me with the whole project."

"Project?"

He tipped his head back and let the water thrum on his face; then he shook it off and looked back at her. "I know I'm not making any sense."

She shook her head slowly, but that smile, that same one that wouldn't go away in the bathroom earlier when she wanted so badly to get her perspective back, spread across her face again. "But you're awfully damn cute about whatever it is that's got you so excited. And to answer the one question you did ask that I did understand . . ." She reached up and cupped his cheek with her hand and slid it around so that her fingers wove into the wet curls plastered against the back of his neck. "I don't mind you staying. Here, in this other place, in a tent for all I care. But no," she said softly, "I definitely don't mind you staying."

Then she pulled his head down and kissed him, hoping he felt the commitment he was wanting from her. Because while she might be thoroughly confused on his plans for his future, she knew the one thing she absolutely wanted in hers.

Chapter 16

Brett worked on the sauce while Kirby chopped vegetables. "This is kind of how I imagined it would be. When I let myself think about things like that. As a kid, I mean."

Kirby looked up from her studious attempt at slicing tomatoes. "Like what would be?"

"Home life. Partnership life."

"I take it you didn't have this kind of life, then? Fixing dinners in the kitchen, that sort of thing?"

He shook his head and stirred the sauce again. "I grew up in and around casinos."

"We're more alike than you think. I grew up in a ski resort."

"Your folks ran one?"

She shook her head. "No, I got abandoned in the restroom of one."

His eyes popped wide and he stopped stirring. "What? When? How old were you?"

"Old enough to walk, but too little to remember any of it."

"What happened?"

"Well, it was a small resort town, and one of the ladies that worked in the food concession part took me in. The closest protective services kind of thing was hours away in Denver, so . . ." She shrugged. "They kind of adopted me. Not formally or anything. But someone made sure I had food and a place to sleep. Dottie was in her sixties—she was the first one to take care of me—and eventually got to where she couldn't really keep up. Then I stayed with—" She tilted her head. "Gosh, I don't even know the whole list at this point, but honestly I really lived at the resort. I was kind of like the mascot or something."

"And no one ever came and got you out of there?"

She shook her head. "Honestly, Brett, it's not hard to fall through the cracks when no one knows you exist."

"They never found out who your mother was?"

"No. When I was thirteen and all angst-ridden like most teenagers, I thought about trying to figure it out, but since I wasn't formally abandoned no search had ever been done and that many years later it was doubtful anyone would ever figure it out. One thing that was for sure was that she never came back to find out."

"Did you wish that she would?"

Kirby went back to slicing tomatoes. "When I was really little, and I figured out how families were supposed to work from watching the folks who came to stay at the resort, I used to wonder, make up stories, and think if I just stayed there she'd always know where to find me." Kirby slid the chopped tomatoes onto the top of the tossed salad greens. "But eventually I got over that. Along with the fairy tale that one of the rich, foreign families would come to stay at the resort would fall in love with me and insist that I come back home with them. To their castle, of course. I'd have a title, at least. And my own pony."

She laughed and shook her head. "Honestly, for the most part, I liked how I grew up. I mean, there were times when I was ashamed a little, or felt bad." She smiled over at him. "They used to dress me from lost-and-found stuff, and I remember thinking that if I could just get two mittens that matched, then people wouldn't know I came from an untraditional home." She laughed. "Like that was the only clue."

Brett was listening, certain his mouth was still hanging open. It was hard to believe this bright, articulate, witty, gorgeous woman had grown up in such a vagabond lifestyle. Maybe that explained her self-assurance. And also why she might have stayed with her former lover for so long, with only a promise of a ring.

"You could have easily passed for royalty," he said, unthinkingly uttering the first thought that had come to mind.

She looked surprised for a moment, then glanced away again, blinking a few times.

He sat his spoon down and crossed the kitchen, laying his hand over her wrist until she put the knife down, then turned her into his arms and tipped up her chin. "I always thought you were."

"Would that be when I was hanging from a tree, or when I had a kitten attached to my midsection?"

He smiled and leaned down to kiss her. "Always."

When he lifted his head a few moments later, she had that bemused look on her face again. Like she was trying hard to figure out if it was okay or not. If he was okay or not. He knew, without doubt, she was attracted, and she'd made it clear, up in the shower, that she was happy he was going to stick around a while, but since they'd come down to start making dinner, he'd catch her looking at him with this considering look in her eyes.

Which made the anxious knot in his stomach only wrench more tightly as he imagined telling her the rest of the news he'd only begun upstairs. She wanted him, but maybe only temporarily. And his thoughts were already racing well past that.

But maybe, given what she'd just revealed, and how her last love affair had gone, maybe she simply refused to think in anything but temporary measures. What she'd started here, what she'd built was clearly meant to last, to be a solid future. But perhaps she saw that future alone. She'd said as much, early on.

Would she take a chance? Play the hand despite the odds?

"I have a pretty unconventional background, too," he reminded her.

"Did your parents run a casino?" she asked, smiling as she rephrased his earlier question.

"Actually, my mother was a showgirl. I haven't a clue who

my father was." Her gaze sharpened on his and he suddenly realized why she'd gone back to chopping vegetables as she'd told
him about her childhood. Clearly she'd long since come to terms
with how she'd been raised, and she had even spoken about it
pretty fondly. But that didn't mean it was easy to share with someone else. Perhaps someone whose opinion might matter to her.

And as much as that thought brought a little unknotting to
the anxiety he was feeling, it didn't help that he had to bear his
soul in the same way with her. He'd also come to terms with it,
but it mattered to him what she would think. "She was also a
prostitute. And a drug addict."

Kirby's mouth shaped a little "o" and her eyes filled with sadness. "Was it just the two of you?"

He nodded. "Until I was about nine. Then we moved into the
boarding house, the one Vanetta runs, that I told you about.
Vanetta couldn't do much at the time, but she went easier on my
mom when she couldn't come up with rent. She'd stopped per-
forming by the time I was twelve. Her lifestyle was taking a toll
on her body and her looks, at least by her bosses' standards. By
then I was already playing cards, working odd jobs at the casinos to make money. Mom, uh . . . well, there were more men
coming around. Vanetta put a stop to that when she found out,
but that just meant that Mom was gone all the time instead. I'd
have to go find her . . ." he trailed off, realizing that Kirby didn't
need to hear the gory details. It was bad enough that he'd had to
deal with finding a parent who'd oftentimes been left beaten up,
or was strung out. He didn't think back to those days much, if
at all, anymore. "She died when I was fourteen. Overdose.
Vanetta kind of did what your friends at the resort did. Made
sure I had food, clothes, that I went to school, though that was
never a chore. I loved school."

"Me, too," Kirby said, the light of true kinship in her eyes.
"It was the most normal thing in my world. And taught me how
big the real world really is. It gave me such a better perspective
of what my possibilities were. I would have stayed there twenty-
four-seven if I could have."

"That's exactly how I felt. Well, there and at the casino. Even though I knew the latter part probably wasn't healthy, it was home for me."

"Maybe the resort wasn't quite the same, in terms of not being so great an environment for a child. But I know what you mean, it was home to me, too."

"Except I never left the casino life, while you grew up to build your own version of home."

She laughed. "Right, where people still come and go and nothing is permanent. But a permanent home for me, I guess."

He leaned back to look into her eyes. "We do what we know. I know cards. You know resorts."

She lifted a shoulder. "Makes sense, I guess."

"If things had gone differently with . . . what was his name?"

"Patrick."

"Right. Say he had married you, been partners at work, partners at home. Would you still have wanted this?" He gestured to the room around them, and what lay beyond.

"You mean did I want the more traditional home? Babies, a puppy, nine-to-five day job, that kind of thing?"

"Yes. I know the resort was never going to be nine-to-five, but you know what I mean."

"I do, and I don't know. Patrick had other properties, but the resort was his baby. We lived on premises, very nice premises, but . . . that was home. A very familiar one to me, of course, though certainly more posh than the one I grew up in."

"Were you happy? Doing that, I mean?"

"I was certainly good at it, given my background. But . . . I don't know that I yearned for the white picket fence world, really. We never really got that far and my life didn't really ever seem suited quite for that. But I did know that if I could do whatever I wanted, I wanted to take what I knew about running hotels and run my own smaller place. Intimate, personal—mine. I think it was maybe my way of combining what I knew with what I wanted to have."

"And now you have."

"Trying to, anyway."

"Is it what you wanted?"

She didn't answer right away. "Yes, and no. Yes, Pennydash Inn is exactly what I wanted, and I love the place. I had pictured being in the West, because my vision didn't extend beyond that, but being here feels very right to me. Possibly because of how things ended out west, starting over truly fresh was not only practical financially here, but emotionally a good move, too."

"And the no part?"

"I'm finding there are things I'm not as personally good at, I guess, as I thought I might be. But I suppose that's to be expected. At least I tell myself that."

"Like?"

"Well, I do like running my own ship, and I like being out from under any kind of corporate presence, both business-wise and personally. So, small, intimate, mine, is definitely the right thing for me. And I'm good with people, though I know I haven't had the chance to prove that so much yet, but I know that's going to be a good fit with me. That's not something I doubted."

"Folks in town like you; you have earned respect here. At least from what I'm hearing as I'm putting together the event."

She smiled more brightly. "Really? That's nice to hear. I've felt very welcomed here, but it's always nice to know I'm not just imagining that part."

"Definitely not. So . . . what's the no part, then?"

"Maybe I'm not as, I don't know . . . proprietary isn't the right word, because I feel that and am that in all senses of the word. Maybe more maternal? That doesn't seem like the right term, either, but . . . I think it's more like . . . when you talk about Vanetta, she sounds nurturing. My 'aunt'—Frieda—is the same. Did Vanetta have kids of her own?"

Brett shook his head. "Married a couple of times, but no. Her boarders are her babies, so she is fond of saying."

"See, I guess I thought it would be that way for me. But despite feeling strongly about this being my place and putting my stamp on it, the business part is really just business to me. I love having guests, making them happy, getting to know them . . . but I don't know that it goes beyond that. Not sure what that says about me, but . . ."

"Did you and Patrick discuss having a family? Do you feel that you missed out on that?"

"We did in a general sense. It was important to him to have someone to carry on the family name, but I never got the impression that he was all that interested in personally being a father."

"And you?"

"I didn't know what kind of parent I would make. Frankly, the idea terrified me for most of my twenties. I'm sure any shrink would tell me it's because of my upbringing and they'd very probably be right. We were both pretty career focused, so it was an easy discussion to put off."

"And now? Any regrets?"

She started to say something, then stopped. "What about you? You're still in that stage where families get started."

"You're forty, not eighty. Families can start at any time."

Her look instantly shuttered, though she held his gaze. "Is that a goal of yours? I mean, it's the natural thing, so not surprising, just—"

"Kirby, I have the same fears as you do, for probably even more reasons than you do. And I definitely don't want to know what any shrink would tell me about the long-lasting effects of my childhood. I think it was a triumph just to get myself raised. I don't know that I was ever anxious about raising anyone else. Don't let that spook you, okay?"

"I wasn't spooked—okay," she added, when he gave her a look that said he clearly knew otherwise. "Maybe a little, but it's a knee-jerk reaction. You see, I was worried about it, but not anymore. I—I can't have kids."

"No?"

She shook her head. "Not by choice. It's a long story, but I found out about eight years ago that I have a few genetic issues that make carrying a baby pretty much impossible."

"Did Patrick know about it?"

She nodded. "He was with me when I found out. We had—well, we had a little pregnancy scare once. I'd missed a few months, but the home tests were negative, so I made an appointment to find out what was going on. Turns out my plumbing isn't exactly normal. Anyway, I was fine, but the end result was finding out that I probably won't ever get pregnant."

"How did he take the news?"

"Well, or so I thought. I mean, like I said, he had made a big deal out of carrying on the family name. He mentioned adopting a few times, but we quickly got absorbed back into our work lives and it never really came up again."

He ducked down to keep her gaze when she would have glanced away. "But?"

"But nothing; there's nothing more to tell. I know it makes me sound like less than a woman, maybe, to say that I'm okay with that future. I never ruled out adoption, but then things turned out like they did, I moved here . . . I'm forty now, and . . . well, I made peace with it."

"What else?"

"Nothing else." She finally sighed when he kept staring. "Okay, okay, so the personal assistant he was with when I walked in on them . . . they're married. She's already had their first child by now, at least I assume so since she was pregnant when I left Colorado."

"Ah. Fresh start a few thousand miles away. Good choice."

"I thought so."

"I'm sorry."

"Don't be. Things tend to work out the way they do for a reason. I don't know that I'd have ever stepped out from his shadow to build my own life. Now we both apparently have what we wanted. It's not a bad thing, Brett."

And it was clear that she meant it.

"I just didn't—"

"Want the pity party. I know. That's not you. And, for what it's worth, I'm kind of glad it worked out like it did, too." He snugged her closer against his body. "Purely selfishly speaking."

She giggled, which made him smile in return. He framed her face with his hands and kissed her. "I guess we're both a couple of misfits, finding our own place," he said.

"Something like that, I guess."

"I like this place, Kirby. Your space. You. This. All of it. I couldn't have said what it was that was going to make me feel content, or at peace. Or excited about life. About what I was going to do next. I should have never stayed in that world as long as I did, but I didn't know where to go. I just knew where I wasn't going. And that was into business with Dan."

"The guy who came to see you?"

"Mmm hmm," he said, bussing her on the nose, then hopping over to the stove when his sauce started to boil. "Turns out he's not as happy for me as I thought he was."

"Oh?" Kirby had picked up her knife again, but put it right back down. "In what way?"

"He was thinking I'd get over this . . . ennui, or whatever you want to call it, and come back and work with him. I worked for his dad as a kid, and with him off and on the whole time I was playing cards. His dad retired about five years ago, moved to Palm Springs. Dan runs their home building and construction company now. And though I enjoy aspects of it, it's not really want I wanted to do full time, or how I wanted to make use of my degrees."

"Which are?"

"Architecture and design theory."

"There wasn't a way to join his world to yours? They sound related."

"Not the type of business he does, no. And . . . frankly, maybe I always knew that I wanted to get out of the desert, take on a new challenge. Vegas and the surrounding counties aren't exactly known for their architectural brilliance, at least beyond the magnificence of the resort casinos. And I don't have any interest in commercial building."

"What did you want to do?"

"That's just it. I only knew what I didn't want to do. And I guess Dan thought he knew me better than I did, and figured I'd finally realize that I was destined to work with him. Things aren't apparently going so well right now, and I've offered to help him out, but he's too proud to accept a loan, much less an outright gift."

"I understand the feeling."

He smiled briefly. "I know you do. And I've tried to be more discreet and creative in the way I offered help, but . . . let's just say it was a sore subject which has been closed for a long time."

"Until this morning?"

He nodded.

"I'm sorry."

He looked over, surprised.

"It's obviously eating away at you. You're a nurturer, Brett. You take care of people. You want to help Dan because you love him. He can't accept your help because it makes him feel less of a man, less of an equal. I don't know what it's like being in Vegas with you, where you're like some kind of rock star poker legend, but I'm guessing it can't be easy on him. So . . . I guess I kind of understand where he's coming from. But it's a shame he can't see the rest, about your future, I mean. Have you told him?"

"About?"

"The rest, whatever it was you discovered today. About the house and whatever that means to you."

"I told him about you."

She looked up; now she was the one with the surprised expression. "You did?"

He nodded. "I wanted him to meet you. And for you to meet him. It's important to me."

"Do you think that's part of why he begged off tonight? I mean, first you turn him down on going back to work with him and I'm guessing he see's me as an obstacle to that." Her eyes widened. "Oh, wow, the charity event. He knows you're helping me? I mean, not directly, but in finding a way to drive guests to the area, to the inn?"

"Not the particulars, but yes."

"It's no wonder he stayed away." She put her knife down. "Maybe you should go over there, talk to him. Spend the evening hanging out, get room service or go out." She lifted a shoulder and smiled that half smile of hers. "Be anywhere other than here playing house with me."

She'd said it affectionately, easily. But that's what they were doing. Playing house. Only he didn't want to play at it. Not forever, anyway. *Slowly, Hennessey. She's had a lot of experience with temporary. Let her get used to the idea of you becoming permanent.* Hell, he still needed to get used to the idea. There was no need to rush anything, anyway. She wasn't going anywhere, and neither was he. She'd realize that sooner or later. He would find his niche here. And it if it was all meant to be, it would all figure itself out in time.

So there was absolutely no reason for him to switch off the burner, cross the short distance to the counter where she was chopping, put her knife down, then scoop her up against his chest and kiss the daylights out of her. But that's exactly what he wanted to do . . . so that's exactly what he did.

"What was that all about?" she said, half laughing, half out of breath when he finally let her feet slide to the floor.

"That is because this is amazingly good."

She beamed a smile, her eyes shining with true affection. "It is kinda, isn't it?"

"Thank you," he said, "for suggesting time with Dan. If you're truly okay with it, then I think maybe that's not a bad idea. Can we maybe shoot for lunch together—all three of us—tomorrow? I've got stuff in the morning, but we should be done by noon, or shortly after. If you want, maybe come up to the resort and we'll have lunch there? I don't mean for you to do any extra work."

"You just don't want to risk me cooking for him," she teased. "Which, good plan. But I think this salad will keep until tomorrow, so maybe that, some ham sandwiches, and I can pick up one of Mrs. Hanson's pies."

He'd been ready to tell her not to take on the extra bother. Until she'd gotten to that pie part. He was a sucker for pie. Which, apparently had shown on his face, because she laughed.

"Strawberry rhubarb. You'll never be the same. Warmed up, with ice cream, it's like sin on a plate."

He moved his pan off the burner and then wiggled his eyebrows at her. "Funny, that's how I think of you."

Her mouth dropped open, then closed, then she rolled her eyes, but there was the most becoming bloom of pink staining her elegantly sculpted cheekbones, he couldn't help but laugh.

She waved him out of the kitchen. "Go on," she said. "I'll clean up here. And if lunch doesn't work out tomorrow, no worries. I'd like to meet him, though, so I hope he's okay with the idea. I'll come to the resort if you think neutral ground is better."

"I'll call you later this evening, let you know for sure." He crossed back to her, eliciting a squeal when he took her by the hips and sat her up on the counter beside the butcher block. He moved between her thighs and took her face in his hands again, planting a kiss that held both the passion he had for her right that second along with the building excitement he had for their potential future. "I want to tell you everything, about the house, my plans. I want you there, for all of it, involved right alongside me."

She still looked a little stunned by the kiss. In a good way. A very good way. "Uh . . . okay. Good," she said, finally finding her voice. "I'll do whatever I can to help."

She still didn't get where he was going with this, that the partnership he wanted with her wasn't about business or friends helping each other out. All of which was wonderful, but the partnership he was interested in was the fully invested one. He knew she'd worked with her ex, so he was going to have to take care in how he presented it to her . . . but if she shared his vision, nothing could stop them.

He kissed her again; then he groaned and pressed his forehead to hers. "I really want to stay. Eat, talk, maybe take another shower." He wiggled his eyebrows again so they tickled her forehead, making her giggle in that way that was coming increasingly more naturally to her.

"The shower's not going anywhere. And neither am I."

Now all he had to do was convince her he wasn't going anywhere, either.

Chapter 17

Brett had tried to reach Dan on his way up to the resort, but he hadn't gotten an answer on the room phone or Dan's cell. He might have been telling the truth about being wiped out and was already asleep, but it wasn't even eight in the evening. And the time change was only two hours. He ducked into the first set of elevators, hoping no one on staff noticed him or any of the early arrivals for the event. One in particular he hoped to avoid. The very last thing he needed at the moment was—

"Ah, Mr. Hennessey, here you are, at last." A beefy hand shot out to prevent the elevator doors from closing. They reopened to show a smiling Maksimov standing just beyond the threshold.

Brett was sorely tempted to hit the CLOSE DOOR button again, but knew he'd have to deal with Maks sooner or later. He'd just been hoping for the latter. He really wanted to talk to Dan, see if the two of them could get back on even ground. That whole situation had really taken him by surprise.

"Could I persuade you to join me in the lounge for a drink? Or perhaps we could talk in your suite, if it's privacy you prefer."

The suite was out. And perhaps a public setting wasn't a bad idea, anyway. "Nothing for me, but let's go ahead and have our little chat." Brett exited the elevator and fell into step beside the much shorter, stockier Russian. "Or we could skip this part and just go right to where I politely decline your offer."

"You haven't even heard me out yet," he said, a smug smile creasing his wide, perpetually shiny face.

"I don't need to. I appreciate the gesture, you coming all the way out here," he said, straining to be polite. He had no real reason to be any longer, other than it was never wise to burn a bridge you didn't have to. "But I'm not coming back to the tables, Maks."

"Except here, where you are playing again."

"It's for charity. One time only. I'm retired and I'm planning on staying that way."

"And yet, there are so many other worthy organizations who could use help from someone like you. Perhaps you have a specific one in mind? We would be happy to help. In fact, I must admit, Rudov wasn't happy when you chose to allow the Bronfield brothers to oversee this event. We have worked tirelessly for you in the past. And we were the first to make you very generous offers when you were starting out."

"And I believe I've filled those very generous coffers back up. Several times, in fact." He paused just outside the entrance to the lobby pub. "I appreciate all you've done for me, as I hope you appreciate what I've done for you in return. I'm working with the Bronfields because they have hotel interests in places other than Vegas and were best suited to handle things this far afield. No personal slight was intended."

Maksimov paused outside the door, and his smile widened as his eyes hardened. This was the more familiar side of Rudov's hired hand that Brett had been hoping to avoid.

"Perhaps you don't understand the offer we are making you."

"I believe I do," Brett responded, hoping the shorter man understood him. "Please tell your boss that I am flattered by the continued attention and his persistence. But I am no longer available, regardless of the beneficiary. If you decide to stay on for the event, I hope you enjoy yourself. But please don't feel as if you have to for appearances' sake. I know Mr. Rudov relies on your assistance, so if your time would be better utilized back in Nevada, I'll certainly understand."

Now even the smile faded. "I don't relish the idea of disappointing Mr. Rudov again. Surely, given your generosity here, you could see your way clear to supporting the good works of a needy organization out west. After all, it is your hometown. Giving back, and all that. We would make the appearance well worth your while, donating your media fees to whatever charity you name." He lifted a hand to stall Brett's reply. "This sport has given you wealth beyond what most could measure."

Brett could have mentioned that he'd earned that money by playing the sport but didn't bother wasting his breath.

"There are others, after you, young and eager."

"Perhaps you should be focusing your largesse on them, then."

"Oh, we are. But it takes time to groom the new talent, expose them properly, build their names. Most don't stay in the sport long enough, and none have shown even a glimmer of your particular talents."

"As you said, it takes time. But better to focus on the future."

"You'd think you would want to be part of that grooming process."

"Perhaps you missed the part where I've given seminars, many for free, for that very purpose, over the past few years. Trying to eliminate the online scam sites and to help bring more organization and a better profile to the sport. I've given at the office, Maks. Now I'm done."

The smile returned now, only it was the kind that made a person's skin crawl. Reptilian, was the word that came to mind. "In this game, in this sport, you are only done when you lose too much to come back. It breaks your heart, this game, and your spirit. That is not the case with you. You will not be walking away, as you claim. Perhaps for a time, but it will bring you back." He reached into his pocket and withdrew a sterling silver business card sleeve. He depressed a button and some hidden mechanism pushed a single, engraved card from one end. He extended the card to Brett. "When that time comes, it is strongly suggested that you contact us first. We will work together again, as we have in the past. It will be good for all concerned."

Brett took the card merely to expedite the end of this little tête-à-tête.

"And you have much to be concerned about, Mr. Hennessey."

Brett had already taken a step back in preparation for heading back to the elevator, glad that their business had been concluded without the whole charade of drinks at the bar. But as he paused and looked back, his gaze narrowed. "Care to explain that comment in more detail?"

"I only meant that there are always those who will rely and depend on you, no matter how far you run. In fact, I believe I noticed one of them here in the hotel, earlier. A friend of yours, I believe. If I'm not mistaken, I believe I overheard him on his phone, while dining a table or two away, looking to find some action on the event this coming weekend. Perhaps he could use your assistance there?"

"I have no idea what you're talking about," Brett said, quite honestly, but the hairs on the back of his neck had prickled a bit at the comment. Maks could be lying to try to get a rise out of him. He wasn't surprised at the veiled comment; it hadn't been the first time. And he hadn't been the only one who was more than a little persistent in trying to woo him back for another round or two. Maks, and his boss, Rudov, were just the only ones he didn't like. Their association had ended a long time ago; though he had played more than a few events at their resort in the intervening years, he'd done no work for them personally in promotion or marketing. Only now that they weren't getting any piece of him did he fully realize to what lengths they were willing to go to get any piece of him back. He could have told Maksimov that that approach alone had already cost him any opportunity that might ever arise. Not that one would.

"Perhaps you should have a little talk with your friend."

Maksimov slid the silver case back inside the breast pocket of his perfectly tailored suit jacket. He lifted a shoulder as if to say that it mattered not to him, one way or the other. "I will be staying through the weekend. We will talk again, I am certain." With that, he tipped a hand to his forehead and turned away from both the pub entrance and the first bank of elevators, strolling through the remainder of the lobby and out the rear doors that led to the private villas.

Brett watched him exit; then he finally turned to the elevators, thankful that no other untimely intrusions occurred, breathing a little sigh of relief when the doors slid shut without further obstruction. He glanced at his watch. Half past. Surely Dan was still up. His friend could nurse a bit of a grudge, but now was not the time to let him wallow in his dissatisfaction. Brett would find some way to make him understand why he'd made the choices he had, and also find some way to help him out. If Maks was telling the truth, then Dan was in far more desperate straights than Brett had realized. Dan would listen to him this time. He wasn't leaving until they had a working solution. To both the business and the friendship issues.

The door opened to the top floor, which housed three suites in this section. His was the larger one at the end of the short hallway. He patted his jacket and realized he'd left the inn without his wallet, which had his other key card in it. So he rapped on the door. "Dan, it's Brett."

He didn't hear anything, but the suite door was thick. Premium rates got you as quiet a room as possible. He knocked again, harder this time. "Dan," he said again, as loud as he dared without risking annoying the other occupants of the floor. He wasn't entirely sure there were any, but thought it best to err on caution's side.

He was just considering heading back down to the lobby for another key, willing to risk pissing his friend off further by letting himself into the room, when the door cracked open. The safety latch was in place.

"Not exactly a hotbed of crime here, you know," he said lightly. "You want to let me in?"

It was dark beyond the small crack of doorway. "I thought we agreed to put this off a day. I'm beat."

He also wasn't showing his face. "What's going on, Dan?"

"Sleep. Or it was, anyway. Till you came banging. Shoulda gotten my own room. What, she kick you out or something?"

"No, I came to talk to you. About . . . well, everything."

"Can't it wait until I get some sleep?"

He either sounded extremely fatigued or a little drunk. Or both. He and Dan had shared a few beers after a particularly grueling workday, but neither of them were drinkers by nature. So he didn't really know what to think. Had he really been that upset? Or were things just that bad? He remembered what Maksimov had told him downstairs. Not that he'd put it past the man to lie, but Brett had a niggling suspicion there was more to that story. "Come on, it's not even nine p.m., which makes it seven back in Vegas. You're not that jet lagged. I thought we could take some time before the true craziness descends in the next day or two to catch up and maybe talk things through a little."

He waited. Dan didn't say anything, but he didn't close the door in Brett's face.

"I feel like I'm standing out here begging for a nightcap; come on."

He thought he heard a short snort. Then the door closed, but just long enough for the safety latch to come off. When the door swung back open, Dan was holding the knob but standing just behind the door in his boxers.

"Mind if we turn a light on in here?"

Dan's response was a short grunt. Fortunately Brett's hand was already reaching for the light switch before the door shut behind him, sinking them both into full darkness. A moment later, soft lighting on low tables situated just beyond the foyer area flickered on, bathing the stylishly decorated main room in a warm glow. Perfect mood setting for that late-night date a guy might bring back to the room, but not much to go on for a regular conversation. He moved into the living area and reached down to turn on one of the end table lamps.

"Can we just—not," Dan finished lamely, as Brett switched on the more high powered lamp.

He turned to see Dan squinting in the sudden light, holding his hand up like a shield. But not shield enough to keep Brett from seeing the nasty bruise on his cheek and the split at the corner of his mouth.

"What the hell happened to you?"

"Ran into a door," he retorted. "Can I get you a beer? Why the hell not," he answered himself, "you're paying for them. Did you know they stock the damn fridge? And I don't mean the minibar. I don't think this room even has one of those." He scuffed bare feet across the thick carpeting as he headed into the more dimly lit kitchen area. It was more a wet bar with a Jenn-air in the middle, and a full-size Sub-zero fridge lodged at one end, then it was a full-fledged kitchen, but it screamed luxury nonetheless. "Wait, what am I saying?" he added dryly as he opened the fridge door, ducking his head a little at the bright interior light. "Of course you know they stock the fridge. You're used to this shit. How in the hell you're tired of the shit, I have no idea. Pretty sweet deal," he added, fishing out two long necks and closing the door with an audible sigh. He grabbed a dish towel and screwed the tops off. "Of course, I guess there's the irony that you score the best free stuff when you can actually afford to pay for it, but why go there?"

Brett was still standing by the couch, watching his friend. Who was clearly at least a little drunk, and definitely no less bitter than he'd left him a few hours before. Possibly more so. "Some door," he said, gesturing to Dan's face with the bottle he'd just been handed.

Dan turned and flopped down in the nearest chair, propping his feet up on the engraved crystal surface of the free form hardwood coffee table now situated between them.

Brett took the couch and propped his feet as well. He took a slow pull from the bottle, trying to figure out the best way to ease into any semblance of rational, constructive conversation. "Ran into Maksimov," he said, deciding that perhaps it was better to start neutral and wind his way back around to the real topic at hand.

"I'm sure he's been laying in wait for you," Dan said, the accompanying chuckle carrying more than a little edge. "He try and woo you back like I said?" He took another pull.

Brett noticed he wasn't maintaining any kind of eye contact; rather he was looking at the bottle, or staring at his feet. "At least, and then some."

"And you said?"

"No. I told you that."

Dan lifted a shoulder in a negligent shrug that said he really couldn't care less. But Brett wasn't so sure about that. He watched Dan start to pick at the label on the bottle, the digging motions proving there was more than a little tension beneath the lazy, drunken sprawl he'd adopted.

"Folks change their minds all the time."

Brett understood the unspoken challenge. "I didn't change my mind. Not about Maksimov. And not about coming back to work with you. I never told you I would. You do know that."

Dan snorted. "You've only done two things in your life. Play poker and work for my dad, then me. When you gave up poker, what the hell was I supposed to think you were gonna do, huh? Of course I thought you'd come over full time. Hell, I was all ready to propose a partnership. I know you want to design shit, with those degrees you have and all. I was willing to accommodate that."

"I don't want to design homes in the desert."

"What, not good enough for the likes of you now?"

"You know better than that. It's just not the challenge I want."

"And what the hell is?"

Brett thought about telling him, about the property he'd found today, about the business idea that had sprung, almost fully formed and too stunningly perfect to be anything but exactly the right thing for him to do. Or at least try. But that business plan involved him . . . and Kirby. Probably not the best time to spring that tidbit on his oldest and dearest friend.

Then another thought occurred to him. Wouldn't have ever crossed his mind before, but that was before he understood the reality Dan was facing. Personally and professionally. What if . . .

"Maybe I'm the one with a proposition for you?"

Dan let his feet slide off the table and thump to the floor as he shoved himself out of the chair and scuffed back to the kitchen for another beer. "I already told you. Not interested."

"I'm not offering a handout, or a loan for that matter. I'm offering a new business venture opportunity."

Dan screwed off the lid of the beer and turned around, facing him fully for the first time.

Brett had to work not to wince as he caught the full scope of the damage someone had done to Dan's face.

"What kind of opportunity?" He lifted his beer in a warning gesture. "Patronize me and I'll kick your sorry, over-educated ass. So you better have a straight plan in mind and not some elaborate scheme to dump some of your money in my bank account. I work for what I have. We might not all have freak talent like you do, but I'm damn proud of what I built, what my father did before me. That means something."

He crossed back into the room and dropped heavily back into the chair, wincing a little as he propped his feet up once again. Giving up all pretenses of pretending his face hadn't been beat all to hell, he rolled the cold bottle over his cheek and groaned a little. "Go on," he said when Brett simply sat there and watched. "I'm not gonna keel over from a little thump to the head. You know it's hard. Take a lot more than a fast fist to put me down."

"You gonna tell me what really happened?"

"Well, obviously, I got in a little fight. It was nothing. Don't worry about it." He propped the beer on his stomach. "Go on.

What's this amazing new deal all about? Funny how you didn't mention it this afternoon, but go on, I'm all ears."

Dan was a little drunk, more than a little pissed off, and a whole lot hurt. So Brett tried to rein in his own temper. He also tried not to feel sad. Dan didn't deserve his pity. What he deserved was a good friend who could find a way out of whatever mess he'd gotten himself into.

"Actually, all the pieces just started falling into place today. Before I ran into you," he added. "It's still in the idea stage, but I think it has real potential."

Dan tried and failed to maintain his look of casual disinterest. His body was still slouched in the chair, feet and beer propped, but his eyes had lasered in quite directly on Brett's now.

Brett wondered if he was more impaired by alcohol or the fight he'd gotten into. Dan wasn't what anyone would call a hothead. He wasn't a gambler, either, that Brett knew about anyway. Running a football pool with some of his employees was about the extent of it. Dan had never gotten into the casino life, leaving that to Brett. He worked long hours, rarely took a full day off, and never took vacations. The occasional strip club night out with some of his crew maybe, but that's about it.

In fact, if he wasn't sitting there with a face that had been used as a punching bag, Brett would have discounted Maksimov's comments as nothing other than trying to stir up some trouble to see what might shake loose.

"Well?" Dan prodded. "You gonna tell me what's got your designer knickers all knotted up or not?"

"They're Levi's," Brett said, trying harder not to get exasperated. He and Dan had their moments, but this was a snide side he'd never heard. "So, I found an old log cabin, up in the hills on a ride today. Falling down, abandoned, lot totally overgrown. Then, on the way down, I passed by an old farmhouse, barn, silo. Beautiful creek running through the property, wide open spaces. Looks like it's been empty for some time now, too."

"Fascinating. What has this got to do with us?"

"It got me to thinking, with the resort newly opened, over time, there will be a need for vacation housing, time-shares, as well as full-time homes for people who are drawn into the growing development, that kind of thing."

"You mean the kind of thing we already have in Vegas?"

"I don't want to build tract housing. Even ridiculously over-the-top Liberace mansion tract housing. I'm talking smaller, intimate, one-of-a-kind places, unique in structure and suited to the landscape here, both mountain and valley." He leaned forward, excited now that he'd finally gotten to tell someone. Saying it out loud wasn't nearly as terrifying as he'd thought it would be. In fact, it was quite the opposite. He was really going to do this. It had already grabbed his heart. "I want to work with what's already here, as well as build new."

"And you think I should take the company that my dad spent his lifetime building, that I inherited, and what, chuck it? Sell it? Move east? Holy hell, Brett, what has this chick done to your brain?" He made a little crazy motion next to his head with the beer bottle. "No, seriously, are you even listening to yourself? I'm asking you to come home—home, bro—and work side-by-side with me, and you turn me down flat. Now you have the nerve to invite me to what . . . work for you? Are you fucking serious?" He downed the beer in one swig and stood, albeit a bit unsteadily. "I'm going to bed. Frankly, I don't care what the hell you do. But as of this moment, I think it's safe to say you can officially leave me out of it. Thanks for nothing." And with that, he tossed the empty beer bottle in the general vicinity of the kitchen, where it bounced from counter to floor—thankfully not shattering—before stalking off to the master bedroom and kicking the double doors shut behind him.

Brett sat, perfectly still, on the couch opposite where Dan had just been sitting, wondering what in the hell had happened to his best friend since he'd left Vegas. That was not the Dan he knew and loved. Granted, maybe he should have thought through his presentation a little bit better, given the status of their relationship when he'd shown up this evening. Hell, he hadn't even been thinking of Dan when the idea had hatched in his head. He'd been thinking of Kirby, and partnering her into the business using her excellent interior design skills. What she'd done with the inn, the personal touches, the local flourishes, the natural warmth she'd created . . . that's how he pictured these places.

He'd design and do the reno, she'd design and decorate the interior, then they'd sell it and move on to the next project. His biggest concern was whether she'd want to take on something like that while running the inn, but he figured his busy season would be her slow season, so perhaps it would be the perfect partnership. He'd help her out in the winter with the inn and guests; she'd jump in with him in the spring and summer.

He hadn't really thought about Dan, or bringing him in, until just about thirty minutes ago. The truth of it was, he really wanted a fresh start, and he wanted to share this new adventure with Kirby. He wanted a break from his past. Not to abandon it, but to move forward. He'd always love Dan, Vanetta, and the rest of the friends he'd made back in Nevada.

But here . . . this was where he wanted to be now. And he'd meant what he'd started to say, he hadn't thought about it, but now that he was, yes, he'd take Dan on, too, form some kind of partnership. If Dan were remotely acting like Dan, anyway. They would make a good team in this endeavor. Dan's strengths were in building solid structures with solid craftsmanship. Brett could design and help with construction, but Dan would make the perfect site manager and project foreman.

He acknowledged that his offer had been seen as an insult, and he even got where Dan was coming from. He'd been clumsy, at best, thoughtless at worst, in presenting it to him as he had. He didn't know what to tell Dan about his dad's company, or where he should go. Maybe Dan needed a fresh start, too. Though good luck convincing his deeply entrenched, routine-loving best friend of that possibility.

He spent a few more minutes considering if there was a way

to expand on the Vegas business and just branch it out. He thought about what Kirby had said, about it being hard on Dan to have a friend who was a well-known celebrity, that his ego could only take so much. So he'd make Dan a full partner in this new endeavor so it didn't come off sounding like he was offering Dan a job in his own damn industry, the one place where Dan was supposed to have the leverage and expertise in their friendship.

He hung his head and let the tension roll from his shoulders. Then he knocked back the rest of the beer before getting up and retrieving the other bottle, throwing them both in the trash.

He let himself quietly out of the suite, trying to decide what the best next step would be. But though the ride down in the elevator didn't bring any answers regarding his friend, he did know what the next step was going to be with Kirby.

Smiling despite still feeling deeply unsettled about the situation with Dan, he climbed on his bike and headed home.

Chapter 18

Kirby carted the last load of quilts and bedspreads through the screen porch and out to the backyard where she'd resurrected the old rotating laundry line. It was still warm and the air fresh and dry enough that she thought it would be nice to give them all a good airing before her guests started arriving that weekend.

So, she might have shaken them loose with a bit more force than was absolutely necessary, but it was a harmless enough way to burn off excess energy. Energy she'd been hoping to burn off another way entirely. Except it didn't appear as if Brett had come back last night. Or if he had, he was already up and out early this morning. He never made his bed and she hadn't done his room yesterday assuming she'd get to it this morning. After they got up. Together.

She snapped out another blanket. Of course it was her fault. She'd told him to go be with his friend, hadn't she? And she'd meant it. But that was when she'd thought he was coming back, when she could serve him the dish she'd kept warm in the oven for him, share a late-night glass of wine, and then maybe carry the bottle upstairs with them.

She swore under her breath as she flipped the heavy quilt up and over the line, then some more as she tugged it so it laid smoothly over the laundry cord. Would it have killed him to have at least called? She'd been all dreamy and thinking about their future after he left and then . . . nothing. She turned around, ready to shake out another blanket, only to discover she'd done them all. She picked up the basket and propped it on her hip, giving the linens a final look over.

Great. "Now what in the hell am I supposed to do?" she muttered.

"Well, they look kind of dry to me already, so you've got me."

She swung around and wished she was slightly less thrilled to see him, that her heart hadn't done a little twist and leap inside of her chest, and that her body hadn't gone on full-tilt alert the moment she laid eyes on his smile. Because it would have been a hell of a lot easier to be at least a little put out with him, or at the very least, more believable.

"I'm airing them out," she said, striving for complete indifference. But well aware that the thin, long-sleeve T-shirt she had on, and the complete lack of bra, was probably making it clear she was anything but. Maybe she could blame it on the breeze. If there was one.

"Do they need monitoring, or could I pull you away?"

Every particle of her being shouted "Pull! Pull!" She didn't even try pulling off the bluff. Brett was definitely not the guy to try that with. "Pull me away where?" Her thoughts had already strayed up to his bedroom, and it was only a miracle of will that her gaze didn't follow.

Then she realized he was holding something behind his back. Which turned out to be a motorcycle helmet. Her particles sank a little.

"I was hoping I could convince you to come on a ride with me. Up in the hills."

If that last part was supposed to reassure her, he had missed the mark. "Why the sudden urge for a road trip?"

"I want to show you something. Two somethings, in fact."

Then it clicked into place. She'd been so busy pouting and being put out by his not coming home to her last night that she'd forgotten all about the thing he'd started to tell her about.

"Does this have something to do with the house you started to tell me about?"

He nodded. "Everything to do with it. Come on, I've been dying to show you, to tell you all about it."

Could have fooled me, the pouty part of her still wanted to say. Fortunately the mature side of her brain prevailed. "Couldn't we take my truck? Then we could talk on the way and you can tell me about it." She cocked her head. "Are you . . . pouting? Did I just see you stick your bottom lip out?" Like he needed to be more adorable.

He lifted the helmet. "I don't want to tell you. I want to show you. And besides, on my bike I can have you all wrapped around me."

Her body leapt right on board with that suggestion. But her body was shallow. Her body wasn't the part that was going to give her nightmares about suffering a road rash fatality. That was her head. The same rational part that was going to turn his suggestion down. Flat.

"You can duck your head behind mine. Close your eyes. But I honestly think once we turn up the mountain road you're not going to want to hide. It's nothing like riding through town or in traffic." At her continued mutinous expression—okay, okay, maybe it was more dubious by then because her damn body wasn't backing down—he added, "If you hate this ride, I won't ask you to do it again. The truck will be the automatic default vehicle." He held up his hand in some configuration, changed it a few times, and then grinned broadly and said, "Scouts honor. At least I'm sure they would honor my word. If I'd been a scout."

She couldn't help it; she laughed. "Okay. But this will be it for me, just saying that up front."

"Wait until you see a mountain sunset from the back of a bike; you might change your mind. At least try and keep an open one."

"Why don't we start with open eyes and go from there?" she said, then added, "Will we be gone that long?"

"I know you have a million and one things to do, and we could postpone until after—"

"No, it's not that. Actually, I've been ready for days now. I'm at the point where I'm rearranging every piece of furniture and second guessing dried flower arrangements—do purple heather or marigolds strike just the right accent with the wedding ring quilt—that kind of thing. Getting out of here for a day would probably be the best thing for me. You'd never know I handled fully booked international resorts in my day. It's silly to be so nervous—"

"Not silly." He set the helmets aside and took the laundry basket from her arms and set that next to them. Then he cupped her elbows, drawing her hands up to his shoulders before pulling her into his arms. "That was a corporate-owned entity, and even if you were part of that corporation, it's not the same. Here you're inviting people into the place you created, the place you call home. It's personal. And I think it shows how great an innkeeper you are that you're so concerned about the details." He tugged her closer to him. "In fact, it's your very attention to detail and your good eye that I'm hoping to exploit."

"Really," she said, her brows quirking. "That's a new approach."

He laughed. "That wasn't sexual innuendo. In that case, I meant it straightforwardly." He tipped her chin up to his. "However, I'm not above—or beneath—a little innuendo if it will get me in tight with the innkeeper."

She smiled up into his dancing eyes. "Now there's an innuendo."

"Isn't it, though?" he murmured, and captured her mouth.

It started as a simple, sweet kiss, with all that banked steamy stuff that was always below the surface with them, just simmering along. But then she might have sighed a little, possibly moaned when he pulled her tight against him so his hips could rock against her stomach. And the kiss dipped right past sweet and dove straight into that carnal place. She definitely moaned then.

Her nails dug into his shoulders and he held her face in his wide palms with more determination, his mouth slanting more heavily over hers as he sought out what he wanted . . . and got it.

She was considering the merits of distracting him from his proposed motorcycle ride with another, far more enjoyable ride, when he broke the kiss and laughed.

That caught her up short. When her eyes finally came back into focus, she said, "What was funny? Did I miss something?"

"No, it was . . . it was us, this. Not a ha ha laugh, more an amazed laugh." He pulled her up into his arms so her feet barely touched the ground, and kissed her mouth, then the tip of her nose, and as he let her slide back down his body—making them both suck in a quick, shuddering gasp—he kissed her forehead, too. It should have felt patronizing, or . . . something. But it was endearing and sweet and made her feel a little . . . cherished. Which might have been silly, but there it was anyway.

"Amazed at . . . ?" she led, knowing she shouldn't fish like that, so blatantly, but she'd been giving a lot of thought to what he'd said before, about staying, about finding something that had sparked his interest—beyond just a fling with the local innkeeper.

And she'd dared, on occasion, when she couldn't shore up her defenses well enough, to think about what it would be like. If he stayed. And the picture that painted was too good, too perfect, too . . . exactly what she wanted most, to allow herself to wallow around in it. Staying in the moment, and enjoying it, were one thing. Planning a future with a guy who had no mapped-out future . . . not so smart.

"What's amazing is this. You. Us."

There's an us? she wanted to ask. Which sounded obtuse, for, as far as she knew, there wasn't anyone else and they clearly were voluntarily staying connected to one another.

"I won't lie to you, Kirby. I've never felt this before. That kind of instant connection. And time is going on, and it feels so new and fantastic, but also like I've been right here, in this place, with you, forever. It's that comfortable. And comforting." He laughed again, but it was with a definite self-deprecating edge. "You're probably wondering how in the hell to tell me that it's just a fling for you. And tell me, Kirby, if that's what this is. Or all it can be, for you." He tipped her chin back up, lowered his mouth again. "And tell me soon. Because I'm falling here. And I really, really like where I'm landing."

Her heart started pounding so hard she didn't know if she'd survive it and another passionate kiss from him. She felt like it was going to pound right out of her chest. "I—" She broke off, and his mouth hovered just above hers. In that split second, she wanted to pour out all the confusing and wonderful and terrifying feelings she was developing for him. After all, hadn't he just handed her the perfect opening, backed up with his own admission? What more did she want? A guarantee her heart wasn't going to be decimated a week from now? A month? A year?

Half her head was telling her to backpedal, to buy more time, to see where things were going when they weren't all caught up like this. Problem was, they were always caught up like this. Even when they were two floors, or half a town, apart. This . . . connection, between them, existed all the time. Which was why half of her heart was telling her to jump, take the risk, what the hell.

"There isn't a thing I'd trade, or change, about this." Except maybe being more certain about where it was going. And that it was going. But she didn't say that part.

His smile stayed, but his gaze took on a more probing look as he used his powers of people reading to look deep into hers. It should have unnerved her, used to. Not so much anymore, she realized. She liked that he got her, that he didn't have to ask a million questions, or just guess. He looked at her. And he knew. It was a little daunting. But it was also a huge relief. Because then she didn't have to find the words.

"You're not sure of me, are you," he said, not making it a question. "I understand that. I do. But if that's all you're worried about, come with me. Up into those hills. I have something I want to show you, something I want to ask you. And maybe then you'll see that I'm not a man of flowery speeches and given to jumping on a whim. But know this, Kirby Farrell. I am a man who takes his time figuring things out when the hand's not clear . . . but when he knows that what he has is a winner, he totally goes for broke." Then he grinned again, and that light was fully back in his eyes. "And when I play like that, I pretty much always win."

He leaned down and took her mouth in a kiss that was both a confident claiming—and he had every reason to believe he had because she certainly kissed him back with equal passion—and felt a lot like a promise.

Then, while she was trying to figure out how to handle all of this, he reached down and plucked up the helmets. "Come on," he said. "Ride with me."

She took the helmet, thinking that climbing on the back of his bike and wrapping herself around him while they flew up the side of a winding mountain road was probably not the smartest thing to do with her head spinning like it was. And her heart tilting. But then she was putting it on and walking around the corner of the house, and a minute later, holding on for dear life as they rolled down the long driveway . . . then took off like a shot toward the outskirts of town.

She was just about to jerk on his shoulder and motion for him to pull over so she could see her life flash before her eyes while sitting still, when he took a turn off the main road, past the edge of town, and suddenly they were in a totally different world. A narrow lane, no houses, no other vehicles zooming past, just trees and more trees as the road wound its way up and around and through them. There were glimpses, on the turns, of the town below on one side, and valley that stretched out below that on the other. She didn't even realize that she'd kept her eyes open until she caught herself craning to look around him, waiting for that next overlook, to see the view.

She slid her arms farther around him, and as they leaned to one side, then the other, as the road became twistier, she started to get the feel of the road, the movement, and they way they wound their way through each bend and turn, their bodies moving as one unit, along with the bike. And . . . she realized she was liking it. A lot.

As they kept climbing, her grip on him went from one of panicked determination to one of desired connection. She liked having him between her legs like this, she realized, with the power of the bike thrumming beneath them. It was rather . . . visceral.

She smiled privately to herself and wondered what she'd say to him when they got to wherever it was they were going. Maybe he already knew, from the way she was holding him, that she'd changed her mind about riding. He always knew.

And that's when it kind of all clicked into place for her. He knew her. Bottom line. He got her, honestly, completely, without reservation. He listened, and he asked, and he talked to her and with her, and it all came so naturally, so easily. There was no effort being made to try, no need to impress or go out of his way—or hers—to do or say things intended to elicit a certain result. They were just being themselves. And that's when she realized that she'd never really been herself in her relationship with Patrick. Not all of herself, anyway. She'd kept a lot to herself, things she didn't think he'd understand, or wouldn't want to hear, thinking that was just the compromise of any partnership.

What she'd failed to see was that she and Patrick really had a partnership only. Yes, it had been both personal and professional, even intimate, but it was a partnership only. With Brett she not only felt those same connections . . . but they also had, were developing anyway, a very wonderful friendship. She could, in all honesty, tell him anything. In fact, for the most part, she had. Certainly more than she'd revealed to anyone else. It could have been because she thought he was transient, so what she divulged wouldn't matter in the long run, but that hadn't been it at all.

Their connection was true and unavoidable, really. She supposed it was possible after all to click with a person. Or not. And they definitely clicked. On levels that far surpassed the lust and even intellectual chemistry. It was easy because it was right.

And maybe that was why she'd been so scared. It was hard to accept that it could be this right, this simple, so quickly.

And now he was telling her things that made her believe he wanted more, too.

How could she not take that chance?

Because if you think Patrick shattered your heart, you're going to be in for the mother of all apocalyptic destruction if you let yourself fall the rest of the way . . . and he turns and walks away, her little voice prodded.

They took another turn, and she didn't even have to think, or tighten her hold on him. They just relaxed into the turn, perfectly in sync. Which is exactly what they were. With each other. She supposed the remaining question she had was how did he think he'd be in sync with all the rest? Was he willing to walk away completely from all aspects of the only life he'd ever known? Not just the poker, he'd already walked from that. But the rest, too. Vegas was home to him. He had people he cared about there. Could his sudden interest in the wilds of Vermont . . . and a certain innkeeper . . . keep his attention long haul?

She had no doubt that he thought he was in it to win it, but could she trust that instinct? Trust him?

And then they were slowing down before reaching the next peak and turning up a dirt road.

"Hold on," he shouted back. "It's a bit rutted."

Like she was going to go "look ma, no hands." But hey, any excuse to snuggle up a little closer . . . she wasn't on the fence about that part.

She winced a few times as they bounced in and out of ruts and went around and alongside a few more. She might have had her face buried behind his back for most of the last run up the hill, because she had to lift her head to peek when they finally rolled to a stop. She breathed a sigh of relief when they weren't inches from a death drop or anything. In fact, they were still deeply in the trees. Then she looked past his shoulder in front of the bike and saw the clearing. And the house.

He turned off the bike and they both climbed off and removed their helmets. He saw she was looking at the house, not at him, and let her look before he said anything.

It was an old log cabin, and not the prepackaged type. This one looked like the logs had been hewn and set by hand. It was still in decent shape, and a decent size as well. Unique, too. There were two plank wood dormers, painted green it looked like—at one point anyway—set equal distance apart in the roof, and there were chimneys rising at both ends. She'd guess it was at least thirty or forty years old, possibly more. A beautifully crafted front porch had been added at some point. Kirby walked a few feet across the front of the lot and saw that there had been an addition put on the back, as well. Also hand-hewn logs, but the color and age were different. It looked either like a small lodge or a big home. Nature had taken the yard over some time ago as there were pines growing almost right up to the porch and no drive or walkway that was clearly determinable anymore.

Brett walked over and stood next to her. "Well, what do you think?"

"Old, still has good bones. If they're not chewed up by termites anyway. Unique structure for a cabin. I like the porch. I'd say it hasn't been lived in for a very long time, so who knows what's on the inside." She shifted her gaze up to him. "So . . . what's the deal?"

He reached in his pocket and pulled out a set of keys. "I bought it. This morning, actually."

Which explained where he'd been all day, but . . . wow. "Um. Bought it?" She looked at the house again. "Just like that? Have you been inside?"

"I've tromped around it enough. And if it's not salvageable, then I'll put something else on the lot."

"Okay," Kirby said, because she wasn't sure what else to say.

"I like the view, the location. Entrance road needs work, but the whole thing will be a huge project, so that's not a huge obstacle. Mostly I got it for the house, though. I hope it's sound."

She half laughed, half snorted. "Me, too. Are you in the habit of just buying things on impulse without doing any research?" All her previous concerns about him rushed right back in. Maybe he was just a compulsive doer. She had no idea if he was as good at finishing what he started, however.

"No, actually. I just knew this was the right first step. I saw the dormer windows glinting in the sun, way down below, when I was out riding."

"Yesterday, right? In one day, you just—"

He turned then and swung her into his arms; then he made her squeal when he spun them both around. "Sometimes a day is all it takes." He plunked her feet down but kept her caught up in his arms. "You know what I mean?"

His eyes were so full of joy, she couldn't help but get pulled in. "Yeah," she said. "I think I know exactly what you mean."

He kissed her, and there was something else there this time, along with the passion and instant ignition of need and want. He wasn't rushing, wasn't pouring himself into it, he was . . . steadied, grounded, like he had the rest of his life to keep doing exactly what he was doing.

And damn if she didn't want a float in that parade. A real big one.

When he finally broke the kiss, he was still grinning, like a kid with a new toy, which, in a sense, he was.

"So, what are you going to do with it once it's rehabbed?" She tried not to hold her breath, waiting for the real answer she wanted to hear. He'd said she wouldn't doubt his intentions after coming up here. Did he really plan to move here? Permanently? She tried in vain to keep from leaping to any assumptions. Maybe it was just a part-time property, that he planned to visit. Occasionally. Maybe he thought that would be enough.

Kirby asked herself, in those very few seconds before Brett responded, whether occasionally was going to be enough for her. And her gut response, before she had time to manage her feelings—or shield her heart—was no. She wanted it all, dammit.

All in. Wasn't that what poker players said when they shoved all their chips to the middle of the table? Well, she wanted to shove chips. Mountains of them.

What worried her was that she'd accept occasionally. Like she'd accepted the half-life she lived with Patrick. And they'd been under the same roof. Hadn't she said she'd never do that again? Settle for less? Compromise herself right out of what mattered most?

She hadn't thought she could ever feel . . . what she was feeling now? It made anything she'd had before pale in comparison.

"Kirby," he said, more soberly, making her realize that she'd completely gotten lost in her thoughts.

She looked up again, into his eyes. Eyes that saw so much. And wondered what he saw in hers now.

"I jumped in, both feet, with this house. I know it seems reckless to you, but it was the right thing for me. I know what I want now. I know what I want to do next, with my life. I'm excited about it. And I want to share it with you. I want you to be part of this. It's all wrapped up together for me. The only regret I have is that I should have maybe brought you up here before I got the keys, made you part of that, too. But—"

"But you can afford to jump impulsively; I can't. If you're that excited by this, then maybe it was better that you just went for it. I don't know what I'd have advised you to do if you'd asked. It wouldn't have been my place to make that decision for you."

"I want it to be your place. I mean that literally, too."

She looked at the house again. "Wh—what?"

"I'm going to renovate the house, Kirby. Then I want to decorate it, furnish it, and turn it over to a management company to run."

"Whoa, whoa, wait." She stepped back, out of his arms, as that loaded piece of information dropped like a bomb into her brain. "So . . . you're not going to live here."

He laughed. "Well, it will feel like it while I'm working on the place. I plan to be involved in every step, hiring out what I can't do. But, if you mean afterward, no."

Her heart squeezed into a tiny little ball. "Then you want to rent it out . . . I'm guessing to skiers, or vacationers."

He grinned like it was the best idea anyone had ever had. "It's going to happen here, Kirby. The snow will come, this season, next season, whatever. And Pennydash will grow. Cabins, chalets, time-shares, will be in increasing demand. I want to be in on the ground floor of that, but I want to design and offer one-of-a-kind, unique locations. Like your inn does."

She crossed her arms over her chest, feeling suddenly cold. To the bone. "So . . . you're going into business to compete against me. More or less. You'll have to pardon me if I'm not exactly thrilled with that idea. I mean, you're right, it's going to happen, but—"

He reached for her, but she took another step back, purely instinctive, and tried not to feel bad when hurt flashed across his handsome face.

"Kirby," he said, "I don't want to compete against you. I want to do this with you."

She let that sink in for a second and then spoke from her heart. "I just want to run my own inn. I don't want to run multiple properties or get back into any kind of—"

"Management companies will run the places. I don't want to run them and you have a place to run. Your place. I just want the challenge of finding and reworking interesting old places, possibly designing my own as well. But I need your help with that. Or, I want your help with that." He lifted his hand. "Yes, it means more places that offer guests a night's stay, but trust me, you have the foot in the door there. You can only take so many guests and I'm offering houses, not rooms."

"So you want me to run my inn and help you run . . . whatever it is you're going to be doing? Brett—"

He stepped forward and tugged her arms from their crossed position. "Come here. Please," he added when she dragged her feet a little.

"I don't think as clearly when you have your hands on me."

He wiggled his eyebrows. "You're on to my evil plan then."

She couldn't help it, her mouth twitched a little.

"Kirby, I wouldn't do anything to hurt you, you know that." He leaned down to make direct eye contact with her. "You do know that."

"I want to know it," she said.

"This is what I was thinking. The bulk of your business is fall and winter. I can only do what I do during spring and summer. I help you during your high season, and you help me during mine. I'll use my off season to research, look at property, work on design ideas, and you can use your more relaxed guest booking times to help me finish the places off when I'm done. If you want to. No pressure."

She laughed. "Right."

He did smile. "Okay, maybe a little. It's not something you have to decide in this exact instant. It's a long ways off before I'm at that stage. I just . . . I want to share this with you. It's partly because of you, because of this place, the mountains . . . I don't know. It's like a whole new beginning, what I've found here. I couldn't imagine you not being part of it. You're such a huge part of it already."

So he was making a commitment. To Pennydash, anyway. Which put him in her world . . . permanently. Or at least for the immediate future. Far more of one than she thought she'd have with him. It was hard to let herself go and embrace that . . . she felt like she was waiting for the other shoe to drop. It was almost too good to be true. And those things usually were.

"You're still not sure of me, are you?" he asked.

"Are you of me?"

"I'm sure that when you commit to something, you do what you set out to do. I trust your word. I trust—yes, I trust you, Kirby. I know people." Something flickered in his eyes then, and she wondered if he was thinking of his friend Dan. "I know enough to be comfortable with my decisions, anyway. Just think about it."

"Okay, I will," she said, knowing she had a hell of a lot more to think about than just whether or not she wanted in on his business venture.

"When do you plan to start?" she asked.

"It will depend on what the weather decides to do over the next few months. There's a ton of preliminary work to be done before any actual work takes place. I've got plenty to keep me busy until spring."

She debated for about five seconds before just blurting out the crux of what was holding her back. "Will you be doing this preliminary work here? Or are you going back to Vegas?"

"Here," he said, clearly surprised at the question. "I meant what I said when I asked about me staying. I am staying, Kirby."

She took a steadying breath. But her heart was already off to the races again. "What about home? Your friend Dan? Vanetta?"

"I tried to talk to Dan about it last night, see if he wanted in on the building phase, but . . . things there . . ." He trailed off, and the sadness and confusion was clear on his face. "I don't know what the hell is going on there, to be honest. But I'm working on that, too."

"So . . . you really are staying."

He reached out to tuck a stray hair behind her ear. "That was my plan." He took her hand, tugged her closer. "Good plan or bad plan?"

"Good plan," she said somewhat distractedly, still trying to sort through the onslaught of questions and emotions this sudden turn of events had set to swirling around inside her head. Along with all the ones she already had. But one thing she knew. "You staying is very good."

"I can move out of the inn, if that makes it better."

"Makes what better?"

"Whatever it is about this that has you feeling . . . I don't know. Trapped? I didn't mean for it to be like that. I know I'm excited about this, and there's no way I can hide that; I don't want to, even if I could. But don't let my enthusiasm for this make you feel crowded and pushed into a corner. I don't—"

278 *Donna Kauffman*

"No, it's not that. I think it's pretty fantastic that you're excited about this. I don't know what I feel about my part; I have
to think about that. I haven't even decently launched my own
place yet, so—"

"So, don't worry, or even think about it. It's months away."

"Months," she echoed, trying to imagine having months with
him. It was everything she wanted. And his excitement about
having her be part of it was flattering and not a little thrilling.
Except—

"Tell me what's going through your mind, right now. Uncen-
sored."

"Okay. I was thinking that I've already had a relationship
with someone I worked side by side with, and to be honest, it
makes me a little nervous to think about—"

"Listen, just scrap what I said, okay? We don't have to mix
business with pleasure. I'm not going to risk what we're starting
for that—"

"I didn't say no. Just that . . . it's all part of the stuff going
through my head. You're not Patrick. And this situation is far,
far from that. Just . . . give me some time. To get used to it." To
get used to the idea of him being around. Of letting herself want
the impossible. Again.

Because it seemed so . . . so very possible, right now. It was
scary. In a very good way. Also in a completely terrifying, "run
for the hills and protect your heart" kind of way.

"You can have all the time you need." He caressed her cheek,
urged her face to tilt up to his. "You sure you're okay with the
me staying part, though? Be honest with me, Kirby. I didn't
come here to cause you trouble. You deserve the life you've
carved out for yourself. I just want to be part of that, and build
my own while I'm at it."

"The problem is I want it too much," she said, baldly honest.
That was the one thing with Brett that made this entirely different. He made bald honesty not only easy, but pretty much

mandatory. "It scares me. How much I want what you're offering. How much I want you."

All in, indeed.

His pupils flared at that, and he might have made a little growling sound in the back of his throat. "That . . ." He stopped, ducked his head, and cleared his throat. "Wow," he managed. "I had no idea how badly I needed to hear you say that. Until you just did."

She smiled a little then, no less terrified, but realizing that she wasn't the only one dancing on a dangerous ledge made facing the terror that much easier. "Kind of scary, right?"

"You forget. I like high stakes."

Her smile spread, and the very beginnings of allowing herself to accept what might be possible started to bloom inside her heart. And her head. And . . . every-damn-where. "You'll have to teach me to play. Poker, I mean. I want to understand more what it is you do. Did. Whatever."

"Deal." Then he laughed and swung her around again. "You feel like taking the inaugural peek inside? We can come back another time—"

She shut him up by placing her hands on either side of his face and pulling his mouth to hers. For once, she was taking the lead. And as soon as she kissed him, and felt him immediately relax, and soften, and take her so easily and perfectly and naturally . . . she understood as she never had before what true power there was to be had in a complete partnership. And it didn't consist of one leader and one follower.

This was nothing like before. This was . . . new. And it was hers to decide what to do with, and how she wanted it to be. At least to work for her. She wasn't surrendering control. She was taking on a new challenge. And damn, but maybe she was up for it after all. Because, the reward, if she pulled if off, was priceless.

When she broke the kiss, she lifted up on her tippy toes to hug him, and he swept her up so they could hug good and proper, everything aligning so perfectly. She kissed the side of his neck and felt his pulse thrumming, which set hers to thrumming, too. "Okay," she whispered in his ear. "I'm all in."

Then she snatched the keys from his unsuspecting grip and wriggled out of his arms. "Come on. Let's go see what you've gotten us into. Last one to the front door is a rotten poker player." And she took off toward the house.

Chapter 19

B rett throttled down as they rolled through town, then punched it a little as they neared the turn up to the inn. He wanted to get home. Where he was going to make love to Kirby and end the perfect day with the perfect night.

He couldn't believe it was all going to work out. She'd loved the farmhouse and his design concept for it as much as she had with the log cabin. He'd called and put an offer on the place on their way back into town. What a lucky, lucky bastard he truly was. Hell, Kirby had even admitted she'd gotten used to the bike. Total package. He had the most ridiculous urge to beat his chest and howl at the moon.

They rolled to a stop in front of the house; the sun had sunk enough to cast the front of the house in deep shadows. The air had a distinct bite to it, and Kirby shivered as she let go of him and climbed off the bike.

"Maybe some wine, have the leftovers from last night?" she asked.

He wanted to scoop her up and head to the nearest bed, but pacing, given the rush he was feeling, was probably not a bad thing.

"Sounds perfect," he said, and meant it. He took her helmet and then slipped his hand in hers as they walked toward the porch. He was thinking about how easily he pictured himself doing just this for a very long time, when she suddenly paused.

"Oh, crap. The quilts and bedspreads, they're still out back. I need to bring them in."

"You want some help?"

She lifted up on her toes and kissed him. "Why don't you go pour the wine and start reheating the food. It won't take me long."

Yeah, he thought as he kissed her back. Definitely lifetime material. Better than he'd ever thought possible. "Okay," he said, his body stirring again as he watched her walk around the outside of the house toward the back of the property. He spent about two seconds contemplating following her around back and getting at least one of those blankets dirty all over again, but it was getting colder by the second. "Dinner. Then play." He took the steps two at a time, put the helmets on the registration desk, slung his jacket over the newel post at the base of the stairs, and then headed straight for the kitchen.

He was smiling as he entered the room and was thinking that maybe he'd snag one of the blankets and start a fire in the front parlor fireplace, turn dinner into a little fireside picnic, but stopped in his tracks when he spied Kirby through the kitchen window.

She was standing in the backyard, hand over her mouth, looking at what was left of her freshly aired antique quilts and spreads. All of which were in shredded ribbons.

Something went hard and cold inside his chest. He was simultaneously furious at whoever had invaded her property, whoever had destroyed a single thing she'd worked so hard to get . . . and sick almost to the point of puking over the unavoidable suspicion that crawled right back into his gut.

No. This wasn't happening. Not again. He thought he was done with that, that he'd left it back in Vegas. That whoever thought this was the right way to get his attention had figured out they were wrong when, instead of caving in, he'd packed up and left town for good.

One face floated through his mind. Maksimov's smug expression as Brett had turned him down flat, like he'd known something that Brett hadn't known. Like . . . he was going to stir up the shit all over again until Brett agreed to another deal. The thing was, he couldn't understand why they thought this was the way to get what they wanted? Whatever it was they thought he could bring to their table, or any promoter or casino owner's table for that matter, regardless of his celebrity when it came right down to it . . . he was just one guy. It wasn't worth this kind of aggravation. For him or for them. That was the one part he couldn't figure out.

But no matter who had been behind the problems back in Vegas, he'd never thought trouble would follow him here.

He pushed through the door to the porch and let himself out the screen door. She looked over to him as he crossed the yard to the clothesline. "I guess we need to call Thad," she said. "File a vandalism report. Was anything done inside? Was it still locked up?"

"Door was locked, nothing looks out of place inside. At least on the main floor. Kirby—"

"Who would do this?" she asked, clearly at a total loss. "We don't really have a lot of school-age kids around here. And certainly not any kind of gang problems. I mean . . . what, a hoard of Clemson's maniacal kitties? What?" She looked back at the shredded quilts and sort of slumped in on herself. "These were antiques. They . . . you can't replace these. I spent a full year hunting these down."

She sounded more sad than pissed, though he suspected the latter would show up eventually. "Kirby, I need to tell you something."

"I guess I shouldn't take them down until Thad can come and file an official report," she said, not hearing him, too upset by what had happened to pay attention to anything other than what was going through her own mind.

She had her arms wrapped around her middle, and Brett suspected that was as much to console herself as it was to ward off the rapidly cooling evening air. He wanted to hold her, console her himself, but he had to tell her first. She might not want him

anywhere around her after he told her what he knew. Or suspected, anyway. He should have told her the rest of the reason
why he'd left Vegas when she'd told him about Maksimov
booking a room. He just hadn't thought it really mattered.

He walked over to her and pulled her arms from where they
were crossed. "Come here." She walked into his arms, and
that's when he could feel her shaking. "Let's go inside, okay?
We'll call the deputy and go ahead and heat up some food."

"I can't eat."

"Okay. But let's get out of the cold."

She nodded against his chest and willingly let him steer her
inside. He noted that she didn't look back at the destruction.
Once they were in the kitchen, she moved away from him and
slipped out of her jacket, still clearly upset. It didn't make him
any happier to have to tell her the rest, but she had to know.

"Kirby, before you call Thad, there's something I need to tell
you."

She had already started toward the cordless that sat on the
counter, but paused to look at him. "Shouldn't we get this re-
ported as soon as possible? It will be dark soon and I'd like to
see if he can get right over here and take a look. I mean, I'm
racking my brain, but even crotchety old Clemson would never
do something like this. And unless he's breeding a whole new
kind of barn cat over there, I don't think they're responsible, either." Then her expression lightened. "Do you think it could
have been some kind of animal? I mean, I can't imagine what
kind, but—"

"No, Kirby, I don't think it was an animal. Not the four-
legged kind anyway. I . . . I think I might know who did this."

She started to respond, then stopped as the rest of what he
was saying sunk in and snapped her mouth shut again.

"When I left Vegas, there were a few other reasons why I
left."

Her eyebrows lifted. "What? Are you saying someone is after
you? Oh, my God, Brett. Why didn't you—"

"I didn't think it would follow me." He crossed the room in three strides, but she folded her arms across her chest, barring him. He respected that. Hated it, but didn't push. She deserved to hear the rest. "It hasn't, actually. But now I've brought the world of poker here, and I guess that problem came with it. I'm sorry. If I thought—" He broke off as her expression changed from one of honest confusion and concern to that shuttered look he hadn't seen in quite some time now. He silently swore and vowed right then that as soon as Thad was done here and he was reasonably certain Kirby was okay left here by herself, he was heading to the resort. Maks wasn't going to touch another person he cared about.

"What kind of trouble?" she asked, a carefully blank tone in her voice.

"I—when I stopped playing, when I retired, not everyone was happy about it. I was the poster boy for a lot of big events and it drew money to the tables, both during the event itself and before and after, just from the publicity of it. I was the biggest name and the easiest money to be made, promotionally speaking. So I know it wasn't a great day for promoters and casino owners when I stepped down. There aren't many others with the easy name recognition that I had and it will likely be a while before someone dominates the sport." He lifted a hand. "I'm not saying any of this to toot my own horn, just—"

"No," she said quietly, "I know you're not like that. Just . . . go on."

"So, there were a series of . . . events. Set up to look like accidents, but after a while, it was too coincidental to have all those things happening to me. Or to people I cared about." Her shoulders slumped then and he couldn't help it, he grasped her folded elbows and tugged her closer. "Kirby, we could never prove anything; the police chalked it up to bad luck. The running joke was all the ridiculous luck I'd had during my career had flipped on me when I left the sport. But I—I didn't want anything bad happening to anyone I cared about. And I needed time and some space to figure out what I was going to do. So I took off, figuring if it was one of the folks hounding me to come back, then they'd either follow me or let up once and for all."

"Did anything else happen after you left?"

Brett shook his head. "No. Dan has kept an eye out and it all stopped as soon as I left. Word got out and people stopped calling. I haven't had to deal with any of that fallout since crossing the Nevada state line. Which you can take as proof it was someone there, or maybe it was just bad luck."

"But you didn't think so."

"No," he said, "no, I didn't."

"What did Dan think?"

"I would have told you that Dan was the one supporting my decision to get out, only now I'm not as sure about that. I was working for him after I quit, which, as I told you before, is something I had done off and on since I was a kid. It wasn't a permanent thing, just helping him and giving myself something to do while I figured out what I wanted to do next."

"But now you think it was someone. And that they're here. Because you're playing again." Her eyes went wide. "That Russian guy? Maks—whatever? You think it's him, don't you?"

"I don't know what else to think. Kirby, honestly, you know I'd have never put you at risk like that if I had any idea—"

"Okay," she said, cutting him off, obviously still trying to process the whole thing. "So, why do you think he's behind it?"

"They were probably the least happy when I retired. I had done a few events for them when they'd started up, and it always went well for them. And for me, I won't lie. So they leaned pretty hard to try and get me to continue on, at least with their events."

"And you turned them down."

"Flat. And then . . . things started happening."

Her carefully controlled expression shook for just a second, but the fear he spied in her eyes was all he needed to see. "I'm going to put an end to it, Kirby. Once and for all. As soon as we report this to the sheriff's office, I'm going up to the resort." He thought about taking Thad with him, then immediately reconsidered. A small town local cop was not going to intimidate Maks. In fact, it was probable he was counting on that. As he was counting on the local female innkeeper not being able to bring much pressure to bear, either.

Well, Maks was about to learn that he was all kinds of wrong on that score.

"I'm going with you."

"What? No. Not because I don't think you can handle yourself and not because you don't deserve a crack at him, but I understand the world we're from. You don't. And I can't—" His grip tightened on her elbows. "I'm not putting you in the middle. I'll leave here before I do that."

"What, and keep running?"

He tried not to wince at that, but she was close enough. "No," he said, and meant it. "If he's left town, I'll go back to Vegas after him. I'll pull every string I have, cash every marker. But I'm done. All done."

She took a deep, shuddering breath. "This is all . . . a lot." She gently disengaged her elbows from his grip. "I—I need to call Thad. And my insurance company, I guess." She blew out a breath, then turned away from him and went to the phone.

Standing by and watching was possibly one of the hardest things he did, but she knew the story now, and how she wanted to handle things, both with Thad and between them, was up to her. Not that he didn't plan on having any influence, but she'd been happy here, going along with her plans for the future. And yes, the lack of snow had put those dreams at risk, but somehow he knew she'd have found a way, even if he'd never shown up.

He turned and looked out the rear window, looking at the shredded quilts in the rapidly fading daylight. Goddammit. If anything had happened to her . . .

He paced the room, half listening to her talk to the deputy, then her insurance rep, his anger building, his patience growing thinner by the second. He tried Dan's room at the resort, planning on having him meet him in the lobby before tracking Maksimov down. Dan was the only other person in town he could trust and it wouldn't hurt to have backup. Or witnesses.

As soon as Thad arrived and Brett gave his statement, he told Thad to please stick by Kirby, that he had some business to attend to at the resort that couldn't wait.

Both Thad and Kirby protested, but he was already out the door and on his bike before they could stop him.

Before the night was over, it was all going to be over.

Brett parked his bike right in front of the hotel and headed inside to the registration desk. "Hi, Bobby," he said to the young man behind the counter. He knew most of the desk staff by now. "Listen, I need to find out where—" He stopped when there was a tap on his shoulder. He turned, half expecting it to be Maks confronting him. He wouldn't put anything past him at this point. But it wasn't Maks, or anyone he'd seen before.

"Mr. Hennessey, sir? If I might have a word with you?" The man was massive. Tall, dark skinned, shoulders wider than most doorways. He gave big a whole new meaning. He opened his jacket to show his security badge. "Privately, please?"

Brett stepped away from the desk, but said nothing.

"Sir," Mr. Big began, "With all due respect, I am supposed to alert you to the fact that we've placed hotel security out front of Mr. Maksimov's villa. He's not to be disturbed until someone from the sheriff's department arrives to talk to him."

"Okay," Brett said. Chalk one up for the small town deputy. "I'll just head up to my room, then."

"I'll escort you," he said cordially enough, but the way he instantly flanked Brett's steps made it clear he wasn't going to be dissuaded.

"Fine."

They rode up the elevator in silence, with Big standing in front, closest to the doors. Brett was fine with letting him play the shield. The doors slid open to reveal an empty hallway. Big stepped out and gestured for Brett to precede him. They both walked over to the door leading to his suite. Brett opted not to knock for Dan. Better to keep him out of this as much as possible until Brett figured out exactly what was going on. He slid his card out, but the security guard already ziplined his out from his jacket and swiped it through the locking mechanism.

The tumblers dropped, and Brett pushed the handle down and went in. He started to turn to thank the security guard for the escort, intending to close the door between them, but suddenly the guard planted one beefy palm on Brett's shoulder and shoved him straight to the floor. Do not pass go, face on carpet.

Brett immediately started to scramble, thinking maybe this was all some kind of elaborate setup by Maks. He'd never have guessed they'd go that route, but what the hell did he know at this point? Except there were no stakes high enough for them to be taking this kind of risk. There had to be cameras in the hallway getting at least some of this, as the door hadn't shut yet. None of this made any fucking sense.

But he barely got his hands beneath him to shove himself up, when he was stomped right back down again, with either a foot or a hand, he had no idea. But when he heard the gun clear the holster, he renewed his efforts. "Don't move," Big ordered. "Stay right here."

Then he released him, stepped over him, and moved farther into the apartment, gun drawn and held steady in front of him, like a cop would breaking into an apartment where he thinks there might be trouble.

Dan.

Should he call out? Warn him? Or would Brett just be drawing attention to his presence?

Well, one thing he wasn't going to do was stay prone on the floor. But just as he got to his feet, he heard Big yell, "Call nine one one!"

Shit. He palmed his cell out of his pocket as he ran through the suite into the bedroom where Big was standing. Over a prone body. Brett's fingers faltered on the dial pad as his heart squeezed into a tight fist. Until he got a look at the whole body and realized it wasn't Dan. Thank God. But . . .

Big was already on his ear piece, notifying the front desk that there was a guest in trouble and needing immediate medical assistance, then he was on the floor, checking the man's pulse.

"Don't move him," Brett cautioned. "You don't know where he's—" He stopped because he'd moved around the room enough to see the prone figure from another angle. One that provided him with a look at his face. And the pool of blood extending out from under his head.

It was Maksimov.

"Dan!" he immediately shouted. He spared a glance at Big, who looked up at him and shook his head, indicating there was no pulse.

Holy— "Dan?" he shouted again, and tore through the suite to the other bedroom. Empty. No one in either bathroom. He checked behind the kitchen counter, out on the balcony. Even, God forbid, down below the balcony. Nothing.

"Will you step back inside, Mr. Hennessey. We need for you to remain calm until the sheriff's department arrives. They're going to want to speak with you."

"Me? I didn't—you were with me when we opened the door." And thank God for that, he realized now. This was not going to look good, not after the way he tore out of the inn. And where the hell was Dan?

"We don't know anything yet. What, when, why. Just stay put. Sir," he added, remaining respectful but clearly not willing to have any discussion about the matter.

Brett didn't argue. Instead he pulled his phone out again and hit the speed dial for Dan. "Come on," he muttered.

"Sir—"

"I'm trying to find out where the gentleman is who was staying here with me, okay? Given what we found, we might want to know that. I want to know that. I don't know what the hell is going on, but I'm not going to sit here and do nothing." He dialed again, but it went straight to voice mail. He dialed the inn, then hung up before Kirby could answer. She didn't need to be any more freaked out than she already was. Hell, she was probably already packing his things for him and putting them by the front door as it was. Goddammit. They go up in the hills for a few hours and the whole world goes crazy.

Medical staff from the resort showed up a few minutes later, followed by the town paramedics. They were in the bedroom, doing . . . whatever the hell they could with Maks.

Brett paced the living room like a caged animal, alternately trying to dial Dan and spending the rest of the time trying to calm down enough to figure out what in the hell was going on.

Thad showed up and Brett was across the room in a blink.

"What's going on? What have you learned?"

"Where's Maksimov?"

"In the bedroom, they're . . . working on him." Brett didn't mention that he didn't think they'd have much success with that. Thad would figure out the rest shortly. "Where's Kirby?"

"Back at the inn. She wanted to come, but I told her to stay put."

"You left her there alone?"

"She's fine," he said, clearly on the job now as there was no kissing up to the local celebrity in his tone. "She'll be safe there, out of the way."

"You have no idea what you're talking about. I can't find Dan, I don't know who the hell did—"

"Who's Dan?" They were pushed aside as what looked like the entire police force of Pennydash rushed into the room, immediately asking Thad questions, with some heading straight to the bedroom.

There was a strong sense of foreboding that crawled over Brett in that moment. Something very, very wrong was going on here, and there was only one person unaccounted for. And Kirby was all by herself in the inn. "I've gotta go," he said. Not that anyone was listening to him.

Brett ducked around Thad, who broke off what he was saying to one of the younger officers and snagged him by the arm. "Where are you going? You need to stay right here until we can get a full state—"

"Ask Mr. Big, the security guy in there. He knows as much as I do. I have to go make sure Kirby is all right."

"I told you—"

"I'm not a flight risk. I'm not going anywhere." And he'd never been so certain of that in his life as he was now. The sheer terror he'd felt when he'd thought anything might happen to her— He pulled his arm free and made a move through the door. "You know where to find me when you're done here." He didn't wait to hear anything else, but hit the stairs and started running.

Chapter 20

By the time Brett got to the inn, his heart was lodged in his throat. The bad sensation in his gut had only gotten stronger the closer to home he'd gotten. And still nothing from Dan.

He almost laid the bike on its side in his hurry to get up the hill, park, and get inside the house. There were lights on and everything looked perfectly peaceful, like any other evening, from the outside. But then, his hotel room had appeared normal, too.

He ran through the front door and immediately checked himself, made himself slow down. With everything else she'd been through today, Kirby didn't need him racing into whatever room she was in looking like an out-of-control wild man. Though that's exactly how he felt.

He blew out a heavy breath, trying to get a grip on himself, but before he could call out to her, he heard voices. Coming from . . . the kitchen? Whatever calm he might have found deserted him completely as he headed through the foyer to the dining room, barely clipping the foyer furniture and dining room table, only to come to an immediate halt when he finally hit the kitchen and saw who Kirby was talking to.

"Dan?"

His friend was sitting at one end of the middle butcher block counter on a stool. Kirby was at the opposite end, also sitting. But after a quick, life-affirming glance at Kirby, who appeared fine, his gaze went right back to Dan, who looked anything but.

If someone had used his face for a punching bag the night before, they'd gone on to take out considerable frustration on the rest of his body today, if the torn shirt, bloody stain on one shoulder, and half-swollen, ravaged face was anything to go by.

"What the hell?"

"Brett, my man," he said, trying to smile, then wincing when it pulled at skin that couldn't handle any more movement at the moment. He seemed . . . not drunk, exactly. High?

Brett couldn't tell. "What the hell happened?"

"You've been to the hotel?"

"Yes. Police are there, paramedics."

Kirby's eyes widened, though her gaze would go to him, then right back to Dan. She had looked calm enough when he'd come in, but now that he'd had a moment to focus, he realized . . . she might appear to be okay, but she was terrified. Her hands were knotted together on the kitchen counter and the set of her shoulders was rigid. He started to walk over to her.

"Let's just stay where you are. For now," Dan said.

He glanced from Kirby to Dan again. "I don't underst—"

Then Dan lifted the hand that was in his lap behind the counter . . . revealing the gun he was holding.

"Jesus, Dan. Man, what the hell is going on here? This is not a good idea. Where did you get the—"

"Well, I thought it would be a good idea to keep Maks from beating the hell out of me with it, before he decided to shoot me. It was self-defense."

"Why was Maks beating you?"

"Do I really have to spell that out for you?"

Brett had no idea what was going on, but walking into the middle of this was like walking into the middle of a nightmare that made no sense, and he couldn't slow his brain down enough to grasp it. "Listen, we'll make this work out. If it was self-defense, then that's what it was. But you need to put the gun down. This isn't going to help. But I can. Let me help you, let—"

Dan erupted in a painful gurgle of laughter. "Right, right. Let you *help* me. What the hell do you think I've been trying to get you to fucking do?" He waved the gun at that last part, making Kirby shift back on her stool as it swung past her direction.

Brett immediately put his hands out. "Okay, okay. I know we can figure this out, but Dan, you have to put the gun down to make that work."

"No point in that now. Can't you see that? You saw Maks, right? You know?"

It was all too surreal. Maks's body in his hotel room, Dan sitting in Kirby's kitchen waving a gun about. Like he'd left Pennydash earlier today with Kirby and found the answer to all his dreams, only to come back home to some kind of alternate universe nightmare. "I saw Maks," he said, trying like hell not to picture that in his head. He needed to keep his wits about him, and at the moment, that was going to take immeasurable focus. "What happened? Start at the beginning." Maybe if he could get Dan talking in some kind of rational form, he could figure their way out of this and no one else would get hurt.

"Put it together, man," Dan said, agitated. "All the shit that went down back home? Me here, Maks here? Come on, you're the college degreed rocket scientist here."

Brett just stared at his friend. Or the man who used to be his friend. He didn't recognize the man seated in front of him now. It was like he was talking to a complete stranger. "Why don't you tell me?"

The room was chilly, and not just because Dan was sitting there, half unhinged, terrifying both him and Kirby, albeit for different reasons. Then he realized the back door to the porch was open, letting in the chill night air. Was that how he'd gotten in?

Brett contemplated heading over to close the door, which meant he either had to circle around behind Kirby, which was the long route, but that would give him a chance to block her at least momentarily from Dan's site range. Maybe give her a chance to duck down and escape the kitchen. Or circle around behind Dan. Maybe disarm him. Somehow.

Brett looked at the back door. Then he caught Kirby's gaze

from the corner of her eye, trying to somehow mentally signal to her what he wanted to do so she could get herself out of harm's way once he made his move. But all he got from her was an almost imperceptible shake of the head.

He looked back at Dan. "Are you saying that what happened tonight—here with the laundry out back, and with Maks at the resort, has something to do with what was happening out in Vegas?"

"Give the man a gold star," Dan said, his clearly barely controlled anger turning snide and even uglier.

Then the pieces tumbled into place. "Wait—"

Dan turned to Kirby and waved the gun in her direction as well, making Brett's heart stop completely. "*Now* he's getting it," Dan smirked nastily. He swung his gaze and the gun back to Brett. "All that damn time, and never once did you figure it might not be all about you for a goddamn change."

Brett was only half hearing his snidely delivered commentary; his brain was spinning, almost out of control as every piece of the puzzle finally shifted to make the right picture. "They weren't coming after me. Maks and Rudov. They were coming after . . ."

"Me," Dan supplied. "I was this close to making the money back. While you were playing. Even after you quit, I thought I had it. We were a team, man. A team. It was all going to be okay; I just had to hold them off a while longer. Then you go and fucking leave and I have no chance to recoup my losses."

"Gambling debts? That's what this is about? Since when did you—"

"The business was in trouble, Brett. Dad didn't exactly stick around to help with the transition, you know? And you. Just when I think I'm good to go, you working the circuit, you up and quit."

"Wait, you . . . bet on me? On the events?" He thought about what Maks had said, about overhearing Dan trying to get some game action while at the bar.

Dan shrugged, seemingly unashamed by his actions, belligerent almost. "Sometimes I bet against you, too. I could always kind of tell when you were hitting burnout stage, figured my chances were better going with number two then."

"I offered to help, you could have come to me."

Dan lifted the gun from his lap. "How many times do I have to pound it into your thick skull? I am *not* your pet charity project! So I bet on you playing, so what? First it was just kind of for fun, but then I won a little. And when things got tight with the business, I'd bet more. And not just on your events. I got in deeper with the company, and deeper with the casino. So . . . they kind of came after me. To collect. I promised them when you came on board, they'd get their money back with interest."

"So why did they vandalize your property? And Vanetta, Dan, how could you let them put her and her life's work in jeopardy like that? I would have paid them off for you; we'd have hashed it out later. I mean, Jesus, Dan, how could you not do some—"

"I was doing something!" he roared. Dan shoved off his stool, sending it skidding backward, where it fell through the screen door. "I was *earning* the money back, Brett. Earning it back."

From the corner of Brett's eye, he saw Kirby's gaze stray again and again to the rear open door. It was really cold now. Maybe she was signaling him to do what he'd been thinking about earlier. But what if he was wrong? He couldn't risk it, risk her.

"I needed one more game, one more, dammit," Dan shouted, his beaten face contorted with pain and rage and tears. "Then you up and fucking quit. All these years I tell you to leave the damn sport, come work with me. It would have been good. No trouble. I'd have been clean. The business would have been strong. But no. *No.* So I get in the game, and get deeper, then you fucking leave? But it's all good, I tell Rudov. I'll recoup the money with you working for me full-time now. But that wasn't fast enough for Rudov. So they sent Maks around to *persuade* me to come up with the money. I didn't know what else to do.

The only sure thing was you playing again, one more time. I could have worked that angle. I thought you'd go back. They all go back. But no, not you! I told him to lean on you, get you to play again. Just once. But . . . but it got out of hand, and Maks got impatient. Then you left, and . . . and I was losing work with you gone."

The tears started spurting from his swollen eyes; his jaw quivered as anger gave way to shame. He looked like nothing more than a trapped, wounded, cornered animal. And for the first time, Brett was really, truly afraid of how this was all going to play out. Dan was so far beyond reason, he wasn't even hearing anything Brett said.

"Then you up and fucking decide to play again. Here, in this godforsaken shit town. So what choice do I have but to get the hell out here? Why do you think Maks came out here, anyway?" He was almost sobbing now. "And even then, I didn't want to do it, any of it. I just wanted you to come home. We'd have made it work, man. It would have fixed everything." He hunched over, slumped, letting the gun dangle down for a moment and in that split second, Brett knew that might be his only chance to do something.

With Dan breaking eye contact, Brett glanced quickly at Kirby to motion her to get down, but her gaze was riveted on a spot somewhere behind Dan.

Just as Brett swung his gaze back, to see what she was looking at, Dan's head came up and he brought the gun up to his temple. "I could solve all our problems, you know," he said, his voice no longer wild with pain, but calm, cold, empty. Too empty.

"No!" Brett shouted. "Dan, put it down. Now. I'll do whatever you want me to do."

"It's too late now. Don't you see? Too fucking late." The gun wavered beside his temple, and Brett was just girding himself to dive over the counter if he had to, when suddenly Dan let out an almost inhuman shriek of pain and pitched violently forward, his body thrashing. The gun went off, the bullet ricocheting up into the ceiling, then all chaos erupted.

Kirby dove for the floor. Brett dove for Dan as he landed on the floor, hand outstretched, still holding the gun. Dan was howling. Kirby was scrambling toward the screen door.

"Run!" Brett yelled at her. "Get Thad."

But instead she scooted behind Dan just as Brett cleared the counter in one leap, then had to almost twist into a pretzel to keep from landing on Dan's back, which had been his intended target. He'd meant to pin him down and kick the gun away. But at the last second, he realized the reason Dan had suddenly had what looked like a violent seizure.

He had demon kitty lodged on his back, nails dug in deep, looking more terrified than she had when she was trapped two stories up in a tree.

That's what Kirby had seen. The stool clattering over, then Dan jumping up and swinging the gun up must have set the cat off. Literally.

"What the hell is that? Get it off me!" Dan was screaming.

Brett kicked at the gun in Dan's hand, sending it skittering as Kirby stepped in with a dish towel to trap the kitten.

She pried the cat loose and Brett hauled Dan up by his shoulders, prepared to level him with a knockout punch if that's what it took to keep him from doing any more harm. To them or himself.

Dan took a swing at Brett, but at that point he was pretty easy to subdue.

When Thad arrived seconds later, Brett had Dan face to the wall, arm pinned behind his back. Dan was sobbing, completely broken. And Brett's heart was breaking as well.

Thad stepped in, and though Brett instinctively moved forward to protect Dan, despite what had happened there that night, Thad quietly but firmly told him to step back and then clear the room once the reinforcements had come into the house as well.

"I've got it from here," he told him.

"He's . . . not well," Brett said, not knowing what else to say. "Don't—just—he's done, okay? You don't have to—"

"We've got it under control," Thad reassured him, still stern, but clearly signaling with the stern set to his face that Brett needed to move back.

Brett did, and he felt what was left of his heart shatter as they cuffed Dan and took him outside to the squad car. Another officer retrieved the gun. Several others stayed behind to ask questions. Kirby was still cradling the bundled cat.

Brett took the towel and went out back on the porch and to the backyard. He crouched down and carefully opened the bundle. The kitten tumbled out, then arched her back and hissed once she was free. "Thanks for the assist, hellion," he said as the kitten continued to yowl. "We're even. Now git before you get impounded as evidence or something." He watched the kitten take off back up the hill, hopefully toward home.

When he turned back around, Kirby was standing in the doorway, arms folded protectively against her middle. Her face was expressionless, but he could hardly blame her for being numb. He wished he was, too.

"I'm so sorry," she said as he climbed the steps and came back on the porch.

He paused on the top step. "My best friend holds you at gunpoint and you're telling me you're sorry?"

"It's . . . sad. He's . . . he's not a well man. It's not your fault, Brett. I know you're going to think you could have done something to prevent this but you couldn't possibly know if he hadn't told you."

She opened the door and he came inside, but before they could say anything else to each other, Thad stuck his head through the kitchen door. "Your turn. We need your statements."

Kirby slipped her hand in Brett's as they stepped inside. It was that small but monumental thing that brought everything into crystal clarity for him.

He tightened his grip, squeezing her hand, wanting to say so many things to her. But first they had to get through the rest of this.

In retelling their story to the police, it settled things inside Brett's mind, if not his heart. He wasn't sure what was going to happen to Dan. The only piece of good news was that Maks was actually going to be okay. Apparently Mr. Big's skills didn't extend to the medical field. He'd missed the pulse because he'd been checking in the wrong place. So, while Dan still faced some very serious charges, thank God one of them wasn't going to be manslaughter.

Morning light was starting to creep over the horizon, the sky as gray as his emotions, as they watched the last squad car pull out from the front driveway. Kirby shivered as they stood, arms around each other's waist, on the front porch.

"What happens next?" she asked quietly.

"I don't honestly know anymore, Kirby. I just don't know." He was past angry and sad. By now, he just felt . . . hollow. His whole world had been turned upside down . . . for good. Then flipped over again with this.

Then she turned in his arms, slid both of hers around his waist. She looked as tired as he felt, but her gaze was steady, her voice certain. "We'll figure out what's best to do. For him. For you."

Brett touched her face, humbled by this woman. But never more certain about where he was supposed to be. "I thought you'd have me packed and out of here. I'm so sorry, Kirby. I didn't know. I'd have never . . ." He closed his eyes and pressed his forehead to hers, trying to shut out the memories of the night before. "When I thought you might be in trouble . . . I haven't been that terrified since I was a kid."

"I was okay. I was talking to him. I didn't think he'd hurt me. He was just . . . mixed up, and hurt, and confused. He's going to need help. More than legal help, I mean."

Brett nodded, then squeezed his eyes more tightly shut as another thought hit him.

"What?" she asked gently, pulling him closer and touching his cheek as she lifted his head up.

"Dan's dad. This . . . it'll break him. I—I should call him."

"I think they're already doing that. I heard one of the deputies say they were trying to reach him."

Brett swore under his breath. "How in the hell did it get that out of hand and I didn't know? I don't miss much, Kirby. And I completely missed this. He's the closest friend I have, and I never saw it. I was so wrapped up in my own crap, I never—"

"Hey," she said, framing his face. "You tried to help him and he was too stubborn, too full of pride, to accept the kind of help that would have put him back on the right path. He's a grown man. He could have chosen the smarter, safer path, even if it meant swallowing his pride. He's the only one to blame here. Not you."

She'd said it quite fiercely, and that, more than anything, cut through his grief and got his attention.

"Brett, we'll figure out how best to help him, if we can, but he's got to help himself now. You do know that?"

He nodded and then held her face in his hands. "We?" he asked.

She held his gaze. "We."

He pulled her tightly into his arms and buried his face in her hair. "When I thought I might lose you, that you might be hurt . . ." He pushed her back enough to look in her eyes. "I don't want to ever lose you."

And though there was still the residual pain and ache from the toll the evening had taken, her mouth smoothed, then finally curved. It was a smile of confidence. And of hope. "That's good, because the man I want is the man I saw today. Who didn't back down when things were hard. The hardest, maybe. Who wanted to protect me . . . and a lifelong friend. We're both misfits, of sorts, you and me, you know that. From backgrounds that weren't easy. But I think that's what makes us strong. And what makes us value what we have, what we've earned. I think that's why we fit, you and me, almost from the moment you climbed off that bike."

"You do fit me, Kirby."

"Are you still planning on staying here? I mean, with Dan's stuff and—"

"I'm not going anywhere. You're right, we'll figure out what we can do for him. For his dad. The company, whatever that might take. But this is where I belong now." He pulled her up close and hiked her up into his arms so their faces were even. She wrapped her arms around his neck as he held her tightly against him. "And one thing I'm not going to do is just play house with you, Kirby. I want to marry you. And I don't want to wait ten years. Or maybe even ten days. I love you, Kirby Farrell. And I want the whole world to know you're mine."

Now the smile did come, shining through tears. But they were tears of joy this time. She wrapped her legs around his hips as he swung her around on the porch.

"Is that a yes?"

"I already told you. I'm all in, Brett. I've never been a gambler, but I'd bet on you. Every time."

"Well, maybe you've heard, but I'm one lucky son of a bitch. I don't like to lose."

"You're not going to lose me."

She slid one hand to his cheek and rubbed her thumb across his lips, making him shudder . . . and forget every damn thing except this moment. And her.

"I love you, too," she said. "So, marry me, Brett Hennessey. Because I think I'm one lucky son of a bitch, too. Look!" she exclaimed, pointing behind him.

He turned them both around to see that it had begun to snow. Hard. If the thick, white flakes were any indication, it didn't look like it was something that was going to let up anytime soon.

"The Hennessey Fortune Factor," she murmured. "Ha!"

"You are all the good fortune I need," he said, then kissed her, hard, before he carried her back inside the house. They'd both go down to the station later, find out what came next, what could be done. But for right now, he was going to celebrate life. New life. New dreams. His dreams.

Their dreams.

"Mind if we start the honeymoon part a little early?" he asked.

"I thought we already had," she said, then squealed as he put her over his shoulder and took the stairs two at a time.

They were both laughing as they landed on his bed. Their bed.

And as he slowly peeled off her clothes and started to make love to the woman who was going to be his wife . . . somewhere out in the white swirl of the dawn snow, they heard cats howling in unison.

They both paused and looked at each other.

"I'm going to take that as a good sign," Kirby said cautiously.

"I'm going to reinforce the screen on that door."

Kirby laughed. "Later."

Brett pulled her under him, felt her arch up, naturally moving with him as he slid deep into her. "Yeah," he said. "Later is good. Now come here my soon-to-be wife and let's see if I can make you howl."

And he did.

Epilogue

"Sure thing, Mr. Deverill. Dev," she corrected, unable to keep the goofy, girlish smile off her face as she cradled the phone between her chin and shoulder and typed in his request to book his room for an additional week. "Will you be needing me to send someone to pick you up after the game is over? Fine, okay. Will do." She hung up the phone and glanced over at the small television set she'd brought in from the kitchen and hooked up at the front desk.

ESPN was covering the third annual Brett Hennessey Foundation poker tournament out at the resort. She smiled with ridiculous pride as she watched her husband sitting in the booth with the announcers, calling the play. She watched with particular interest as they talked about the young Irish player, Iain Summerfield. In the past three years, he'd become something of a new sensation and was threatening to topple some of Brett's long-standing records. Brett was not only not bothered by this, he seemed kind of excited for the kid.

Vanetta came around the corner just then and Kirby dragged her gaze away from the action. "I need to see if we can get Tommy to head over to the resort to pick up Dev. He's already out of the tournament, but he just called to extend his stay." Her smile turned a bit cheeky. "I think there's a certain French ski team racer who caught his eye."

Vanetta fanned her face with her hand. "If I was only a few

years younger, I'd show that scamp what a real woman could do."

Kirby laughed, as she often did when she spent any time around the older woman. Vanetta had come east during Dan's trial and had never gotten around to going back. Brett had ended up setting up another management company out west to run her boarding house. He'd tried to talk Dan into sticking around, too, but he and his father had ended up in Palm Springs, both wanting a fresh start without the past haunting them. Brett respected their need for privacy and kept his shadow from looming anywhere over them, but he still kept in contact, and Kirby thought that someday, if he had anything to say about it, they'd find their way back to a solid relationship.

Vanetta had turned out to be a godsend to them both, managing a good part of the day-to-day business of the inn while Kirby helped Brett with his flourishing home rehabbing business. Kirby had found a profound happiness there, working side by side with Brett, indulging her own creativity that fulfilled her in a way she'd never thought possible. They'd never formally hired Vanetta on; she'd just sort of worked her way into their lives. By now Kirby couldn't imagine what she'd do without her.

"Why don't you head on over to the resort," Vanetta was saying, turning the TV around so she could watch. "Go see that handsome husband of yours, and bring Mr. Dev back yourself. I can hold the fort down. Besides, looks like another storm is coming. Supposed to be another record snow year." She rubbed her elbows. "Might be time for a bit of buttered rum. Keep the joints working," she grumbled. As she always did during the winter season. Brett had tried to talk her into staying out west during the cold months, to which she'd frostily replied, "What, and leave this place to fall down around your ankles?"

They both knew that Vanetta was happiest when she was working, or tending to something. And what she most wanted to tend to was the two of them. They were family. Even Aunt Frieda had started to make routine visits, which had gotten longer and longer each fall season.

What a family they'd become, Kirby thought as she scooted out from behind the desk, barely missing tripping over Elvira. Barn cat turned loyal companion. She'd never left that night after they'd taken Dan away. She'd caught Brett feeding her out back, and after a while, she'd just kind of ended up staying. So far she hadn't attacked a single guest.

Kirby slapped her thigh and whistled for Elvis. The big, lumbering mutt trotted out from her office and then perked right up when he saw her slipping on her coat. Brett had found him on the side of the road by the first farmhouse they'd rehabbed. He'd been a permanent guest ever since.

She gave his head a good scratch and then gave Vanetta a quick hug. Always discombobulated the older woman, which was half the reason why she did it. "I think I saw Clemson hanging around the foyer," she told her. "Maybe he'd like to join you for that buttered rum," she added with a wink as she snagged the truck keys from the front board, where they hung next to Brett's bike keys. And her own bike keys.

"Old coot," Vanetta grumbled. "Can't find something better to do than to get in my way." But Kirby caught her patting at her hair as she walked into the foyer.

She grinned to herself as she opened the front door and headed out to her truck, Elvis trotting by her side. It started snowing again. Big fat flakes swirling through the air. She stuck her tongue out, letting a few land there and melt, and raced Elvis to the truck.

She climbed in and pulled the seat belt across her lap, then laid a protective hand on her slowly burgeoning belly. A medical miracle, her OB had called it. But, at forty-three, all was going blissfully, almost ridiculously well. By the end of summer, there'd be another permanent guest at the inn.

Yep, the Hennessey Fortune Factor was still going strong.

If you liked this book,
you've got to try Mary Wine's
IN THE WARRIOR'S BED,
out now from Brava!

S he was a fool.

Bronwyn felt her heart freeze, because the man was huge. The hilt of his sword reflected the last of the daylight. His stallion was a good two hands taller than her mare. It could run her down with no trouble at all. Worse yet, the man wore the kilt of the McJames clan. With her father and brothers raiding their land, he had no reason to treat her kindly. His body was cut with hard muscles, and where his shirt sleeves were rolled up, she saw the evidence that spoke of his firsthand knowledge and skill with that sword. She scanned the ridge above him quickly, fearing that the McJameses had decided to repay her father's raids by doing a few themselves.

But there was no one in the fading light. Her teeth worried her lower lip as she returned her attention to him. She'd never considered that a McJames warrior might enjoy an afternoon ride the same as she.

"Good day to ye, lass." His voice was deep and edged with playfulness. He reached up and tugged on the corner of his knitted bonnet, a half smile curving his lips. His light-colored hair brushing his wide shoulders, a single thin braid running down along the side of his face to keep it out of his eyes. He wore only a leather doublet over his shirt and the sleeves of the doublet were hanging behind him. There was a majestic quality to him. One that was mesmerizing. Her brother Keir was a very large man and she wasn't used to meeting men who measured up to his size. This one did. He radiated strength from his booted feet to his blond hair. There was nothing small or weak about him. In his presence she felt petite, something she was unaccustomed to. Almost as though she noticed that she was a woman and that her body was fashioned to fit against his male one.

"Good day."

She had no idea why she spoke to him. It was an impulse. A shiver raced down her back. Her eyes widened, heat stinging her cheeks, her mouth suddenly dry. A shudder shook her gently, surprising her. Beneath her doublet, her nipples tingled, the sensation unnerving.

His gaze touched on her face, witnessing the scarlet stain creeping across it. A flicker of heat entered his eyes. It was bold but something inside her enjoyed knowing that she sparked such a look in him.

"It's a fine day for riding."

His words were innocent of double meaning, but Bronwyn drew in a sharp breath because her mind imagined a far different sort of riding. Her own thoughts shocked her deeply. She'd never been so aware of just what a man might do with a woman when they were alone, and now was the poorest time for her body to be reacting to such things. It felt as though he could read her mind. At least the roguish smile he flashed her hinted that he could. His lips settled back into a firm line. She had to jerk her eyes away from them but that left her staring into his blue eyes. Hunger flickered there and her body approved. Her nipples drew tight, hitting her boned stays.

"Ye shouldna look at me like that, lass." He sounded like he was warning himself more than her, but her blush burned hotter because he was very correct.

"Nor should ye look at me as ye are."

A grin split his lips, flashing a hint of his teeth. "Ye have that right. But what am I to do when ye stand there so tempting? I'm merely a man."

And for some reason she felt more like a woman than she

ever had. Something hot and thick flowed through her veins. There was no thinking about anything. Her body was alive with sensations, touching off longings she'd thought deeply buried beneath the harsh reality of her father's loathing to see her wed.

"A man who is far from his home." Her gaze touched on his kilt for a moment, the blue, yellow, and orange of the McJames clan holding her attention. "I'm a McQuade."

"I figured that already, but its nae my clan that keeps us quarrelling."

He let his horse close the distance again. The mare didn't move now, she stood quivering as the large stallion made a circle around her. The same flood of excitement swept through Bronwyn, keeping her mesmerized by the man moving around her. Bronwyn shook her head, trying to regain her wits.

"But I'm thinking that we just might be able to get along quite nicely." His eyes flickered with promise. "Ye and I."

"Ye should go. Ye're correct that it is my clansmen that seek trouble with the McJameses. Ye shouldna give them a reason to begin a fight."

"And ye would nae see that happen? I'm pleasantly surprised."

His stallion was still moving in a circle around her. Bronwyn had to twist her neck to keep him in sight. Every time he went behind her, her body tightened, every muscle drawing taut with anticipation. Such a response defied everything that she knew.

"Surprised that I've no desire to see blood spilt? Being a McJames does not mean I am cruel at heart. What is yer name?" he asked.

Fear shot through her, ending her fascination with him. Being the laird's daughter meant she was a prize worth taking. Riding out alone so far had been a mistake she just might pay for with her body. Few would believe her if she told them her father wouldn't pay any ransom for her. Beyond money, there were men who would consider taking her virtue a fine way to strike back at her clan.

"I'll no tell ye that. McQuade is enough for ye to know."

"I disagree with ye. 'Tis much too formal only knowing your clan name. I want to know what ye were baptized."

"Yet ye'll have to be content for I shall nae tell ye my Christian name." He frowned but Bronwyn forced herself to be firm. This flirtation was dangerous. Her heart was racing but with more than fear. "If ye get caught on McQuade land, I'll no be able to help ye."

"Would that make ye sad, lass?"

"No." He was toying with her. "But it would ruin supper, what with all the gloating from the men that drove ye back onto McJames land. There would be talk of nothing else."

One golden eyebrow rose as the horse moved closer to her. He swung a leg over the saddle and jumped to the ground. Her belly quivered in the oddest fashion. But she had been correct about one thing—this man was huge.

"Are ye sure, lass? I might be willing to press me luck if I thought ye'd feel something for me."

"That's foolishness. Get on with ye. I willna tell ye my name. Ye're a stranger; I dinna feel anything beyond Christian good will toward ye."

"Is that so?"

"It is."

He flashed another grin at her, but this one was far more calculating and full of intent. "Afraid I might sneak into yer home and steal ye if I know who's daughter ye are?"

He came closer but kept a firm hand on the reins of his mount. Authority shone from his face now, clear, determined, and undeniable. This man was accustomed to leading. It was part of the fibers that made up his being. He would have the nerve to steal her if that was what he decided upon. There was plenty enough arrogance in him, for certain. She felt it in the pit of her belly. What made her eyelashes flutter to conceal her emotions was the excitement such knowledge unleashed in her.

"Enough teasing," she said. "Neither of us are children."

"Aye, I noticed that already."

Her face brightened once more. His eyes swept her and his expression tightened. Maybe she had never seen a man looking at her like that afore but her body seemed to understand exactly what the flicker of hunger meant. She stared at it, mesmerized.

"Tell me yer name, lass."

Don't miss Kathy Love's latest,
WHAT A DEMON WANTS,
available now . . .

Jude stood in the doorway of a shotgun cottage that looked as if it had fallen out of the pages of a fairytale. He half-expected children in lederhosen to answer the door.

But instead of Hansel or Gretel, the door was jerked open by a tall man, fit and tough enough to be a bodyguard himself.

"Jude Anthony?"

Jude nodded. "Yes."

The man extended his hand. "Maksim Kostova. I'm the one who contacted you on behalf of my sister."

Jude guessed as much. He accepted the man's hand, giving a brief, firm shake. As he released it, he fought the urge to wipe his hand on his pants as if there was something thick and slimy clinging to his fingers.

Demon. That particular preternatural aura affected him more than some others. The energy from Maksim was strong and heavy, coating Jude's palm and fingers, creeping up his arm like a living thing. The Blob from horror movie legend.

Damn, he hated that sensation. He flexed his fingers, trying to subtly shake the sensation off.

Maksim raised an eyebrow, obviously aware that Jude had had some reaction to him, but he didn't inquire. Instead he stepped back, opening the door wider.

"Come in."

Jude moved past him, keeping a good distance between them.

This male was clearly a powerful, high ranking demon. Jude could even feel his aura just in passing.

Jude steeled himself to the sensation, but was pleased to step into a fair-sized sitting room. More space was always better.

He could do this. Just a few more jobs, and he'd be done with this life. No more paranormal creatures. No more of this existence. He would reinvent himself.

With renewed determination, he turned his focus away from the demon and to the room they'd just entered. His impression again was that of being in a fairy tale world. Lavender walls, gold brocade furniture, and beaded lamps gave the room a feeling of a princess's private parlor.

But the woman who entered the room was no fairytale character. Not unless fairytales had changed greatly since he'd last read one. She was hugely pregnant, making her hard to miss. Her belly protruded, almost comically large when compared to her slight frame. Then his gaze moved to the tall, dark-haired woman following the waddling pregnant one.

She was stunning. Definitely princess material here . . . except instead of a flowing gown she wore a faded concert T-shirt which clung to her small, pert breasts and slender midriff.

Dark washed jeans encased her long legs, accentuating the flare of her hips and cupping what he had no doubt was a great ass—not that he could see that, but he just knew. Pale bare feet with her toes painted cherry red peeped out from under the cuffs of her jeans.

Jude's body tensed at the sight of her, very aware—of her.

Just an observation, he told himself. What he was paid to do. Notice—things. But his body told him it was more than a detached opinion. He reacted. Instantly. Viscerally.

Don't let this be Ellina Kostova. Please don't let this be her.

He tried to ignore his response, relieved when Maksim spoke. "Jude, this is my wife, Jo," Maksim said, gesturing to the very pregnant woman, drawing Jude's attention away from the beauty.

His wife stepped forward and offered her hand. The briefest

touch revealed she was human. A welcome sensation after making contact with her husband. No supernatural residue there.

But of course, Maksim redirected him back to the other woman. "And this is Ellina, my sister. The one you will be protecting."

Shit. He'd been hoping this wasn't her. She certainly didn't fit his image of Ellina Kostova, the recluse, the eccentric author who preferred to stay in her world of demons, monsters, and other things that went bump in the night.

He hadn't expected her to be so young . . . or so lovely. She had an almost ethereal quality to her features. Full lips, large pale eyes, creamy skin.

She moved closer and offered a hand to him. Her fingers were slender, elegant. A beautiful hand.

But she was paranormal, he reminded himself. So really, would she be anything less than perfection? On the outside, at least. That was the way of preternaturals.

He reached for her hand, waiting for the same clinging, distasteful aura to encompass him. The aura that would remind him that not all things were as beautiful on the inside as they were on the outside. He knew from the information her brother had given him that she was only half-demon, but half was all it would take for his preternatural awareness to kick in.

But instead of that sickening, clinging, creeping sensation, her touch sent tingles up his arm. Tangible, electric pulses. Pulses that were anything but unpleasant.

As if in utter synch, they released each other, both stepping back from one another.

But unlike him, Ellina didn't show any outward reaction to the touch. Her lovely face was as serene as a mannequin. Certainly she didn't show any indication she'd felt the same shockwaves passing between them. Instead her pale eyes roamed over him, taking very obvious inventory, although her expression revealed nothing of her thoughts. Just an assessment. Testing his musculature, his strength. Like appraising a horse about to be purchased.

Except he was no stoic equine. His body tightened further. His mind imagining what her fingers would feel like moving over him. Those tiny pulses radiating from her fingers into him.

His spine straightened, and he forced his attention, and his reaction, away from the woman who'd managed to affect him more with one fleeting brush of her fingers than hundreds of paranormals before her.

He turned to Maksim.

"I'm sorry. I'm not the right man for this job."

And be on the lookout for
INSTANT TEMPTATION by Jill Shalvis,
coming soon from Brava . . .

"I didn't invite you in, T.J."

He just smiled.

He was built as solid as the mountains that had shaped his life, and frankly had the attitude to go with it, the one that said he could take on whoever and whatever, and you could kiss his perfect ass while he did so. She'd seen him do it too, back in his hell-raising, misspent youth.

Not that she was going there, to the time when he could have given her a single look and she'd have melted into a puddle at his feet.

Had melted into a puddle at his feet. Not going there . . .

Unfortunately for Harley's senses, he smelled like the wild Sierras; pine and fresh air, and something even better, something so innately male that her nose twitched for more, seeking out the heat and raw male energy that surrounded him and always had. Since it made her want to lean into him, she shoved in another bite of ice cream instead.

He smiled. "I saw on Oprah once that women use ice cream as a substitute for sex."

She choked again, and he resumed gliding his big, warm hand up and down her back. "You watch Oprah?"

"No. Annie was, and I overheard her yelling at the TV that women should have plenty of both sex *and* ice cream."

That sounded exactly like his Aunt Annie. "Well, I don't need the substitute."

"No?" he murmured, looking amused at her again.

"No!"

He hadn't taken his hands off her, she couldn't help but notice. He still had one rubbing up and down her back, the other low on her belly, holding her upright, which was ridiculous, so she smacked it away, doing her best to ignore the fluttering he'd caused and the odd need she had to grab him by the shirt, haul him close and have her merry way with him.

This was what happened to a woman whose last orgasm had come from a battery operated device instead of a man, a fact she'd admit, oh, *never*. "I was expecting your brother."

"Stone's working on Emma's 'honey do' list at the new medical clinic, so he sent me instead. Said to give you these." He pulled some maps from his back pocket, maps she needed for a field expedition for her research. When she took them out of his hands, he hooked his thumbs in the front pockets of his Levi's. He wore a T-shirt layered with an opened button-down that said *Wilder Adventures* on the pec. His jeans were faded nearly white in the stress spots, of which there were many, nicely encasing his long, powerful legs and lovingly cupping a rather impressive package that was emphasized by the way his fingers dangled on his thighs.

Not that she was looking.

Okay, she was looking, but she couldn't help it. The man oozed sexuality. Apparently some men were issued a handbook at birth on how to make a woman stupid with lust. And he'd had a lot of practice over the years.

She'd watched him do it.

Each of the three Wilder brothers had barely survived their youth, thanks in part to no mom and a mean, son-of-a-bitch father. But by some miracle, the three of them had come out of it alive and now channeled their energy into Wilder Adventures, where they guided clients on just about any outdoor adventure that could be imagined; heli-skiing, extreme mountain biking, kayaking, climbing, *anything*.

Though T.J. had matured and found success, he still gave off a don't-mess-with-me vibe. Even now, at four in the afternoon, he looked big and bad and tousled enough that he might have just gotten out of bed and wouldn't be averse to going back.

It irritated her. It confused her. And it turned her on, a fact that drove her bat-shit crazy because she was no longer interested in T.J. Wilder.

Nope.

It'd be suicide to still be interested. No one could sustain a crush for fifteen years.

No one.

Except, apparently, her. Because deep down, the unsettling truth was that if he so much as directed one of his sleepy, sexy looks her way, her clothes would fall right off.

Again.

And wasn't that just her problem, the fact that once upon a time, a very long time ago, at the tail end of T.J.'s out-of-control youth, the two of them had spent a single night together being just about as intimate as a man and woman could get. Her first night with a guy. Definitely not his first. Neither of them had been exactly legal at the time, and only she'd been sober.

Which meant only she remembered.